THE HIGH HOUSE

Honor Arundel wrote her first children's book to entertain her two youngest daughters who wanted to read about ordinary children in ordinary circumstances. The book was a great success and Miss Arundel went on to write a number of novels for children. She lived in Scotland until her death in 1973.

The High House is the first title of the well-known 'Emma' series. Emma goes to live with her scatter-brained artist-aunt in Edinburgh. At first she hates her new disorganized life but gradually comes to love Aunt Patsy and her chaotic ways.

Emma's adventures are continued in *Emma's Island* and *Emma in Love*, both also published in Piccolo.

HONOR ARUNDEL

THE HIGH HOUSE

Cover illustration by Mary Dinsdale
Text illustrations by Eileen Armitage

A Piccolo Book

PAN BOOKS
LONDON AND SYDNEY

First published 1966 by Hamish Hamilton Ltd
This edition published 1972 by Pan Books Ltd,
Cavaye Place, London SW10 9PG
2nd printing 1976
© Honor Arundel 1967
© Illustrations by Eileen Armitage 1967
ISBN 0 330 23217 7

Made and printed in Great Britain by
Cox & Wyman Ltd, London, Reading and Fakenham

Chapter One

AUNT PATSY arrived the morning after the accident and as she had always lived in Edinburgh and we had always lived in London and neither of us had had enough money for the fares, we had never met her before.

She was Mother's sister, tall and thin, with dark straight hair so smooth it looked polished, grey eyes, a pointed nose and long nervous hands. She came on the overnight train and arrived just as Richard and I were thinking about breakfast. I say thinking because we both knew we couldn't eat. But I boiled an egg for Aunt Patsy and made some tea and she ate and drank in an absent-minded way. She hadn't said much. She hugged us when she arrived but without kissing – I hate the way most relations think they have the right to kiss you whether you know and like them or not.

She was quite different from Aunt Laura, Father's sister, who arrived with Uncle Edward from their home in Exeter later in the morning and immediately took charge.

Aunt Laura was square and brisk and she wore

a black suit and a black hat (Aunt Patsy was wearing green corduroy and no hat) but she looked as if she would be more at home in baggy country tweeds.

Uncle Edward, who was a lawyer, was also square and brisk, with rimless glasses and thin grey hair. They both kissed us and Aunt Laura cried and called us 'poor little orphans' and kept repeating, 'It's so terrible. I can't believe it. I just can't believe it.'

Mother and Father had been killed in a car smash on their way home from visiting friends. I can't write about it.

As I said, Aunt Laura took charge; she sent Richard and me upstairs to rest and bustled into the kitchen, clattering things. Uncle Edward settled beside the telephone and Aunt Patsy was left in the living-room, smoking, and staring out of the window.

Richard and I crept upstairs but we didn't seem able to rest. Instead, we went into Richard's room and Richard stood by the window kicking the carpet and I sat on the divan. Sometimes, when something terrible has happened you can't feel it. It's like cutting yourself really badly. At first it doesn't feel at all and then very gradually it begins to ache. We were still at the numb stage.

Richard is fifteen, two years older than me. He is tall for his age and he has dark copper-coloured hair and lots of freckles. My hair's the same colour

but somehow I have escaped the freckles. He is
a terribly nice brother and quite unlike most boys
you meet because he doesn't show off or think he's
a superior person just because he's a boy. He is
going to be a musician. But the best thing about
him is that he always knows how I feel and never
laughs when I say stupid things accidentally.

I remember that bit of the morning very clearly, the sound of Aunt Laura in the kitchen, the bumble of Uncle Edward on the telephone and the sound of bird-song coming through the open window.

We live in a fairly new suburb and there aren't many trees big enough to be called proper trees, but there is one which must have been there already, a sycamore, a lovely round symmetrical tree and it's at the bottom of our garden. Every now and again some stupid neighbour wants to cut it down but we won't let him. That morning, it was early September, the tree was just beginning to turn yellow and every now and again a leaf would be blown off and fall very gently on to the grass. And this seemed very sad although the sun was shining. On any other day it wouldn't have seemed sad at all because I love autumn.

At last I said: 'If we're orphans will we have to go into a Home?'

'I don't know,' Richard said.

Somehow saying the word 'orphans' made me want to cry for the first time.

'Perhaps one of the aunts will take us,' Richard went on.

I simply couldn't think clearly what that would be like. My head ached and my eyes ached – we'd been up most of the night – and I felt tired with that dreadful dragging sort of tiredness which stops you going to sleep. But I longed to sleep and sleep and then wake up to find it had all been a terrible dream.

Then Aunt Patsy knocked at the door and came in. We didn't want to talk to her at all but she said we must: it was only fair that we should know what was happening.

9

'Have we got to go into a Home?' I asked.

'Homes aren't so horrible nowadays, more like boarding schools,' Aunt Patsy said with the ghost of a smile. 'Not like Oliver Twist at all. But there is an alternative.'

'You mean we could live with you or Aunt Laura?' Richard said.

'I wish you both could but I simply haven't room. And Aunt Laura can't afford it. But she says she'll take Richard if I take you, Emma.'

'You mean we couldn't be together?' I asked horrified.

'That's what I want to talk about. If you went to some sort of a Home you could be together.'

'What about a boarding school?' said Richard.

'Too expensive, at the moment anyhow. But it might be managed later.'

'So it's a choice,' said Richard gloomily, looking down at his feet. 'Together in some ghastly Home or separately with the aunts.'

'Yes. I thought you ought to choose. Aunt Laura's boy, Colin, is just about your age, Richard, so you would have someone to do things with.'

'He was a horrible boy last time I saw him.'

'Most boys grow out of being horrible,' said Aunt Patsy. 'I know it's difficult to choose, especially at a time like this. And especially for Emma because she's never met me before. But there's a spare room in my flat and there are lots of nice things to do in Edinburgh. I'm untidy and bad-tempered and I'm used to living on my own, but we could try it as a temporary arrangement. If you hate it too much or I hate it too much we'll have to think of something else.'

I liked her saying that, I mean not pretending that she loved me or promising to make me happy or saying she would be a second mother. I didn't want another mother. I felt I ought to thank her or something but I just couldn't.

'Well, what do you think?' Aunt Patsy asked. 'Or do you want to talk it over?'

I looked at Richard and Richard looked at me. My look said, 'Please not a Home, I couldn't bear it,' and Richard's look said, 'I'll put up with Aunt Laura if you put up with Aunt Patsy.'

'OK,' said Richard slowly, 'I'll give Aunt Laura a try.'

Aunt Patsy smiled again, this time a proper smile. She wanted to say something cheering or comforting, I knew, but what was there to say? She went towards the door and then turned and said:

'You know, nothing stays the same. We won't always feel like this.'

At this I started to cry and lay on Richard's bed and stuck my head in the pillow. The numbness had gone and the ache I had been expecting was so sudden and so dreadful that I felt there weren't enough tears in the world to drown it.

I don't remember anything about the rest of the day, or rather I don't want to remember. I just remember the sycamore tree and the leaves falling off, sadly, one by one.

Chapter Two

AUNT PATSY and I arrived at Waverley Station, Edinburgh, about seven o'clock in the morning. I realized that she was the sort of person who feels cross and prickly in the early morning so I didn't say much and neither did she except 'I hope you managed to sleep' and 'We'd better get a taxi.'

A strange town looks twice as strange first thing in the morning with no one about and I felt too blurred and excited and confused to notice anything except the coldness and freshness of the air and the cold grey tall buildings. The taxi drove up a steep hill and then turned right and went on climbing.

'I live near the Castle,' said Aunt Patsy. 'It's the oldest part of Edinburgh.'

When we got out I realized what she meant. The buildings were all tall and twisty and some of them looked as though they would fall down at any moment. I couldn't imagine how anyone could live in them and said so.

'Well, I do,' said Aunt Patsy, a little sharply, as she paid the cab driver.

'How are you going to manage with the trunk,

lady?' he asked, slamming the door behind us.

'I'll take one end,' said Aunt Patsy, and to my horror she and the cab driver began walking down a flight of stone steps beside one of these huge crumbling buildings, carrying my trunk between them, leaving me to follow with the suitcases. I couldn't think where they were going. Surely Aunt Patsy couldn't live here?

I paused for a moment at the top of the steps and looked blearily down. At the bottom a wide road curled round like a snake and then more steps went down another hill until they disappeared among hundreds of tall dark buildings, all with puffing chimneys.

I walked slowly down the steps and joined Aunt Patsy and the cab driver who had put the trunk down outside a shabby-looking red door.

'We'll leave it at the foot of the stairs and I'll get it carried up later,' said Aunt Patsy, who didn't even seem to be panting.

'How far up are you?' asked the cab driver.

'Fourth floor,' said Aunt Patsy.

He eyed the trunk doubtfully and then shrugged his shoulders.

'I'll do it,' he said, 'though it'll probably be the death of me.'

It'll probably be the death of me too, I thought, as Aunt Patsy opened the door and led the way into what looked and smelt like a cellar.

The cab driver managed to hoist the trunk on to

his shoulder (of course, it wasn't a very big trunk
but still!) and set off after Aunt Patsy up the
winding stone stairs, and I brought up the rear.
The paint was peeling off the walls, one of the
stair windows was broken and the steps had great

15

sags worn in the middle of them. I felt gloomier and gloomier – I mean, this was practically a slum.

I was panting a bit myself because the suitcases were jolly heavy and the stairs seemed to go on for ever but we finally stopped at a blue door with P. Grieve written on a brass plate.

The driver up-ended the trunk and mopped his brow.

'They stairs'll keep you fit,' he grunted.

'They do,' said Aunt Patsy smiling.

Aunt Patsy opened the door, gave the cab driver some more money, told him he was an angel, told me to dump the cases anywhere and began pottering round the flat the way people do when they have been away, picking up letters and newspapers and putting them down again and wandering about in a clueless way.

Inside, the flat wasn't too bad, at least nothing like as bad as I had thought it would be judging from the stairs, but it was still pretty weird. And I realized that she'd not been joking when she said she was untidy because the whole flat was in a frightful mess.

Off the hall was the kitchen and the sink was full of washing-up that hadn't been done and generally littered with odds and ends; then came the bathroom which was tiny, and then Aunt Patsy's bedroom with the bed unmade and lots of clothes and stockings lying about.

16

'This will be your room,' said Aunt Patsy opening another door.

I nearly died. It had obviously been used as a junk room and though there was a divan bed and a chest of drawers there were no curtains or carpet. And everywhere was junk, piles of books, an umbrella, a broken table lamp, a deck chair and a sewing machine.

'It's in a bit of a mess,' said Aunt Patsy offhandedly, 'but we'll soon have it shipshape.'

'How? When?' I wanted to ask but I felt too miserable to speak. I thought of our lovely house in London, all clean and new and tidy, and my lovely room with the curtains I had chosen myself and my desk and my bookcase. It was terribly difficult not to sit down and howl.

Aunt Patsy must have realized a little of what I was feeling because she said:

'We'll make it nice, I promise. And we'll get the things you specially like sent up from London. Now come and see my studio.'

She led the way up a little flight of stairs into a huge room, a sort of attic with slopey ceilings and two skylights as well as dormer windows. It was all painted white and had a wooden polished floor with shabby rugs on it. There were dozens of pictures, mostly unframed and pinned with drawing pins, and curious lumps of stone that could have been anything and a stone jar full of dead brown hemlock.

And untidy – I couldn't imagine how anyone could live in such a room. There was a piano with stacks of music just about to fall off the top. There was a long thin table covered with papers and books and coffee cups and ashtrays. There was a sofa and a couple of ancient armchairs that looked as though they would collapse if you sat on them. And one half of the room was full of painting things, an easel, stacks of paper and canvases, a drawing board, bottles of this and that and jugs full of paintbrushes and pencils. (Aunt Patsy is the sort of artist who does illustrations for books and magazines and designs for dress materials and things like that.) I remembered that Mother had said she was 'artistic', and now I knew what she meant.

'Come and look at the view, Emma,' said Aunt Patsy. 'Isn't it marvellous?'

You must have been able to see the whole of Edinburgh from those windows, miles and miles of buildings and trees, low hills (which Aunt Patsy said were called 'the Pentlands') and even what looked like the sea in the distance.

'That's the Forth,' said Aunt Patsy.

And bang in front was a wide square, at the far end of which was a gaunt rocky lump with houses and towers on it.

'That's the Castle and the Esplanade. Well, what do you think of my house?'

I decided not to say what I really thought, that

it was weird and horrible and badly needed tidying up and that I couldn't imagine how I would ever settle down there.

'I never imagined it would be like this,' I said lamely. 'Are all Edinburgh houses like this? I mean, aren't there any new houses?'

'Of course. As I told you, this is the oldest part of the city. But I love it. I hate little modern match-boxes.'

I had thought that perhaps a modern house would be too expensive, because I knew she hadn't much money, but to think of anyone choosing to live in a place like this!

I turned away from the window. The view was really too much of a good thing: it made me feel dizzy and overwhelmed and lonely. I'd rather have had a sycamore tree than a castle any day.

'What we need is some breakfast,' said Aunt

Patsy suddenly. 'Oh dear, there isn't a thing in the house.'

We went down to the kitchen again and she poked about in a cupboard and looked in the fridge. 'Not a thing!' she said, but not as if she were surprised or sorry. 'I'll tell you what, Emma, I'll put the kettle on and you run down to the dairy for milk and eggs and some morning rolls.'

She gave me a latch key and a ten-shilling note and I climbed down the four flights of stairs and then up the steps into the main street. I was certainly going to get plenty of exercise in Edinburgh, I thought bitterly. I'd probably wear my legs to stumps.

I found the dairy quite easily and bought the things Aunt Patsy had asked for. I wondered if she had Nescafé, which I always like for breakfast, and decided she might easily not, so I bought a small tin.

The street was beginning to wake up and look more cheerful, but I couldn't get used to those tall black buildings, and when I thought of our nice tree-lined streets and little houses with gardens it was even worse.

When I got back (down the steps and up the stairs) Aunt Patsy had cleared the table and put out mugs and plates and butter and marmalade.

'I didn't know if you had Nescafé so I got some,' I said. 'I hope that's all right.'

'You're a very intelligent girl, Emma,' said Aunt Patsy and she smiled, a really warm smile as if, for the first time, she thought she might like me. I smiled back.

'Here's your change,' I said. 'I wrote down what everything cost and it came to—'

Aunt Patsy interrupted. 'For goodness sake,' she said impatiently. 'I can't add up, and life's too short to count change.'

'But—' I was really shocked. I had been keeping accounts for years whenever I did shopping for Mother; she was most strict about every penny and said it was good training.

'Let's eat a huge breakfast and then we'll make plans. There's a terrible lot to do. You'll have to tell me all sorts of things—' Her voice trailed away. 'I mean I haven't the faintest idea what girls of your age should do or wear or eat or what they like or anything.'

'First I shall clear out my room,' I said firmly.

'Yes, of course. Put all the junk outside the front door and I'll arrange for the dustmen to collect it. There are clean sheets in the airing cupboard. Then we'd better paint the walls – is there any special colour you'd like? Tell me and I'll go out and buy some emulsion paint. Then we'll measure the windows and you can choose curtain material. I wish I could afford a carpet but I won't be able to until I get a pretty fat cheque. But we might manage a rug. Can you use a sewing machine?'

'Yes,' I said. Mother believed in girls being able to sew and cook and things like that.

'Oh good, because I never can remember how to thread up the wretched thing.'

Just then the phone rang and I heard Aunt Patsy say: 'Of course. Do come to lunch and meet my nice niece.'

Honestly! Think of asking someone to lunch on a day like this.

While Aunt Patsy talked to the voice at the other end of the telephone, I stacked the dishes in the sink. At least I could get the washing-up out of the way.

Chapter Three

WHEN I had finished washing up and put every-thing away – probably in the wrong places – and mopped the floor, I surveyed the wreckage of the room that was going to be mine. Aunt Patsy had disappeared. I hoped she was tidying the studio.

First I cleared out all the junk and stacked it neatly outside the front door. This left the divan, a chest of drawers, a rather saggy basket chair, a sort of ottoman thing and a table. Then I swept the floor, dusted and washed down the paintwork. It certainly made a faint improvement.

Aunt Patsy wandered in at this point.

'I'm going out to do the shopping,' she said. 'My, what a transformation! You're a genius, Emma.'

I looked at her sourly.

'Where shall I put the things from the chest of drawers? And is there any clean shelf paper?'

'Use newspaper,' said Aunt Patsy. 'And put the things – oh anywhere. In the ottoman for the moment.'

'That's full too.'

'Oh dear. Well, put them on my bed and I'll go through them and chuck out what I can. How does one accumulate so much stuff? You know, Emma, you're exactly like Christine.'

I couldn't help flinching to hear my mother's name but Aunt Patsy went on:

'We used to share a room when we were little and I used to drive her mad with my untidiness. We used to draw a chalk line down the middle of the floor and if she found any of my things on her side she used to kick them over the line, but she wouldn't pick them up. I can see I'm going to drive you mad too.'

'I like things to be tidy,' I mumbled.

'You're absolutely right. But don't try to reform me, I'm past redemption. What is in the chest of drawers, by the way?' She flung open a drawer. 'Oh, photographs. You must look.'

She took out the drawer and sat on the divan.

'Look, here we are in our ghastly school uniforms. And this was on a picnic in the Pentlands. And this is Granny, doesn't she look a scream?'

She handed me photo after photo, exclaiming and laughing. I daresay she didn't mean to be cruel but every time she said 'Christine' or 'your mother' it was like walking on knives. Suddenly she noticed I was crying.

'Emma, I didn't mean to upset you. But you see, we had such jolly times when we were children and I like to remember them.

'We'll look at them some other time. Now I must fly and don't bother with the rest of the room if you're tired. What colour paint shall I get? White?'

I nodded. What did it matter what colour my room was? Aunt Patsy disappeared and I heard the front door click.

I lay back on the divan and remembered too. I remembered Mother reading to me when I was ill in bed in her special reading-aloud voice; and Father coming home from work saying 'Surprise' because he'd brought us sweets or flowers; and how we'd all sit and plan summer holidays, whether we'd go to a farm in Devon or a seaside cottage in Cornwall or climb mountains in North Wales; and the time Richard fell off his bicycle and broke his arm – and then the door bell rang.

Honestly! Aunt Patsy! Here was a strange person coming to lunch and she was out and I was in a ghastly mess and feeling like death.

I ran a comb through my hair, and rubbed a dust mark off my face with a handkerchief before I opened the door. There was a strange man outside and for a moment I stared at him blankly. Then I remembered my manners. (Mother had always been particularly keen about good manners.)

'Won't you come in?' I said as graciously as I could. 'Aunt Patsy's gone to do the shopping. I'm Emma Langham, her niece.'

'Hullo, niece Emma. My name's Stephen McTaggart and I've been invited to lunch.'

He was rather crummily dressed in a navy donkey jacket and scuffed suede shoes, and he wore a dark-green jersey instead of a shirt and tie. He had light-blue eyes, a crooked sort of nose and his smile showed rather bad teeth.

'I'll hang up your jacket,' I said and then he followed me upstairs to the studio. He used a lot of swear words when he talked but I won't put them in.

'Typical of Patsy to be out. She has no more sense of time than a seagull. I hope she hasn't forgotten she invited me to lunch,' he went on as he sank heavily into an armchair. 'And what about offering me a drink? I'm as thirsty as a camel. What do you think of Edinburgh? Have you come to stay for long?'

So Aunt Patsy hadn't even told him about me and of course she hadn't tidied the studio.

'I don't know where she keeps the drinks,' I said disapprovingly. Mother and Father never had a drink before lunch except a glass of sherry on Sundays.

'Well I do, if you'll get the glasses from the kitchen.'

I fled downstairs carrying two empty coffee cups and an ashtray, and looked for glasses. I wasn't sure what he was going to drink so I brought two tumblers, in case it was beer, and two small glasses, in case it was sherry.

Actually he wanted gin and vermouth.

'How about you?' he asked.

'I don't drink.'

'Try a little vermouth.'

'No, thank you.'

'Mum disapprove?'

To my horror I burst into tears. 'My mother's dead – that's why I'm here,' I managed to blurt out.

He was as nice as possible or tried to be. He gave me his handkerchief and insisted upon my trying some vermouth which didn't taste too horrible after all.

'I'm terribly sorry, Emma, behaving like a clown, when you must be feeling wretched. Now drink up like a good girl and forgive me.

'So you're coming to live here? I think that'll be an excellent thing for Patsy, she's getting eccentric from living alone and I can see you're going to be a thoroughly good influence on her. You'll settle down in no time. Edinburgh's a great place to live. Are you interested in history? If you are I'll show you one or two places.'

Actually, history is one of the things I am interested in so I said Yes, that would be very kind of him.

Then he started telling me about the Old Town and all the famous people who had lived there, poets and philosophers and artists and scientists, so that by the time Aunt Patsy arrived I had more or less recovered.

She burst into the room carrying two string bags bursting with shopping, a bottle of wine, a bunch of flowers and a long loaf of French bread.

Mr McTaggart got up and kissed her.

'My poor Patsy,' he said. 'You should have told me.'

For a minute Aunt Patsy's face looked as though she might cry too, but then she smiled.

'This is going to be a special lunch to welcome Emma. We're not going to be sad.' Then she turned to me. 'Would you like to get some knives and forks and plates and things and bring them up and we'll eat in here.'

While I was downstairs I washed my face and brushed my hair and put on a clean jersey and then rummaged in the kitchen. I was glad I had done the washing-up.

Aunt Patsy had brought a cold chicken and tomatoes and little cartons of salady things and a chocolate cake. Mr McTaggart was opening a bottle of pink wine, and he poured some into three glasses.

'We're going to drink to you, Emma,' he said. 'Welcome to Edinburgh!'

It seemed a funny sort of lunch to invite some-one to, it was more like a picnic really. At home when we had visitors we always had everything very nice, flowers and the best table mats and butter knives and matching plates and coffee afterwards in tiny cups.

I didn't talk much but Aunt Patsy and Mr McTaggart chattered away about all sorts of people and things and about their work – it turned out he was the Art Editor of a magazine she some-times worked for – and they used a lot of words and technical terms I didn't understand. Every now and again they tried to bring me into the conversation but it was difficult because they didn't know what to say to me and I couldn't think of anything to say to them. Although the chicken was very nice I wasn't hungry. Suddenly I felt dreadfully tired. Too much had been happening too quickly and it was as if my brain had stopped and refused to think a single other thought. I sat curled up in one of the shabby armchairs and my eyes just wouldn't keep open although I knew it was terribly rude to fall asleep in company.

Then Mr McTaggart noticed me.

'Patsy, that poor child is dropping with fatigue. Do something about it.'

I blinked.

'Come on, Emma,' said Aunt Patsy. 'Trot off and have a sleep.'

'But I haven't made my bed,' I mumbled.

'You can use mine.'

I meant to explain and apologize but it was too difficult. I let Aunt Patsy take me into her room and turn down the bed and draw the curtains.

'I'll wake you up at tea-time,' she said as I took off my skirt so that it wouldn't get crushed.

'But I never sleep in the daytime.'

'It's different when you've been travelling all night.'

My eyes were shut almost before she was out of the door.

Chapter Four

I woke up very slowly as if I had been wrapped in swathes of cotton wool and it had to be moved away bit by bit. I kept my eyes shut for a long time after I was actually awake and tried to sort out where I was and what I was going to do. I always like to do this when I wake up so that I can remind myself to take gym shoes or a tennis racket to school or take a last look at my French verbs or check a history date. Now I was remembering slowly and painfully that I was in Edinburgh, that my room was still in a mess, and that Aunt Patsy would probably still be sitting upstairs talking to Mr McTaggart. I wondered what time it was.

But she wasn't. She and Mr McTaggart were in my room; he was standing on a chair rollering the ceiling and she was sloshing emulsion paint on to the walls with a big brush. She was wearing an old green shirt instead of an overall and her head was tied up in a duster.

'Ever done any painting, Emma?' she asked. 'If so you'll find an old shirt in my room and you can do the window and the door. I've got the non-drip sort of paint but if you should spill any mop it up quickly before it dries.'

She showed me how to do the windows, starting with the insides in the top left-hand corner and leaving the outsides till the end, and how to take a little piece of rag to wipe off any paint on the glass. It was pretty tricky and I got a crick in my neck twisting myself into knots to see into the corners but, in a way, I was enjoying myself. We didn't talk much but Mr McTaggart kept swearing when he put too much paint on the roller and it sprayed into his eyes, and in between he sang songs which I liked although they were Scotch and difficult to understand.

At last he said: 'Well, girls, let's call it a day. I'm exhausted and asphyxiated and urgently in need of sustenance.'

'Shall I make some tea?' I asked.

'No, in return for treating me to a magnificent lunch I shall treat you to a humble supper. Go and scrape the paint off your faces and we'll away.'

I finished the last little patch of door and then stood up and surveyed the room. It really did look nice, all clean and white and sparkling and I suddenly saw flowery curtains at the window, in green and blue and white, and a blue carpet and divan cover. Tomorrow I'd paint the wooden chair white too, and when my books arrived I'd arrange them in the shelves in the alcove and put my ornaments on the mantelpiece.

We walked down the horrible stairs and up the horrible steps and then down the street they call the Royal Mile because it leads from the Castle to Holyrood Palace. There were funny little passages leading off the street called names like 'Advocates Close' or 'Riddles Court', mostly full of dustbins and boarded-up doors secured with barbed wire, but through some you could see right down to Princes Street and then to the sea. Mr McTaggart stopped to show me where Robert Burns had stayed and where a philosopher called David Hume had lived, and one big court where there was an old stone turreted house that used to belong to someone called Lady Stair and was now a museum.

Aunt Patsy became impatient.

'I thought you said you were hungry, Stephen. Emma has bags of time to rootle about and discover who lived where and why. I'm starving.'

So was I, though I was interested in what Mr McTaggart was telling me. What I couldn't understand was why, if this was the Royal Mile, it should be allowed to get into such a frightful mess. Lots of the windows were broken or boarded up and I actually saw grass growing in one of the gutters. When I asked, Mr McTaggart snorted and said:

'Have you no feeling for history?'

'History's all right but no one wants to live in a ruin,' I said sharply.

'You've got a point. If only stupid local authorities wouldn't let places fall to pieces before they realize their historical and architectural importance.

'Still, some renovations have been done. I'll show you Whitehorse Close, some time. It looks as if it was an illustration for Grimms' Fairy Tales.'

'Food,' said Aunt Patsy.

So we went into a little restaurant and ate spaghetti and fruit salad with ice cream.

*   *   *

The next few days I was so busy I didn't have time to feel homesick. We found the curtain material and I machined the curtains myself – they weren't exactly the same length but Aunt Patsy said it didn't matter. And we shopped for school clothes and in between I did mounds of washing-up because Aunt Patsy always forgot. She said there were two types of people, those who washed up after meals and those who washed up before, and she was the second sort. I didn't think I would ever get used to her ways. She was the most disorganized person I had ever met.

To start with, about meal-times. 'Aren't we going to have lunch?' I would say, and she would reply: 'Oh dear, are you hungry again? We'd better scramble some eggs,' as if it was unnatural and incomprehensible for me to be hungry at one o'clock.

Sometimes we had nothing but bread and cheese for supper and at other times she would say, 'I feel like a feast,' and spend hours in the kitchen making some complicated dish with rice and prawns and mushrooms and green peppers, followed by chocolate soufflé with whipped cream; and there would be wine for her and ginger beer for me, though she always said I could have wine if I wanted.

She was always running out of quite ordinary things like salt or coffee or butter and I would have to dash out and buy some at the last minute.

Luckily for her there was a little shop which seemed to be always open, even on Sundays. After a bit I started checking the larder and the fridge every morning and telling Aunt Patsy what we needed.

She was also disorganized about money. I couldn't make out if she was rich or poor. Sometimes she'd come home with a new gramophone record or bunches of flowers and at other times she'd say: 'We can't send any laundry this week – we'll have to wait till my cheque arrives.' It took me a long time to broach the subject of pocket-money because she must have had to spend pounds on my room and my uniform. But all the same a girl does need the odd shilling for sweets or paper hankies or pencils. I spent about a pound of my savings before I nerved myself to ask her.

'You should have told me,' she said crossly. 'How much do you want?'

'Mother used to give me five shillings every Saturday.'

'Well, here's a pound and tell me when you need some more.'

'I don't want a pound. I want five shillings every week. Otherwise I can't plan.'

'Do you have to be so methodical?' she burst out, and then stopped and smiled. 'All right, you shall have five shillings every Saturday.'

But of course she forgot and sometimes when I reminded her she hadn't got any money and then

I would have to remind her again. It was awful!

I discovered after a time that she was what you call a free-lance which meant she didn't get paid regularly, only when one of her illustrations or designs was accepted. But at first I couldn't understand why she didn't have a pay-day like other people. At home Father had always handed Mother the housekeeping every month when he got his salary cheque and she used to put so much aside for things like shoes and winter coats. But when a cheque did arrive Aunt Patsy would say: 'Goodie, goodie, let's go on the spree. What would you like? A new jersey or some roller skates or something for your room?' And how could I say what I wanted when I thought I might get left without a mackintosh or stockings?

We didn't exactly quarrel because during those first few weeks together we were both on our best behaviour. I was conscious how kind she was to look after me so that I didn't have to go to a horrible Home, and she was conscious that I was an orphan and needed to be cherished. Whenever she noticed that I was bored or unhappy she would ask me politely what I would like to do, go to a cinema or visit the Art Gallery or something like that. And I'd mutter she needn't bother and go and lie on my bed and think how much I hated Edinburgh, or write long letters to Richard explaining just how impossible Aunt Patsy was.

Richard wrote back long letters too and told

me what life with Aunt Laura was like.

'It appears that we have chosen the wrong aunts,' he wrote. 'You like being organized, so you would fit into Aunt Laura's house like a glove. We have meals on the dot and the same meals every week: roast beef on Sunday, cottage pie on Monday, sausages on Tuesday, and so on. And she asks Colin and me before every meal if we have washed our hands. And every evening at half past nine she says, "Well, boys, time for bed." She always says "boys", never our names. She talks about "boys" all the time – boys are always hungry, boys make too much noise, boys are untidy, boys like football. She doesn't think it's at all boyish when I want to play the piano or go for walks by myself. Colin is just as horrible as I remember. He's always wanting to wrestle and talks about football all the time and knows the name of every single player in every single team, and he won't learn to play chess. Uncle Edward plays with me sometimes but he does pretty well what Aunt Laura says because he is a "boy" too.

'The nice thing is that there is a really good music master at school, and he's going to teach me composition and harmony and all that jazz out of school hours. He says if I work hard I might get a scholarship to the Academy but I must practise three hours a day and with Aunt Laura sniffing and looking down her nose it's very difficult. She says I may practise an hour before breakfast and another hour between tea and supper but she's always finding reasons why it's inconvenient. And the piano is lousy.

'Still, I'm keeping a stiff upper lip. "Boys" always do! Shall I try and wangle you an invitation for Christmas? Or shall I come to Edinburgh?'

It seemed a marvellous idea, being with Richard and having meals on time and living in an organized household. If only Aunt Laura could have taken us both. You see, Richard is very different from me. He's always been terrifically independent and he likes being alone with his music or looking things up in encyclopaedias; he doesn't need people so much as things. And I don't mean he's one of those sissie boys – he's a super swimmer and he was in the tennis team at his old school and one of his ambitions is to be a rock climber. But he's never been like those boys who are always rolling on the grass wrestling or kicking balls about or making extraordinary noises like tractors or machine guns. It really was a pity we had got the wrong aunts because I could see quite clearly that Richard wouldn't be annoyed by Aunt Patsy at all. She'd be at her drawing board making squiggles and he'd be at the piano playing scales and when they were hungry they'd eat and when they were tired they'd go to bed without bothering about the time at all.

And I wouldn't mind being called 'girls' by Aunt

Laura or being asked if I'd wash my hands or told when it was bedtime. I don't think Aunt Patsy would have noticed or cared if I stayed up till midnight. At first I used to look at the clock around half past nine and wonder if she would say: 'Time for bed, Emma!' But she never did. I used to yawn and fidget and then say: 'Don't you think it's time I went to bed?'

'If you want. No one's stopping you.'

I couldn't help missing the way Mother used to get my milk and biscuits, and say she'd be up in half an hour to turn my light off, and kiss me goodnight. Sometimes she'd just kiss me and tell me to sleep well, and at other times she'd sit on my bed and we'd have a cosy chat about school or what colour I'd like my winter coat or things that happened to her when she was a little girl. It made me feel very lonely and cut off to choose my own bedtime and turn off my own light.

If only I could persuade Aunt Laura that I was the sort of girl she'd like and persuade Aunt Patsy that Richard was the sort of boy she'd like, without being rude or ungrateful!

Chapter Five

I WAS dreading my first day at school. New schools of any sort are bad enough. I hated it when I started Grammar School in London and had to get used to new teachers and different rules. It's partly because I'm what Mother used to call 'a creature of habit' and partly because although I'm not shy at meeting one or two strange people, a lot of strangers make me feel terribly tongue-tied and stupid.

But after all in London I already had several friends and I did start at the beginning of the term. Also I had Mother to boost my morale when I got home and Father to help me with my Latin and Geometry homework.

Starting school in Edinburgh was going to be sheer murder, I thought gloomily. The term had already started and everyone would know I was an orphan and feel sorry for me. And everything would probably be taught differently in some stupid Scottish way, and instead of being near the top of the class, I'd probably be the prize dunce.

Aunt Patsy had rung up the Education Committee and fixed for me to go to what is called a

Senior Secondary School. (They don't appear to have Grammar Schools in Edinburgh.) It was called Parkhill.

'All schools are pretty awful in my opinion,' said Aunt Patsy. 'I know I never learnt a thing but it's the law. So there's nothing we can do about it.'

'But you have to be educated,' I said, rather horrified.

'Education!' Aunt Patsy sniffed. 'What have square roots, and the date of the Battle of Trafalgar, and being able to translate some Roman general's reminiscences into pidgin English to do with education? I'd throw children into public libraries and art galleries and see what happened.'

'But then we'd never pass our exams.'

'Quite!' said Aunt Patsy.

I found out later that she had left school at fifteen and done all sorts of horrible jobs like working in a bakery and serving in a shop until she won a scholarship to Art School.

'If I don't get "A" level in at least three subjects,' I said, 'I'll never find an interesting job.'

'I did,' said Aunt Patsy.

I was just going to say, 'But that was in the olden days,' then I thought it would be rude so I said instead: 'It's different if you're an artist.'

Anyhow to school I had to go, and we bought an alarm clock and Aunt Patsy, rather unwillingly, agreed to go with me. 'It gives me the shudders just going into a school,' she said, 'and as for being smarmy to headmasters...'

I wanted to say, 'All right, if that's the way you feel I'll go alone,' but I couldn't bring myself to. I just hoped and prayed she wouldn't wear her

slacks and look too eccentric. However, she wore her green corduroy suit and actually looked rather smart.

'And you will be here when I get back?' I asked.

'I daresay.'

Parkhill is in what they call the New Town because it is only about a hundred years old! It's quite different from the Old Town, and has squares and gardens and terraces built in circles called circuses and crescents, rather like some parts of London. And a lot of the buildings have pillars and funny bits of statuary. I liked it because of the trees and the gardens, and because the houses didn't look as though they would fall down any minute, the way they did in the Old Town.

Naturally the school wasn't new. It looked rather like my idea of a prison or a reformatory – a great square high building in sooty stone surrounded by a concrete playground with high spiky railings. The date over the door was 1899. Probably, I thought, it's still lit by gas and we have to write on slates.

'Aren't there any new schools?' I asked Aunt Patsy as we stepped off the bus.

'Oh yes,' said Aunt Patsy. 'In the suburbs they've built several, all glass and concrete and bright coloured tiles. I must say, this does look rather awful. But never mind. It's supposed to be quite a good school – as schools go.'

To be honest, it wasn't quite as bad inside as I had feared. It was light and the paintwork was pale blue and it didn't remind me of a prison at all.

But something else struck me.

'Do you mean there are boys too?' I asked.

'Of course. Nearly all Scottish schools are co-educational. Didn't you know?'

I gulped. It had just never occurred to me. I'd heard people discussing coeducation, and Mother had always said it was a bad thing because boys and girls developed at different speeds and were good at different things.

The place seemed suddenly full of boys – great

tall, practically grown-up boys, and middle-sized pimply boys with weird hair styles, and little midgetty boys staggering under the weight of enormous school bags, all looking exactly like what Aunt Laura meant when she said 'boys'.

I followed Aunt Patsy up the stairs to the headmaster's room feeling worse and worse.

The headmaster was small and fat and grey with an india-rubbery face and a toothy smile. He shook both our hands.

'Ah, Miss Grieve,' he said, 'and this is Emma.'

As I obviously was Emma there didn't seem anything to reply. So I sort of smirked.

'I'm afraid it will all seem rather strange at first,' he said to me, 'but I'm sure you'll settle down soon.'

Again I gave a tepid smile.

'You've been doing Latin and French, haven't you, so I've put you into Miss Morrison's class, number five, and we'll see how you get on. I'll just get one of the prefects to take you to your classroom, that is unless there's anything you would like to ask me.'

I did want to ask him something frightfully badly, but it was difficult.

'Please, could you not tell anyone about' – I gulped – 'my parents.'

'Of course not, my dear child. Now,' he picked up his telephone, pressed a knob, and said:

'Miss Vaughan, would you find one of the prefects and ask her to take Emma to Miss Morrison's class, please.' A minute later there was a knock on the door. I shook hands with the headmaster again, Aunt Patsy gave me a rueful look as if to say, 'I told you schools were awful and headmasters fools but what can we do?' and I followed a very tall snooty-looking girl down the stairs again.

The classroom was on the ground floor but the windows were too high up to look out of. The desks were all double ones but I was relieved to find that the boys sat on one side of the room and the girls on the other. Miss Morrison, our class teacher, was youngish and quite pretty, and gave me a smile. She wrote my name down, handed me hundreds of books and exercise books (they call them jotters) and introduced me to the class: 'This is Emma Langham, and she's from London, so I hope you'll all help her to find her way about.'

The girl she put me to sit beside was called Elizabeth Cameron. She had shoulder-length mouse-coloured hair in such a very long fringe I couldn't see much of her face but what I could see seemed nice. All the same it was horrible to have to sit so close to a perfect stranger – no privacy at all.

'Have you come to stay here?' she whispered.

'No, I'm just on a visit,' I whispered back.

'Is your father in the Army?'

'No. He's an engineer. My mother's in hospital so I'm staying with an aunt.'

'How long for?'

'I don't know. Probably till Christmas.'

I don't approve of lies but you can't go round telling people that you're a very new orphan because they just get embarrassed and don't know what to say. I remember a girl at my other school whose mother died and of course we all wanted to be specially nice to her but we didn't know how.

The first lesson was Maths and we were given a perfectly easy problem but for some reason I couldn't concentrate. Ordinarily I'm pretty good at Maths.

After a few minutes Elizabeth Cameron nudged my elbow and pushed a piece of paper on to my desk with the answer written on it. I was furious. As if I wanted any help! I scrumpled it up and dropped it on the floor and shook my head violently.

'Sorry I'm sure,' she whispered in a huffy voice.

Then the Maths teacher, who was red-faced and bald and called Mr Hamilton, did the problem on the board and asked whoever had it right to put up their hands.

'And you-er-Emma,' he said, 'are you familiar with this type of problem?'

I blushed and nodded. I daresay he was trying to be helpful but it's beastly to be picked on on your very first day.

At break we all went into the horrible concrete

playground and most of the girls said Hello to me, and asked me the same questions, and I elaborated a bit, and told them my mother had rheumatic fever but they'd just discovered some absolutely super new drug so that she'd be well again in no time. And I'm afraid I boasted that Aunt Patsy was a famous artist who lived in a historic house near the Castle that had been in the family for generations, and that my school in London was the very latest design. (Actually it was quite old too.) Once you start lying it's difficult to stop. I saw how I'd like everything to be and I couldn't resist the chance to make it that way even though, at the same time, I knew it was stupid.

After a bit the girls became bored and started talking about who was gone on who, and wasn't the Maths teacher a beast to have given us so much homework, and other school gossip, and as it was all about people I had never heard of I got bored too and drifted away. Then the bell rang.

We had History next which was confusing, because it was the history of Scotland, and the only things I knew were about Mary, Queen of Scots being beheaded, and Robert Bruce winning the Battle of Bannockburn. But the History teacher was nice and made it all as interesting as possible.

The Latin teacher was a little bright-eyed old lady with white hair and a pink face who seemed to think Latin was so dull she must cheer it up by telling us lots of jokes and describing her holidays in Italy where her knowledge of Latin 'had been so useful'. I had a suspicion that the class had heard her jokes before but they all laughed politely. And I couldn't help thinking, too, that Italian would have been a great deal more useful than Latin for a holiday in Italy.

Elizabeth Cameron didn't try to help me again and I put a stack of books at my side of the desk so she couldn't see what I was writing.

Dinner was the worst part of the day because the dining-room was so crowded we all had our elbows practically in each other's plates, and the mince was gristly, and the custard too sweet, and the sponge was full of dates that tasted like penicillin tablets. But then, in my experience, school dinners always are vile.

I felt very tired when eventually the bell rang at a quarter to four and I filled Aunt Patsy's old music case, which she had lent me, with all the books I had been given. It weighed a ton and I didn't look forward to lugging it up the hill.

'Do we have to take all our books home?' I asked Elizabeth.

'Of course.'

'What a bind!'

At the bus stop there was a great jostling queue and the bigger boys simply smashed their way through it. A girl who was standing beside me gave one of them a smart kick on the ankle and darted on to the bus while he looked round. Fortunately there weren't so many people for my bus so I didn't have to resort to such drastic tactics.

Still I was pretty exhausted when I finally staggered up the stairs and let myself into the flat.

'Yoohoo,' I called, which was what I always did at home when I got back from school.

There was no reply. The kitchen was empty, except for the usual pile of washing-up, and the studio was empty except for the usual trail of coffee cups and bulging ashtrays. Aunt Patsy was out.

Mother was always home at four o'clock and she always had tea ready, and suddenly I felt utterly miserable. I sat down at the kitchen table and cried. Horrible Edinburgh! Horrible school! And horrible Aunt Patsy.

Then I pulled myself together, filled the kettle and lit the gas and laid the table for two – surely Aunt Patsy would be back soon. I tackled the washing-up while the kettle was boiling. Then I made the tea and toasted two bits of bread. Still no Aunt Patsy. I leaned out of the window but apart from the usual silly tourists coming to look at the

Castle there was nobody. So I ate my tea by myself.

Aunt Patsy didn't get home till six o'clock. I heard her call 'Emma!' but I was lying on my bed and I didn't reply. I was too angry with her. She knocked on my door and came in.

'Hullo. How are you? How was school?'

'You weren't in,' I said accusingly. 'I made tea and everything and you didn't come.'

'Emma, I'm sorry, I just had to go and see someone about a job.'

'I bet you forgot,' I mumbled.

'I didn't forget. I just couldn't make it.'

'You don't care.'

Aunt Patsy went pink. I thought for a moment she was going to be angry and tell me I was a bore and a nuisance and I could jolly well go into a Home for all she cared. Instead she tightened her mouth and looked out of the window. In a way I wanted her to be angry but she just spoke very quietly.

'Look, Emma, I have to earn my living and if a chance of a job comes up I simply have to take it. Sometimes I'll be in and sometimes I won't and you'll have to put up with it. You're quite old enough to be reasonable.'

The trouble was I didn't feel at all old enough to be reasonable. So I went on lying on my bed feeling sorry for myself until Aunt Patsy told me supper was ready. We were very polite at supper about passing the butter and the salt, and we didn't talk. After supper she went up to the studio and I went back into my room and did my homework.

Chapter Six

I DON'T know exactly when it was that I stopped hating everything so much. It was like when you've been ill in bed for a long time and you wake up one morning and think 'I'm well' and you actually feel hungry for breakfast. Mother used to give me, on these occasions, a lightly boiled egg and brown bread and butter cut very thin and I used to eat it very slowly because it tasted so delicious. And then I'd get up and go into the garden and everything would look and smell clean and new, especially the sycamore tree.

Something like this happened to me now. I woke up one morning and thought, goodie, History today, and I shot out of bed and looked out of the window and suddenly realized I liked looking at all the slatey-blue roofs and chimney-pots and the green hill they call Arthur's Seat. And I liked hearing the milkman's horse clop-clopping up the hill and the chink of bottles and the scruffy-looking starling that sat making wolf-whistles on the gutter.

As I got washed and dressed I felt conscious of the beautiful way all the bits of my body were joined together and I thought how clever my muscles were to do so quickly what I wanted them to do. And I smiled at myself in the mirror as if I were being introduced to someone who would say, Who is that beautiful and talented girl?

I decided to make bacon and eggs for breakfast and I put Aunt Patsy's on a tray and knocked at her door and said, 'Surprise,' just like my father used to say when he did it for me or Mother.

Aunt Patsy blinked and mumbled something but I just drew her curtains and brought up a chair to put the tray on.

'Emma,' she protested. 'What on earth's got into you?'

'It's a marvellous morning,' I said. 'You can't waste it asleep.'

I discovered later that she loathed breakfast in bed and that bacon and eggs first thing in the morning gave her indigestion but she put on a very convincing act of thanking me and saying she felt like a duchess.

Recently, Aunt Patsy and I had been awfully polite to one another without ever really saying anything. She had made a great effort to be in at four o'clock and had almost resigned herself to doing the washing-up after instead of before meals. She always asked me how I had got on at school and I always asked her if she had had a good day but we had just been strangers living in the same house, certainly not friends or relations.

And I suddenly thought what a bind it must have been for her to alter her whole life for someone I could hardly believe she even liked.

So after breakfast I went back into her room and said: 'You don't have to be in for tea. I don't really mind.'

She grinned, though she was still rather sleepy and hadn't made much headway with her breakfast. Then she said: 'Let's have something nice for supper. What would you like? I might ask Stephen and make it a party.'

'Can we have it all laid out properly with table mats and butter knives?'

'Your word is my command.'

'And flowers?'

'Why not?'

'I mean, can we afford it?'

'We can. I got a very good cheque this week.'

'Then let's have roast pork and apple sauce and trifle with lots of cream.'

'Ugh, I can't bear to think of food at this time of the morning.'

'Well, you asked me.'

'So I did.'

'And can we have salted nuts and cheesey biscuits to nibble while we're waiting?'

'Ugh,' said Aunt Patsy again and shut her eyes.

I don't mean from all this that I had given up my plan of exchanging Aunt Patsy for Aunt Laura. I knew that Aunt Patsy and I just weren't suited. But I also knew that she was being as nice to me as she could and probably a great deal nicer than I deserved. And I knew that Mother would strongly disapprove if I went on sulking and narking. It suddenly seemed very easy not to sulk and nark. After all it would only be until Christmas.

I met the postman on the stairs – and don't think I had suddenly decided to like *them* – and he gave me a letter from Richard which I read on the bus.

'All sorts of plots and plans are brewing,' he wrote. 'To start with the insurance money has come through which has cheered Aunt Laura up no end – I mean "boys" are so expensive, always growing out of their clothes, etc. It also appears that she has been appointed our guardian and so will be able to decide whether you are being properly looked after, or not, as you seem to think. She definitely disapproves of Aunt Patsy, with her nasty bohemian habits, irregular hours, unsuitable friends and so on. The money having arrived, she is now talking about sending me to boarding school and going to Edinburgh to investigate the appallingly unsuitable conditions she is sure you are living in, ha ha! I think if she finds that you are a "nice" girl and liable to fit into a "nice" home she might consider taking you into "the bosom of". As for me, I am in disgrace for being so unboyish as to prefer music to football.

'At first I wasn't sure about the boarding school idea but, as you know, I am not such a home body as you and when I talked to Mr Chator (the music master) he said he thought I could get a scholarship to a really super school where music is taken seriously.

'I'm pretty sure that M-O-N-E-Y counts more with Aunt Laura than anything else so if she finds one of those schools that are all discipline and keeping a stiff upper lip and a healthy mind in a healthy body, I shall be able to make a counter-suggestion with a scholarship cheque clutched in my unboyish hand.

'Is Edinburgh really so awful? Are you sure it's Aunt Patsy and not just you? Think twice, dear sister, before you exchange your crumbling bohemian attic for a nice suitable home.'

This was a terribly exciting letter. I thought Richard was being just too stupid about Aunt Laura. Of course money was important. It was important to Aunt Patsy too; perhaps with the insurance money she'd be able to buy the blue carpet she'd promised me.

Then I remembered that by Christmas I'd be living in Exeter, Richard would be back for the holidays and life would be marvellous. It would be nice, too, for Aunt Patsy who must be bored to death with my fussing about the washing-up and having meals on time.

School started off well. I even smiled at Elizabeth Cameron and didn't put a pile of books between her desk and mine, and I was top of the History test.

Now I want to make it clear before I describe what happened next that the teachers at Parkhill were, as teachers go, all reasonably nice. They had their quirks and oddities of course but in general, if you behaved adequately, they treated you as a human being. There are days when even the nicest teacher obviously has a headache or indigestion or the beginning of flu and then if anyone plays up they tend to go mad. And in any class there are always one or two pupils, especially boys, who aren't interested and who do everything they can to get a rise out of a teacher. They ask silly questions and drop things and talk and throw india-rubbers at each other. And they don't apparently mind being caned, or getting the belt as it's called in Scotland.

But Mr Hamilton, the Maths teacher, seemed to suffer from permanent headaches (or indigestion or flu) because he was always in a bad temper. His big red face used to go even redder and he would shout and bang his hand on the desk and wave his belt around like a cowboy with a lassoo. Even when he wasn't angry he always spoke in that nasty sarcastic way: 'I wonder if I could trouble you to rise from your seat and approach the blackboard,' or 'It appears that our mathematical genius in the back row is under the impression that two and two make five,' which we all hated.

I used to do quite well in Maths but it was more to spite him than to please him. I liked to do a problem very quickly and then, as if bored, sit looking at the ceiling. When he thought he had me napping and asked if I could bear just giving him a quarter of my attention, I would give the right answer in a superior voice.

I knew he was dying to catch me out and I was determined that he shouldn't. One day I even found a mistake in one of his calculations. Delighted I put up my hand. 'Excuse me, sir, but I don't understand.'

'You don't understand? I thought that with your experience in the southern part of the island there was little we poor Scots could do to puzzle your superior knowledge.'

'The figure on the right,' I said. 'I don't understand why it's 59 and not 58.'

'What? What?' he barked. 'Oh I see. Yes, yes.'

He scowled at me and I looked as innocent as possible and one of the boys tittered but as he was looking at me he didn't see which one. So he gave us all extra homework to relieve his feelings.

This particular morning he was even worse

than usual. Perhaps he had quarrelled with his wife because she had burnt the toast or he had left his umbrella on the bus.

He stormed into the classroom, gave us all a row for not standing up fast enough and told us we were the laziest set of nincompoops he had ever had the misfortune to teach. He was going to give us a test and anyone who got less than ten out of twenty would be given double homework.

'And anyone who gets less than five,' he snarled, taking out his belt and giving it a swish, 'will make closer acquaintance with Oscar here.' (He always called the belt 'Oscar' – stupid!)

One or two people snickered nervously and then we all bent over the test. Even though I knew I wasn't likely to get less than ten I couldn't help feeling nervous and my heart beat in the way that makes you feel everyone must be able to hear it.

Elizabeth, beside me, was even more nervous. I could hear her giving little sighs of desperation and she kept licking her lips.

When I was nearly through I looked round and caught her eye and gave her an encouraging smile. She shook her head and turned her eyes towards the ceiling. I glanced at her paper and saw that she had only got as far as number four.

Although we often help each other with our homework or ordinary classwork it's understood that when we do tests it's each man for himself.

Still, every rule has its exception and I felt this certainly was cause for one.

I tilted my papers sideways so that Elizabeth could see at least some of my answers, but she was hunched over her desk and didn't look up. I gave her a tiny kick on the ankle and nodded as if to say, 'It's all right, go ahead.' Then I became very absorbed in the next question and didn't dare to see if Elizabeth was taking advantage of my help or not.

'Elizabeth Cameron!' boomed out the voice of Mr Hamilton.

'Y-yes, sir,' she stammered.

'When I give tests I expect the results to be the unaided efforts of your own brain, however woefully inadequate that organ is, not the joint efforts of you and the distinguished scholar on your left.'

'Yes, sir,' said poor Elizabeth.

Her face was always half-hidden behind her hair but the bit of it I could see was crimson.

'Oscar would like a few words with you, Elizabeth.'

Elizabeth stumbled up to his desk and held out her hand. I was so furious I didn't care that I was playing right into Mr Hamilton's hands.

'It's unfair!' I shouted.

Mr Hamilton glared at me.

'Oh?' he drawled.

'It was my fault. I wanted to help her.'

64

'I don't know what the custom is in the southern part of the island,' he sneered, 'but in Scotland cheating is regarded as dishonourable.'

I knew it was crazy to answer a teacher back (any teacher) but I couldn't stop, in spite of Mr Hamilton looking apoplectic and running his belt through his fingers. Although red-haired people are supposed to have hot tempers I don't often lose mine; but when I do it's like a galloping horse.

'Helping isn't cheating,' I burst out.

'Really? How interesting! How informative!'

'And in any case,' I went on in a rush, 'she could have done the test perfectly well if you hadn't made her so nervous.'

'So the age of chivalry is not dead,' drawled Mr Hamilton. 'If you wish to suffer alongside your friend, who am I to stand in your way? Approach the desk, please.'

So I walked up and stood beside Elizabeth and he hit us both with his beastly belt. It was horrible. No one had ever hit me before in my life. I don't mean I'm always angelically well-behaved. From time to time I've been sent to bed early or had my pocket-money docked or just been given a talking to. But hit – never. I didn't know I could feel so angry.

Elizabeth was crying when we went back to our desks but I wasn't. I was just seething with fury. I stuffed my books angrily into my school bag and stumped straight out of the classroom, giving Mr

Hamilton what I hoped was a withering look.

Just as I reached the main hall the bell rang for the dinner break but I didn't go into the dining-hall. I went out of the door and across the play-ground and out into the street. The lollipop man in his white coat was standing by the bus stop for the primary children who mostly went home to dinner.

'Going home early?' he asked. He was a nice cheery man.

'I'm not feeling well,' I said and let him stop the traffic for me to go across the road to my bus stop on the other side.

'You don't look so good and that's a fact,' he said sympathetically. 'There's a lot of flu going round.'

It's funny that whenever you have a cold or a sore throat someone always tells you that there's a lot of it going around.

All the way home in the bus I kept saying to myself, 'I'll never go there again. The beast, the absolute beast.'

I simply raced up the stairs and rushed into the flat. Aunt Patsy was sitting in the kitchen drinking coffee and reading the paper and before I had thought what I was going to do or say I had flung my arms round her and burst into tears.

Aunt Patsy was utterly bewildered but she held me tightly and kept saying: 'What happened, Emma? What's the matter, darling?'

I choked and sobbed and then I blew my nose and sat down beside her and told her the whole story. At the back of my mind I realized that she had never called me Darling before.

She was just as angry as I had been. She kept exclaiming, 'Disgusting! Revolting behaviour! What a swine!' and she lit cigarettes and stamped round the room and said that I need never go to school again, that all the School Inspectors in the world wouldn't force her to send me, that she'd go to jail first, and other comforting things.

'The spectacle of a grown man beating little girls makes me spew,' she spluttered. 'Now don't worry, Emma, there's no headmaster in the world who can frighten me.'

When I had calmed down she wanted me to have some lunch but I felt I'd be sick, so I just had a cup of tea and a piece of toast and Marmite. And then Aunt Patsy strode to the telephone as if she were going to impale it on a bayonet, dialled the number with savage little jabs of her finger and asked to speak to the headmaster.

I felt rather cosy and exhausted sitting in the kitchen listening to Aunt Patsy's voice.

'I hear from my niece that she has been attacked by one of the vile sadistic thugs you employ to instruct her in Mathematics ... Either you sack him immediately or I shall go to the Education Committee and raise Cain ... It's abominable that grown men are allowed to hit little girls under your revolting system of so-called education ... I shall take him to court and charge him with assault ... I won't allow my niece to set foot in your deplorable school again ...'

Then she came back into the kitchen looking smug.

'I've scared him out of his wits,' she said with a chuckle. 'He wants me to go to the school this afternoon and tell him exactly what happened and then he will "take steps". He is deeply apologetic, ha ha! Didn't you think I was impressive on the phone, Emma?'

'You were marvellous. I don't suppose anyone's ever spoken to him like that before in his life.'

'I don't suppose so. And it's high time someone did. Now Emma, why don't you lie on your bed with a book and when I come back with his head on a spear we'll have tea together. And after that we'll cook our delicious celebration supper.'

Chapter Seven

SUPPER that evening was a great success. I cleared the table in the studio and laid it with matching cutlery and plates – Aunt Patsy did have nice things, she was just too lazy to use them half the time. We arranged some lovely white chrysanthemums in a red jug and polished the furniture, and the whole room looked quite civilized for once.

Aunt Patsy had made the trifle and put it in the fridge but she had allowed me to decorate it with whipped cream and cherries and chopped nuts. I also arranged the before-supper drinks on a tray with the salted nuts and potato crisps and cheesey biscuits in little bowls.

So when Stephen McTaggart arrived everything was ready, both Aunt Patsy and I were clean and brushed, wearing nylons without snags in them, and the new corduroy pinafores we had just bought: Aunt Patsy's was pale blue and mine was honey colour.

She had come back from her interview with the headmaster in high spirits but she just said: 'I'll tell you about it at supper. It's so boring to have to tell a story twice. Everything's going to be all right.'

So I felt rather gay too and to my surprise I quite enjoyed telling Stephen what had happened at school and imitating Mr Hamilton; in fact I even made them both laugh. It's peculiar that things which make you furious or upset at the time can make you laugh when you tell them afterwards.

Then Aunt Patsy told Stephen about her telephone conversation and she made us laugh too. So when she came to describing her interview we were all quite giggly.

I don't know exactly what she said to the headmaster because often when you tell a story you slightly improve what you said and what he said, but apparently he had been very nice and understanding. He said he had been trying to get a replacement for Mr Hamilton for some time as he had not been satisfied with his teaching methods, but that there was a terrific shortage of teachers. He'd go immediately to the Education Department and insist on a replacement but he'd be hardly likely to get one until next term.

Aunt Patsy said in that case she'd keep me at home for the rest of the term and if anyone asked why, she'd jolly well tell them.

The headmaster gave his personal assurance that Mr Hamilton wouldn't lay a finger on me again. What about the other girls? Aunt Patsy had asked. She didn't want anyone to be beaten. A man who threatened defenceless children with physical violence wasn't fit to be entrusted with teaching them.

Well, the headmaster said, he quite understood but there were limits of his powers of interference. The whole question of corporal punishment was under review and many teachers were against it nowadays; he personally was in favour of restricting it to really serious offences but, because of the shortage of teachers, overcrowded classes and so on and so forth . . .

Aunt Patsy snorted: she hadn't yet given up the idea of reporting the whole matter to the Director of Education, charging Mr Hamilton with assault, and giving the story to the press.

The headmaster promised he would look into the whole matter immediately and let her know within the next few days. But he did feel it would be a mistake to deprive a promising scholar of half a term's work. It might seriously prejudice my chances in the exams.

So then Aunt Patsy told him exactly what she thought about exams. I wish I had been there.

'So here you are and here you stay,' said Aunt Patsy triumphantly, 'until that monster has been removed.'

While we had been unfolding our tale Stephen had been chuckling and saying, 'Good for you,' and 'You're absolutely right,' and 'The thug,' and things of that sort. But when she had finished he stared at Aunt Patsy in quite a different way and said: 'Patsy, you're marvellous!'

Until now I hadn't noticed anybody or anything except as they'd appeared to me. I suppose I had been completely self-centred. But now I looked at Stephen and Aunt Patsy in quite a different way, looking at them both as they must appear to each other.

Aunt Patsy, sitting on a tufftie by the electric fire, in her nice blue corduroy pinafore that made her eyes look blue too, was flushed and almost pretty. And although you couldn't call Stephen handsome he did look distinguished and interesting as he sat on the sofa and leaned forward to touch her hand when he told her she was marvellous. He always wore dark green or dark blue shirts with peculiar ties or polo-necked sweaters and his donkey jacket was a disgrace. His teeth weren't good and he had a round bald patch on the top of his head. But his light-blue eyes had a sort of electric sharpness and there were little lines on his face that made him look kind, and his smile always seemed as though he were really smiling, not just being polite.

I decided they must like each other very much indeed and that I liked them both very much too. So I got up and went downstairs to make coffee. Of course I hadn't the faintest intention of staying away from school. That would have been stupid because I knew the value of exams even if Aunt Patsy didn't. I wasn't really frightened of Mr Hamilton and now that I had recovered and been made a fuss of and eaten a delicious meal (the trifle was fabulous) I was even looking forward to going back to school and having a good gossip with everyone. So I hummed happily to myself as I made coffee and put Aunt Patsy's best coffee service on a tray. (I discovered it at the back of a cupboard where she had forgotten it.)

Perhaps Stephen had seen a completely 'new side' to Aunt Patsy and now he would fall in love with her. Then she'd have someone to pay the laundry bills and she could move into a civilized new house with a garden, and perhaps (I'm a bit ashamed of thinking this) I'd even have my blue carpet.

When I returned to the studio with the coffee they were both sitting on the sofa which I thought was an encouraging sign.

'What did we ever do without Emma?' Stephen said smiling. 'Butter plates and paper napkins and coffee in the best cups! What a transformation! What a reformation!'

Aunt Patsy and I looked at each other and for a moment I thought *she* looked annoyed and that *I* felt annoyed, but then we both laughed.

'Soon I'll be wearing gloves and a hat,' Aunt Patsy said.

'Never!' said Stephen.

'Sipping tea, with my little finger curled up, with all the best Edinburgh ladies,' continued Aunt Patsy simpering.

'Learning to play bridge and writing letters to the papers about the Decline of Modern Youth.'

'Please, no!'

'The people in Castlehill will set their watches by me because of the punctuality with which I dispatch my duties and when I die they'll put on my gravestone: "By her sobriety, godliness and righteousness she set an example to the people of this parish".'

'Promise,' said Stephen to me, 'that you won't reform Patsy too much.'

I smiled rather smugly. It was intoxicating to think of reforming anyone, even a little, let alone too much. Privately I thought I had made very little headway and that if Aunt Patsy wanted to get married, to Stephen, for instance, she still had a long way to go before she would make him a suitable wife.

At that moment the door bell rang and Stephen said: 'Oh, by the way, as you felt like a party, I asked some of my students to drop in.' (Stephen taught part-time at the Art College.)

I felt a bit disappointed because we were having such a cosy time, just the three of us, but I went down to open the door and four or five people burst in, carrying guitars and tins of Coca-Cola and beer, all laughing and talking. They were a pretty weird lot, mostly wearing jeans and jerseys which could have done with a wash, and with hair badly in need of cutting. They all had names like Lil or Bett or Jim or Dave and I could never remember which was which. (Some of them had visited us before but I usually went to my room to get out of the way.)

This time they all became very excited looking at some new designs of Aunt Patsy's. They made me quite ashamed that I'd never really found out what she was doing when she sat up late at night at her drawing-board. Apparently one of those boutique shops had asked her to design some tiles and one of the students, Jim (or Dave), was going to fire them for her.

I looked at the designs and really they were rather nice. There were some in splodgy blues and greens with butterfly shapes and some in splodgy oranges and browns in flower shapes.

While the others were admiring them I fetched more glasses and a beer-can opener and rescued the precious coffee cups from possible accidents. By the time I had returned, one of the girls was playing the piano. Then Dave tuned his guitar and sang some folk songs, and soon everyone was talking and drinking and joining in the songs, and talking and drinking again. I did not talk much because they were all a lot older than me and I don't know anything about art. I just filled their glasses and passed ashtrays so they wouldn't drop ash on the floor.

It wasn't the sort of party I usually like but because of my special mood I found I was enjoying myself. We had drawn the curtains and the lamplight made shadows on the white walls; the piano, which we had polished till it shone, reflected the light; and the guitar made a nice twangy background noise.

In fact after all the excitement and the good food I felt rather as if my body had gone to sleep and that the rest of me was floating on some sort of cushiony cloud, so that I could think and notice with a special sharpness without being able to move or talk. I could see Aunt Patsy and Stephen sitting on the sofa talking earnestly together; and the students mostly on the floor, with glasses in their hands, jabbering away, except for the one called Jim who was bent over his guitar, and the one called Lil who was leaning against the mantelpiece singing a song about a lassie with a yellow coatie.

I don't know how long this mood lasted but quite by accident my eyes wandered to the clock on the mantelpiece. It was usually wrong but I had set it right before the party. And to my horror I found it was half past eleven, long past my bedtime. What would Mother have said, I suddenly thought with a pang: at home I'd only been allowed to stay up late on very special occasions like Christmas and my birthday and then certainly not later than half past ten. There wasn't a hope that Aunt Patsy would look up and say: 'Gracious, child, it's high time you were in bed!'

But then, I reflected, Aunt Patsy couldn't help it. She had never had a daughter and didn't know what mothers are expected to do, and after all she had shown that she had my interests at heart. So when she looked across at me and smiled and said, 'Enjoying yourself, Emma?' I just smiled back and went on floating on my cloud. After all it was Saturday tomorrow and we'd be able to have a late breakfast.

I didn't look at the clock again but presently everyone started getting ready to go home. They made a terrific noise galumphing down the stairs and I couldn't imagine what the neighbours would think; and then Aunt Patsy and I were left alone, yawning and blinking at each other.

'Let's leave the washing-up till tomorrow,' said Aunt Patsy coaxingly.

For a moment I was going to say No, we'll do it now; then I relented.

'Let's,' I said.

Chapter Eight

THE next morning Aunt Patsy and I got up rather late, about nine o'clock. We spent an hour clearing away and washing up after the party and then settled down to a quiet breakfast of boiled eggs and lots of toast and marmalade (for Aunt Patsy) and honey (for me) and tea (for Aunt Patsy) and Nescafé (for me). We were both rather sleepy so we didn't talk much but over our second cups Aunt Patsy said, 'Stephen and I are thinking it would be rather nice to get married. What do you think?'

'I think it would be super,' I said quickly. 'I mean he's awfully nice and you have got Art in common even though—' I choked back what I was going to say next.

'Even though what?'

'He's a bit bald,' I mumbled shamefacedly.

Aunt Patsy roared with laughter so I knew I hadn't hurt her feelings.

At that moment, just as I was going to ask all sorts of questions, the postman arrived with Aunt Laura's letter. Aunt Patsy read it with, every minute, her eyebrows going higher, her nose getting longer, and the corners of her mouth turning in a satirical way.

'Well, well, well!' she said. 'Laura has all sorts of ideas about your future – about all our futures, in fact.'

'Tell me,' I begged.

'I don't know' – began Aunt Patsy – 'but, oh well, it's your future so you ought to hear the letter itself, not just what I think of it.'

She began to read.

Dear Patsy,

The Will has appointed me as guardian to poor Richard and Emma and now the insurance money has come through it will be possible to do the sort of thing that Christine would have wished.

In the case of dear Richard I feel the answer is clearly a good boarding school. He has not really settled down to our way of life and cannot be said to have fitted in, though I have done my best for him. He is not a very cooperative boy.

As for Emma, I have no doubt that she has been somewhat an inconvenience to you, knowing the free-and-easy life you lead, and that you will be pleased to hear that it will now be possible to send her to a boarding school too.

On the other hand, from what I learned about her from Christine and the chance remarks of her brother, she seems essentially the sort of girl who would benefit from family life and, if I am satisfied that she would fit in, I would consider taking her under our roof and providing the sort of background for her that I am sure she would appreciate.

I realize that it was your keen sense of duty and family obligations that led you to give Emma a temporary home in Edinburgh but I am sure that you will be pleased to be freed of that obligation now that a suitable alternative offers itself.

As for myself, it is hardly necessary to tell you that I want the best for my dear nephew and niece.

I am coming up to Edinburgh in the near future when we can discuss the matter. Please do not offer to put me up as I know of your cramped surroundings and I would not dream of inconveniencing you.

> Yours affectionately,
> Laura

On hearing this letter I was filled with so many conflicting feelings I didn't know what to say.

First I felt Hooray! Aunt Laura will find out how nice I am and how unsuitably I am being looked after and she will take me back to Exeter, and I shall live in a nice family house in the country. On the other hand I realized I liked Aunt

Patsy and I liked living in Edinburgh, and I didn't want to go to a boarding school or stay in a house where I was just a 'girl'. I'd rather have had irregular meals and bedtimes and be treated as a person. Still, if Aunt Patsy was going to marry Stephen they wouldn't want to start off with a great lump of ready-made family (me); I mean people just don't, they like their own children but not other people's.

It all led to two conclusions: if I behaved nicely, Aunt Laura would whisk me off to Exeter; and if I behaved badly she would whisk me off to boarding school. And I suddenly and most violently did not want to do either.

I saw Richard's letters in quite a new light. Obviously he had been wretched because Aunt Laura was a narrow-minded stupid woman. He had just tried to be cheerful for my sake. And now she was coming to rescue me and I didn't want to be rescued.

It might have been different if Aunt Patsy had really wanted me to stay but why should she? I was an awful expense, I knew, and a nuisance, always being hungry and needing white shirts ironed for school and even help with my homework. And if she married Stephen I would be even more of a nuisance.

'Well, what do you think?' asked Aunt Patsy.

I took a gulp of my nearly cold coffee.

'I don't know,' I said limply.

We stared at each other across the kitchen table, with Aunty Patsy trying to discover my thoughts on the matter and I trying to find out what she really thought; but we didn't know each other well enough.

'Aunt Laura on the warpath,' said Aunt Patsy, 'coming to inspect me and see whether you keep regular hours, eat suitable food at stated intervals and meet my unsuitable friends! Grrr.'

At the remembrance of yesterday I couldn't help giggling, and Aunt Patsy giggled too. In fact we became quite uproarious and I spilt my coffee.

'Darling Emma,' said Aunt Patsy. 'I can't decide your future. You will have to decide yourself, though I think it's unfair when you're so young. But it would be even more unfair if I tried to decide for you. Do you understand?'

I nodded. I did, in a way. But I wished, all the same, that she would simply take charge and tell me what to do. Aunt Laura undoubtedly would and that was why I still had a sneaking feeling that life with her would be much simpler and more peaceful (if not quite so interesting) than life with Aunt Patsy.

Chapter Nine

I HAD quite a struggle before Aunt Patsy would let me go back to school on Monday.

'Are you sure you want to go?' she kept asking.

'Of course. I don't want to get behind.'

'Why you have this absurd addiction for exam-passing I'll never understand.'

'It's not just exams. I like school.'

'You're an unnatural child!'

'I think it would be much more unnatural not to like it,' I retorted.

'OK,' said Aunt Patsy smiling. 'You win. But if you have any trouble with that moronic charac-ter, let me know.'

'I won't,' I said confidently.

While I was waiting in the playground for the bell to ring some of the girls pounced on me.

'Where did you go?'

'I just went home,' I said loftily.

'Fancy making all that fuss about getting the belt.'

'I wasn't making a fuss. I just don't choose to have a horrible beefy old man like Mr Hamilton hitting me. Besides it was unfair. He has no business to terrorize us.'

'Of course it was,' said Elizabeth, linking her arm through mine. 'I think Emma was dead right. I wish I'd had the nerve.'

'Oscar would like a few words with you,' said one of the girls, mimicking Mr Hamilton. 'He's a real nit!'

'Can't teach for toffee.'

'I hate Maths anyway.'

'I wonder what he'll be like today.'

I was just going to boast about the awful things Aunt Patsy had told the headmaster and then I thought better of it.

Maths was third period but instead of Mr Hamilton our class teacher came in and introduced a student. She said Mr Hamilton was ill (I wonder if he really did have flu?) and that we were to be specially helpful and well-behaved to the student whose name was Miss Ogilvie.

She was young and thin and earnest and though we teased her a little – you can't somehow help it with students – we were pretty nice to her on the whole.

Nothing much else happened except that the Lady Adviser gave us one of her stupid lectures. She is a sort of matron who sees that everyone is clean and tidy; if someone has a headache she gives them an aspirin and lets them lie down for half an hour. She was always urging us to bring our little problems to her but of course we never did. Every few weeks she would give us a talk: about why we should wear school uniform, and be a credit to the school, and behave quietly on buses, and would warn us that girls wearing jazzy stockings would be sent home, and that if we modulated our voices and learnt to speak like ladies we'd all get much better jobs, and a lot of nonsense no one ever listened to.

This morning she found fault with Elizabeth's hair and stuck in two horrible kirby grips to keep it behind her ears. The moment she bustled through the door to lecture some other class Elizabeth promptly took them out again.

I went in to dinner with Elizabeth. I usually found it a bit difficult to talk to her because I didn't watch the telly and she was always describing to me the programme she'd seen the night before. But today we had Mr Hamilton to talk about and I told her, in confidence, how Aunt Patsy had torn into the headmaster. She was terribly impressed and kept saying, 'Jings, your aunt's got a nerve.'

'I wonder if he really has got flu,' I said.

'I think he's got the boot,' said Elizabeth.

Then when we were coming out of the dining-hall we ran into the History teacher. He stopped us and said: 'Emma and Elizabeth, just the girls I wanted to see. Can you spare me a moment?'

Of course we could, and he explained that there was going to be an exhibition of students' work at the end of the term and he wanted a pictorial chart made of medieval Scotland, with a plan of a village and a town and photographs of people and buildings and little pictures of this and that and an example of what an illuminated manuscript looked like.

'If you two could get together sometimes after school you might have a stab at it,' he said. 'Elizabeth is good at drawing and Emma's handwriting is a thing of beauty and a joy for ever. What do you say?'

'It might be fun,' I said cautiously, looking sideways at Elizabeth to see if she looked enthusiastic under her fringe.

'Now the thing is, do you live reasonably near each other and would your mothers let you gad round in the evening?'

'My mother wouldn't mind,' said Elizabeth quickly, 'as long as I'm home by ten.'

'Well, see if you can fix something up and then I'll give you the materials.'

He beamed at us both and strode off down the passage.

'Would your aunt mind?' Elizabeth asked me.

'No, of course not. She never minds!' I said proudly.

'Well, I'd ask you round to my place but there are kids all over and we wouldn't have peace to work. Could I come round to you?'

For a moment I felt a twinge; after all I had described Aunt Patsy's flat as an 'historic' house; and then I thought, well, after all, it *is* an historic house. As far as I could make out all the houses round there were historic.

'Come round after school and we'll ask my aunt if she'll lend us pens and paints and things.'

So Elizabeth came back with me. I wondered

what she'd say to the stairs but she didn't say anything. I hoped that it would be one of Aunt Patsy's good days and that she'd have tea ready, but she was working in her studio, wearing very grubby slacks and a huge black sweater, with an old shirt which she used instead of a proper painter's smock flapping round her shoulders. Her hair was on end and she had some paint on her cheek.

'This is Elizabeth,' I said and then I told her about the history project.

She was most helpful, promised a pen with a thick italic nib and some indian ink for the lettering but we'd jolly well have to find our own paints as she wasn't having hers mucked up. 'You'd better go and buy some,' she said, rootling in her bag and produced a scrumpled ten-shilling note.

'I have enough pocket money saved,' I said with dignity.

'Don't bite the hand that feeds you or look a gift horse in the mouth,' said Aunty Patsy.

'Can I give Elizabeth some tea?'

'Of course. Eat anything you like as long as you don't disturb me. I'm working at high pressure.'

She disappeared into her studio again and Elizabeth and I went into the kitchen.

'Gosh, your aunt's rather weird,' whispered Elizabeth – she had been staring at Aunt Patsy as if she had never seen anyone like her before.

'That's because she's an artist,' I said haughtily.

'Oh, I know. I didn't mean she wasn't nice.'

'What would you like for tea? Shall we have toasted cheese? And there may be some chocolate biscuits left.'

After tea I showed Elizabeth my room: she was very envious as she had to share with her little sister, but she couldn't get over us not having the telly.

'You can come round and watch ours if you like,' she offered.

After tea we went out and bought a paintbox and some brushes and some pencils and a big soft rubber and then I chummed her to the bus stop.

'Is your Mum getting better?' she asked while we waited for the bus.

'She's gone abroad,' I said quickly. 'She has to live in a warm climate.'

Then the bus came.

When I got home again I arranged my drawing materials on my desk but I felt lonely and wanted someone to talk to. I went up to the studio, knocked at the door and opened it.

'What is it now?' Aunt Patsy barked, looking up crossly from her drawing-board.

'I got the paintbox and things.'

'Good.'

'What are we going to have for supper?'

'You're not hungry again, are you?'

'Well, I soon will be.'

'Then for goodness sake, Emma, go and stuff yourself, but please, please, please leave me alone until I've finished this.'

I hesitated and then to my disgust found myself saying in a whiney voice.

'I wish we had the telly.'

'Well, we haven't and we're not going to. I loathe and abominate it.'

'All the girls at school have sets.'

'Emma! Scram!'

I scrammed. I shut the door with a bang, and stamped down the stairs and went into the kitchen. Of course I wasn't hungry. I just wanted to talk. How beastly Aunt Patsy was. I sat and glowered out of the window at the roofs and chimney-pots and hated everyone. I wished, oh how I wished that everything was different. It was difficult not to cry and I was just getting that chokey feeling in my throat and hot feeling behind my eyes when the doorbell rang. It was Stephen.

He just said, 'Hullo chick,' and bounded up the stairs into the studio, and I hated him too. 'She'll have time to talk to him,' I thought and felt even more aggrieved.

But within two minutes he had bounded down again.

'Why didn't you tell me Patsy was working?' he asked me ruefully.

'You didn't give me time.'

'Grrr,' he said. 'Patsy's a menace when she's trying to meet a deadline. She flew at me like a wild cat.'

'She flew at me too,' I admitted. We grinned at each other.

'She promised I could come to supper and she's completely forgotten,' Stephen grumbled.

'I could make you some supper,' I said, cheering up.

'Could you really?'

'If eggs and bacon would do? I can't find anything else.'

'Eggs and bacon would suit me admirably. Now, tell me, what happened at school today? Is the monster still in evidence?'

I told him about the student, what the girls had said, and about the pictorial history, and he said he had some material that might be useful. So we ate our bacon and eggs and chatted like mad.

At about nine o'clock Aunt Patsy appeared, kissed Stephen as if nothing had happened, and said: 'Emma, I'm starving to death. What have you two been guzzling? Can I have some too?'

I thought Aunt Patsy might have apologized, and that Stephen might have pointed out that it was very rude to invite someone for supper and then forget, but neither of them mentioned it.

So I found some more bacon and eggs and

cooked her a big plateful. Then I decided I would have a bath and go to bed.

'Don't forget the washing-up,' I said as I left them, getting my own back at last.

Chapter Ten

THE next couple of weeks passed pleasantly although Mr Hamilton did come back. He was much the same, except that he ignored me completely. But when he found one of the boys, Thomas Macintyre, reading a comic under his desk, instead of belting him there and then he said:

'I understand that some of our more sensitive scholars do not care for encounters with Oscar. How do you feel about it, Thomas?'

Thomas wriggled and muttered:

'I don't know, sir.'

'You don't know, Thomas? You don't know if you would prefer six words with Oscar to, let us say, an hour's extra homework?'

'Gie's the belt, sir,' Thomas said, going scarlet with embarrassment.

'No, Thomas. Curiously enough my intention is not to consider your wishes. If you study comics when you ought to be studying algebra it seems only right that you should study algebra when you might be titillating your imagination with stories of spacemen and private eyes. Take problems 7 to 13, inclusive, please Thomas, to redress the balance.'

Of course Thomas was furious, and he and several other boys made rude remarks to me during break but the girls were on my side, especially Elizabeth.

We had become friends. We had been working on our history project off and on. Stephen found us a nice bit of illuminated manuscript to copy, with a capital letter entwined with birds and flowers and a strip at the bottom of funny little men shooting a deer with bows and arrows. I copied the lettering and Elizabeth did the pictures and it looked splendid.

I also went down the hill to Stockbridge to her house to watch the telly. So I was able to discuss with the girls who was fabulous in the Top Twenty and what we thought was going to happen in the serial.

Elizabeth was a peculiar girl. Her mother liked her to wear nice clothes, frocks or frilly blouses and skirts but she liked to wear scruffy jeans and big jerseys. So she used to put her old clothes in a duffel bag and dive into the nearest public lavatory to change whenever she went out. I thought she was bonkers!

She lived in a super new block of flats, and she and her family – three younger sisters and a jolly fat baby – were always sitting together cosily in the kitchen watching telly and drinking cups of tea.

Her mother was quite nice except she would keep asking Elizabeth why she didn't wear her hair short like mine.

'But it's the fashion, Mum,' Elizabeth would explain hopelessly, and I would chip in: 'You can't wear curly hair long – it would make me look like a spaniel. But long straight hair is super.'

'I think it looks a proper mess,' her mother would snort.

Elizabeth had a thing on one of the boy prefects. She was always hanging about the corridors hoping to catch sight of him or planning to sit next to him in the bus. Once at the bus stop a pencil fell out of her school bag and he actually picked it up. She talked about it for weeks. I couldn't understand what she saw in him: he had awful sticky-out ears and his name was Gilbert.

One evening when she'd been at my house she said: 'Let's knock off early, Emma. There's a smashing coffee bar I'm dying to go to. But I can't go alone.'

'I'll make you some coffee,' I suggested.

'No, I want to go out. But you must chum me.'

'Oh all right.'

Aunt Patsy was out and I thought maybe I ought to leave her a note but then I thought, why bother? She probably wouldn't even notice.

So we went to this coffee bar. It was all furnished in wood, and there was a juke-box, and the air was full of steam and cigarette smoke. The people were mostly teenagers: boys with floppy hair that they were always combing; and now I understood about Elizabeth because all the girls there looked the same. I felt a bit odd myself wearing a skirt and having short hair.

We stood in a queue to get our coffee, and Elizabeth led the way to a table. I realized then why she had wanted to come. Gilbert was sitting at the next table.

Of course she was dying to talk to him but she was far too shy so she just sat, with her hair hiding her face, sipping her coffee and making the odd remark.

'Lend us a threepenny bit,' she said at last. 'I want to play *You're the only girl.*'

'OK.'

She got up very slowly and walked over to the juke-box, waited until the record dropped into place, and walked slowly back again, all the time stealing glances at Gilbert from under her fringe. I suffered for her because Gilbert was talking to a couple of other boys and took no notice at all.

'If you're lonely, girl, remember that you're the only girl for me,' sang the juke-box.

Then just as Elizabeth was level with his table Gilbert looked up, smiled at her and said, 'Hi.'

That was the only thing he said to her until we left, and then he said, 'Chow' (which is what a lot of people were saying at that time), but I could tell Elizabeth was as pleased as punch.

'Fancy him being there,' she kept saying as we waited at the bus stop. 'Fancy him noticing me. Fancy him speaking to me.'

'You're a nut case,' I told her. 'An absolute out and out nut case.'

'I know Emma, but he's so gorgeous.'

'Here's your bus, goodnight.'

'Goodnight, and thanks for coming.'

The lighted bus swung down the street with

Elizabeth waving frantically and I walked back up the hill home, chuckling to myself. I hoped I'd never get that way about a boy, especially one with sticky-out ears called Gilbert.

When I opened the front door Aunt Patsy literally pounced on me.

'Emma, where have you been? It's terribly late.'

'I've just been with Elizabeth to a coffee bar,' I explained. 'I didn't realize it was so late.'

'It's half past ten,' Aunt Patsy exploded. 'I came back an hour ago and there wasn't a sign of you. I've been worried stiff.'

I stared at her in absolute amazement. Aunt Patsy worried stiff! I could hardly believe my ears. I didn't realize she even knew the meaning of the word 'late'.

Recently we had been getting on rather well together. Of course, she still forgot my pocket-money and snapped my head off if I interrupted her when she was working; and I still grumbled about not having a telly and she would complain about my always being hungry; but this was somehow more natural and friendly than our polite stage. Still she had never fussed or made me feel I had to ask her permission to do anything – I just told her. I think she must have noticed my surprise because she calmed down and murmured sheepishly: 'You might have left a note.'

'I'm terribly sorry.'

'Well, don't do it again.'

'I promise. I just never thought.'

'I never thought either,' began Aunt Patsy and then changed what she was going to say. 'Was it fun in the coffee bar?'

So I told her about Elizabeth and she laughed like anything.

Although it was so late I lay thinking for a long time before I went to sleep. The wind was whooshing round the gable end so that I felt as if I were living in a lighthouse with the sea surging all round. I liked lying there with the eiderdown pulled under my chin, listening to the wind, and I listed all the reasons why I was happy.

I had got used to Aunt Patsy's way of life and now even liked it: the way she didn't try to 'bring me up' but treated me as an equal, and how, if I was working on my history chart, she never interrupted to ask me to go out and buy some eggs or make coffee. I could stay up if I felt sociable or go to bed if I felt sleepy; I could bring Elizabeth home when I wanted and go out when I wanted. (Leaving a note to say where I'd gone was completely different from having to ask permission.) I liked our movable meal-times, so that sometimes we had breakfast at lunch-time and supper any time from six o'clock to midnight. I had even got used to living up the terrible stairs in Castlehill, and I actually liked the crumbly old Royal Mile (though I still thought it ought to be tidied up as soon as possible). In a way, it was rather marvellous to be in the middle of so much history. I used to wander into the wynds and closes and wonder what James Boswell and David Hume and Robert Burns had been like, what clothes they had worn and what they had talked about. No wonder Mary, Queen of Scots had been depressed, I thought, living in gloomy old Holyrood Palace with the mist sliding over Arthur's Seat wishing she could go home to France. And I definitely liked school. It was fun being near the top of the class, and trying to outwit Mr Hamilton, and finding new things for the history chart, and being friends with Elizabeth.

Of course I still missed Mother and Father but it didn't hurt so much. It was rather as if they had gone away, and I could think my thoughts as if I were writing them a letter, and they would understand and be pleased with me.

Just as I was dropping off to sleep I remembered Aunt Laura's visit. But I said firmly to myself, 'I'll think about that tomorrow.'

Chapter Eleven

WHEN I did come to think about Aunt Laura I decided the only person who would understand my feelings was Richard. So the next evening, after I'd finished my homework, I wrote him a long letter.

Dear Richard,

I've changed my mind and don't say, Ha ha, girls always do. I really want to stay with Aunt Patsy. I've got used to everything now and even like it. But the awful thing is I don't know if Aunt Patsy wants me to stay. She and Stephen are going to get married at Christmas but she never says things like 'when we're married we'll all do such and such,' or tells me if we're going to go on living in Castlehill, or what will happen to me if they go away on a honeymoon. If only Aunt Laura's letter hadn't arrived at the exact moment it did I would have been able to ask all these questions, but now I simply can't. Aunt Patsy does appear to like me but that is different from her wanting me to go on staying after she is married. Perhaps she is just waiting for Aunt Laura to carry me off so that she and Stephen can be left in peace.

The other evening something most peculiar happened. I went out with a friend to a coffee bar and when I got home Aunt Patsy, who usually doesn't care a hoot where I am or what I'm doing, was furious. She said she was worried about me! I still can't make up my mind if it was because she is fond of me or because I'm a nuisance.

I don't think I could bear to be uprooted again and have to start getting used to someone else's ways. And I don't think I like the sound of Aunt Laura.

Richard wrote back that I wasn't to worry, and he was sure that if I was happy, Aunt Patsy must be happy too because, living so closely together as we did, I couldn't have been happy if Aunt Patsy hadn't felt the same.

It wasn't a very satisfactory letter!

So I started worrying all over again. How ought I to behave during Aunt Laura's visit so that she would let me stay in Edinburgh? If I behaved too nicely, and was tidy and polite, and went to bed early she might think I would 'fit in' with her family. And if I was very noisy and teenage-ish, and played pop records very loudly, and left all the towels on the bathroom floor, she might insist that I was immediately packed away to a good boarding school.

Suppose, too, that Aunt Patsy was in one of her working moods, wearing her old slacks with her hair on end, and forgot about meals, and invited Stephen's friends to a noisy party. And suppose Stephen used bad language or forgot to shave, and he and Aunt Patsy had one of their conversations about the stupidity of the educational system.

It was all terribly worrying: I almost stopped feeling hungry and, when I went to bed, I tossed and turned as I imagined all the things that could go wrong with the visit.

Aunt Laura wrote that she was coming for the weekend and would get in touch after her arrival on the Friday. When Aunt Patsy read the letter aloud to me I felt a horrible thud at the bottom of my stomach.

All that day at school I couldn't concentrate and the teachers accused me of wool-gathering and told me that if I didn't pay more attention, I'd fail my exams.

When school finished I didn't know whether to hurry home to see if Aunt Laura had arrived or to hang around and put off knowing the worst for a little longer. However, there was a nice prefect at the bus stop who actually kept the queue in order, and stopped the boys from pushing the girls out of their way; so I got on an early bus, and the church clock at the corner was just striking four as I began very slowly to climb the stairs.

I remembered that first morning I had climbed them: how disgusted I'd been at the way the stairs sagged in the middle, at the paint flaking off the walls, and at the peculiar musty smell. And now I didn't mind at all. I hardly noticed.

When I reached the last flight I heard the sound of a piano being played. Now sometimes Aunt Patsy did play the piano but she wasn't very good, and this was fast ripply sort of playing, quite different from hers. I thought it must be the radio but while I was taking off my coat I saw the transistor on the kitchen table: so it couldn't be the radio.

I rushed upstairs and burst into the studio, hardly daring to hope; but I was quite right! There, sitting at the piano with his copper head bent over the keys, looking perfectly at home, was Richard.

'Richard!' I squeaked, rushing at him, and completely forgetting that boys don't like being hugged. But he didn't seem to mind and hugged me back, and then we both looked at Aunt Patsy who was curled up on the sofa, smiling at us.

'Richard just got here about an hour ago,' she said. 'I must say, you play the piano remarkably well, Richard.'

'It's a nice piano,' said Richard, 'but it needs tuning.' He did a quick little arpeggio and shuddered.

I looked at Aunt Patsy to see if she thought he was being rude but she seemed to think he was quite right to tell her, and promised to get it seen to directly.

I thought how like both of them it was to be talking about pianos and music instead of any of the questions that people usually ask: where he should sleep, if he had eaten lately, and why he hadn't rung up. I suspected she hadn't even asked whether he had had permission from Aunt Laura to come or had merely walked out of the house. Aunt Patsy seemed to take it for granted that it was all the most natural thing in the world.

But I didn't.

'How did you get here? Why have you come? Does Aunt Laura know? When did you get here? Oh Richard!' I was quite breathless and silly with excitement.

'I hitch-hiked,' said Richard calmly, 'on an overnight lorry. I'm not having family conferences taking place behind my back.'

'But does Aunt Laura know?'

'I don't think she does because I left after she did. Oh, it's all right. The police won't be scouring the countryside for me. I left a note in the approved fashion.'

'On a pincushion?' giggled Aunt Patsy.

'No, on the hall table.'

'That was sensible.'

'I must say I hope I never have to be a long-distance lorry driver,' said Richard. 'You have to sit all bent up like a hairpin and the engine makes so much noise it practically deafens you. And the food at transport cafés is absolutely vile.'

'Talking about food,' said Aunt Patsy, 'shall we have some?'

'Gorgeous idea,' said Richard. 'I don't suppose you have a horse, but I could certainly eat one.'

So we all went down to the kichen. Fortunately it was one of Aunt Patsy's good days and there were plenty of things in the fridge and the cupboard.

Aunt Patsy cooked onion soup which made us all cry, and while the onions were sizzling in butter Richard grated cheese to put in it. I opened a tin of ham and made a huge salad with curly lettuce and watercress and thin slivers of cucumber. To make quite sure it would be enough I opened a tin of pineapple and added chunks of that.

Soon we were all sitting round the kitchen table, eating and talking like mad, about Edinburgh, and my school and Mr Hamilton, and whether the Scottish National Orchestra was any good, and Richard's school, and his chances of a scholarship, and Aunt Patsy's tiles, and my history project.

The only thing we didn't talk about was Aunt Laura.

After we had finished, Richard was still hungry so he topped up with brown bread and cheese.

'I see big appetites run in the family!' said Aunt Patsy. 'Can I press you to a chocolate biscuit, Richard?'

'I wouldn't say no,' Richard said, wiping the crumbs off his mouth.

'Then we'll take some upstairs with our coffee,' Aunt Patsy suggested. 'And perhaps – if you're quite sure you've eaten enough, Richard – you might play us some more music. That is, unless the piano's really too awful.'

'It isn't that bad,' admitted Richard. 'Compared with Aunt Laura's it's a marvel.'

When he had finished playing he sat down on the sofa, and began yawning and yawning and yawning. Then quite suddenly he was asleep.

'How stupid of me!' exclaimed Aunt Patsy. 'I'd forgotten he'd been up all night.'

So we arranged him on the sofa with a pillow under his head. We couldn't help giggling while Aunt Patsy loosened his tie and edged his shoes off: he felt so limp and funny, but he was so fast asleep he didn't wake up. Then Aunt Patsy fetched a couple of rugs to keep him warm when we turned off the fire.

'What a nice brother you have,' she whispered as we tiptoed downstairs. 'How dreadfully you must have missed him!'

I nodded. I didn't feel I needed to speak.

Chapter Twelve

WHEN I woke up next morning I heard Richard playing the piano again and I hoped Aunt Patsy wouldn't be cross at being disturbed. It was lovely to lie in bed and to know that we would have a whole day together. The sun had just arrived round the corner of Arthur's Seat, and I could see the golden glow in the sky from my bed. It was actually going to be a fine day.

But I couldn't lie still for long. I jumped out of bed, dressed and washed, and started frying large quantities of bacon for breakfast. Richard came in looking sleek and well-brushed.

'Do I smell bacon?' he asked. 'I thought so. It's my favourite smell first thing in the morning. How efficient you are!'

'Somebody has to be,' I retorted smartly.

Then Aunt Patsy came in yawning in her dressing gown.

'Do you have to play the piano so early in the morning, Richard?' she asked.

'Well I do rather,' said Richard smiling.

'I suppose I should be grateful it wasn't boogie-woogie.'

'Honestly, Aunt Patsy!' I said. 'No one plays boogie-woogie nowadays. It's terribly old-fashioned.'

After breakfast we sat around talking and Richard examined some of Aunt Patsy's designs and my history chart until Aunt Patsy broke it up.

'Delightful though all this social life is, I must get down to work, and you two are a distracting influence. Why don't you go out and see the town? And if I provide the wherewithal you can eat lunch out and leave me in peace till tea-time.'

'Good-oh!' said Richard.

So we spent the day exploring Edinburgh. We climbed the stairs to the Outlook Tower where **a** camera throws an enlarged picture of the city on to a circular white screen; we poked our noses into all the courts and wynds, and visited all the museums in the Royal Mile

We didn't go into Holyrood Palace because you have to go on a conducted tour and the guide tells you hundreds and hundreds of names and dates. Instead we climbed Salisbury Crags. I stuck to the path but Richard couldn't resist showing off his rock climbing which made me nervous though I didn't dare say so.

From the top you can see for miles: fields, woods, hills, blue sea, and the whole city spread out below like the view from an aeroplane.

Richard is usually rather solemn and grown-up but sometimes he goes mad and behaves as if he were a ten-year-old. Suddenly he whooped like an Indian and began racing down the hill. 'Come on, Emma,' he shouted. 'Let's run all the way down.'

'You're crazy,' I shouted after him. There were a lot of loose stones which you could easily trip over and I had no intention of falling on my nose.

He was sitting on a rock when I panted up to him.

'I think Edinburgh's fabulous,' he said.

'It is rather.'

'I wonder if I should go to the University here, that is, if there's a good music department.'

'Oh do!' – and then I remembered – 'What about Aunt Laura?'

'I refuse to think about Aunt Laura on a lovely day like this. She's not going to run my life whatever she thinks.'

'I'm afraid she's going to run mine,' I muttered miserably.

'Nonsense!'

'Well, she is our guardian.'

'She needs,' said Richard grandly, 'a little handling, that's all.'

I told him my idea of acting the 'Terrible Teenager' but he shut me up.

'Don't be such a nit, Emma. Be yourself. It's the only way. Besides, you're a lousy actress. You couldn't keep it up for ten minutes.'

'But—' I began.

'But me no buts. Aunt Laura is Forbidden Topic number one. Besides I'm hungry. Let's go and find some grub.'

We found a rather nasty café and ate fish and chips, and ice cream. Then we went for a walk in Princes Street Gardens. The gardeners were brushing up the fallen leaves, and there was the bitter-sweet autumnal smell of a bonfire. The north slope of the gardens was in shadow but there was still enough sun to catch the castle rock and turn it pink. Although we could hear the roar of the traffic at the West End and a diesel train hooting Whoo-hoo as it went into the tunnel, the gardens seemed very peaceful.

I should have liked to stay but it was too cold and I shivered.

'Shall we plod homewards now?' asked Richard. 'It'll be tea-time by the time we get back.'

So we crossed the little humped railway bridge and after we had puffed up the long hill home I was quite warm again.

When we got back there was the sound of voices coming from the studio, and when we opened the door there were Aunt Laura and Aunt Patsy having tea together.

Richard was as calm as a cucumber, shook hands politely, and then sat down and poured himself some tea. I, however, stopped short, blushing furiously and wishing I could fall through a hole in the floor.

Aunt Laura rose to her feet and made a swoop at me. She pressed me to her bosom, and actually

began sniffling down my neck and saying, 'You poor child!' I was absolutely furious and extricated myself as soon as I could, mumbled that I was fine, thank you, and stood there feeling an utter fool.

'Come and have some tea, Emma,' said Aunt Patsy, and I saw by the glint in her eye and the curl of her lip that she was as disgusted with Aunt Laura's behaviour as I was. So I sat down and accepted a cup of tea, but my hand shook so much that I nearly spilt it.

'I didn't expect to find you here, Richard,' said Aunt Laura, sitting down too.

'I acted on impulse,' said Richard in a lordly way.

'It's not usually considered good manners to descend on people without warning,' Aunt Laura said severely.

I thought Richard was going to snap back but Aunt Patsy smoothly intervened.

'Oh, Richard has always had a standing invitation,' she said. 'I'm only sorry he didn't come before. Do have a piece of cake, Laura.'

By this time I had calmed down, and I noticed several surprising things. The room was beautifully tidy. The tea was served in the best tea service (instead of mugs), and there was actually a clean cloth on the table. There was cake and little sandwiches, a knife for the butter and jam in a little dish instead of the jam pot. And Aunt Patsy herself was dressed in a dark wool frock, her face was nicely made-up, and her hair like a smooth dark helmet. She looked absolutely respectable.

And then I realized why. She wanted me to stay with her! She wanted to impress Aunt Laura that she was a fit and proper person to look after me.

I wanted to shout Hooray, and jump up and hug her but, of course, I couldn't. I just looked across at her and gave her an enormous grin.

Meanwhile Aunt Laura asked me questions.

'And how do you like Edinburgh, Emma?'

'I love it,' I said happily.

'And how are you doing at school?'

'Quite well, I think. It was a bit queer at first but I like it now.'

'There's a very good girls' school in Exeter,' said Aunt Laura.

'Edinburgh schools are famous,' said Aunt Patsy hypocritically. 'And I've had very good reports of Emma's work from the headmaster.'

'I'm glad you have made such a good adjustment,' said Aunt Laura. 'And I'm sure you, Patsy, have had to make an adjustment too. Girls of Emma's age are not always easy to handle.'

'Emma doesn't need handling,' said Aunt Patsy.

'Still I think we should speak frankly,' said Aunt Laura. 'Young girls do need a stable family life as a background.'

'There's nothing particularly unstable about my life,' said Aunt Patsy, with a trace of acid in her voice. 'In actual fact I'm getting married at Christmas.'

'My dear Patsy, congratulations!' exclaimed

Aunt Laura. 'I'm so happy for you. And who is the lucky man?'

'His name is Stephen McTaggart. He lectures at the Art College, and is Art Editor for a magazine called *Scottish Homes*.'

'Then that clarifies everything,' said Aunt Laura. 'Obviously a newly-married couple don't want—' she paused delicately.

'On the contrary,' retorted Aunt Patsy. 'This newly-married couple does want. We want very much. I've talked about it to Stephen and he thinks it's a marvellous idea to start off with a bit of ready-made family.'

'Still, I do feel,' said Aunt Laura, 'that in my position as guardian I should accept the responsibility of Emma's upbringing. I'm sure she will be very happy with us in Exeter.'

Here Richard interrupted. 'I think, if you don't mind my butting in, that you should ask Emma what she wants.'

'A child may know what she wants but does she know what is best for her?' demanded Aunt Laura.

'Just what objection exactly do you have to her staying with me?' demanded Aunt Patsy with an edge to her voice.

'My dear Patsy, there's no need to be offended. I only referred to your lack of experience. After all, you've never been married and had children of your own. And I don't feel that all these artistic people you mix with—' again she paused.

I was almost in despair. How could anyone prove they were right in such an argument. I could see the glitter in Aunt Patsy's eyes which meant she was really angry and even Richard looked pink. At any moment now someone was going to be rude. But when Aunt Patsy spoke again her voice was as smooth as silk.

'Don't let's argue, Laura,' she said. 'I know we're very different people—'

'That's why Emma should decide,' broke in Richard. 'After all, what you both want is for her to be happy and even if she is only thirteen she's a jolly sensible thirteen. It's horrible to be argued over.'

'Of course it's up to Emma,' agreed Aunt Patsy quickly, giving me a smile.

Aunt Laura sighed and tightened her lips. 'Well, Emma?' she said pompously.

What I wanted to do was to burst into tears and scream that I wanted to stay with Aunt Patsy and that no one, no one, no one would ever take me away and that I loathed Aunt Laura and the thought of going to Exeter. But now I saw that this was childish and stupid. Richard had said I was old enough to make up my own mind but I had to do it politely and tactfully. I took a deep breath.

'It's terribly kind of you, Aunt Laura, to offer to have me in Exeter,' I said, 'and I'd love to come and visit you some time. But, honestly, I do feel I've settled down now, and I love living here with Aunt Patsy, and if she and Stephen won't find me a nuisance, then please let me stay.'

I smiled at Aunt Laura as I spoke. I suppose I had been turning her into a monster in my imagination but now I saw she was quite an ordinary well-meaning woman who probably did want me to be happy. Anyhow, she smiled back and said:

'If that's the way you feel, dear, then of course there's no more to say. But I must say it's rather surprising. I never thought of you having maternal feelings, Patsy.'

'They're not maternal feelings, just auntly feelings!' said Aunty Patsy.

Just then the doorbell rang.

'That will be Stephen,' said Aunt Patsy, and I ran down to let him in.

'Has she arrived?' he whispered.

'Yes, and everything's all right. I'm going to stay with you.'

'Goodie, goodie,' whispered Stephen, squeezing my arm. 'Now I must go and be polite. How do you think I look?'

He was actually wearing a dark suit and a clean white shirt; he was beautifully shaved, and had had his hair cut. He, too, looked absolutely respectable.

'Smashing,' I said. 'For once.'

He gave me a quick cuff. 'Don't be cheeky.'

He came upstairs and was introduced. We had
some sherry and everyone made polite conversation but I didn't bother to listen. I was too
busy making plans. At last Aunt Laura said she
must go back to her hotel. She kissed me again and
said she did hope that everything would work out
for the best, and that I must write often and tell
her how I was getting on.

The moment the front door had clicked shut
Richard sat down at the piano and played a wild

polka, while Aunt Patsy, Stephen and I danced round the room singing all sorts of words to the music.

'That's the way to treat Aunt Laura – that's the way to treat them all – Aunt Laura's through the door-O – and we can have a ball.'

'Thank goodness, now I can relax,' said Aunt Patsy, taking off her shoes and falling back on the sofa laughing.

'I told you so,' said Richard to me.

'I hardly recognized you,' said Stephen to Aunt Patsy.

'I hardly recognized you!'

'Let's have a picnic supper,' said Aunt Patsy. 'I'm so exhausted at being a stable family background I couldn't lift a finger. Richard and Emma, do you think you could bring up everything edible you can find in the fridge, and we'll be messy and—' she looked at me doubtfully. 'Or do you want to go on being respectable?'

I hesitated for a moment. After all it would be rather nice to have an elegant supper. Then I thought, 'What did it matter? What matters is that we're all together, and we'll laugh and talk and enjoy ourselves, and make plans. There'll be lots of other opportunities for elegant suppers.'

'I don't mind a picnic,' I said, 'but I insist on the tea things being washed up first.'

Richard groaned. 'As far as I'm concerned your

appeal falls on deaf ears,' he said. 'Don't be such a fanatic.'

But I didn't reply. I just carried the tea things downstairs to the kitchen.

Piccolo fiction

Monica Dickens
Follyfoot 40p
Dora at Follyfoot 30p
The House at World's End 35p
Summer at World's End 35p
World's End in Winter 35p
Spring Comes to World's End 35p

Rudyard Kipling
The Jungle Book 50p
The Second Jungle Book 50p
Puck of Pook's Hill 50p
Rewards and Fairies 50p
Just So Stories 40p

Lavinia Derwent
Sula 25p
Return to Sula 25p

Maria Gripe
Josephine 25p
Hugo and Josephine 25p
Hugo 25p

Piccolo non-fiction

Piccolo picture surveys

An abundance of information and good solid facts, presented in these special format books with photographs on every page.

Picture Survey of Horses and Ponies
Lawrence Dunn

Picture Survey of Racing and Sports Cars
G. N. Georgano

Picture Survey of Aircraft
Maurice Allward

Picture Survey of Ships
Lawrence Dunn

Picture Survey of Motor Cars
Colin Munro

Picture Survey of Locomotives
Brian Reed

All at 50p

You can buy these and other Piccolo books from booksellers and newsagents; or direct from the following address:
Pan Books, Cavaye Place, London SW10 9PG
Send purchase price plus 15p for the first book and 5p for each additional book to allow for postage and packing

While every effort is made to keep prices low, it is sometimes necessary to increase prices at short notice. Pan Books reserve the right to show on covers new retail prices which may differ from those advertised in the text or elsewhere.

Born in New Delhi, India, in 1961, Vikram Chandra (chandra@ mindspring.com) now divides his time between Bombay and Washington, DC, where he teaches at George Washington University. His stories have appeared in the *New Yorker* and the *Paris Review*. He is the author of *Red Earth and Pouring Rain*, which was awarded the David Higham Prize for Fiction and the Commonwealth Writers Prize for the Best First Published Book. *Love and Longing in Bombay* was published in 1997 and won the Commonwealth Writers Prize for the Eurasia region.

Further acclaim for *Love and Longing in Bombay*:

'An interlocking of stories, five main stories, out of which dozens of other shorter narratives unfold, one story begetting another and another in the concentric kind of narrative structuring Chandra evidently loves. The result, in a prose so lucid and transparent as to be endlessly reassuring, is a maelstrom of loss, desire and romance . . . Extremely readable, Chandra's prose is shot through with moments of psychological clarity, beauty and revelation.' *Scotsman*

'When *Midnight's Children* first appeared on the scene, it became necessary to re-evaluate stories from and about India. With Vikram Chandra's collection – his second book – it is time to take stock again . . . Chandra's Bombay is linguistically multiplanar and authentic . . . breathtaking in the accuracy of its detail.' Farrukh Dhondy, *Observer*

Acclaim for Vikram Chandra's *Red Earth and Pouring Rain*:

'A dazzling first novel . . . It has passages of epic grandeur and desolation worthy of Thomas Mallory. It has jokes and grotesqueries and flights of madness and it has a handful of episodes in which Chandra is imagining and writing with such originality and intensity as to be not merely drawing on myth but making it.' Lucy Hughes-Hallett, *Sunday Times*

'Vikram Chandra's first novel makes its British counterparts look like apologetic throat-clearings. Verbally lithe, astute, marvellously vivid, it brings the Indian gods into compelling play with our soiled strivings, where telling a story – hundreds of them – becomes its own life-preserving act.' Adam Thorpe

Love and Longing in Bombay

Vikram Chandra

faber and faber

First published in 1997
by Faber and Faber Limited
3 Queen Square London WC1N 3AU
This paperback edition first published in 2000

Printed in England by Mackays of Chatham plc, Chatham, Kent

A CIP record for this book
is available from the British Library

ISBN 0–571–19208–4

4 6 8 10 9 7 5 3

For
my first readers:
my sisters,
Tanuja and Anupama;
and
Margo True

Contents

Acknowledgments

I'm grateful, as always, to my parents, Navin and Kamna. Also, for friendship, information, aid, and inspiration, my thanks to: Eric Simonoff; Linda Asher; David Davidar; Jordan Pavlin; Nicholas Pearson; Lekha Rattanani; Vidhu Vinod Chopra; Vir Chopra; Sheela Rawal; Smruti Koppikar; Arun Subramaniam; Rakesh Maria, Additional Commissioner of Police, Crime Branch, Bombay; Mahesh Bhatt; Farah Khan; Sanjay Leela Bhansali; Vikram Chopra; Kathy and Glenn Cambor; Cece Fowler; Marion Barthelme; Claire Lucas; Christa Forster; Amy Storrow; Leslie Richardson; Susan Davis; David Harvey; Rifka Tadjer; Lu Wiu; A. S. Samra, Director General of Police, Bombay; Deepak Jog, Deputy Commissioner of Police, Bombay; Viral Mazumdar; Lieutenant Colonel H. L. Saluja (Retd.); Colonel N. B. Kanuga (Retd.); Shelina Kukar; Comilla Shahani Denning; Namrita Shahani Jhangiani; Anuradha Tandon; Brig. Harish Chandra; Shanti Chandra; Brig. Sudhir Arora (Retd.); Anne Bogle; Rebecca Flowers; Paulette Roberts; Sanjay (Pinku) Desai; Pam Francis; Amy Georgia Buchholz; Jack Brandt; Leslie Nigham; Wendy James; Ashish Balram Nagpal.

Dharma

CONSIDERING THE LENGTH of Subramaniam's service, it was remarkable that he still came to the Fisherman's Rest. When I started going there, he had been retired for six years from the Ministry of Defence, after a run of forty-one years that had left him a joint-secretary. I was young, and I had just started working at a software company which had its air-conditioned and very streamlined head offices just off the Fountain, and I must confess the first time I heard him speak it was to chastise me. He had been introduced to me at a table on the balcony, sitting with three other older men, and my friend Ramani, who had taken me there, told me that they had been coming there for as long as they had worked and longer. Subramaniam had white hair, he was thin, and in the falling dusk he looked very small to me, the kind of man who would while away the endless boredom of his life in a bar off Sasoon Dock, and so I shaped him up in my mind, and weighed him and dropped him.

I should have noticed then that the waiters brought his drinks to him without being asked, and that the others talked around his silence but always with their faces turned towards him, but I was holding forth on the miserable state of computers in Bombay. The bar was on the second floor of an old house, looking towards the sea, and you wouldn't have known it was there, there was certainly no sign, and it couldn't be seen from the street. There were old trophy fish, half a century old at least, strung along the walls, and on the door to the bathroom there was a picture of a hill stream cut from a magazine, British by the look of it. When the wind came in from the sea it fluttered old flowered curtains and a 1971 calendar, and I was restless already, but I owed at least a drink to the courtesy of my friend Ramani, who understood my loneliness in Bombay and was maybe trying to mix me in with the right circle. So I watched a navy ship, a frigate maybe, wheel into the sun, sipped my drink (despite everything, I noticed, a perfect gin sling), and listened to them talk.

Ramani had been to Bandra that day, and he was telling them about a bungalow on the seafront. It was one of those old three-storied houses with balconies that ran all the way around, set in the middle of a garden filled with palms and fish ponds. It sat stubbornly in the middle of towering apartment buildings, and it had been empty as far back as anyone could remember, and so of course the story that explained this waste of golden real estate was one of ghosts and screams in the night.

"They say it's unsellable," said Ramani. "They say a Gujarati *seth* bought it and died within the month. Nobody'll buy it. Bad place."

"What nonsense," I said. "These are all family property disputes. The cases drag on for years and years in courts, and the houses lie vacant because no one will let anyone else live in them." I spoke at length then, about superstition and ignorance and the state of our benighted nation, in which educated men and women believed in banshees and ghouls. "Even in the information age we will never be free," I said. I went on, and I was particularly witty and sharp, I thought. I vanquished every argument with efficiency and dispatch.

After a while my glass was empty and I stopped to look for the bearer. In the pause the waves gathered against the rocks below, and then Subramaniam spoke. He had a small whispery voice, a departmental voice, I thought, it was full of intrigues and secrets and nuances. "I knew a man once who met a ghost," he said. I still had my body turned around in the seat, but the rest of them turned to him expectantly. He said, "Some people meet their ghosts, and some don't. But we're all haunted by them." Now I turned, too, and he was looking straight at me, and his white hair stood clearly against the extravagant red of the sunset behind him, but his eyes were shadowed and hidden. "Listen," he said.

On the day that Major General Jago Antia turned fifty, his missing leg began to ache. He had been told by the doctors about phantom pain, but the leg had been gone for twenty years without a twinge, and so when he felt a twisting ache two inches under his plastic knee, he stumbled not out of agony but surprise. It was only a little stumble, but the officers who surrounded him turned away out of sympathy, because he was Jago Antia, and he never stumbled. The younger lieutenants flushed with emotion, because they knew for certain that Jago Antia was invincible, and this little lapse, and the way he recovered himself, how he came back to his ramrod straightness, this reminded them of the metallic density of his discipline, which you could see in his grey eyes. He was famous for his stare, for the cold blackness of his anger, for his tactical skill and his ability to read ground, his whole career from the gold medal at Kharakvasla to the combat and medals in Leh and NEFA. He was famous for all this, but the leg was the centre of the legend, and there was something terrible about it, about the story, and so it was never talked about. He drove himself across jungle terrain and shamed men twenty years younger, and it was as if the leg had never been lost. This is why his politeness, his fastidiousness, the delicate way he handled his fork and knife, his slow smile, all these Jago quirks were imitated by even the cadets at the Academy: they wished for his certainty, and believed that his loneliness was the mark of his genius.

So when he left the *bara khana* his men looked after him with reverence, and curiously the lapse made them believe in his strength all the more. They had done the party to mark an obscure regimental battle day from half a century before, because he would never have allowed a celebration for himself. After he left they lolled on sofas, sipping from their drinks, and told stories about him. His name was Jehangir Antia, but for thirty years, in their stories, he had been Jago Antia. Some of them didn't know his real name.

Meanwhile, Jago Antia lay on his bed under a mosquito net, his arms flat by his sides, his one leg out as if at attention, the other standing by the bed, and waited for his dream to take him. Every night he thought of falling endlessly through the night, slipping through the cold air, and then somewhere it became a dream, and he was asleep, still falling. He had been doing it for as long as he could remember, long before para school and long before the drop at Sylhet, towards the hostile guns and the treacherous ground. It had been with him from long ago, this leap, and he knew where it took him, but this night a pain grew in that part of him that he no longer had, and he tried to fight it away, imagining the rush of air against his neck, the flapping of his clothes, the complete darkness, but it was no use. He was still awake. When he raised his left hand and uncovered the luminous dial it was oh-four-hundred, and then he gave up and strapped his leg on. He went into the study and spread out some maps and began to work on operational orders. The contour maps were covered with markers, and his mind moved easily among the mountains, seeing the units, the routes of supply, the staging areas. They were fighting an insurgency, and he knew of course that he was doing good work, that his concentration was keen, but he knew he would be tired the next day, and this annoyed him. When he found himself kneading his plastic shin with one hand, he was so angry that he went out on the porch and puffed out a hundred quick push-ups, and in the morning his puzzled *sahayak* found him striding up and down the garden walk as the sun came up behind a gaunt ridge.

"What are you doing out here?" Thapa said. Jago Antia had never married. They had known each other for three decades, since Jago Antia had been a captain, and they had long ago discarded with the formalities of master and batman.

"Couldn't sleep, Thapa. Don't know what it was."

Thapa raised an eyebrow. "Eat well then."

"Right. Ten minutes?"

Thapa turned smartly and strode off. He was a small, round man, not fat but bulging everywhere with the compact muscles of the mountains.

"Thapa?" Jago Antia called.

"Yes."

"Nothing." He had for a moment wanted to say something about the pain, but then the habit of a lifetime asserted itself, and he threw back his shoulders and shook his head. Thapa waited for a moment and then walked into the house. Now Jago Antia looked up at the razor edge of the ridge far above, and he could see, if he turned his head to one side, a line of tiny figures walking down it. They would be woodcutters, and perhaps some of the men he was fighting. They were committed, hardy, and well trained. He watched them. He was better. The sun was high now, and Jago Antia went to his work.

The pain didn't go away, and Jago Antia couldn't sleep. Sometimes he was sure he was in his dream, and he was grateful for the velocity of the fall, and he could feel the cold on his face, the dark, but then he would sense something, a tiny glowing pinpoint that spun and grew and finally became a bright hurling maelstrom that wrenched him back into wakefulness. Against this he had no defence: no matter how tired he made himself, how much he exhausted his body, he could not make his mind insensible to his phantom pain, and so his discipline, honed over the years, was made useless. Finally he conquered his shame, and asked—in the strictest confidence—an Army Medical Corps colonel for medication, and got, along with a very puzzled stare, a bottle full of yellow pills, which he felt in his pocket all day, against his chest. But at night these pills too proved no match for the ferocity of the pain, which by now Jago Antia imagined as a beast of some sort, a low growling animal that camouflaged itself until he was almost at rest and then came rushing out to worry at his flesh, or at the memory of his flesh. It was not that Jago Antia minded the defeat, because he had learnt to accept defeat and casualties and loss, but it was that he had once defeated this flesh, it was he who had swung the *kukri,* but it had come back now and surprised him. He felt outflanked, and this infuriated him, and further, there was nothing he could do about it, there was nothing to do anything about. So his work suffered, and he felt the surprise of those around him. It shamed him more than anything else that they were not disappointed but sympathetic. They brought him tea without being asked, he noticed that his aides spoke amongst themselves in whispers, his headquarters ran—if it was possible—even more efficiently than before, with the gleam of spit and polish about it. But now he was tired, and when he looked at the maps he felt the effort he had to make to grasp the flow of the battle—not the facts, which were important, though finally trivial—but the thrust and the energy of the struggle, the movement of the initiative, the flux and ebb of the chaotic thing. One afternoon he sat in his office, the pain a constant hum just below his attention, and the rain beat down in gusts against the windows, and the gleam of lightning startled him into realizing that his jaw was slack, that he had been staring aimlessly out of the window at the green side of the mountain, that he had become the sort of commander he despised, a man who because of his rank allowed himself to become careless. He knew he would soon make the sort of mistake that would get some of his boys killed, and that was unacceptable: without hesitation he called the AMC colonel and asked to be relieved of his command for medical reasons.

The train ride to Bombay from Calcutta was two days long, and there was a kind of relief in the long rhythms of the wheels, in the lonely clangings of the tracks at night. Jago Antia sat next to a window in a first class compartment and watched the landscape change, taken back somehow to a fifth-grade classroom and lessons on the crops of the Deccan. Thapa had taken a week's leave to go to his family in Darjeeling and was to join up in Bombay later. Jago Antia was used to solitude, but the relief from immediate responsibility brought with it a rush of memory, and he found the unbidden recall of images from the past annoying, because it all seemed so useless. He tried to take up the time usefully by reading NATO journals, but even under the hard edge of his concentration the pain throbbed in time with the wheels, and he found himself remembering an afternoon at school when they had run out of history class to watch two fighter planes fly low over the city. By the time the train pulled into Bombay Central, he felt as if he were covered not only with sweat and grit, but also with an oily film of recollection, and he marched through the crowd towards the taxi stand, eager for a shower.

The house stood in a square plot on prime residential land in Khar, surrounded by new, extravagant constructions coloured the pink and green of new money. But it was mostly dark brown, stained by decades of sea air and monsoon rains, and in the late-afternoon sun it seemed to gather the light about it as it sat surrounded by trees and untidy bushes. There was, in its three stories, in the elegant arches on the balconies, and in the rows of shuttered windows, something rich and dense and heavy, like the smell of gun oil on an old hunting rifle, and the taxi driver sighed, "They don't build them like that anymore."

"No, they're draughty and take a fortune to keep up," said Jago Antia curtly as he handed him the money. It was true. Amir Khan the housekeeper was waving slowly from the porch. He was very old, with a thin neck and a white beard that gave him the appearance of a heron, and by the time he was halfway down the flight of stairs Jago Antia had the bags out of the car and up to the house. Inside, with Amir Khan puffing behind him, he paused to let his eyes take to the darkness, but it felt as if he were pushing his way through something substantial and insidious, more clear than fog but as inescapable. It was still much as he had left it many years ago to go to the Academy. There were the Victorian couches covered with faded flower prints, the gold-rimmed paintings on the wall of his grandparents and uncles. He noticed suddenly how quiet it was, as if the street and the city outside had vanished.

"I'll take these bags upstairs," he said.

"Can't," Amir Khan said. "It's been closed up for years. All just sheets on the furniture. Even your parents slept in the old study. They moved a bed into it."

Jago Antia shrugged. It was more convenient on the ground floor in any case. "It's all right. It's just for a few days. I have some work here. I'll see Todywalla too."

"What about?"

"Well, I want to sell the house."

"You want to sell the house?"

"Yes."

Amir Khan shuffled away to the kitchen, and Jago Antia heard him knocking about with cups and saucers. He had no intention of using the house again, and he saw no other alternative. His parents were dead, gone one after another in a year. He had been a distant son, meeting them on leave in Delhi and Lucknow while they were on vacation. Wherever they had met, far away from Bombay, he had always seen the old disappointment and weariness in their eyes. Now it was over, and he wanted not to think about the house anymore.

"Good, sell this house." It was Amir Khan with a cup of tea. "Sell it."

"I will."

"Sell it."

Jago Antia noticed that Amir Khan's hands were shaking, and he remembered suddenly an afternoon in the garden when he had made him throw ball after ball to his off side, and his own attempts at elegant square cuts, and the sun high overhead through the palm trees.

"We'll do something for you," said Jago Antia. "Don't worry."

"Sell it," Amir Khan said. "I'm tired of it."

Jago Antia tried to dream of falling, but his ache stayed with him, and besides the gusts of water against the windows were loud and unceasing. It had begun to rain with nightfall, and now the white illumination of lightning threw the whole room into sharp relief. He was thinking about the Academy, about how he had been named Jago, two weeks after his arrival. His roommate had found him at five o'clock on a Saturday morning doing push-ups on the gravel outside their room, and rubbing his eyes he had said, "Antia, you're an enthusiast." He had never known where the nickname Jago came from, but after the second week nobody except his parents had called him Jehangir again. When he had won the gold medal for best cadet even the major-general who was commandant of the Academy had said to him at the reviewing stand, "Good show, Jago." He had been marked for advancement early, and he had never betrayed his promise. He was thinking of this, and the wind flapped the curtains above him, and when he first heard the voice far away he thought it was a trick of the air, but then he heard it again. It was muffled by distance and the rain but he heard it clearly. He could not make out what it was saying. He was alert instantly and strapped on his leg. Even though he knew it was probably Amir Khan talking to himself, flicking away with a duster in the imagined light of some long-gone day, he moved cautiously, back against the wall. At the bottom of the hallway he paused, and heard it again, small but distinct, above him. He found the staircase and went up, his thighs tense, moving in a fluid half-squat. Now he was truly watchful, because the voice was too young to be Amir Khan. On the first landing, near an open door, he sensed a rush of motion on the balcony that ran around the outside of the house; he came to the corner, feeling his way with his hands. Everything in the darkness appeared as shades, blackness and deeper blackness. He darted a look around the corner, and the balcony was empty, he was sure of it. He came around the corner, back against the wall. Then he heard the movement again, not distinct footsteps but the swish of feet on the ground, one after another. He froze. Whatever it was, it was coming towards him. His eyes ached in the darkness, but he could see nothing. Then the white blaze of lightning swept across the lawn, throwing the filigreed ironwork of the railing sharply on the wall, across Jago Antia's belly, and in the long light he saw on the floor the clearly outlined shape of shoes, one after another, the patches of water a sharp black in the light, and as he watched another footprint appeared on the tile, and then another, coming towards him. Before it was dark again he was halfway down the stairs. He stopped, alone with the beating of his heart. He forced himself to stand up straight, to look carefully about and above the staircase for dead ground and lines of fire. He had learnt long ago that professionalism was a much better way to defeat fear than self-castigation and shame, and now he applied himself to the problem. The only possible conclusion was that it had been a trick of the light on the water, and so he was able to move up the staircase, smooth and graceful once again. But on the landing a breath of air curled around his ankle like a flow of cool liquid, and he began to shiver. It was a freezing chill that spread up his thighs and into his groin, and it caught him so suddenly that he let his teeth chatter for a moment. Then he bit down, but despite his straining he could hardly take a step before he stopped again. It was so cold that his fingers ached. His eyes filled with moisture and suddenly the dark was full of soft shadows. Again he heard the voice, far away, melancholy and low. With a groan he collapsed against the banister and slid down the stairs, all the way to the bottom, his leg rattling on the steps. Through the night he tried it again and again, and once he made it to the middle of the landing, but the fear took the strength from his hips, so that he had to crawl on hands and knees to the descent. At dawn he sat shaken and weak on the first step, his arm around the comforting curve of the thick round post.

Finally it was the shock in Thapa's eyes that raised Jago Antia from the stupor he had fallen into. For three days he had been pacing, unshaven and unwashed, at the bottom of the stairs, watching the light make golden shapes in the air. Now Thapa had walked through the front door, and it was his face, slack, and the fact that he forgot to salute that conveyed to Jago Antia how changed he was, how shocking he was.

"It's all right," Jago Antia said. "I'm all right."

Thapa still had his bag in his right hand and an umbrella in the left, and he said nothing. Jago Antia remembered then a story that was a part of his own legend: he had once reduced a lieutenant to tears because of a tea stain on his shirt. It was quite true.

"Put out a change of clothes," he said. "And close your mouth."

The water in the shower drummed against Jago Antia's head and cleared it. He saw the insanity of what had gone on for three days, and he was sure it was exhaustion. There was nothing there, and the important thing was to get to the hospital, and then to sell the house. He ate breakfast eagerly, and felt almost relaxed. Then Amir Khan walked in with a glass of milk on a tray. For three days he had been bringing milk instead of tea, and now when Jago Antia told him to take it back to the kitchen, he said, "Baba, you have to drink it. Mummy said so. You know you're not allowed to drink tea." And he shuffled away, walking through a suddenly revived age when Jehangir Antia was a boy in knickers, agile and confident on two sunburnt legs. For a moment Jago Antia felt time slipping around him like a dark wave, but then he shook away the feeling and stood up.

"Call a taxi," he said to Thapa.

The doctors at Jaslok were crisp and confident in their poking and prodding, and the hum of machinery comforted him. But Todywalla, sitting in his disorderly office, said bluntly, "Sell that house? Na, impossible. There's something in it."

"Oh don't be ridiculous," said Jago Antia vehemently. "That's absurd."

Todywalla looked keenly at him. Todywalla was a toothless old man with a round black cap squarely on the middle of his head. "Ah," he said. "So you've heard it too."

"I haven't heard a damn thing," Jago Antia said. "Be rational."

"You may be a rationalist," Todywalla said. "But I sell houses in Bombay." He sipped tea noisily from a chipped cup. "There's something in that house."

When the taxi pulled through the gate Thapa was standing in

the street outside, talking to a vegetable seller and two other men. As Jago Antia pulled off his shoes in the living room, Thapa came in and went to the kitchen. He came back a few minutes later with a glass of water.

"Tomorrow I will find my cousin at the bank at Nariman Point," he said. "And we will get somebody to come to this house. We shouldn't sleep here."

"What do you mean, somebody?"

"Somebody who can clean it up." Thapa's round face was tight, and there were white crescents around his temples. "Somebody who knows."

"Knows what exactly? What are you talking about?"

Thapa nodded towards the gate. "No one on this street will come near this place after dark. Everyone knows. They were telling me not to stay here."

"Nonsense."

"We can't fight this, *saab*," Thapa said. After a pause: "Not even you."

Jago Antia stood erect. "I will sleep tonight quietly and so will you. No more of this foolishness." He marched into the study and lay on the bed, loosening his body bit by bit, and under the surface of his concentration the leg throbbed evenly. The night came on and passed. He thought finally that nothing would happen, and there was a grey outside the window, but then he heard again the incessant calling. He took a deep breath, and walked into the drawing room. Thapa was standing by the door, his whole body straining away from the stairs. Jago Antia took two steps forward. "Come on," he said. His voice rustled across the room, and both of them jerked. He read the white tightness of terror around Thapa's mouth, and as he had done many times before, he led by example. He felt his legs move far away, towards the stairs, and he did not look behind him to see if Thapa was following. He knew the same pride and shame which was taking him up the stairs would bring Thapa: as long as each saw himself in the other's eyes he would not let the other down. He had tested this in front of machine guns and found it to be true. So now they moved, Thapa a little behind and flanking, up the stairs. This time he came up to the landing and was able to move out, through the door, onto the balcony. He was moving, moving. But then the voice came around a corner and he stood still, feeling a rush in his veins. It was amazing, he found himself thinking, how localized it was. He could tell from moment to moment where it was on the balcony. It was not a trick of the wind, not a hallucination. Thapa was still against the wall, his palms against it, his mouth working back and forth, looking exactly where Jago Antia was. It came closer, and now Jago Antia was able to hear what it was saying: "Where shall I go?" The question was asked with a sob in it, like a tearing hiccup, so close that Jago Antia heard it shake the small frame that asked it. He felt a sound in his own throat, a moan, something like pain, sympathy. Then he felt the thing pause, and though there was nothing but the air he felt it coming at him, first hesitating, then faster, asking again, where shall I go, where, and he backed away from it, fast, tripping over his heels, and he felt the railing of the balcony on his thighs, hard, and then he was falling.

The night was dark below. They plummeted headfirst from the belly of the plane into the cool pit at a thousand feet, and Jago Antia relished the leap into reality. They had been training long enough, and now he did not turn his head to see if the stick was tight because he knew his men and their skill. The chute popped with a flap, and after the jerk he flew the sky with his legs easy in the harness. The only feature he could see was the silver curve of the river far below, and then quite suddenly the dark mass of trees and the swathe of fields. There were no lights in the city of Sylhet, but he knew it was there, to the east, and he knew the men who were in it, defending against him, and he saw the problem clearly and the movements across the terrain below.

Then he was rolling across the ground, and the chute was off. Around him was the controlled confusion of a nighttime drop, and swiftly out of that formed the shape of his battalion. He had the command group around him, and in a few minutes they were racing towards their first objectives. Now he was sweating freely, and the weight of his pistol swung against his hip. He could smell the cardamom seeds his radioman was chewing. In the first grey, to the east, the harsh tearing noise of LMG fire flung the birds out of the trees. *Delta Bravo I have contact over.* As Jago Antia thumbed the mouthpiece, his radioman smiled at him, nineteen and glowing in the dawn. *Delta Bravo, bunkers, platoon strength, I am going in now.* Alpha Company had engaged.

As the day came they moved into the burning city, and the buildings were torn by explosions and the shriek of rockets skimming low over the streets and ringing off the walls. Now the noise echoed and boomed, and it was difficult to tell where it was coming from, but Jago Antia still saw it all forming on his map, which was stained black now with sweat here and there, and dust, and the plaster knocked from the walls by bullets. He was icy now, his mind holding it all, and as an excited captain reported to him he listened silently, and there was the flat crack of a grenade, not far off, and the captain flinched, then blushed as he saw that Jago Antia was calm as if he were walking down a golf course in Wellington, not a street shining with glass, thousands of shards sharp as death, no, he was meditative and easy. So the captain went back to his boys with something of Jago Antia's slow watchfulness in his walk, and he put away his nervousness and smiled at them, and they nodded, crouched behind cracked walls, sure of each other and Jago Antia.

Now in the morning the guns echoed over the city, and a

plummy BBC voice sounded over a Bush radio in the remnants of a tailor's shop: "Elements of the Indian Para Brigade are said to be in the outskirts of Sylhet. Pakistani troops are dug in . . ." Jago Antia was looking at the rounded curves of the radio on the tailor's shelf, at the strange white knobs and the dial from decades ago, at the deep brown wood, and a shiver came from low on his back into his heart, a whisper of something so tiny that he could not name it, and yet it broke his concentration and took him away from his body and this room with its drapes of cloth to somewhere else, a flickering vision of a room, curtains blowing in a gusting wind, a feeling of confusion, he shook his head and swallowed. He curled the knob with the back of his hand so that it snapped the voice off and broke with a crack. Outside he could feel the fight approaching a crisis, the keen whiplash of the carbines and the rattle of the submachine guns and the heavier Pakistani fire, cresting and falling like waves but always higher, it was likely the deciding movement. He had learnt the waiting that was the hardest part of commanding, and now the reports came quickly, and he felt the battle forming to a crescendo; he had a reserve, sixty men, and he knew now where he was going to put them. They trotted down the street to the east and paused on a dusty street corner (the relentless braying scream of an LMG near by), and Jung the radioman pointed to a house at the end of the street, a white three-storied house with a decorative vine running down the front in concrete, now chipped and holed. "Tall enough," Jago Antia said: he wanted a vantage point to see the city laid out for him. He started off confidently across the street, and then all the sound in the world vanished, leaving a smooth silence, he had no recollection of being thrown, but now he was falling through the air, down, he felt distinctly the impact of the ground, but again there was nothing, no sound.

After a while he was able to see the men above him as he

was lifted, their lips moving serenely even though their faces were twisted with emotion, they appeared curved and bent inwards against a spherical sky. He shut and opened his eyes several times, searching for connections that seemed severed. They carried him into a house. Then he was slowly able to hear again, and with the sound he began to feel the pain. His ears hurt sharply and deep inside his head, in a place in which he had never felt pain before. But he strained and finally he was able to find, inside, some part of himself, and his body jerked, and they held him still. His jaw cracked, and he said: "What?"

It was a mine on the corner, they told him. Now he was fighting it, he was using his mind, he felt his strength coming back, he could find his hands, and he pushed against the bed and sat up. A fiercely moustached nursing-assistant pushed at his shoulders, but he struck the hands away and took a deep breath. Then he saw his leg. Below his right knee the flesh was white and twisted away from the bone. Below the ankle was a shapeless bulk of matter, and the nursing-assistant was looking for the artery, but as Jago Antia watched the black blood seeped out onto the floor. Outside, the firing was ceaseless now, and Jago Antia was looking at his leg, and he realized that he no longer knew where his boys were. The confusion came and howled around his head, and for a moment he was lost. "Cut it off," he said then. "Off."

But, said the nursing-assistant, holding up the useless bandages, but I have nothing, and Jago Antia felt his head swim on an endless swell of pain, it took him up and away and he could no longer see, and it left him breathless and full of loss. "No time. Cut it off now," he said, but the nursing-assistant was dabbing with the bandages. Jago Antia said to Jung: "You do it, now. Quickly." They were all staring at him, and he knew he could not make them cut him. "Give me your *kukri*," he said to Jung. The boy hesitated, but then the blade came out of its scabbard with a hiss that Jago Antia heard despite the cease-less roar outside. He steadied himself and gripped it with both hands and shut his eyes for a moment, and there was impossi-bly the sound of the sea inside him, a sob rising in his throat, he opened his eyes and fought it, pulled against it with his shoulders as he raised the *kukri* above his head, against dark-ness and mad sorrow, and then he brought the blade down below his knee. What surprised him was the crunch it made against the bone. In four strokes he was through. Each was easier. "Now," he said, and the nursing-assistant tied it off. Jago Antia waved off the morphine, and he saw that Jung the radioman was crying. On the radio Jago Antia's voice was steady. He took his reports, and then he sent his reserve in. They heard his voice across Sylhet. "Now then," he said. "Finish it."

The room that Jago Antia woke up in had a cracked white ceil-ing, and for a long time he did not know where he was, in Sylhet (he could feel an ache under his right knee), in the house of his childhood after a fall from the balcony, or in some other room, unknown: everything seemed to be thrown together in his eyes without shape or distinction, and from moment to moment he forgot the flow of time, and found him-self talking to Amir Khan about cricket, and then suddenly it was evening. Finally he was able to sit up in bed, and a doctor fussed about him: there were no injuries, the ground was soft from the rain, his paratrooper's reflexes had turned him in the air and rolled him on the ground, but he was bruised, and a concussion could not be ruled out. He was to stay in bed and rest. When the doctor left Thapa brought in a plate of rice and *dal,* and stood at the foot of the bed with his arms behind him. "I will talk to my cousin tonight."

Jago Antia nodded. There was nothing to say. But when the exorcist came two days later he was not the slavering tribal magician that Jago Antia was expecting, but a sales manager from a large electronics company. Without haste and without stopping he put his briefcase down, stripped off his black pants and white shirt and blue tie, and bathed under the tap in the middle of the garden. Then he put on a white *dhoti* and daubed his forehead with a white powder, and meanwhile Thapa was preparing a *thali* with little mounds of rice and various kinds of coloured paste and a small *diya,* with the wick floating in the oil. Then the man took the *thali* from Thapa and walked slowly into the house, and as he came closer Jago Antia saw that he was in his late forties, that he was heavyset, that he was neither ugly nor handsome. "My name is Thakker," he said to Jago Antia before he sat cross-legged in the middle of the living room, in front of the stairs, and lit the *diya.* It was evening now, and the flame was tiny and flickering in the enormous darkness of the room.

As Thakker began to chant and throw fistfuls of rice from his *thali* into the room Jago Antia felt all the old irritation return, and he was disgusted with himself for letting this insanity gather around him. He walked out into the garden and stood with the grass rustling against his pants. There was a huge bank of clouds on the horizon, mass upon mass of dark heads piled up thousands of feet high, and as he watched a silver dart of lightning flickered noiselessly, and then another. Now his back began to ache slightly, and he shook his head slowly, overwhelmed by the certainty that he no longer knew anything. He turned around and looked up the path, into the house, and through the twilight he could see the tiny gleam of Thakker's *diya,* and as he watched Thakker lifted the *thali* and walked slowly towards the stairs, into the shadow, so that finally it seemed that the flame was rising up the stairs. Then Thapa came out, and they stood in the garden together, and the breeze from the sea was full of the promise of rain. They waited as night fell, and sometimes they heard Thakker's voice, lifted high and chanting, and then, very faint, that other voice, blown away by the gusts of wind. Finally—Jago Antia did not know what time it was—Thakker came down the stairs, carrying the *thali*, but the *diya* was blown out. They walked up to meet him on the patio, under the faint light of a single bulb.

"It is very strong," he said.

"What is it?" said Jago Antia angrily.

Thakker shrugged. "It is most unmovable." His face was drawn and pale. "It is a child. It is looking for something. Most terrible. Very strong."

"Well, get it out."

"I cannot. Nobody can move a child."

Jago Antia felt a rush of panic, like a steady pressure against his chest.

Thapa said, "What can we do?"

Thakker walked past them, down the stairs, and then he turned and looked up at them. "Do you know who it is?" Jago Antia said nothing, his lips held tightly together to stop them from trembling. "It is most powerful because it is a child and because it is helpless and because it is alone. Only one who knows it and who is from its family can help it. Such a person must go up there naked and alone. Remember, alone and naked, and ask it what it seeks." Thakker wiped away the white powder from his forehead slowly, and then he turned and walked away. It was now drizzling, fat drops that fell out of the sky insistently.

Out of the darkness Thakker called. "You must go." Then a pause in which Jago Antia could hear, somewhere, rushing water. "Help him."

At the bottom of the stairs Jago Antia felt his loneliness like a bitterness in his nostrils, like a stench. Thapa watched from the door, remote already, and there seemed to be nothing in the world but the shadows ahead, the creaking of the old house, the wind in the balconies. As Jago Antia walked slowly up the stairs, unbuttoning his shirt, his pulse was rushing in his head, each beat like an explosion, not out of fear anymore but from a kind of anticipation, because now he knew who it was, who waited for him. On the landing he kicked off his shoes and unbuckled his belt, and whispered, "What can you want from me? I was a child too." He walked slowly around the balcony, and the rain dashed against his shoulders and rolled down his back. He came to the end of the balcony, at a door with bevelled glass, and he peered through it, and he could dimly make out the ornate curves of his mother's dressing table, the huge mirror, and beyond that the bed now covered with sheets, he stood with his face against the cool pane. He shut his eyes. Somewhere deep came the poisonous seep of memory, he felt it in his stomach like a living stream, and his mother was looking at him, her eyes unfocussed in a kind of daze. She was a very beautiful woman, and she was sitting in front of her mirror now as she always did, but her hair was untidy, and she was wearing a white sari. He was sitting on the edge of her bed, his feet stuck out, and he was looking at his black shoes and white socks, and he was trying to be very still because he did not know what was going to happen next. He was dressed up, and the house was full of people, but it was very quiet and the only sounds were the pigeons on the balcony. He was afraid to move, and after a while he began to count his breaths, in and out. Then his father came in, he stood next to his mother, put a hand on her shoulder, and they looked at each other for a long time, and he wanted to say that they looked like their picture on the mantlepiece, only older and in white, but he knew he couldn't so he kept himself still and waited. Then his father said to his mother, come, and they rose and he walked behind them a little. She was leaning on his father, and they came down the stairs and everyone watched them. Downstairs he saw his uncles and aunts and other people he didn't know, and in the middle of the room there was a couch and on it lay his brother Sohrab. Sohrab had been laid out and draped in a white sheet. There was a kind of oil lamp with a wick burning near Sohrab's head, and a man was whispering a prayer into his ear. There was a smell of sandalwood in the air. Then his mother said, "Soli, Soli," and his father turned his face away, and a breath passed through the room, and he saw many people crying. That was what they always called Sohrab. He was Soli, and that was how Jehangir always thought of him. His mother was kneeling next to Soli, and his father too, and he was alone, and he didn't know what to do, but he stood straight up, and he kept his hands by his sides. Then two men came forward, and they covered Soli's face, and then other people lifted him up, and they took him through the door, and for a long time he could see them walking through the garden towards the gate. His mother was sitting on the sofa with her sisters, and after a while he turned around and walked up the stairs, and above there was nobody, and he walked through the rooms and around the balcony, and after a while he thought he was waiting for something to happen, but it never did.

Jago Antia's forehead trembled against the glass and now he turned and walked down the corridor that ran around the house, through darkness and sudden light, and he walked by a playroom, and then his father's study, and as he walked he felt that it was walking beside him, in front of him, around him. He heard the voice asking its question, but his own desperate question seemed to twist in his throat and come out only as a sound, a sort of sob of anger. It went into the room that had been his room and Soli's room, and he stopped at the door, his chest shaking, looking at the floor where they had wrestled each other, the bureau between the beds on which they had stacked their books and their toys. The door creaked open under his hand, and inside he sat on this bed, in the middle,

where he used to, and they were listening to the Binaca Geet
Mala on the radio, Soli loved his radio and the Binaca Geet
Mala. He was lying on the bed in his red pyjamas and the song
went *Maine shayad tumhe pahale bhi kahin dekha hai,* Soli sang
along with it, Jehangir was not allowed to touch the radio, but
when Soli was away he sometimes played with the knobs, and
once he switched it on and heard a hiss and a voice far away
speaking angrily in a language he didn't understand, it scared
him and he ran away from it, and Soli found his radio on, and
then there was a fight. Jehangir lost the fight, but Soli always
won, even with the other boys on the street, he was fearless,
and he jumped over walls, and he led them all, and at cricket
he was always the captain of one side, and sometimes in the
evenings, still in his barrister's clothes, their father watched
their games in the garden, and he said that Soli had a lovely
style. When he said this the first time Jehangir raised his head
and blinked because he understood instantly what his father
meant, he had known it all along but now he knew the words
for it, and he said it to himself sometimes under his breath, a
lovely style, a lovely style. Now Soli raised himself up in bed
on an elbow, and Amir Khan brought in two glasses of milk on
a tray, and then their mother came in and sat as she did on Soli's
bed, and tonight she had *The Illustrated Weekly of India* in her
hand, folded open to a tall picture of a man with a moustache
and a bat, and she said, "Look at him, he was the Prince." So
she told them about Ranjitsinhji, who was really a prince, who
went to England where they called him nigger and wog, but he
showed them, he was the most beautiful batsman, like a
dancer he turned their bouncers to the boundaries with his
wrists, he drove with clean elegance, he had good manners,
and he said nothing to their insults, and he showed them all
he was the best of them all, he was the Prince, he was lovely.
After their mother left Soli put *The Illustrated Weekly* in his
private drawer, and after that Jehangir would see him take it

out and look at it, and sometimes he would let Jehangir look at it, and Jehangir would look at the long face and the pride in the stance and the dark opaque eyes, and he would feel a surge of pride himself, and Soli would have his wiry hand on his shoulder, and they would both say together, Ranjitsinhji, Ranji.

That summer one Sunday afternoon they were dozing in the heat when suddenly Burjor Mama came in and tumbled them both out of bed, roaring what a pair of sleepyhead sissy types, and they laughed with delight because he was their favourite uncle. They knew his arrival meant at least two weeks of unexpected pleasures, excursions to Juhu, sailing trips, films, shows, and sizzling forbidden pavement foods. Their mother came in and hugged him close, and they were embarrassed by her tears, Burjor was her only younger brother and more precious for his profession of soldiering, she was exclaiming now how he was burnt black by the sun, what are they doing to you now, and he was really dark, but Jehangir liked his unceasing whiplike energy and the sharp pointed ends of his handlebar moustache. Barely pausing to thump down his hold-all and his suitcase, he gathered up the whole family, Amir Khan included, and he whisked them off for a drive, and he whistled as he drove. On the way back Jehangir, weighted down with ice cream, fell asleep with his head in his mother's lap, and once for a moment he awoke and saw, close to his face, his mother's hand holding her brother's wrist tenderly and close, her delicate fingers very pale against his skin with the strong corded muscles underneath.

And Jago Antia, walking down the corridor, walking, felt the sticky sleep of childhood and the cosy hum of the car and safety. And then he was at the bottom of a flight of stairs, he knew he had to go up, because it had gone before him, and now he stumbled because the pain came, and it was full of fear, he went up, one two three, and then leaned over, choking. Above him the stairs angled into darkness and the roof he knew so well, and he couldn't move, again he was trembling, and the voice was speaking somewhere ahead, he said, "I don't want to go," but then he heard it again. He knew his hands were shaking, and he said, "All right you bastard, naked, naked," and he tore at the straps, and then the leg rolled down the stairs to the bottom. He went up, hunching, on hands and knees, his lips curled back and breathing in huge gasps.

Burjor Mama bought them a kite. On Monday morning he had to report in Colaba for work, and so Jehangir's mother brought up his pressed uniform and put it on the bed in the guest room. Jehangir lay on the bed next to the uniform and took in its peculiar smell, it was a deep olive green, and the bars on the front were of many colours but mainly red and orange, and above a breast pocket it said, B. MEHTA. Jehangir's mother sat on the bed too and smoothed out the uniform with an open palm, and then Burjor Mama came out of the bathroom in a towel. As he picked up the shirt, Jehangir saw under the *sadra,* under and behind his left arm, a scar shaped like a star, brown and hard against the pale skin. Then Jehangir looked up and he saw his mother's face, tender and proud and a little angry as she looked at Burjor. After breakfast Soli and Jehangir walked with him to the gate, and he said, "See you later, alligators," and in the afternoon they waited on the porch for him, reading comics and sipping at huge glasses of squash. When the taxi stopped at the gate they had run forward, whooping, because even before he was out they had seen the large triangle of the kite, and then they ran up without pause to the roof, Soli holding the kite at the ends, and Jehangir following behind with the roll of string. Jehangir held the roll as Soli spun off the *manjha,* and Soli said, watch your fingers, and Burjor showed them how to tie the kite string, once up, once down, and then they had it up in the air, it was doing spirals and rolls, and Soli said, "*Yaar,* that's a fighting kite!" Nobody was flying to fight with nearby, but when their father came up he laughed and watched them, and when they went down to tea Soli's fingers were cut from the *manjha,* and when Jehangir asked, Burjor Mama said, "It's ground glass on the line."

Now he came up the stairs, his stump bumping on the edges of the stone, and his palm scraped against something metal, but he felt the sting distantly and without interest. The next day Soli lay stretched across the roof, his mouth open. Jago Antia pulled himself up, his arms around a wooden post, and he could see the same two-level roof, Amir Khan's old room to one side, with its sloping roof coming to the green posts holding it up, beyond that the expanse of brick open to the sky, and then a three-foot drop with a metal ladder leading to the lower level of the roof, and beyond that the treetops and the cold stretch of the ocean. He let go of the post and swayed gently in the rain. Soli walked in front of him, his hands looping back the string, sending the kite fluttering strongly through the sky, and Jehangir held the coil and took up the slack. It flew in circles above them. "Let me fly it," Jehangir said. "Let me fly it." But Soli said, "You can't hold this, it'll cut you." "I can hold anything. I can." "You can't, it'll hurt you." "It won't. I won't let it." And Jehangir ran forward, Soli danced away, light and confident, backwards, and then for a moment his face was surprised, and then he was lying below, three feet below on the ground, and the string flew away from him. Jago Antia dropped to his knee, then fell heavily on his side. He pulled himself through the water, to the edge, next to the metal stairs, and he peered down trying to see the bottom but it seemed endless, but he knew it was only three feet below. How can somebody die falling three feet? He heard the voice asking its question, where shall I go, and he roared into the night, "What do you want? What the hell is it you want?" But it wouldn't stop, and Jago Antia knelt on the edge and wept, "What do you want," and finally he said, "Look, look," and he pushed himself up, leaned forward, and let himself go, and he

fell: he saw again Soli backing away, Jehangir reaching up trying to take his hand away from the string, Soli holding his
hand far up, and Jehangir helpless against his strength. Then
Soli smiling, standing, and Jehangir shouting and running forward and jumping, the solid impact of his small body against
Soli's legs, Soli's look of surprise, he's falling, reaching wildly,
Jehangir's hand under the bottom of Soli's shorts, he holds on and
tries, holds and pulls, but then he feels the weight taking him
over, and he won't let go, but he hasn't the strength, he's falling
with Soli, he feels the impact of the bricks through Soli's body.

When Jago Antia stirred weakly on the roof, when he
looked up, it was dawn. He held himself up and said, "Are you
still here? Tell me what you want." Then he saw at the parapet,
very dim and shifting in the grey light, the shape of a small
body, a boy looking down over the edge towards the ocean. As
Jago Antia watched, the boy turned slowly, and in the weak
light he saw that the boy was wearing a uniform of olive green,
and he asked, "Where shall I go?" Jago Antia began to speak,
but then his voice caught, because he was remembering his
next and seventh birthday, the first party without Soli, and his
parents holding him between them, soothing him, saying you
must want something, and he looking up at their faces, at the
lines in his father's face, the exhaustion in his mother's eyes.
Burjor Mama sits on the carpet behind him with head down,
and Amir Khan stands behind, and Jehangir shakes his head,
nothing. His mother's eyes fill with tears, and she kisses him
on the forehead, "Baba, it's all right, let us give you a present,"
and his heart breaks beneath a surging weight, but he stands
up straight, and looking at her and his father, he says, "I want a
uniform." So Jago Antia looked at the boy as he came closer, and
he saw the small letters above the pocket, J. ANTIA, and the sun
came up, and he saw the boy clearly, he saw the enormous dark
eyes, and in the eyes he saw his vicious and ravenous strength,
his courage and his devotion, his silence and his pain, his

whole misshapen and magnificent life, and Jago Antia said, "Jehangir, Jehangir, you're already at home."

Thapa and Amir Khan came up the stairs slowly, and he called out to them, "Come, come. I'm all right." He was sitting cross-legged, watching the sun move in and out of the clouds.

Thapa squatted beside him. "Was it here?"

"He's gone. I saw him, and then he vanished."

"Who?"

Jago Antia shook his head. "Someone I didn't know before."

"What was he doing here then?"

"He was lost." He leaned on both their shoulders, one arm around each, for the descent down the stairs. Somehow, naked and hopping from stair to stair, he was smiling. He knew that nothing had changed. He knew he was still and forever Jago Antia, that for him it was too late for anything but a kind of solitude, that he would give his body to the fire, that in the implacable hills to the north, among the rocks, he and other men and women, each with histories of their own, would find each other for life and for death. And yet he felt free. He sat on the porch, strapping his leg on, and Amir Khan brought out three cups of tea. Thapa wrapped a sheet around Jago Antia, and looking at each other they both laughed. "Thank you," Jago Antia said. Then they drank the tea together.

Shakti

W E HAD BEEN TALKING about Bombay that evening. Somebody, I think it was Khanna, was telling us about Bahadur Shah, who gave the island to the Portuguese for their help against the Moghuls. "At the beginning of everything great and monstrous," said Khanna, "is politics."

"You're forgetting the other half," Subramaniam said. "Remember, the Portuguese gave the island to the British as part of Catherine of Braganza's dowry."

"Meaning what?" I said.

"Meaning this," said Subramaniam. "That the beginning and end of everything is a marriage."

What you must understand about Sheila Bijlani is that she was always glamorous. Even nowadays, when in the corners of parties you hear the kind of jealous bitching that goes on and they say there was a day when she was nothing but the daughter of a common chemist-type shopkeeper growing up amongst potions and medicines, you must never forget that the shop was just below Kemp's Corner. What I mean is that she was a shopkeeper's daughter, all right, but after all, she saw the glittering women who went in and out of the shop, sometimes for aspirin, sometimes for lipstick, and Sheila watched and learnt a thing or two. So even when you see those early photographs from the Walsingham School — where she was, yes, the poor girl — what you should notice is the artistic arrangement of the hair, which she did herself, and the shortness of the grey skirt, which she achieved every morning with safety pins when she reached school. Even in those days there was no argument that Sheila had the best legs at Walsingham, and so when she finished with college and next we heard that she was going to be a hostess with Air France, it all made sense, I mean who else would you imagine pouring champagne for a movie star in some Frenchly elegant first class cabin or running down the steps of the Eiffel Tower, holding her white stilettos in one tiny and graceful hand — it had to be Sheila.

Air hostessing in those times didn't mean tossing dinners at drunks on the way back from Dubai or the smell of a Boeing bathroom after a sixteen-hour one-stop from New York. Remember, travelling abroad was rare then, and so all the air hostesses were killingly beautiful and St. Xavier's graduates, and they all had this perfume of foreign airs which they wafted about wherever they went, and Sheila was the most chic of them all. It could break your heart, the way she smoked a True, placing it ever so delicately between her lips and leaving just a touch of deep deep red on the very tip. And the men came around, the princes and the *Jamsahebs* in their convertibles, promising adventure, the cricketing knights in their blue blazers of glory, the actors' sons offering dreams of immortality. We used to see Sheila then in a flash as a car roared around the curve on Teen Batti, and we would sigh because somewhere there was a life that was perfect and wonderful.

So we were expecting a prince for Sheila — at least, a flashing star of some sort — but she disappointed us all when she married Bijlani. He was U.S.A.-returned and all, but from some place called Utah and what was electrical engineering anyway when you had Oxford cricketing royalty on the phone — but

Sheila liked Bijlani and nobody knew why. He was square and, later, fat and mostly quiet and he told everyone he wanted to make appliances, which was all very well and good, but four-speed electric mixies weren't exactly dashing, dammit. They met at a party at Cyrus Readymoney's and Bijlani was sitting quiet in a corner looking uncomfortable, and Sheila watched him for a long time, and when she asked, Readymoney said, "That's Bijlani, he used to be in school with us but nobody knows his first name. He wants to make mixies." Then Readymoney, who was dressed in black, snapped his fingers and said, "Let's boogie, baby," but Sheila looked up her nose at him—what I mean is she was a foot shorter than him but she somehow managed to look him up and down like he was a worm—and she said, "Why don't you go into a corner and squeeze your pimples, Cyrus?" and then she went and took charge of Bijlani. Now, you must understand that when nowa-days you see old Bijlani looking hugely regal in a black silk jacket it all started that night when Sheila took him out of his corner and tucked in his shirt at the back and took him around, never mind his sweating, and kept him by her side the whole evening. I don't think he ever tried to understand the whats and whys of what happened, I think Bijlani just took his blessings gratefully into his bosom and built mixies for Sheila. Everyone made fun of him at the start, but they went and got married, and people rolled their eyes, and a year passed and then another and another, and then they suddenly reappeared with an enormous flat on Malabar Hill, and there was a huge intake of breath clear down to Bandra, and now the story was that she had married him for his money. If you tried to tell someone that the first mixie was built with Sheila's money from a thousand trips up and down an Air France aisle, the next thing you heard was that she was paying you in cash and kind, and more, to say nice things about her. Her success drew out the venom up and down the coast of Bombay, let me tell you, it's a wonder the sea didn't curdle and turn yellow.

So now Sheila was on the hill, not quite on the top but not quite at the bottom either, and from this base camp she began her steady ascent, not quickly—she had patience and steadiness. It was done over years, it cost money, and the hill resisted, it fought back right from the start. In that first year Sheila threw cocktail parties and lunches and Derby breakfasts, and it became clear to her that the top of the hill was the Boatwalla mansion, which stood on a ridge surrounded by crumbling walls, overlooked by the frame of a new apartment building coming up just above. The mansion wasn't really on top of the hill, and it was dingy and damp, but Sheila knew it was where she had to go to get to the real top, the only one that mattered. For that first year Sheila sent invitations to Dolly Boatwalla every other week and received typed regrets one after the other, she saw Dolly Boatwalla at parties, and finally she was introduced under an enormous chandelier at a plastics tycoon's birthday party. Dolly Boatwalla was long and horsy-looking, she looked down an enormous nose and murmured, "*Ha-aaloo*," and looked away into the middle distance. Sheila understood that this was part of the rules of current diplomacy and was happy all the same, and even when the next weekend at the racecourse somebody by mistake introduced them again and Dolly said "*Ha-aaloo*" as if for the first time, Sheila didn't mind a bit and took it as part of her education. Sheila smiled and said, "You look wonderful, what a lovely scarf." She was willing to let Dolly have her way, and if Dolly had been a little less Boatwalla and a little more sagacious, she could have adopted Sheila and taught her and patronized her in a thousand little ways, but Dolly saw only a little upstart, which Sheila was, Dolly didn't see the ferocious political will, that hidden glint. This is how wars start.

How it all really began was this: finally Dolly accepted one of Sheila's invitations. Actually she had no choice but to accept, which may be why she went from being coolly condescending to openly sarcastic. And it started. What happened was that Sheila had finally been able to join the Lunch Club. Not many people in Bombay knew that the Lunch Club existed. Most of the people who knew what it was also knew that they couldn't be in it. The women in the Lunch Club met once a month for lunch at one of the members' houses. After lunch they played cards. Then they had tea and went home. That was it, nothing very exciting on the face of it, but if you knew anything you knew that that was where marriages were arranged and sometimes destroyed, deals were made, casually business was felt out, talk went on about this minister in Delhi and So-and-So's son who was school captain at Mayo. It was the real stuff, you know, *masala*-grinding, how the world works. So Sheila's name came up, naturally, several times, and, every time, Dolly sniffed and said, Not our type, really, and that finished off Sheila's chances. But then Sheila made friends, fast ones, and they pushed it, they liked her, for her money, for her nippy wit, for her snap, and maybe it was also that some of them were tired of Dolly, of her Boatwalla sandwiches served soggy but with absolute confidence, of her pronouncements and the delicate way she patted her pursed lips with a napkin after she ate pastries. So they insisted, and it was clear there would be either agreement or a direct struggle, and Dolly decided that it wasn't worth risking defeat, so finally she flung an eyebrow towards the roof, sighed, and said, "All right, if you must, can we talk about something else, this is really so boring."

So this was how they all gathered at Sheila's home. Her new house, that is. It was a white two-storied mansion, really, with a bit of lawn in front and a little behind, and of course even though it was big money for the time it was nothing on the sprawling Boatwalla jungles from colonial times, when you could buy land on the hill for nothing. Still, a house was something, actually it was a lot, and the Lunch Club oohed and exclaimed as they came up the short flight of stairs and into the front room, Sheila had it absolutely right, there were the big double doors inlaid with brass and then a carved wooden elephant's foot with walking sticks in it and a Ganesha that was chipped and old and grey stone and it had to be some major antique, two huge plants on either side, and a diffused white gleam through a skylight, and in the halo, changeless and eternal as the day that Bijlani threw his future kingdom at her feet, was Sheila, her skin glowing, her hair as dark as a Malabar wave on a moonless night. She welcomed them silently, smiling as they chattered around her, she led them through a long hall, past a study with a huge brown desk and a brass lamp, past a room full of leather-bound books and brown-and-red Kashmiri rugs, and finally into the dining room, where on a stone-topped dining table gleamed twelve place settings in silver. Here, finally, Sheila spoke her first words of the afternoon, "My son," because a young boy was standing near the table peering at the fantastic ikebana flower arrangement at its centre. Sheila ruffled his hair, and he turned his head to look at her, and the ladies murmured. He was certainly very good-looking. Bijlani's stolid bulk had passed into a sort of slow, unblinking expressiveness in his eyes, a kind of silence, and he had Sheila's sharp features. "Say hello," Sheila said, and he did, shaking hands with each one of them. Mani Mennon laughed over her shoulder as he gravely bowed over her hand, and she said, "Better watch out for this one." Meanwhile Sheila leaned into the corridor and called, "Ganga! Take Sanjeev to his room, will you?"

Ganga came in, a short wiry woman with her hands still wet from dishes. She had her red sari pulled between her legs and she pushed back a strand of loose hair with one hand. As Sheila walked Sanjeev to the door, Ganga took his other hand, and they smiled at each other over his head. "Isn't he so cute?"

Mani Mennon said, and as she did, Sheila turned and saw the look on Dolly's face, a kind of absurd pursing of the nostrils, an unmistakable look of offense, as if she had just begun to smell something bad. As everyone went towards the table, Mani Mennon hung back and whispered at Sheila, "She has *French* maids." It was true. They weren't actually French, usually Keralans, but all the same the petits fours at the Boatwalla mansion were served by maids in black dresses and those frilly things around their heads. Mani Mennon rolled her eyes. She was Sheila's main supporter in the Lunch Club, her sponsor, and she hated Dolly Boatwalla but was absolutely silenced by her, robbed of speech and presence of mind by Dolly's height and ruthlessness and way of commanding a room. Mani Mennon was short and funny and plump and couldn't think of any reasons why she should be silenced by Dolly, but always was anyway. "Boatwalla bitch," Mani Mennon hissed. Sheila shrugged and took her calmly by the elbow and led her to the others.

"Have some quail," she said. The food was unusual, small and spicy, made by a Lucknow cook from a Nawabi family. The tastes were light and chased each other across their palates with such foreign essences that they had to exclaim that it was all perfect, because they had never tasted anything like it before. Dolly held a silver fork at an angle and sawed at a tiny wing, and even she was puzzled and pleased, you could see that. Afterwards they sat on the sofas, luxuriously sunk in the pillows and lingering over the sweet dish, a concoction of almonds and cream so light you barely felt it on the tongue. Dolly began to be funny. She sat on a couch by herself, one leg bent over the other, in her cream pants suit, all long lines from the silk sheen of her leg to the nose, which was a little bony but very elegant. She told cruel little stories about people they all knew. All the stories were about people doing silly things or embarrassing themselves or just being stupid and not knowing about something that everybody knew. Dolly had a great sense of timing and was a good mimic and it was impossible not to laugh at her stories. The women sat in a little semicircle around her and laughed. Sheila laughed, and Mani Mennon laughed. Mani Mennon whispered to Sheila, "She must tell stories about me, too," and then she laughed at a story about a Punjabi woman at the club who pronounced "pizza" the way it was written and who dressed her daughters in too much gold.

Finally everyone grew quiet in an afternoon haze of contentment. There was no doubt it had been an enormously successful lunch, and Dolly had been allowed to dominate it completely. Now it was almost over, and there was a quietness in the air as everyone relaxed with the thought that it would actually finish without any horrendous tension, and as they walked towards the front door everyone was exhausted from the relief and strange disappointment of it all. Then Mani Mennon startled everyone by squeaking, "Hussain!" They were passing by the room with the bookshelves, and what Mani Mennon had noticed on the wall opposite the hallway was a large canvas, the chariot of the sun, gold and red. She went fluttering into the room with her arms held out, and stood swaying in front of the painting. It was quite overwhelming, with its rich swirl of colour and the horses as if they would burst from the canvas, and everyone clustered in front of it. Dolly hung back in the hallway, but then everyone crowded forward and she was alone, so she came forward reluctantly and stood behind them all. "It's your second one, isn't it, Sheila?" said Mani Mennon. "It's wonderful. Look at those yellows." And then, seeing Dolly behind the others, she said, smiling, "It's a Hussain, Dolly."

Dolly tilted her head back. "Is it?" she said. Her head tilted further. "Oh. Is that what it is?" She smiled. "Freddie has a few of those at his office."

Sheila was standing next to her. Without a word, Sheila

turned and walked back into the hallway. They followed her, and she walked to the door, opened it, and held it open. They walked past, saying thank yous, and she smiled, but her eyes were opaque and she never took her hand off the doorknob. Dolly walked past and murmured, "Thank you so much, darling." Sheila shut the door and the click was very firm and crisp and everyone knew then that something had started.

Sheila sat in her office among the books and tried to think about what she had felt in that moment. It hadn't been anger, more a kind of recognition. In that instant she had felt suddenly outside of her body, standing somewhere else and looking at both of them. What she had seen was that she was herself perfect—she was petite, she had an acute sense of colour and line and so her clothes fell on her exactly and well, her features were small and sharp, her hair was thick, and her vivacity came from her intelligence. Dolly was not perfect, she was long everywhere, she was sallow, she wore old jewelry sometimes missing a link here and there, today she wore a tatty green scarf over her shirt, and that was just it. Sheila was perfect, and she knew that however hard she tried she could never achieve the level of careless imperfection that Dolly flaunted. It had nothing to do with perseverance or intelligence and it took generations. It couldn't be learnt, only grown with the bone. It was absolutely confident and sure of itself and easy. Dolly had it and she didn't: looking at it honestly, Sheila knew this. She knew it and she was absolutely determined that if it took her the rest of her life she would defeat Dolly. That it had come to open conflict she knew, and she would not stand losing.

"*Memsahib.*" Ganga was standing in the doorway, leaning against the side, a hand cocked on her hip. She was wearing a dark red sari with a gold-stamped border. Ganga was dark and very thin, she flung herself at her work with such velocity that it was necessary to put the glassware by the side of the washbasin — otherwise, as she sped through the plates, crystal would inevitably crunch somewhere in the pile. Ganga had been recommended by Sheila's next-door neighbour. She worked, as nearly as Sheila could tell, in another dozen houses up and down the hill, and she sped from one to another without a pause the entire day, after which she stood in a local train for an hour and fifteen minutes to get out to Andheri, where she lived. It had taken Sheila six months to get her to eat lunch, which she did squatting in a corner of the kitchen and holding a plate directly in front of her face for greater efficiency.

"It was a good lunch?" Ganga said.

"Yes," Sheila said. For the first year they had known each other, Ganga had been courteous but dry, her face always expressionless and impossible to read. Then one day, on her way out, seeing Sheila sitting at her desk in the study as usual, she paused in the hallway, her whole body still pointed at the front door, to ask, What do you do in here? Accounts, Sheila had said, for our business, pointing at the ledgers piled up and the sheets of paper that folded out to cover half the room. Ganga had nodded silently and gone on her way, back up to her normal speed with the first step, but since then, she would stop in the doorway, one foot in front of the other, leaning sideways, one elbow angled out, and they would talk for a few minutes.

"Well," Sheila said. "It went well."

Then they talked about their children. Ganga had a daughter named Asha. Then Ganga tightened her *dupatta* about her waist and it was time for her to leave. "Going," she said, clipping the word now, and she went.

When Ganga got home it was seven-thirty. She put down a small packet of *jira* and set about making dinner. There was a single light bulb in the single room, and Asha was sitting under it studying, or at least flipping the pages of a book. Asha was dressed in a flowered shirt and a skirt that reached to her ankles. Her hair was pulled back and neatly oiled, and around her plait she wore a single string of white *mogra* flowers. She was sitting cross-legged with her spelling book in her lap, her chin in her hands, and now she darted a quick look from huge brown eyes at her mother.

"All right, all right," Ganga said. "Come eat."

They sat near the doorway and ate from steel plates, which were old but shiny. Outside, people were still passing, and occasionally somebody would say something to Ganga. The lane was narrow, and whoever walked by had to brush close to the door. Across the lane, there was a narrow gutter which flooded in the rains, and behind that more shacks made of wood, cloth, cardboard, and tin. Later, when it was dark, Ganga would sit in the doorway and talk to her neighbours. Most of them were from the same village in the Ghats near Poona, but to the left, where the lane curved, it became a mostly Malayalee locality. Today they mostly talked about a man in their own community who drank so much that he finally lost his watchman job. "He's a fool," Ganga said. "You always knew that." It was true. They had all known him and they had always known that.

Ganga had arrived in Bombay eleven years before with her husband, who had come back to his village to marry, and since then she had lived in the same place. Ramesh, the husband, had been a millworker in the days before the labour disputes and the big lockouts. He was a Marxist, and he was killed, stabbed, in a quarrel with another union the year after Asha was born. Ganga remembered him mostly as a melancholy sort of man who seemed to cultivate his own sadness. It was only in the month after his funeral that she found out that he was said to have killed two men himself in the same union fight. But anyway, now the mills were closed and the years had passed. Now it seemed that Ganga was going to move, and this was the news she had to give to her neighbours. Two stops up on the Western line she had found an empty plot, and she planned to build her *kholi* there.

"*Pukka?*" said Meenu, her neighbour, her voice a little breathless, because brick would cost more, and everyone knew that Ganga worked so much that she must have money, but nobody knew how much.

"Yes," Ganga said. "Ten thousand for the land, five for the construction."

"Fifteen," Meenu said.

"Yes," Ganga said. "I don't have it."

"How will you manage?"

Ganga shrugged. She didn't tell them what she planned, because she wasn't sure she would get the money and she didn't want to sound sure before she was. That afternoon it had occurred to her to ask Sheila for a loan. Sheila had said that the lunch had gone well, but the concentrated expression on her face, the set of her shoulders as she sat among her books was not that of a happy woman. Looking at her then, Ganga had realized that this was after all a woman of business, somebody who wanted things from the world, and had realized that she should ask Sheila for the money. She wanted to wait for a few days, let the thought sit in her stomach, because she had learnt from the world to be careful when one could, since often there was no time for care. Now she had a month from the owner of the plot to come up with the money, and so she waited for a week. It still made sense, so one day after lunch she asked Sheila, and Sheila said, "Of course," went into the bedroom for a few minutes and came back with a stack of notes. It was no fuss. They talked terms, and it was decided that Ganga was to pay it back monthly over six years.

But leaving was a fuss. They had lived in that nameless lane for a long time, Asha since she was born, and Meenu organized the people up and down the street to give them a send-off. They rented a television set and a video player and they watched films all night long, and it was very very late when Asha finally fell asleep with her head in her mother's lap. Ganga sat in the darkness, an arm over her daughter, and felt the loss as a tightness in the stomach, a kind of relentless wrenching, and the coloured light from the screen flickered on her face as she wept. But the next day, when they loaded up their belongings into a handcart, she was crisp and organized, and she led the way, holding Asha with one hand and a bundle with the other and tireless in her stride, until the men pushing the handcart leaned against it and begged for mercy.

Their new *kholi* was small, but during the rains it was dry, and Ganga kept it in good repair. There were some two-storied houses on their street, built very narrow on tiny plots, and at the end of the lane there was a grocery shop built like a cupboard into a gap between two walls. Also there was a *paan* seller who sold cigarettes and matches and played a radio from morning till night. Their years in this street were ordinary, and Ganga continued her work as before, coming and going with a regularity that her neighbours began to depend on.

Finally, what disturbed their life was Asha's beauty. When she was fifteen a local bootlegging *tapori* fell in love with her. He was at least ten years older than she was, a grown man with some reputation in his chosen trade of gangsterism and with some style, he wore tailored black shirts always, and he fell in love with her ripeness. She was not tall, but there was a certain weight about her body, a youthful heaviness that she made a great show of hiding. She was a student of the movies, and always had flowers in her hair, white or yellow ones. His name was Girish, and he fell in love with a glance that she threw at him coming out of a morning show of *Coolie*. After that he spent his time sitting on the raised platform at the end of their lane, waiting for her to pass, polishing his dark glasses on his shirt. When she did, she never looked at him, but the force of his yearning caused her to duck her head down and blush darkly, amazed and a little frightened and feeling something that was not quite happiness.

Ganga knew nothing about this until the neighbours told her. She had seen him sitting on the platform, spreading out a handkerchief before he sat down, but she had paid no attention, because it had nothing to do with her. The evening when she found out, she sat in her doorway for a long time. When she shut the door, she came in and found Asha sitting on her *charpai,* reading a film magazine. As she watched, a wisp of hair fell across Asha's cheek, and the girl pushed it back behind her ear, only to have it fall forward again. Idly, Asha flicked it away, the hair was heavy and thick and dark brown, and as Ganga watched her daughter's fingers move across her cheek and linger, the danger of it all pressed her heart like a sudden weight. She knew instantly and completely the violent allure of the black glasses, the coiled stance that projected danger, the infinitely dark and attractive air of tragedy.

"Tomorrow I will take you to your grandfather's," Ganga said, louder than she had intended.

"What?" Asha said. "In the village?"

"Don't argue," Ganga said. "You're going."

But Asha wasn't arguing, she was silent, caught somewhere between heartbreak and relief. Her sobs that night in her bed weren't full of grief, or even of sorrow, but of the tension of weeks. She left quietly and obediently with her mother, and in the train she smiled at the mountains and the zigzagging ascent of the tracks and the birds floating in the valley below. But in the village—called Saswadi—she grew sulky at the endless quiet of the long afternoon. Ganga was in no mood for sulks, having spent an unexpected two hundred rupees on the tickets and travel, and she put Asha to work straightaway, in the kitchen and with the cows in the back. Ganga's father was small and very lean, as if every last superfluity of flesh had been burnt away by season after season of a farmer's sun. She had brought him two shirts from Bombay, which he would wear on very special occasions. She spent two days in the village, straightening out the house and seeing to the repair of a waterway that came down the hill into their land. When she left, she hugged Asha briefly, and she felt the youthful sigh more than she heard it. "Don't be silly," Ganga said. "What have you seen of suffering yet?"

It was afternoon when she opened her door in Bombay. She went in and put down her bundle, smoothed her hair once in a single movement, tucking back and tightening all at once, and then she reached forward for the *jhadoo*. She was sweeping under the bed with it when she heard the voice: "What have you done with her?"

When she turned he was looming in the doorway, tall and silhouetted. The sunlight was blinding behind him, and she could see the glint of the perpetual dark glasses at the sides of his face.

"What?" she began, and then her throat closed up from the fear. She stood holding the *jhadoo* in front of her with both hands, handle up, clutching it.

"If you married her to someone else," he said hoarsely. "If you married her." He moved in the doorway slightly and Ganga's head reeled, her eyes dazzled. "If you married her I'll kill you and her. And myself."

He came in, closer to her, and now she could see him clearly. "Where is she?" he said. "Where?" But his head was moving from side to side and she understood that it was very dark in the *kholi* for him. He reached up and took off the glasses and she saw his eyes, red-rimmed. He was very young, and under the sleeve of his black shirt his wrist was thin and bony.

She spoke: "Don't you have a mother?"

A tear formed slowly and inexorably on his eyelid and

rolled down his cheek, and she knew he could do exactly what he had said. She looked at him, into his eyes, and the seconds passed.

"Go home," she said.

Another moment, and then he turned and stumbled out of the doorway. She stood still, holding her *jhadoo,* for a long time, looking towards the door, until the light changed outside and evening came.

On the hill, it was generally agreed that the Shanghai Club was Sheila's masterstroke. There was a whole faction that insisted that Mr. Fong was only a front man, that the money behind Shanghai was actually some of the Bijlanis' industrial lucre, that, having diversified from mixies into plastics and transportation and pharmaceuticals, they had resources to spare. Of course, there was no proof for any of this, but what was clear and needed no proof was that the whole thing started when the Bijlanis were blackballed at the Malabar Gym. Sheila and Dolly had conducted a ruthless but fiercely polite war for years, in which the victories were counted in receptions given and famous writers annexed and huge sums collected for causes, and the casualties were the bruised egos of the partisans of either side, who cut each other in Derby boxes and flicked razor-sharp looks over shoulders at openings. But there were some rules, a certain code of conduct that kept it all civilized until the incident of the blackball.

The Bijlanis had applied for membership to the Malabar Gymkhana, a little belatedly but they were busy people, this was understood, and their son was now old enough to want to play tennis and rugby at the Gym, and the passing of the application was a foregone conclusion. And then came the blackball, which was actually not a black ball but a little slip of blue paper at the quarterly meeting of the membership committee, and the blue paper had on it the single word "No." Everyone looked at each other, astounded, but they all avoided looking at Freddie Boatwalla, because the process was of course anonymous but of course who could it be but him? There was nothing to be done about it, the rules were clear and ancient and unamendable, a blackball was a blackball, if you weren't in you were out, there was no middle ground. The chairman burnt the slips according to rule, but those who saw it said the letters were blocked out and firm, and even before the meeting was over the members were talking about the indisputable fact that Freddie had after thirty years of membership suddenly put himself up for the committee — why now unless there was a plot, a plan — and that this was an unprecedented escalation. Freddie left the meeting without talking to anyone and afterwards he was seen drinking a stiff whisky-and-soda downstairs in the Jockey Bar. The bartender said he had come in and made a phone call first and then asked for his drink. Sitting outside on the long patio with the lazy ceiling fans and the field beyond, the commentators related this and said no more, the implications were clear.

Now everyone waited for the inevitable response from Sheila, and nothing happened. It was unbelievable that she had accepted defeat, and yet this was what some believed, and others insisted that it was merely a tactical feint, this doing nothing, watch and wait. The months passed, and in the fullness of time a Mr. Fong announced that he was going to start a place called the Shanghai Club, and nobody noticed. No one knew who Mr. Fong was, and there was no reason for anyone to ask, and nobody was interested in his club. Then it was known — nobody knew where this came from — that the Shanghai Club would admit only women as members, and furthermore only by invitation. That to do the inviting there was a committee of ten prominent women who were to remain anonymous — and suddenly the phones started ringing all over Bombay. Who was the committee? Nobody knew. Then the first invitation arrived, in a plain white envelope without a stamp, hand delivered at the house of Bubbles Kapadia, of the Ganesha Mills Kapadias. "We are pleased to offer you a charter subscription to the Shanghai Club," it said. "We request the pleasure of your company at the opening on January 26th." At about the same time, in what must have been a sublimely managed leak, it became known—seemingly in the exact same minute—from Nepean Sea Road to Bandra that Sheila Bijlani and Mani Mennon were one-fifth of the committee, and that only a hundred memberships were to be offered. Now there was wild conjecture, endless lists were drawn up and debated, memories were searched for histories of friendship and betrayal, and suddenly that plain white envelope was the most coveted thing in the city. Mr. Fong received so many calls that he changed his home number seven times, and still he was woken up in the middle of the night by desperate pleas from councilmen and captains of commerce. "I'm afraid I can't do anything about it" was his standard reply. "I don't control the committee. They tell me what to do." The Chief Minister himself made a resigned call to Mr. Fong on behalf of the Storrow toothpaste heiress, who sent a hundred and fourteen baskets of fruit to various houses in a scattershot attempt to flush out the committee. Nothing worked.

The white envelopes came in a trickle through October and November, and nobody could tell where one would show up next, and the exact count was tabulated and maintained with increasing tension as the months passed. Those who got one let it slip casually: "Oh, guess what was under the door today!" And those who didn't affected not to care: "I can't believe everyone's so crazy about this stupid Mr. Fong's club." Some pretended to sniff at the kind of people who were getting invitations: a policewoman—a deputy commissioner, but still; a documentary filmmaker; several journalists, some of them of the television variety. And when Ramani Ranjan Das, the erotic poetess, was invited, a whole faction of the Gym set, at the very north end of the patio, declared very dramatically and at great length that they were withdrawing from the Shanghai race, until Bubbles Kapadia asked how they knew they were in it. In the dead silence that followed, Bubbles flicked her ashes onto the table, drew long and at great leisure on her green cigarette holder, then got up and turned and disappeared in a great white cloud of triumphant smoke.

Of course Dolly behaved as if the Shanghai Club did not exist and never would. It was at the Gym, at lunch, that somebody first brought up the subject in front of her. The words dropped, and suddenly silence spread around the table like a ripple. Everyone waited, but Dolly was staring into the middle distance, her eyes calm and genial, absolutely imperturbable, as if she were suddenly a stone-deaf idol, elegantly dressed. She had not heard it, even though the softly spoken words were heard from one end of the oak table to the other. After a while she picked up her knife and fork and cut a tiny little piece of quiche and ate it slowly and with pleasure. As the weeks passed and the hysteria mounted and the rumours flew and everyone talked about nothing but the Shanghai Club, she continued not to hear anything. She was absolute and unshakable. The commentators argued: she must really be upset, some said, she must go home and cry in the bathroom. Nonsense, said the other, stronger, school of thought, it is all truly beneath her, she doesn't care a whit. As January the twenty-six drew nearer, she grew more and more to resemble a kind of stately ship in sail, constant and beautiful, unmoved by choppy waters, and her supporters grew delirious with admiration. It was true: she was magnificent in her dignity. One of the north-patio commentators said, in a tone that mingled exactly equal amounts of envy and quiet pride, "After all, she is a Boatwalla."

All this was true until the evening of January the fifteenth. Bijlani came home, drew Sheila into their bedroom, locked the door, and related a strange and wondrous tale. He had been sitting, as was his custom, on the balcony of the Napier Bar above the Dolphin Club swimming pool, sipping at his nightly martini. He did this every evening after his fifteen laps and massage, with the cane chair creaking gently under his bulk and the breeze in his hair. On this evening, he was startled out of his meditation by a man's voice: "Hello, T.T." Bijlani had acquired, over the years, with his increasing financial weight, with his famous and many-faceted magnitude, a name and a dense, magisterial composure. So his quick turn of the head, his spilling of his drink, was unprecedented but understandable — the man who stood uncomfortably over him, shifting from leg to leg, was Freddie Boatwalla.

Bijlani waved him into a chair, and when he sat Bijlani could see his face clearly in the light from the door. Freddie had always been thin, but now, in the single light against the darkness, he looked like a paper cutout, one of those black shadow figures from another century, nineteenth or maybe eighteenth or something. Bijlani knew the Boatwalla shipping company had been through some ups and downs, but who hadn't, it was no cause for this kind of deterioration. Bijlani waved to a bearer. "Drink?" Bijlani said.

"Thanks, old boy," Freddie said. "Gin and tonic." He crossed his legs, and Bijlani had a moment of hideous, bilelike envy: Freddie's crease above the knee was absolutely straight, without needing a tuck or pull or even a pat. The white pants fell just so, like everything else. His name was actually Faredoon Rustam Jamshed Dara Boatwalla, but he had always been Freddie, son of Percy Boatwalla, grandson of Billy. There had been a great-grandfather, whose name Bijlani could never remember but who stood in full life-size glory in a niche near Crawford Market, haughtily ignoring the pigeons swarming around his feet.

"Nice evening, isn't it?" Freddie said.

"Very." Bijlani was remembering the story about Freddie that everyone told again and again, that he had in the golden days of his youth bowled out Tiger Pataudi twice in two consecutive innings during a match at Cambridge.

"Heard about your pharmaceutical deal with the French. Good show," Freddie said.

"Thanks."

"We've been thinking in that direction ourselves. International hookups. Collaborations."

"Yes."

"Negotiating with an American party, ourselves. Difficult."

"Really?"

"Oh, very. Arrogant sods. Full of themselves. But really it's the only way."

"I'm sure."

"Change, you know. Adaptation."

"Absolutely."

Freddie's drink came and they sipped in a silence that was not exactly companionable but at least businesslike. Above them the lights of the tall buildings made a rising mosaic, and a swimmer's slow splashing in the pool beat a sleepy rhythm to and fro. Freddie put his glass down.

"Thanks for the drink. Have to be getting along. Dinner, you know." He stood up. "Can't stay away. Family. You know how these women are." He laughed.

Bijlani tilted his head back, but Freddie was against the door now and it was hard to make out his face. "Family," Bijlani said. "Of course."

"You know, old boy, you ought to resubmit."

"What's that?"

"Your application, I mean," Freddie said. "At the Gym. I'm sure that whole business was a mistake. Error. Lapse. Awful. Happens. Resubmit. We'll take care of it." And with that he was gone.

When Bijlani told Sheila about this conversation, she sat

very still for a moment, so immobile that she might have been frozen. Then only her eyes moved, and she looked up at Bijlani. "How interesting," she said at last. "Let's go down to dinner."

That Freddie and T.T. had talked was known by everyone half an hour after it happened, and there was much speculation about what had actually been said. It was clear that some sort of deal had been made, that negotiations had happened, and now Dolly-watching took on a strange, fresh piquancy. When she received her white envelope, what would she do? Would she say something casually about the Shanghai Club at a lunch? Would she now hear the words that had rendered her deaf and blind? Everyone wanted to be there at the event itself, whatever and whenever it was, because it was completely unprecedented and sure to be delicious in many ways. But nothing happened. Dolly remained casually unaware and went about her business, and the days passed. It was now awfully close to the Shanghai opening and everybody was wound tight, what with fittings and appointments and plans. In those last few days you only had to say to someone, "Has anything happened?" and they'd know what you were talking about.

But of course nothing did happen. Sheila told no one anything either, she was infuriatingly and politely private and unrelenting. Only Mani Mennon knew, because she had been there on the afternoon of the twenty-third, in Sheila's study, looking through a list as Sheila worked with a calculator and her endless files. "*Memsahib.*" Ganga came in, picked up her half-pay from the desk, and paused long enough to watch Sheila make a notation in a long list of her installments. As Ganga left, Sheila smiled at her. The phone rang, and Sheila picked it up and said, as she had many times that afternoon, "Sheila Bijlani." Then there was a moment of silence, and Sheila stared at the receiver as the silence went on, from awkwardness into significance, and she looked at Mani Mennon and both of them knew instantly who it was.

"Hello," the phone finally said, a little staticky and hissy. "This is Dolly Boatwalla."

"How are you, Dolly?"

"Very well, thank you. How are you?"

"I'm fine."

There was another little moment there, and then Dolly cleared her throat. "I've been very busy, what with the children being at home. Trying to keep them amused is so trying. Freddie told me he saw T.T. at the pool."

"Did he? Yes, he did."

"Keeping fit, that's good. I have to practically send Freddie out with his clubs. Listen" — now a little laugh — "have you heard anything about this Shanghai affair?"

Sheila took a deep breath. One by one, she relaxed her fingers on the receiver and settled back into her big leather chair. She wriggled her shoulders a little. Then, completely calm, she slowly said the word she had been saving for so long: "No."

"Ah."

Mani Mennon began to laugh into a pillow, holding it to her chest and shaking violently.

"Well, it was nice talking to you," Dolly said. "I hear the children coming in. I should go."

"It was nice," Sheila said. "*Namaste.*"

Mr. Fong stood at the door of the Shanghai Club in a dinner jacket and a bow tie, his hair solid black and with a sheen, looking dashing and mysterious and exactly right. Inside, if you looked closely, you could see that the club was really a little too small, that the tables were the same kind that Bhendi Bazaar furniture-makers copied from Danish catalogues, that the drinks were a little diminutive for so much money, that everything was quite ordinary. But it was all transformed that night by an extraordinary electricity, a current of excitement that made everyone beautiful, a kind of light that came not from the dim lamps but from the air itself. Ramani Ranjan Das wore all white, white *mogra* in her hair and a white *garara* suit and a silver nose ring, and she came with a film director twenty years younger. The Deputy Commissioner of Police wore slacks and turned out to be quite charmingly shy. Sheila wore a green sari and came a little late. She and T.T. sat in the middle of the crowded, smoky room and the air was filled with a pleasant chatter against the faint strains of music, and though it was photographed and written about, nothing ever really caught that feeling. It felt new, as if something was starting, and it was somehow oddly sexy, at least six new affairs and two engagements started that night, but that wasn't all of it. It was the certainty of it, the feeling that for a few hours there was nowhere else in the world to be and nothing else to do, it was that cusping of time and place and history and power and effort that lifted the Shanghai Club that night into romance and made it unutterably golden.

We thought then that Sheila was invincible, but we had forgotten that even the strongest will in the world is easily defeated by its own progeny. Inevitably, Sheila's son came back to Bombay a poet. Sanjeev had been gone a long time, first to school at Doon and then to the States — he went not to his father's college but to Yale, where he took many classes in photography and art history, and broke many hearts with a dark curl of hair on his forehead that gave him a look of sad nostalgia. He had learned to ski, and had an easy physical grace that was quite different from his mother's nervous energy, her focus, and his father's thumping walk. He was indolent and he had a little smile just a little tinged with arrogance, but we all forgave him that because he wrote such lovely poetry. Mani Mennon was the first one outside the family to meet him that summer, and she watched him for a long time, and then she said to nobody in particular, in a tone of wonder, "You know he looks always like he's just gotten off a horse." When she said that, she had said everything. Bijlani said to Sheila, "I don't know what to say to him, and he's not quite what I expected, but he's very wonderful." Sheila nodded, overwhelmed by her love. She treated her son like a jewel, standing between him and the world, willing not only to give him anything but to take whatever he wanted to give, a poem if that was it. She already understood that getting what you wanted from the world meant that your own struggles became grubby and irrelevant to your children, which was as it should be, that was after all why you gave them what you didn't have. But like all parents she never really believed he would fall in love.

This is how it happened. A week after coming home, Sanjeev wandered away from the house, feeling rested in the body but exhausted by loneliness. He said later that he was discovering the strange terror of coming back to a familiar city and not knowing anyone, and he thought that seeing the playing fields of his childhood, the streets and the corners, would fill the gap in his heart. So he wandered off the hill and down to Pastry Palace, and as he crossed the flyover bridge he was trying to recall the excitement that once had really made the place a palace, that teenage feeling of seeing a cluster of friends and knowing that everything was possible. But now it just looked ordinary. It was disappointment that made him trudge on into the Palace, a bitter determination to see it all through.

So there are opinions and opinions about what happened next. Some say it was just this — that he needed a way to reconnect, you see, to hold on to something. Others contend contemptuously that it was just the narrative force of history that pushed them into their headlong affair, that it was the ferocity of the feud that made them long for each other. "What a bloody cliche," we heard on the balcony of the Gym. "What atrocious Hindi-movie taste to allow themselves." The best of us believe that it was merely love. But, of course, nobody really knows what happened, except the essential facts, and they tell us precisely nothing: that afternoon, seated at Pastry Palace with her friends, was Dolly's daughter Roxanne, eighteen years old, finishing at Cathedral that year. She was a fair girl, with that milky Boatwalla complexion, dark straight hair, dark eyes, a little plump, sweet and quiet and a little shy, very charming but nothing spectacular, you understand. She and Sanjeev had known each other by sight before, but the last time he had seen her was when she had just turned thirteen. They talked, we know this for certain, but nobody knows what happened next — did they meet again at Pastry, how did they call each other, was it at a friend's house, what exactly went on? Certainly Sheila didn't know. What she did know was that three months later, at the end of the summer, Sanjeev told her that he wanted to marry.

When she heard who it was, Sheila didn't flinch. She asked calmly, "Did Roxanne tell her mother yet?"

"Yes," Sanjeev said. "We thought she should."

Looking at his face, Sheila suddenly felt old. He was confident of the future. He knew there was a problem, but of course he had the essential belief that the wars of the past were fought because of benighted ignorance, that good sense would after all prevail. She wanted to tell him that the past was responsible for him, for his beauty, but of course there was nothing to say, no possible way to explain. After a few minutes of her silence, he asked, "Are you angry?"

"No," she said. It was true; she was baffled. She had no idea what to do next. But as the afternoon passed, as she and Sanjeev sat together in her office, she couldn't endure doing nothing. She picked up her phone and began to make calls. After the first few it became clear that Dolly did know what to do: she had left the city with Roxanne. They had left by the four-o'clock flight for London. They had been seen being driven to the airport, and the report was that Roxanne had looked tearfully out of the window all the way, but this, Sheila was sure, was dramatic value added on as the story passed from phone to phone. In any case, they were gone.

Now Sanjeev looked stunned and wanted to go to London. "Don't be silly," Sheila said. "How do you know you'll find them there? And what'll you do when you find them, tear her away?" Dolly had two other daughters, one married in London, one in Chicago—Roxanne could be anywhere in the world.

So they waited. Sheila was sure that Dolly wouldn't leave Freddie alone for too long, not at this time, she would return soon. Sheila had no idea what she would do when Dolly did return, she thought about it often but could come up with no satisfactory plan. In the meantime she looked after Sanjeev, who was causing havoc as he suffered. He grew thinner, and, with the dark circles under his eyes, his forelock of hair was completely irresistible, women old and young pined after him, they left him notes and waited for him in the pubs he was known to frequent, and they pursued convoluted paths to introductions to him, but it was all useless, he forgot them a minute after meeting them. He saw nothing and heard nothing except the memory of his Roxanne. Sheila understood that every minute he spent apart from Roxanne bound him more irrevocably to her, and she also understood that if she as a mother told him to forget her, Roxanne would become as unforgettable to him as his own childhood. Sheila had to keep quiet. It was a trap finely honed for her by the years of victory. Even now she had to appreciate the justice of its bitterness.

After sixty days, Dolly returned. Bijlani had friends at customs, so they knew even before she was through the green channel that she was back, that she had come alone on a Pan Am flight from Frankfurt. Sheila let forty-eight hours pass, and then on a Saturday afternoon she asked for the car. She sat by herself in the back as it went through a couple of turns, up a long slope to the left, and arrived at the Boatwalla mansion. She could have walked in about ten minutes, but in all the years they had lived so close to each other, she had never actually seen the mansion. The lane that ran up to the gate was shadowed with branches that came over high walls, so that when you actually got to the gate you were surprised by the expanse of lawn beyond. The gate itself was wrought iron, with some kind of coat of arms at the centre, but Sheila noticed with a quick forward leaning of surprise that the marble on the left gatepost was unmistakably cracked. The car went by the gateman, who saluted the Mercedes and let it through without question, and as it swept around the circular drive she saw the whole place clearly for the first time — the white columns, the ornate windows, the facade with its grand curls and flourishes, all of it stained and patchy. The front door was opened, incredibly, by a maid in a black uniform, and suddenly Sheila had to hold back a laugh, but then she noticed that the woman had a head of white, very fine white hair, and that she was peering at her with a concentration that was absolute and unwavering.

"Please tell Mrs. Boatwalla that Mrs. Bijlani is here," Sheila said, stepping past her. The woman's stare held for a moment, her hand stiff on the doorknob, and then she turned and shuffled away. "Mrs. Bijlani," Sheila called after her curved shoulders, but the maid did not turn her head. The only light came through the open front door, catching a myriad of motes that barely moved. In the dim dark, Sheila could see two ottomans against the wall, under a picture of workmen toiling on a dock. The carpet was worn and, near the door, stained with patches of deep brown. There was a very slight smell of damp. There was no light switch that Sheila could see, and so she waited near the door. Finally a sibilant scraping came close and the maid appeared out of the darkness.

"Madame is not in."

"It's very important," Sheila said. "Tell her that it's very important."

"Madame is not in."

The woman was saying it without impatience, standing with her hands loosely holding each other in front of her white apron. Sheila had no doubt she would say it again. Sheila nodded and turned away. She heard the door click gently before she was halfway down the steps. As the car pulled away she looked back at the house, but there was no sign of life in any of the windows. Before the car went through the gate her strategy was clear in her head, fully formed. The thought came to her that way, precise and whole. She was going to buy the mansion. She would buy them out complete: lock, stock, ship, and house. Finally it came down to this vulgarity—that they had the pride and she had the money. She sat alertly in the back of the car that she had earned, paralysed no more, her mind moving quickly. It was, after all, she thought, only inevitable. It was time and history.

Sheila and T.T. sat together late that night, figuring the exact liquidity of their cash. That had always struck her as a strange phrase, because money was, if anything, hard, impersonal. But now she saw how it could be like a stream, unpredictable and underground, and she was going to turn it into a torrent that would flow up the hill instead of down, crumbling the bloody Boatwalla gate like paper. It was going to burst out of the hillside under the mansion like a fountain from the interior rock —surprise, surprise. It was two o'clock when they stared down at a figure at the bottom of a white pad, at the long string of zeros they had spent a lifetime accumulating.

"Is it enough?" T.T. said, rubbing his eyes. "Is it enough?"

"It's enough," Sheila said. "Let's sleep." They went up the stairs to the bedroom, and Sanjeev's light was on under his door. She resisted the impulse to knock and went on, but when the lights were off she couldn't sleep. She could see the shapes of the companies they owned, how they fit together, and she moved the segments against one another like the pieces on a chessboard, looking for the nuance that would give them the edge four moves down. She got up once to drink water and was shocked by the hour gleaming at her from the bedside table. Again she tried to sleep, but now it was only the zeros that spun before her, symmetrical and unchanging. *Shunya shunya shunya*, the words came to her in her father's high voice teaching her some forgotten childhood lesson: *shunya* is zero and zero is *shunya*. She felt very tired.

The exhaustion passed, but something else remained. As they began their bid, which Sheila insisted was not hostile but necessary, as they began their slow and audacious assault on Boatwalla Shipping International & Co. (since 1757), she found that all the pleasure was gone. The takeover was the most complicated puzzle that she had ever faced, and she was perfection itself, her memory was prodigious, her stamina unquenchable, and her charm of course was gleaming and soft and unstoppable. But she felt the gears grinding inside her. She told herself to remember whom she was doing it for, after all; she looked at her son's face and remembered the way he had learned to walk by clinging precariously to her sari and his jerky little steps, but still every morning she lay awake in bed gathering the vitality, a little from here a little from there, for the great effort to get up and war with the day. But the only true thing was that her taste for the game in itself was gone. Suddenly it felt like work, but even when it was over for the day she could only sit silently, staring sometimes at the television, feeling lost. She tried to hide it, and Sanjeev, who had begun to write page after page of poetry, never noticed, but T.T. was uneasy. He said nothing but he looked wary, as if he had smelled something dangerous in the shifting air but wasn't quite sure what it was, where it came from, what it meant.

It was now, in this, Sheila's time of ashes, that Ganga came to her one Sunday. She was wearing a new, bright blue sari, and with her was Asha, also in a sari, a green one. It was a formal call: they stood in Sheila's study, the mother a little in front.

"How pretty you look, Asha," Sheila said.

As the girl blushed, Ganga spoke. "She finished her nurse training last week."

"Very good, Asha!" Sheila said, touching her on the shoulder.

"She's getting married next month," Ganga said. "We came to give you the card. He's a schoolteacher."

Sheila took the envelope, which was huge, a foot square. Inside, the card was red, with a gold vine that went around the borders. It invited the reader to a ceremony and reception at the Vivekananda School Hall, Andheri.

"Will you come?" Ganga said.

Sheila was looking at Asha. For some reason, she was thinking suddenly about her first flight on an Air France plane, the leap of her stomach when the machine had escaped the ground.

"Yes," Sheila said. "Of course."

"Bring Sanjeev Baba, too."

"Yes, I will." Sanjeev hadn't left the house for days, even weeks now, and Sheila was sure she couldn't get him to come out of the edifice of his grief, she had already stopped asking him, but she said, "We'll all come."

Ganga nodded. "Come," she said to Asha, who smiled over her shoulder at Sheila. She ran down the hall to keep up with her mother, the silver *payals* at her ankles tinkling with every step. Sheila sat down slowly at her desk. The girl's eagerness hurt her, the small musical sound pressed against her abdomen and gave her a feeling of discovering a new emptiness. She remembered—remembered driving in a bus with the other hostesses in the early morning, to the airport, the red lights far away in the cool blue dawn, a plane thundering overhead with its running lights twinkling, and the glad feeling that it was all an invitation, a promise. They used to sing together, sometimes, Hindi film songs, from Marine Drive to Bandra, and sometimes in Paris on the road to Orly, with the French drivers smiling at them.

Now Sheila waited, with her hand on the phone, collecting herself before the next call. There were a lot of calls to make. The takeover was not going as planned. The Boatwallas had conducted the sort of political manoeuvring that had been expected, and that was easily countered — in fact it was welcome, because it revealed their connections and their understanding of their own predicament. It had become clear as the weeks passed that Boatwalla International was even more overextended than T.T. and she had thought. The interest on their debt alone was barely within the Boatwallas' means. But when it seemed that they must surrender or be reduced, there had come a sudden influx of cash. Like a transfusion, it had revitalized them, fleshed them out and made them capable of resistance: Freddie appeared on "Business Plus," pink and ruddy under the studio lights, and declared that it was all over, they were safe. Sheila knew they had borrowed money, lots of it at unheard-of rates of interest, but when she tried to find out who had lent it there was no answer. Her intelligence sources all over Bombay and beyond dried up like the city reservoirs in May, there was no information to be had. She and T.T. called in their favours and doled out some more, but still, nothing. If they could get a name, everything would be possible: politics could be made to interfere with the vital flow of money, fine legal quibbles could bring down the whole ponderous sickly-white elephant. Once in a similar situation they had even purchased outright and cleanly the entire lending corporation. But without a name, without that vital secret, they could do nothing, everything was meaningless.

So now she picked up the phone and looked at it, at the

numbers on the keypad. There was a time when she had handled it like a fine instrument, her fingers used to fly over the keys without her looking, it had been her delight, her sitar and her stiletto. Now she just stared at it. I can't remember people's numbers anymore, she noted with a kind of dull surprise. Then she opened her book and began dialing.

When they drove out to the Vivekananda School Hall a month later, the problem was still with them. Boatwalla International stayed perversely healthy, like a patient sprung from the deathbed and made up with rouge. And for Sheila and T.T. the outcome was not quite a draw. In the eyes of the market, the stalemate was their defeat. It was not only for this that Bijlani was silent and distraught; his uneasiness was the trouble of a man whose life has lost its accustomed centre. Sheila knew that her own doldrums becalmed him even more than her, but her best attempts at revitalization seemed false to her. She could feel the muscles of her mouth when she smiled. There seemed to be no way out, so she endured from day to day, and he with her. Now they sat, apart, in the back seat behind the driver, Gurinder Singh, who besides having been with them for a long time was also a friend of Ganga's.

When the car drew up outside the Vivekananda School, Ganga was waiting outside for them. She welcomed them in the midst of a jostling crowd. As they walked in, a pack of children in their shiny best raced around them, staring unabashedly. The hall had been done up with ribbons, and there was a *mandap* at the middle, with chairs arranged in untidy rows around it. "Sanjeev was busy," Sheila was saying as they walked up to two ornate chairs, thrones of a sort, really, all gilt and huge armrests, that had been placed in front of the *mandap*. They sat down and Ganga took her place by her daughter, who was sitting cross-legged next to the man who was becoming her husband. The priests were chanting one by one and in chorus, and throwing handfuls of rice into the fire. Asha smiled up at them with her head down, looking somehow very pretty and plump and satisfied. Sheila nodded at her, thinking of Sanjeev. He was not at all busy, in fact he had been sitting on their roof with his feet up on a table, but he had said he was tired.

It was the first time that Sheila had ever seen Ganga sitting absolutely still. She seemed at rest, her knees drawn up and her hands held in front of her. The priests droned on. Meanwhile, nobody paid attention to the ceremony at all. Children ran about in all directions. Their parents sat in the chairs around the *mandap* and talked, nodding and laughing. Occasionally somebody would come and stand in front of the thrones and stare frankly at Sheila and T.T., whispering to friends. Sheila had her chin in one hand and she was lost in the fire and the chant. Then suddenly the ceremony was over and the couple were sitting on a dais at the end of the hall, on thrones of exactly the same magnificence as those provided for the Bijlanis. Sheila and T.T. were first to go through the reception line, and Sheila hugged Asha, and T.T. shook hands with her husband, whose name was Rakesh. Then Sheila and T.T. sat on their thrones, which had been moved to face the dais, and food was served. Everyone was eating around them. Sheila ate the *puri bhaji* and the *biryani* and the sticky *jalebis,* and watched as Ganga moved among her seated guests, serving them herself from trays carried by her relatives behind her. She gave Sheila and T.T. huge second helpings, and they ate it all.

After the food, Ganga gave gifts to the women at the wedding. She walked around again and gave saris to her nieces and aunts and other relatives. She came up to Sheila, who said without thinking, "Ganga, you don't have to give me anything."

Ganga looked at her, her face expressionless. "It is our custom," she said. Sheila blushed and reached up quickly and took the sari. She held it on her lap with both hands, her throat tight. She felt perilously close to tears. But there were two girls, sisters, seven and eight, leaning on her knees, looking up at her. She talked to them and it passed, and finally she was sitting on one side of the room, away from the lights, not on a throne but on a folding chair, tired and pleasantly sleepy. T.T. was on the other side of the room, talking about the stockmarket scandals with a circle of men. Ganga's father sat beside him, quiet but listening intently. Sheila thought drowsily that T.T. looked animated for the first time in months.

Then Ganga walked up. She paused for a moment and then sat beside Sheila, on a brown chair. They looked at each other frankly. They had known each other for a long time and they liked each other well enough, but between them there was no question of love or hate.

"How did you manage this, Ganga?"

"I sold my *kholi*."

"You sold it?"

"For thirty thousand rupees."

Sheila looked around the hall. A song was ringing out, and a group of children were dancing, holding their arms up like Amitabh Bachchan in *Muqaddar ka Sikandar*.

"Thank you," Sheila said in English, gesturing awkwardly at the sari that she held in her lap.

For a moment there was no reaction, and then Ganga smiled with a flash of very white teeth. "We got them at wholesale," she said. "I know someone." She pointed with her chin at a man Sheila had noticed earlier bustling about, herding people from here to there. "Him."

"That's good," Sheila said.

"You speak English well," Ganga said.

"I learned it as a child."

Ganga settled herself in her chair with the motion of someone who is very tired. "I have heard that Boatwalla speak English."

"You work for her, too?"

"For longer than for you."

"I didn't know. I didn't ask."

"I didn't tell you. I wash dishes and clean the kitchen. Their other people don't do that. I never see her."

"I see."

"Except now and then, once or twice every year, when she comes into the kitchen for something."

"Yes."

"But she never sees me."

"You mean you're hiding?"

"No, I'm right there in front of her.'

"Then what do you mean?"

"I mean that she doesn't see me. If she's talking to someone she keeps on talking. To such high people the rest of the world is invisible. People like me she cannot see. It's not that she is being rude. It's just that she cannot see me. So she keeps on talking about things that she would never talk about in front of you or somebody else. Once she saw me, but it was because she wanted to get water from the fridge and I was mopping the floor and she had to step over my hand."

Ganga's voice was steady, even. Sheila shifted the packet on her lap a little.

"Even then she kept on talking. Once, I heard her say bad things about her elder daughter, the London one."

"Ganga, do you . . ." Sheila stopped.

"Understand English? A little, I think. I've worked for you for twenty years, haven't I?"

"You have indeed."

"Last week, she came in to shout at the cook about the bowls he used for the sweet after lunch. Her husband lagging behind her. These people, she said. She sent the cook to get all the bowls in the house. She said something about meetings, and her husband wrote down something on a piece of paper. How she talks in English, chutter-chutter-chutter, like she's everybody's grandmother in the world, she asked something about the American business, then she said something about a Hong Kong bank, all the time going here and there in the kitchen."

"Bank?" said Sheila.

Ganga straightened up at the sound of Sheila's voice.

"Yes. Bank."

"In Hong Kong?" Ganga said nothing in the face of Sheila's sudden needlesharp focus. "Ganga. Did she say the name of the bank?"

"Maybe."

"Do you remember it?"

"Is it important?"

"Yes. Very."

Ganga threw back her head and laughed, and two children running by stopped to gawk at her. "It was Fugai Bank. Foo Ga. Foo Quay."

In the car, Sheila reached out and took T.T.'s hand. She said nothing and looked out of the window as they went down the length of the city. Gurinder was playing cassettes of old songs, he was humming along with the music, his mood lightened by the food and the amiable chaos of the wedding. Bombay's night hadn't yet quieted down, and everywhere there were people, and at some intersections the cars and scooters honked at each other madly. As the car came around a curve, Sheila saw a family sitting by the side of the road, father and mother and two children around a small fire. There was a pot on the fire, and the flames lit up their faces as they looked up at the car going by.

At home, Sheila walked ahead as T.T. gave Gurinder a couple of fifty-rupee notes. She could hear their voices murmuring behind her, a cricket chirping, and the rustle of the wind in leaves. She had said nothing to T.T., and the name of the bank balanced precariously in her stomach, not unpleasant but not quite welcome, there was something moving in her, something not fully born yet and still unknown. The anticipation kept her awake, and finally, much later, she left her bed and went up to the roof. Now everything was dark, it was a moonless night, and the scrape of her *chappals* against the cement was loud. She found a garden chair and sat in it, her hands held together in her lap. Sometimes a freshness billowed up against her face, barely a breeze but cool and moist. It came again, and she was remembering her father. She remembered him as a small, balding man with a potbelly, dressed always in *chappals* and black pants and a bush shirt in white or brown. He kept the shop open till late in the evening and opened it early, so that Sheila saw him usually at night, when he ate his dinner alone. When she was growing up she had always thought he was a simple man. But once a year he liked to take his family away from the city, to a resort or a hill station, for a week, two weeks. She remembered waking once while it was still dark. She was ten or eleven, they were in some place on the banks of a river, a small hotel, she couldn't remember the name of the river. But she remembered the cold lifting off the water when she went outside and saw her father sitting in the sand on the river's edge below. In the dark, she could see the white of his *kurta* and his head shining above. She walked through a garden with flowers and down the steps that led to the river, and sat beside him, her leg resting on his knee. He smiled at her, then looked away, across the river where the water melted into mist. She shivered a little. There was white speckled into his stubble, which she knew he would shave later with a Wilkinson razor. His name was Kishen Chand, and he was a small man. Later, after he was dead and she was older, she would remember his gaze over the water and think that nothing and nobody was simple. Later, she would remember the old story of schisms and horrors, how he had left half his family murdered in Lahore, two brothers, a sister, a father. They had a shop, which was burned. Partition threw him onto the streets of Bombay, but he still spoke of his Lahore, his beautiful Lahore. It was something of a family joke. She huddled beside him as the river emerged from the grey light. She remembered her geography lesson and whispered to her father, Is this a sacred river? It must be, he said. It is, he said. What is that smell? she said. He said, Wood smoke. She asked, Smoke? He said, Fire. What fire? she said. He said, Cooking fires, hearth fires, hay fires. Funeral fires. Ceremonial fires. Even the firing of refuse, of things that are thrown away. Home fires and factory fires. It's starting to be day and there are fires everywhere. And she saw the white smoke drifting slowly across the surface of the water.

Sheila heard a footstep and lifted a hand to her face. It was wet with tears. She wiped it with her sleeve and when she looked up she saw that the sea, far below, was gold. She stood up and felt the light hot on her face. Sanjeev came up beside her and subsided lankily into the chair. She smiled down at him. He had a book in his hand and looked very handsome in a kind of tragic way.

"You were out late last night," he said.

"Yes."

"You went on to one of your parties?" His mouth was pouty with disdain.

Sheila laughed. As she looked down she could see on his T-shirt a blond, scruffy-looking man and the single word "Nirvana." She said, "Sanju, you're my son, but it would take a lifetime, two lifetimes, to tell you all the things you don't know about the world." As she walked away, she ruffled his hair.

In her bedroom, she laughed to see the mountainous bulk of her husband under the bedclothes. She pulled at his toe. "Come on. We have work to do." He followed her down the stairs, rubbing his eyes, to the office. He sat in front of her as she leaned back in her chair and picked up the phone.

"What are we doing?" he said.

She put her feet in his lap. He rubbed them, smiling, because in her flowered nightgown and with her hair pulled back she looked like a child, and she looked at him sideways from lowered eyes, naughty and a little dangerous. Her fingers moved so quickly over the keys of the telephone that the beep- ings came out as a kind of music. She grinned. "Ah," she said. "I thought we might make a few calls to Hong Kong."

What we remembered from the wedding was not the scale of it and not the celebration, not even how beautiful the couple was or the speculations about their honeymoon in France. It wasn't even the sight of Sheila and Dolly walking hand in hand into the reception. It wasn't the sight of Tiger Pataudi and a very boozy Freddie re-creating their second innings so that T.T. and Mani Mennon could judge whether there had indeed been a flannelled Pataudi leg before the wicket. It wasn't at all the news that Ganga had bought a large shed in Dharavi, where she was going to put in a cloth-reclamation factory. After it was all over, what stayed in the mind was a strange moment, before the double ceremony (one for each religion), when the two families had moved into the centre of the huge *shamiana*. On one side we could see Sheila's aunts, large women in pink and red saris with bands of diamonds around their wrists and necks, and, on the other, Dolly's relatives, in particular one frail, tall old lady in a white sari and a pair of pince-nez glass- es, with pearls at her neck, and all these people looking at each other. Then all the talking died away, there was a curious moment of silence, it was absolute and total, even the birds stopped chirping in the trees. Then two of the children ran through the *shamiana*, it was Roxanne's second cousin who was chasing Sheila's niece, both squealing, and the moment was broken and everyone was talking. Yet there had been that strange silence, maybe it was just that nobody knew what to do with each other. But I think of that moment of silence whenever I realize how much changed because of that marriage. What I mean is the formation of the Bijlani-Boatwalla Bombay International Trading Group, then the Agarwal loan scandal, the successes of the B.B.B.I., the fall of the Yashwant Rao Ghatge government, and the meteoric rise of Gagganbhai Patel, and what happened after that we all know. But that's another story. Maybe I'll tell you about that another evening.

Kama

THAT SUMMER I was heartbroken. I was weary of myself, of the endless details like prickly heat, and the smell of hopelessness in my armpits. It was after all very boring, nothing but something that someone else and I had thought would go on forever, and it had come apart savagely and with finality. It seemed so ordinary, so average in its particulars that I found it sordid to think about, and yet I could do nothing but think about it. I knew I was supposed to drink it away, but liquor just made me even more tired and sleep eluded me anyway. I went slouching sullenly about the city and waited for the monsoon to break, without faith, without belief in its powers, waiting only for something to change.

One evening they were talking of a murder. I say "they" because lately I had been slumped over in my chair for weeks, silent but always nervous, shifting from one side to another incessantly. Subramaniam had been watching me all this time. Now I was very interested in the details of the murder. I wanted to know how they had been killed. It was a husband and wife and they had been found bloodied in their apartment in Colaba. The papers were full of it. The fact that there were no signs of a struggle gave me a particular satisfaction. I nodded rapidly. The others watched me, uneasy.

"No great mystery there," I said. "It must have been love. Sex, you know."

"Or gold," Desai said. "Property. It says that the police are questioning the servants."

"Something like that," I said. "Simple and stupid."

"Or the most complicated thing of all," Subramaniam said suddenly.

"What's that?"

"Don't you know?"

He was smiling gently. I collapsed suddenly. I must have been insufferable, and they had been very patient and very kind.

"No, sir," I said. "Why don't you tell me?"

He laughed, his shoulders shaking. Then his face became serious, and he looked at me for a long time. He nodded with that peculiar motion of his, from side to side.

"All right," he said. "Listen."

The body was almost submerged in the ditch, but what Sartaj noticed about it as he squatted beside it was its expression of pride. One arm was curved out of the water and rigid. The passerby who had found the body was a driver on his way to the milkstand for his *memsaab's* bottles, and he had seen through the rain a hand, reaching up out of the rushing stream as if for something. It had been raining for three days and three nights and through the morning now, and the water was actually roaring as it pushed below a culvert. The dead man was jammed in between the curving brick wall and the broken metal grill. The driver had stood next to the ditch and shouted until people in the nearby buildings had come out, and then he had stood guard until the police came. He seemed to think that somehow it was his responsibility since he had found it, but now he was trying not to look down at it. The skin on the palm of the hand that emerged from the water was a strange bluish grey.

Sartaj Singh, who was an inspector in Zone 13 and used to bodies, was squatting carefully next to the ditch, looking at the ground, but there was running water everywhere and it was likely that the body had drifted. He walked the few yards to the next culvert, feeling his boots sink into the mud. A gust of wind blew water into his face. The flashbulbs were freezing the drops in the air in their sudden glare. It was the first heavy rain of the monsoon, and he knew that the next few weeks would be miserable with mud, with clumsy raincoats and flooded streets, clothes that always seemed wet, and the impossibility of keeping a crease in one's pants. Anyway there was nothing to be found. The photographers had finished.

"All right," Sartaj said. "Get him out."

They put a crowbar against the grill and pulled at the dead man's arm, his shoulders. Finally one of the constables, whose name was Katekar, shrugged, took off his boots, and got into the water. It beat against his waist and chest as he strained and finally the body came free. The driver gasped as they dragged the body out and over because under the chest, on the right side of the belly, the flesh had been eaten away. The rats had been at him before the water took him and covered him over. But the face was unconcerned and smug.

"Turn around," Sartaj said to the driver. "What's your name?"

"Raju."

"Raju, take a look at him quickly. Do you know him?" Finally Sartaj had to take Raju by the elbow and steady him. "Look," Sartaj said. Raju was in his early twenties and Sartaj knew that he had never imagined his own death. Now in the early morning he was looking at a corpse. He shook his head so violently that Sartaj felt the jerks in his arm. "All right. Go over there and sit down. We'll need your statement."

"Robbed, sir," Katekar said as he pulled on his boots. He pointed with his chin at the white band of skin around the dead man's wrist, which showed up clearly even after his colour had drained away into the water. "Must have been a good watch."

"It was a big one anyway," Sartaj said. "Big enough to get him killed."

He had been dead at least eight and not more than twelve hours when he was found. The cause of death was a single stab wound, under the sternum, only an inch and a quarter long but deep. The blade had pierced his heart.

"What was taken?" Parulkar said. Parulkar was Sartaj's boss. He had been promoted up to deputy commissioner from the Maharashtra police service, and still lived in Ghatkopar in what he called his ancestral abode.

"Wallet," Sartaj said. "And a watch."

"Ah, I see," Parulkar said. "Bombay was never like this."

Sartaj shrugged. "It's a new world. He was fifty or thereabouts, no distinguishing marks."

He looked up and Parulkar was smiling. Sartaj had been cleaning his boots with a moist rag, scrubbing away the mud caked around the tread and the ankles.

"It'll get on again as soon as you go out," Parulkar said.

Sartaj nodded. "Yes, sir. But the point is to keep trying?"

"Of course, of course," Parulkar said, standing up and hitching his pants over his considerable belly. His uniform was always bunched up somehow, looking as if it had been made for someone else. "Young fellows must be tip-top. Carry on, carry on." But he was still smiling as he walked out of the room.

Sartaj stood up and walked across the room to a map of the state. In the glass, over the dark borders and the blue roads, he could see himself, and he checked his shoulders, the tuck of his shirt, the crispness of his crease. Now when the moisture hung in the air it was difficult to come close to the perfection he wanted to see in the glass, but he patted his turban and ran a finger over his sagging collar. He did not mind Parulkar's smile at all, because he was a dandy who came from a long line of dandies. His father had retired as a senior inspector in Zone 2, and every street urchin had recognized the swagger stick with the shining steel tips and the gleaming black boots. Sartaj's grandfather's upturned moustaches had been acknowledged as the most magnificent in all of Punjab, and he had died in service as a *daroga*, in a gun battle with Afghan smugglers near Peshawar. The legend went that when he was hit he was eating a *dusseri* mango. He sat down, not far from a *babul* bush, finished the mango, crossed his legs, held out his hand for a napkin that his seniormost *havaldar* was holding for him, wiped his fingers, dabbed at his mouth, twirled his moustaches, and died.

Sartaj had never been able to eat a mango without thinking of the old man, who he had met only through the garlanded portrait that hung in his mother's house. Next to that picture was a portrait of Guru Nanak, another one of Guru Gobind Singh, and then one of Sartaj's father, who had made it to retirement and had passed one night in his sleep, resting on his back with his hands folded neatly on his chest. Sartaj was eating a mango now, holding a slice with his fingertips as he leafed through the reports from the Missing Persons Bureau with his other hand, stacking the probables to the left, face down, and the rejects to the right. He was looking mainly for the age, but also for the kind of man who would have wanted what the dead man wanted. He had it down to fifteen when the phone buzzed angrily. In the quietness after the rain it was very loud.

"Are you still in the office, you sad man?" a boy's voice said.

"Yes, I am," Sartaj said.

"Doing what?"

"Eating the last *alphonso* mango of the season."

"You should go home."

"You're still up. You must be very happy or very sad." It was Rahul, his wife's younger brother, who was now in his second year at Xavier's and therefore always falling in love with someone or out of it.

"Happy, actually," Rahul said quietly. "I bought a new shirt at Benneton today." They had a mutual interest in clothes, although they mystified each other with their choices. They talked for a while about this shirt, and then suddenly Rahul said, "When's the exam tomorrow?" Sartaj flipped over another report as Rahul talked nonsense about college. What that meant was that someone had come into the room, and Rahul was pretending that he was talking to a college friend. Finally Rahul said, "See you at college tomorrow. Go to sleep soon. Night," and hung up.

Ten minutes later the phone rang again. "Hello, Sartaj," his mother said. "I just called home and of course you weren't there." She lived alone in Poona, with a rose garden and one aging Alsatian. When Sartaj's father had been alive, they called every Sunday, but now she allowed herself a daily call.

"*Peri pauna,* Ma," Sartaj said.

"*Jite raho, beta,*" she said. "Did you find a cook?"

"No, not yet, I've been busy." Which, of course, was no excuse. Sartaj held the phone loosely against his ear, and turned pages, and his mother spoke at length about bad diets and nutrition. He could see clearly the sofa she was sitting on, the little table next to it, her small feet which he had just touched in devotion, her hands with which she had blessed him, and the sari wrapped around her plump shoulders, and the garlanded pictures on the wall.

"It's too late, Sartaj," she said finally. "Go home and rest."

"Yes, Ma," Sartaj said. But he stayed for another two hours before he walked home. Even then he walked slowly, stopping sometimes to watch the water as it roiled around the gutters and made whirlpools. He leaned against a wall and scanned the layered many-coloured mess of movie posters and political slogans, dominated by the latest broadside bearing the crossed spears of a right political party. He read all this with the concentration of an archeologist smoothing away layers of ancient dust. What he was avoiding was the small bundle of foolscap paper that sat on his dining table, wrapped in a white ribbon. Rahul's sister had sent him these papers, and he couldn't bring himself yet to say the word for what she wanted. But he was supposed to be distinct now from her and her family, disengaged. He had been told that they considered him dead. Which was why Rahul made phone calls late at night: maybe that's when you talk to the dead.

Sartaj found the next of kin, whose name was Smt. Asha Patel ("wife of missing person"), but not on the batch of missing persons reports that he had. It was in another stack that came three days later from the Missing Persons Bureau. The name of the dead man was Chetanbhai Ghanshyam Patel and the age was right, but what clinched it of course was the entry under distinguishing marks and features: "Wearing a gold Rolex watch, value Rs. 2,18,000/-." Chetanbhai was then a man who liked people to know the make of watch that he was wearing and its exact and precisely calculated value. Sartaj did the missing-property paperwork (in triplicate as required), and out of habit made some phone calls to his usual official and non-official sources, although he had no hope that he would ever see this grand keeper of time, but in this he was wrong because that same afternoon there was a phone call from the station at Bandra. Two of their constables, at seven that morning, had picked up one Shanker Ghorpade, a known bad character, beggar, suspected pilferer, and drunkard. The suspect had been observed in the very early morning hours to be staggering proudly through the bazaar at Linking Road, wearing an ornamental timepiece clearly beyond his means and needs.

Since he was unable to provide a satisfactory explanation they had brought him in, and had already been commended for their alertness.

The station house was hardly alert in the sudden, sultry heat of the afternoon when Sartaj held the watch up to the light. It was indeed a Rolex, large and heavy and very yellow, with a pleasing glistening feel under the thumb. Moitra, the Bandra inspector who had pulled it out of her desk, was leaning back and rubbing her eyes with the palms of her hands.

"Big fucker," Moitra said. "It should tell more than the time."

Sartaj was turning it over and then over again. "Like what?"

"I don't know," Moitra said. "Moon phases. The time in Tokyo. Whatever shit people think they need to know."

"We all want to know the time in Tokyo. Come on. Let's see him."

In the detection room Ghorpade groaned as he came through the door, hunched over and shuffling.

"Have you been third-degreeing him?" Sartaj said.

"For what?" Moitra said. "Why to waste energy? He's a fucking *bewda*. By tonight, for a drink, he'll confess to killing Rajiv Gandhi. And haven't you received the memorandum from up high? No third degree, ask them questions with love and caring and tenderness."

She laughed. It looked to Sartaj that the confession might actually come sooner than nightfall, judging from the trembling of Ghorpade's hands. "Sit down," he said flatly. It was his interrogation voice. He knew his head was leaning forward from his shoulders, and that his eyes had become opaque.

"Have fun," Moitra said as she left. For a long moment afterwards Sartaj could hear her whistling down the corridor.

"We found the man, Ghorpade," Sartaj said.

"What man?"

"The one you knifed."

"I'm a *bewda*. I don't kill anyone. I just wore his watch."

Sartaj had to lean closer to him to hear the words in the voice full of phlegm. Ghorpade had a small, lined face, dry lips, and days of grey stubble on his cheeks. He stank of sweat and monsoon damp.

"Why did he let you take it?" Sartaj said.

"He was lying down."

"On his back?"

"No. Face down. So I took it."

"Did you know he was dead?"

Ghorpade looked up with yellowed eyes. He shrugged.

"Was he in the gutter?"

"Yes."

"Was it full of water?"

"No. It was just starting to rain. There was just a trickle."

"Was there any blood?"

"No."

"None?"

"No."

"What time was it?"

Again Ghorpade shrugged.

"Did you look for a wallet?"

"It wasn't there."

"Why didn't you sell the watch?"

"I was going to. A little later."

"Later till what?"

"I just wanted to wear it for a while." Ghorpade wrapped his arms around himself. "It was a good gold watch."

"Do I look like a fool to you?"

Ghorpade shook his head, slowly.

"But I must look like a fool to you. Otherwise why would you be telling me this fool's story?"

Ghorpade was quiet. His ruin seemed complete.

"All right," Sartaj said. "I'll be back to talk to you more. You think about what you've done. About this children's story you're telling me."

Ghorpade was absolutely still, with his head lowered.

"I'll be back," Sartaj said. He was almost at the door when Ghorpade spoke, and the words were indistinct, and his face was turned away. Sartaj took the three steps back and leaned forward, narrowing his eyes and blinking against the smell that hung over Ghorpade. "What did you say?"

Ghorpade turned his face close to Sartaj, and Sartaj saw that he was really not very old, young perhaps, in his thirties. "I'll be dead," Ghorpade said.

"Nobody's going to kill you."

"I'll die," Ghorpade said. There was no fear in his voice. It was a statement of fact, and it required no sympathy in response, or any other kind of emotion. Sartaj turned and walked away.

The door to Chetanbhai Ghanshyam Patel's sixth-floor apartment was made of dark wood inlaid with criss-crossing copper bands and raised ivory studs, with Chetanbhai's name in gold at the centre. It was a door that belonged in some last-century *haveli*, with an elephant parked outside and *durbans* in *safas*. Now a window opened at the middle of it and a young face peered out through the bars.

"Yes?"

"Police," Sartaj said. The boy's eyes took in Sartaj, and the bulk of Katekar's shoulders behind him. Sartaj was watching him carefully. This was something that Parulkar had taught him: go to their homes, watch their fear, and you will learn everything.

The door opened and Sartaj stepped in. "Regarding the matter of one missing person Chetanbhai Patel . . . Your good name?"

"I'm his son. Kshitij Patel." He was about nineteen, a little shaky.

"Who else is in the house?"

"My mother. She is sleeping, not well. She was very worried. The doctor has given her some medicine."

Sartaj nodded and walked past him. The drawing room was large by Bombay standards, and cluttered with brass lamps and furniture and many-coloured hangings on the wall. The sofas were huge and an alarming red. On the wall to the left there was a long painting of a brilliant sunrise and another of a sad shepherd. Against the back wall there was an Apsara pouring water. Sartaj walked over to it and saw that she was almost life-size, with deep round breasts and huge eyes. She was all white, plaster, and quite startling to find in an apartment in the Narayan Housing Colony, far north and west of Andheri West.

Kshitij was watching him, and Sartaj felt the edge of his resentment without surprise. He used his ability to stalk into people's lives as another tool. What they felt about him was usually instructive.

"Please come to the morgue with us," Sartaj said.

In the long moment then he saw recognition, regret, the usual struggle for control, and then Kshitij said, "Yes." But he did not move.

"Do you want to put on some shoes?" Sartaj said. He followed Kshitij into his room, which was shocking in its austerity after the gaudy brilliance of the rest of the house. There was a shelf stacked neatly with books, a desk, a bed, and a calendar with a goddess on it. There was a window that opened out onto an expanse of swampy vegetation. It had begun to drizzle again. "Is there somebody to take care of your mother?"

Kshitij looked up from his laces, startled. He blinked twice and then said, "I will tell my neighbour." Sartaj noted his thick black Bata shoes, his well-worn white shirt and brown pants. When they came out of the bedroom Kshitij shut the door firmly behind him. "I'm ready," he said.

"I need a photograph of your father," Sartaj said.

Kshitij nodded, turned, walked away. The photograph he brought back was a picture of a happy family, Chetanbhai and his wife in front, stiff and square shouldered in a blue suit and green sari, and Kshitij behind, standing straight in a white shirt, his hand on his mother's shoulder.

He was remarkably steady at the morgue. Sartaj was impressed by his self-possession in the face of the damp walls, the yellow light, and the searing smell of formaldehyde that brought tears to the eyes. Sartaj forgave him a little then for his drab owlishness, his youth entirely lacking in dash or energy or charm. There was a sort of blunt and unprepossessing iron in him. Sartaj had brought some there who had been broken down by the dark corridors even before the room with the rattling metal trolleys and the atmosphere of congestion, but Kshitij identified his father without a tremor. He stood with his arms folded over his thin chest and said, "Yes. Yes." Outside, as they swayed in the police department Gypsy jeep, on the pitted roads, he asked, "Has the police found out anything about the murder?" When Sartaj told him he couldn't talk about the investigation he nodded understandingly and lapsed into silence. But afterwards, at the station, he couldn't stop talking. He drank cup after cup of tea and told Sartaj that he was pre-med at Pateker. He was an only son. He wanted to specialize in neurology. He had been second in the state in the H.Sc. exams, falling short by three marks mostly because of a bad mistake in Physics, which was his worst subject. It had been a sort of trick question in electricity. But other than that everything was moving according to plan.

When Sartaj asked about Chetanbhai Patel, Kshitij fell silent for a minute, a cup suspended halfway to his lips, his mouth open. Then, looking down into the cup of tea, he talked about his father. Chetanbhai was mostly a textile trader. He travelled often, to the interior sometimes, and they had thought he was late coming back from Nadiad this time, which is why they reported him missing two days after he was supposed to have returned. He did some export, mostly to the Middle East, but some to America and of course he wanted more. It was a long-established business, from before Kshitij's birth. Like many businessmen he had sometimes been the victim of petty crime. Once a briefcase with cash in it had been stolen from a local train.

"Did he seem afraid?" Sartaj said. "Any enemies that you know of?"

"Enemies? No, of course not. Why would he have enemies?"

"Somebody in business that he had a quarrel with? Somebody in the locality?"

"No."

"What about you?" Sartaj said. "Do you have any enemies?"

"What do I have to do with it?"

"Sometimes people die because they get caught in their children's fights."

Then there was again that flare of resentment in Kshitij, muted in the eyes but so strong in the shoulders and in the coil of his body that it was a kind of hatred.

"Do you have fights? Quarrels?" Sartaj said.

"No," Kshitij said. "Why would I?"

"Everyone has enemies."

"I haven't done anything to make enemies." He was now assured and confident and calm.

"Right," Sartaj said. "I think now we will look around your house. And I would like to meet Mrs. Patel."

In the jeep Sartaj considered his own vanity. He was sensitive to other people's feelings about him, and had still not learnt to be indifferent to the fear he caused, to the anger of those he investigated. He hid this uneasiness carefully because there was no place for it in an investigator's craft. To be hated was part of the job. But in college he had wanted to be loved by all, and Megha had teased him, you're everyone's hero. Then yours too, he had said. No, no, no, she said, and she shook her head, and kissed him. You have a terrible Panju accent, she said laughing, and your English is lousy, but you are just beautiful, and then she kissed him again. They had married out of vanity, their own and each other's. He had been the Casanova of the college, with a *dada*'s reputation that her friends had warned her about. But she had been so very sure of herself, of her very good looks like a hawk and that shine she had of money, and they were so handsome together that people stopped in the streets to look at them. After they married they liked to make love sitting facing each other, his hair open about his shoulders so they were like mirror images, hardly moving, eyes locked together in an undulating competition towards and away from pleasurable collapse. The memory rose into his throat and Sartaj shook it away as the Gypsy rocked to a halt. A double line of young men in khaki shorts was plunging across the road.

"Bloody idiots," Sartaj said. "Won't even stay home in the rain."

"They're *Rakshaks*, sir," Katekar said, grinning. "Tough boys. A little rain won't stop them. After all they want to clean up the country."

"They'll all catch colds," Sartaj said. The banner carried at the rear of the procession was soggy and limp, but Sartaj could see one of the crossed spears. "And their mothers will have to wipe their noses."

Katekar grinned. He rattled the gearshift to and fro and the Gypsy jerked forward. "How is Mata-ji?" he said.

"She's very well," Sartaj said. "She remembers you often." Katekar was a great devotee of Sartaj's mother. Every time she stayed with Sartaj, Katekar made a special point of coming up to the flat, and touching her feet, not once but three times, bringing his hand up to his throat. Sartaj knew Katekar's mother had died just after Katekar had joined the force.

"Please tell her I said *pranaam*."

Sartaj nodded, and looked over his shoulder. Kshitij was staring dully at the window and crying. His hands were locked together in his lap and the tears were sliding down his face. Now Katekar cursed softly as the jeep growled through a long patch of flooded road, leaving a wake behind. Sartaj turned away from Kshitij and shifted in his seat. Katekar was leaning forward, peering through the regularly spaced waves of water that the wipers were making on the windshield. He was cursing the water, the streets, and the city. His hands around the black plastic of the steering wheel were thick, with huge bulky wrists. He looked at Sartaj and smiled, and Sartaj had to grin back at him. In the rearview mirror, Sartaj could see Kshitij's shoulder, the line of his jaw, and he thought, it's always hard on the serious ones, they were always tragic with their earnestness and their belief in seriousness. He remembered two boys who were the grandsons of farmers in his grandfather's village near Patiala. He recalled them vaguely from a summer visit to the village, remembered them in blue pants and ties. There had been a celebration of their results in the seventh class exams, and he had tried to talk to them about the test match that everyone was listening to but had found them boring and un-informed. After that he had never seen them again and had not thought of them for years until his father had mentioned them during a Sunday phone call. They had been caught by a BSF patrol as they came over the border in the dunes near Jaisalmer laden with grenades and ammunition. They had tried to fire back but had been neatly outflanked and machine-gunned. The papers had reported the death of two Grade-A terrorists and had reported their names and their affiliations. There had been a grainy black-and-white photograph of sprawled, bloodied fig-ures with open mouths. Sartaj had never heard of their organization but had no doubt it was a very serious one.

The Apsara stood among a crowd of mourners, holding her pot tipped forward. The door to the apartment was open and Kshitij was surrounded by young men as soon as they stepped from the lift. In the front room neighbours sat and talked in whispers, and an older man embraced Kshitij for a long moment. Then Kshitij stood facing the door to the bedroom at the back of the house, and the seconds passed, and in his shoulders there was a huge reluctance, as if the next step were from one world into another. Finally the old man took Kshitij by the elbow and led him forward. Sartaj and Katekar followed behind closely, and over many shoulders Sartaj saw a woman sitting on the ground, surrounded by other women. They were holding her by the shoulders and arms, and she had one leg curled under her and the other straight out in front. She looked up with a blank face and Kshitij stopped. Sartaj wanted very much to see the boy's reaction, and he started to push gently past the old man but suddenly the woman started to keen, it was a long wailing sound that arched her back and the others strained to keep her still. It came again and Sartaj shivered, it was somehow quite expressionless, like a long blank wall stretching forever, and as stunning. Kshitij stood helplessly before it, and the room was very close, bodies pushed up to each other and the light broken up somehow into fragments of faces, and then Sartaj turned and walked out of the room. It was bad technique but he couldn't bring himself to look at them any more. The rest of the house was also filled and stifling, and Sartaj jostled shoulders and pushed until he was out.

Sartaj sat wrapped safely in the loneliness of his flat. It was very dark, moonless, and the small space between the gleams on the furniture held him comfortably in its absolute silence.

He knew that if he disturbed nothing, not even the shadows on the floor, he could hold on to the madly delicate balance of peace that he had struggled himself into. He was trying not to think, and succeeding from moment to moment, and then the phone shrilled across the back of his neck. He held on for an instant, but on the third ring he turned his head and reached behind and picked it up. His hand was damp on the receiver and now he felt the sweat running down his sides.

"Ride?" Rahul said. Rahul practised a terseness which he had picked up from watching at least one American film a day on laser disc.

"I don't know, Rahul," Sartaj said.

"I'm ten minutes away."

Sartaj took a breath and tried to recall the thin quiet from a moment ago, but already there was laughter, and tinny music, spilling in over the windowsill. He was dizzy suddenly from the pounding in his head. "All right," he said. "But I have to dress. Give me twenty."

After a quick shower, and with the crisp collar of a freshly starched white *kurta* against his neck he felt cool again: it was a simple Lucknowi *kurta*, but the very thin gold chain threaded through the tiny gold studs made all difference. The studs had belonged to his grandfather and he always stood a little straighter when he wore them. Rahul arrived with his customary honk downstairs, and he came up and they regarded each other acutely. This was a ritual of noticing each other's style, but this time Sartaj was aware only of the boy's long chin, of his nose which suggested his sister so strongly that Sartaj felt again that mixture of anger and longing. Finally he had to make a conscious effort to note the new haircut with sideburns, the loose red shirt, and the slightly flared black jeans.

"I have seen the look before," Sartaj said. "A long time ago."

"Yeah?" Rahul said, without interest. "I guess."

"Yes," Sartaj said. He thought, suddenly and apropos of

nothing, that too young to know cycles is too young to know anything.

Rahul drove fast and well, with the assurance of the moneyed in a good car, or in this case a new red Mahindra jeep with a very good removable tape player. The music they listened to was completely foreign and remote to Sartaj, and as always it was played with a loudness that hovered on the edge of real pain.

"So how're your girlfriends?" Rahul shouted above the music.

"My what?"

"You know. Women."

"I don't have any."

"None? Such a big famous cop and all?"

Sartaj had been in the afternoon papers twice, both times for encounters with minor gangsters. The second confrontation had ended with gunfire, and a dead body on the floor in a dark corridor. Sartaj had fired six shots, and only one had hit. He had crouched, blinded and deafened and trembling, spilling shells onto the floor, but he had never told Rahul about that, or about the small spot of urine on the front of his pants. His picture, a formal studio portrait with retouched lips, had been in *MidDay* the same afternoon. "No, not even one woman. Slow down." Rahul was speeding and then braking the jeep with a violence that was rattling the sleek little tape player in its housing.

"You're a real sad case, you know," Rahul said.

Rahul had girlfriends and broke up with them and then had others with a speed and complexity that dazzled Sartaj, and he was worldly in a way that had been impossible all those years ago when Sartaj and Megha had been the talk of the campus. They had twisted against each other in cinema halls, desperate and hungry, but now Rahul and his friends were too bored with sex to talk about it. It had all changed and he had never seen it change. "I'm just a poor old fogey, what to do, *yaar?*" Sartaj said with a laugh, and Rahul looked at him quickly but then had to swerve around a green Maruti 1000.

"Let's get a beer," Rahul said.

"How old are you, sonny?" Sartaj said and Rahul laughed.

"Don't do the *tulla* thing on me now, Inspector *sahib*," he said. "I need a beer. You do too."

"I do?"

Rahul ignored the question and sped past a timber and wood merchant's shop into a parking lot full of cars. A blue neon sign announced loudly that this was The Hideout, and inside the walls had been painted to look like the walls of a cave, and the floor was littered with barrels and crates. They were seated by a waiter in a black leather jacket, and above their table there was a large black-and-white print of Pran standing with legs wide apart, in black boots, flexing a whip. On the opposite wall a black-hatted foreign villain, one that Sartaj didn't know, glared over his left shoulder, caped and sinister.

"I arrested somebody on this street once," Sartaj said.

"Yeah? A bad guy?" Rahul said, waving to somebody over the heads of the sleek and the young.

"Bad?" Sartaj said slowly. He was staring down at the price of the beer. "Not really. He was greedy." It was actually a quite dusty and unprepossessing commercial street, full of trucks and handcarts and the smell of rotting greens. The man Sartaj had arrested had been named Agha, and he had worked as a clerk for a company dealing in plastic goods. After they put the handcuffs on him he had looked at the owner of the company and said quietly, I have five children, and it was hard to tell whether that was an explanation for taking money or a cry for mercy, but it didn't matter anyway. "I think he must still be in jail."

"Everyone's looking at you," Rahul said sullenly. "Why do you dress like a Hindi movie?"

"This?" Sartaj said, running a finger over the collar of his *kurta*. "You're the one who brought me here."

The waiter brought their beer in what was obviously some designer's idea of roughneck tin mugs that belonged in a low den, and Rahul bent over his beer. Sartaj took a long gulp and was shocked by the pleasure of the thick cold curling against the back of his throat, and he wondered if things tasted better when you paid more for them. He took another long drink and sat up, revived, to look around and to listen to the pleasant buzz of music and the hum of voices that sounded sophisticated even when it was impossible to tell one word from another. He was trying to pin what it was exactly, and after a while he decided it was that they sounded smooth, like there was a lubrication over it all, an oil that eased everything except that it was of course not greasy.

"She's getting married," Rahul said.

"Who?" But even before he spoke it the frightening pitch and yaw of his stomach told him who it was.

"Megha."

"To?"

"She told me not to tell."

"I'll find out."

Rahul looked up then. "Yes, you will." His Adam's apple ducked up and down and his face trembled, but then with a shake of his shoulders he said, "Raj Sanghi. You know."

Sartaj knew. This was the son of a friend of Megha's family, and Megha and Raj had known each other since childhood and the families had always thought that they were good together. He knew about all this. Now he sat with his hands on his thighs and found himself looking for a way to stop it, for a place where he could apply pressure until something snapped.

"Sorry," Rahul said, and Sartaj saw that he looked frightened, terrified. He knew why: during one of their quarrels Megha had screamed at him that in his anger he had a face like a terrorist, looked as if the next thing he said or did would be complete and irrevocable, forever. He had looked at her then dumbly, made desolate and foreign by her choice of words. She had cried then and said she didn't mean *that* at all. They had broken parts of each other like that all through the time at the end, and he tasted these strange victories that left him empty and wishing for nothing more than endless sleep, like the last man on a battlefield where even the blades of grass were dead. Finally it had seemed better never to say anything at all.

"No, no," Sartaj said. "It's all right." He reached across the table and awkwardly patted Rahul's wrist. He had to swallow before he could speak again. "I don't think I should drink any more."

It was morning and sparrows swirled madly through the arches of the police station. Ghorpade was sitting on the bench with his eyes closed when Sartaj and Katekar came into the detection room.

"Wake up," Sartaj said, kicking one of the legs of the bench sharply. Ghorpade opened his eyes and Sartaj saw that he was not sleeping, or even sleepy, but that every moment was a struggle against some monstrous hunger. He had both his hands squeezed between his thighs, and he looked at Sartaj as if from some great distance. Katekar took his usual interrogation stance, legs apart and behind the suspect.

"Have you been thinking about what you did?" Sartaj said.

"I didn't do what you said," Ghorpade said. His eyes were yellowish, rheumy.

"You better decide to tell me the truth," Sartaj said. "Or it'll be bad for you."

Ghorpade shut his eyes again. Katekar widened his stance, and flexed his shoulders. But Sartaj shook his head, and said, "Ghorpade, where do you live? Do you have a family?"

Ghorpade spoke without opening his eyes. "I don't live anywhere."

"Do you have a wife?"

"I had."

"What happened?"

"She ran away."

"Why?"

"I beat her."

"Why?"

Ghorpade shrugged.

"How old are you, Ghorpade?"

Sartaj could hear the sparrows in the yard outside. Then finally Ghorpade spoke: "I was born the year before the Chinese war."

Outside, under the sky which was clouded again, Sartaj considered the slight possibility that he and Ghorpade shared birthdays. He had no idea why it seemed important. Now Moitra, whose first name was Suman, roared into the yard in her new Jeep. They had been batchmates in Nasik, and on the first day of the course she had let them know that she was twice as intelligent and thrice as tough as any of them. Sartaj had no problems with this, especially since it was probably true.

"Did he confess?" she said, bounding up the stairs. "Closing the case?"

"I'm investigating," Sartaj said. "This is an investigation, Moitra. Remember?"

"Investigating what?" Moitra said over her shoulder as she sped down the corridor. "Investigating whom?"

"Where is your mother?"

Kshitij was standing square in the middle of his doorway, his shoulders taut.

"What do you want with my mother?"

"Where is she?"

"She's here. Resting. She's not well. She's sleeping."

"I want to talk to her."

"Why?"

"This is a murder case. We talk to everyone concerned."

"What does my mother have to do with a murder case?"

"She was married to your father," Sartaj said, stepping forward. Kshitij stayed where he was and Sartaj put the palm of his hand against the boy's chest and pushed. Kshitij stumbled back, and Sartaj went past him into the drawing room.

"What do you want? Do you have a warrant? Why are you here? I heard you have a suspect in custody," Kshitij said, following closely, but then Katekar had him by the arm and against the wall. Sartaj turned and Kshitij swallowed and subsided. Sartaj leaned forward and put his face close to Kshitij and watched him for a long moment, let him look and feel the pace of his anger as they listened to each other's breathing. Then he turned away abruptly and stalked through the room, towards the bedroom. Inside, the cupboards stood open, and the double bed and the floor were littered with paper. She was sitting on the balcony that opened out onto the swamp, and far away across muddy patches of green, the silver haze of the sea.

"Mrs. Patel?"

When she turned to him her face was dense with grief. He cleared his throat and set forth briskly into his questions, when did you last see your husband, did he seem worried recently, were there any phone calls that upset him, were you aware of enemies and quarrels, were you aware of money difficulties, were you. She answered each time with a shake of the head, holding a hand at her throat. Her age was forty-nine, but her hair was a brilliant black, lustrous even in its disarray, and Sartaj looked at her, and thought that just a few days ago she must have been very pleasantly attractive, and that fact also settled into the confusion that surrounded the life and death of Chetanbhai Ghanshyam Patel.

Finally he asked: "Can you tell me anything else? Is there anything else I should know?"

"No," she said. "No." But the word was heavy with regret, and Sartaj followed her glance over his shoulder to the doorway to the bedroom, past Katekar, to the corridor where Kshitij's shadow lingered. When he turned back to Mrs. Patel she was weeping, holding the end of her *pallu* to her eyes. And Sartaj, to his own surprise, felt a swell of emotion, rising like a knot in his chest.

In the bedroom, two of the cupboards were stacked full of shirts. Sartaj ran a finger up and down the row of the suits, rattling the wooden hangers against each other. The two other cupboards, against the opposite wall, were empty. He squatted and picked up a small booklet and flattened it out against his knee. It was a bank chequebook, with neat little tick marks in blue pencil next to the cheques and deposits. The closing balance was one lakh forty-six thousand rupees. He put the bank book in his pocket, and straightened up. There was a kind of grief in the wild litter across the room. Over these debris Sartaj began a quick but methodical survey, in a back-and-forth grid. In this practised routine there was a kind of relief.

"Aren't you supposed to have two witnesses for a *panchnama* if you do a search?" Kshitij said from the doorway.

"Am I doing a search?" Sartaj said.

"It looks like you are."

"I'm just looking around. Why is all this on the floor?"

"I, I was just cleaning up. Sorting things out."

"Yes, I see," Sartaj said. After a murder some people tidied up. Others cooked, made huge quantities of food that nobody would or could eat. But every time there was an attempt to find one's way back to ordinary days. And all the paper on the floor was a record of the most innocuous kind of life: birth, insurance, deposits, loans, payments, the bills for hard-won purchases kept carefully for years. Now it was over. Sartaj looked across the room, towards the balcony, and she was staring out at the sea again.

Outside, in the hall, Sartaj ran his hand over the small row of books. The biography of Vivekananda, two Sidney Sheldon novels, *How to Be a Better Manager.*

"He was robbed, wasn't he?" Kshitij said, behind him. He looked tired and slight in his white shirt.

"We are investigating," Sartaj said. The Apsara was gone, disappeared from her space by the wall.

"Is there any progress? What about this suspect? Who is he?"

Sartaj was thinking about the curve of the Apsara's shoulder. He turned his gaze with an effort and then said very directly, in his policeman's voice, "We are investigating. We will let you know as soon as we find out anything."

Outside, in the stairway that wound around the lift shaft, Sartaj leaned against the wall, breathless, hunted by something he had never known.

"Are you all right, sir?" Katekar said.

"I'm fine," Sartaj said. But it was a loneliness so huge and so feral that he wanted to give up and collapse into the thick green swamp he could see far below, through a barred window. Even after the papers had come, after they had been sitting on their dining table for a week, he had never believed that the word "divorce" meant something real. In his whole life he had never known anyone who had been divorced. He had never known anybody whose parents had been divorced. He couldn't remember a friend who had known anybody who had been divorced. Divorce was something that strange people did in the pages of *Society* magazine. His breath came dragging through the pain in his throat. He took a step forward and the green swirled dizzyingly under him, and he lurched forward and it pounded in his head, but then the white wall scraped across his shoulder. Katekar put a hand under his elbow. Sartaj followed his glance: on his own uniform, there was a streak of plaster from the wall, bright against the khaki.

Sartaj stood erect, feeling the muscles in his back, and he

scraped the plaster off his shoulder with his right hand. He thumped it sharply and the white came off in little clouds. Sartaj shook his head. He tucked his shirt in, pulled up his belt, with both hands he felt the slant of his turban and corrected it. Then he smoothened his moustache, said, "I'm all right. Come on." He walked down the stairs, to his work.

"Mr. Patel was a very helping kind of man," Kaimal said. Kaimal was in his sixties, a retired merchant navy captain who lived two floors below the Patels in a flat of the same size and floor plan. "We bought together," Kaimal said. "Seven years ago, almost exactly. Before that we rented in the same building in Santa Cruz."

Mrs. Kaimal brought out coffee in small steel tumblers, and Kaimal rubbed his forehead absently and ran a finger around the edge of the glass. A moment passed and Mrs. Kaimal sat down beside her husband and put a hand on his wrist. Behind them Katekar, who was a tea drinker, sniffed suspiciously at his glass. "He was very much younger than I am," Kaimal said quietly.

"Was he well liked in the building here?" Sartaj said.

Kaimal looked up and nodded. "He was president of the building society for three years in a row. He organized all our functions." Leaning forward, Kaimal said decisively, "He got jobs for the children of many people here." He sat back, and said again, "He was younger than I am."

"You must have seen Kshitij grow up," Sartaj said.

"Yes. He is a very intelligent boy."

"Did his father think so?" Sartaj said.

Kaimal looked at him consideringly, and Sartaj could see the beginnings of distaste. This was familiar: the policeman's assumption of grief and deceit hidden in every happiness was frightening in its simplicity. It implicated everyone.

"Of course. He was very proud of him. Very proud."

"And his mother is proud too?" Sartaj said.

"What else? Of course. Kshitij is a very good son to her. It is good to see a young man with such respect for his mother these days."

"And were they happy together?"

"Who?" Kaimal said.

"Mr. and Mrs. Patel," Sartaj said. "Were they happy?"

"Happy?" Mrs. Kaimal said, shaking her head, exasperated. "They were husband and wife. What else would they be?"

Sartaj finished his coffee. It was very good coffee indeed. In people like this, decent and hospitable, loyalty to the departed was always the most unbreakable bond. They were telling a truth that had become sharp and clear in the sudden glare of death, and he knew he couldn't persuade them to turn them back towards the shadowed ambiguities that were so crucial to him. That would cause them to break with their obligations.

"I see," he said slowly. "I see." He looked at Mrs. Kaimal until she shifted uncomfortably, and then both husband and wife seemed to shrink against the faded lily pattern of their sofa. Then Sartaj said quietly, "Were you aware if Mr. Patel was in any kind of trouble? Did he seem afraid? Had he told you of any threats? Quarrels?"

"Threats?" Kaimal said. "No."

As Sartaj stood up they watched him apprehensively, turned their heads to watch Katekar's thumping walk. He thanked them for the coffee, told them to contact him if they remembered anything, and then he shut the door quietly behind himself and Katekar. They were a nice old pair, handsome and fine-drawn and cultured, but he had no regret for inflicting fear on them. It was what his job required of him, this distance from the rest of the world, their wariness of him, it was inevitable and necessary and he knew that very often it was this very thing that made it possible for him to grasp the truth, to see the secret and fix it, forever. Usually he thought nothing of it, never needed to, but today the click of the lock brought with it a bitter little bubble of loneliness in his mouth. He looked up and down the stairs, leaned towards the grilled door that covered the lift-shaft, and spat into the long pit. Then they went on to the next flat. As the day went on, as they walked down the stairs, from one home to another, Sartaj watched the sweat stain grow between Katekar's shoulder blades and spread across the large breadth of his back.

By late afternoon, from the fragments of many conversations, from hesitations and allusions and things left unsaid, he had teased out these unremarkable facts: the father was a genial man, full of humour, ready to backslap and also to come to one's help when needed; the son was known for his intelligence, for his first rank in every exam, for his quietness; the mother was a good cook, she doted on her son and laughed at her husband's jokes, the husband and wife went for drives every Saturday, long drives.

Sartaj learnt about Patel's passion for his red Contessa as he stood next to it in an incense-filled garage. Patel's driver, a tall, bulky man named Sharma, was polishing the car with a kind of melancholy patience, inch by inch and with many flourishes of a waxy rag. He had two *agarbattis* burning in front of a picture of Shiva—they let forth, now and then, undulating drifts of white smoke, full with the aroma of *chameli*, an aphrodisiacal essence of moonlight and river water and rain. Katekar strolled around the periphery of the room, looking at the cans on a shelf, the calendars on the wall.

"He liked to listen to *ghazals* in the car," Sharma said. "Every new cassette, we got. We just got new speakers."

Between the driver's seat and the passenger's there was a box full of tapes. A tape with blue writing on it was in the deck.

"What's that one?" Sartaj said.

"His favourite. Mehdi Hassan. He listened to it again and again." Sharma reached into the car and a moment later the song drifted out into the garage: *Voh jo ham me tum me karaar tha, tumhe yaad ho ke ya na yaad ho . . .*

"When was the last time he was in the car?"

"Last Saturday. I don't come for duty on Saturdays. But he must have gone for a ride."

"Where?"

"I don't know. Around. But he must have gone."

"Are you sure?"

"I've worked for him for thirteen years and every Saturday he went for a drive with *Memsaab*. I used to pull the seat forward every Friday night for him. He liked cars. This one specially. Last weekend he even washed it."

"Washed it?"

"Outside and in. It was shining clean when I came in on Monday morning."

It was a very long car that filled up the garage so that Sartaj had to squeeze behind it. He opened a door and leaned in. The seats were spotless, and the interior smelt of soap and ammonia. The song was gentle and a little sad and very sweet.

"Was he worried in the last few days? Afraid of something? Upset?"

Sharma stopped rubbing at the metal and looked up at Sartaj. "No. But I'm worried now. What will happen now to Kshitij Baba?"

"Kshitij? Why?"

"He has to take care of his mother. Very much love between them. Often when he was tired and had a headache he would lie with his head in her lap. I saw this when I would go up to give the car keys back in the evenings. But he's very young. How will he manage? So young."

Sartaj took the rag from him and sniffed at it. "Are you afraid for your job?"

Sharma laughed aloud. He straightened up, away from the car, and he was at least three inches taller than Sartaj, and not at all afraid. "Inspector, you know there are jobs for drivers in Bombay. No, I'm worried for him. He looked very tired today."

"Did he take the car out?"

"No, no. When I came this morning I saw him taking rubbish out of the building. Then again an hour later."

"Rubbish?"

"Out to the dump, over there behind the wall. He looked very tired."

Now Mehdi Hassan sang the emperor's old complaint about *baat karni mujhe kabhi mushkil aisi to na thi,* and Sartaj searched the car. He scraped under the seats and rolled the grit off the floor mats between his fingers. The glove compartment held a receipt book from a petrol pump in Santa Cruz, vehicle booklets in a plastic wrapper, a pack of playing cards, and, held together by a black metal office clip, a stack of parking receipts.

"Where was his office?" Sartaj said.

"Andheri East. Near Natraj Studio."

The receipt on top was rubber-stamped "Colaba Parking." Getting out of the car, Sartaj thumbed through the stack, and it seemed that Chetanbhai had gone to Colaba often. Sartaj opened the front passenger door again and knelt, trying to get as close to the floor mats as possible. A quick run of the forefinger over the underside of the front passenger seat, over the shiny metal at the very bottom, and then back, left an impression of some faint roughness, a texture across the metal. He reached into his pocket for the penknife on his keychain, and scraped with it and then held it up to the light, and there was a flakey rust on the blade, an innocuous brown the colour of farm earth after rain.

"Look at this," he said, holding it up to Sharma.

"What is it?" Sharma said, peering. "Rust?"

Sartaj's eyes moved, and Katekar caught Sharma by the collar, bent him suddenly forward at the waist, and with a full high turn of the shoulder hit him on the broad of his back with an open palm. The crack was shockingly loud and Sartaj hissed into Sharma's astounded face, "Did you kill him? Why did you kill him?"

"I had nothing to do with it."

Sartaj looked up at Katekar, and again Katekar's broad hand went up and came down like a piston.

"This is blood," Sartaj said. This was not a fact, it was less than a theory, but Sharma believed it. His eyes were full of tears, and he was panting, holding his chest with both his hands. "You didn't know it's very difficult to get blood cleaned, did you? No matter how much you clean there's always a bit left. Did you wash the car?"

"I tell you I don't know anything about this. I swear to you."

"Why are you still here?"

"I get paid for the month on the thirtieth. *Sahib,* I'm just a poor man. I would have gone but I get my payment on the thirtieth. Nothing else."

Sartaj was willing to wait and see who tried to flee. The guilty always ran. It was like starting an unknown animal out of a thicket. You tossed in a rock and waited to see what came out. "All right," he said, and Katekar let Sharma go and stepped away. But Sharma stayed bent over, huddled to his knees, his face red. "But don't speak to anyone regarding this matter. Don't touch this car. Lock up the garage now and give me the key." Sartaj said to Katekar, "Watch the garage until we can get somebody from the forensics lab down here to take a look at the car."

"Sir," Katekar said, nodding, still looking at Sharma. He took a blue-and-white checkered handkerchief out of his pocket and wiped his mouth, his cheeks.

Sartaj bent over until his face was close to Sharma's. "And you. Don't go anywhere, friend, don't leave the city. We'll be watching you."

We'll be watching you, Sartaj said under his breath as he

walked out behind the building. We'll be watching you. This was a lie he had learnt to tell easily. It was an illusion that suspects believed in easily, and it worked even when there was absolutely no truth in it. Parulkar had once forced a confession, and a nervous breakdown, from a domestic-murder suspect who had started to believe that there were policemen everywhere, on the roof of his house, in his bathroom, and behind his new Godrej fridge. The dump was on a road built out into the swamp, past the buildings under construction and the sodden mounds of earth. At the very end of the road, as it petered out into the thick green bushes, it was covered with a thick layer of paper, bones, and things liquified and rotted. Flies buzzed around Sartaj's head as he carefully placed one foot after another. Sartaj walked by two children with bags over their shoulders, picking out the plastic from the mixture. Further on, three yellow dogs stopped eating to watch him over their shoulders, not moving an inch as he edged past them with a flutter in his stomach. Ahead, there was a huge blackened ring that smouldered across the road. He could see the edges of it trembling with heat. He kicked at the wet surface of the waste and it fell away, and underneath the fire was working relentlessly. He put his hands on his knees, bent over, and walked slowly around the curve of the black circle. Faces and old headlines blurred away as he watched. He straightened up, took a large stride over the border, and went into the circle.

Now the ashes clung to his feet as he walked. Sartaj bent over a twisted piece of plastic and turned it over. It was the casing from a video tape, half melted away. The clouds shifted and suddenly the sun moved across the swamp. The smell filled his head, rank but full and rich. Two egrets came gliding over him and he turned his head full around to watch them. He was at the other edge, near the water. Leaves scraped across his face. He bent down and peeled a soggy curl of paper away from his shoe. It was a picture from a calendar, an almost-nude model in designer tribal clothes, smiling over her shoulder. He scraped at the muck with the side of his shoe and layers of paper parted. He bent quickly, then, to peer at the handwriting on a blackened fragment. "Patel," it said, in the neat script from the chequebook. He squatted, and tried to turn it over, but it broke crisply in half. He took his ballpoint pen from his pocket and used it to poke at the debris. Under a piece of plastic he found a torn page with printing on it. He held it up between his forefinger and thumb. It was thick paper, and he could make out the writing. ". . . having got up in the morning and performed his necessary duties, should wash his teeth, apply a limited quantity of ointments and perfumes to his body, put some ornaments on his person and collyrium on his eyelids and below his eyes, colour his lips with *alacktaka,* and look at himself in the glass. Having then. . . " As he read, it tore across from its own weight and dropped. The sweat dripped down his neck. He could hear the dogs barking.

The wall in front of Parulkar's house was crumbling even as Sartaj watched. As he waited at the door, he watched the rain carry away tiny pieces of stone and brick into the flowing gutter. But inside the floor was cool and polished as he bent to take off his shoes. Parulkar's youngest daughter, Shaila, her hair swinging in two enormous plaits behind her, watched him gravely. She was fourteen, and she wore steel-rimmed spectacles at the very end of her nose. When he had first met her she had loved to be tickled behind the ears. It made her weak with laughter. Now she was a very dignified young woman.

"You're starting to look like someone, Shaila," Sartaj said.

"Who?"

"Oh, I don't know. A model? A movie star? Madhuri Dixit, maybe . . ."

She looked at him sideways, but with a little smile. "I've decided I'm going to IIT," she said. "I'm going to do computers."

"Really?" Sartaj said. "No more Parulkars in physics?" Both her older sisters were physicists, one at ISRO and the other at Bombay University.

"Bo-ring," Shaila said. "That's old stuff, don't you know? Computers are hot, hot, hot."

"Which I don't know anything about."

"As if you know anything about physics."

"You'll have to teach me."

She took him, with both her hands, by the wrist and pulled him down the corridor to the drawing room, which was large and sparsely filled by its two divans and *chatai*. This forward-leaning walk, at least, was something she hadn't decided to outgrow yet.

"Sit," she said, as she went back into the corridor. "Papa will be out in a minute."

Sartaj didn't mind the minute, or more, at all. He had always liked this room. It was long and opened out on one end into a small garden, which actually had a tree in it. The branches hung over the window and now the water dripped slowly, and the light was gentle and green. This light was the surprise the house hid behind its shabby walls, and today Sartaj was particularly glad for it.

"Anything new?" Parulkar said, as he came in, rolling up the sleeves of his *kurta*, which was a starched bluish white. He looked very elegant when he was not in uniform. Sartaj told him about Ghorpade and Kshitij and the mother.

"The forensic report came from Vakola this morning," Sartaj said. "The interior of the Contessa seemed to have been washed with a three-ten mixture of hydrogen peroxide. There were no traces of blood, or any other suspicious substance. The car was scrubbed down, clean. It was wiped down very professionally. No fibres, nothing

"But what has the car to do with any of it? You could close the case really," Parulkar said. "You have the watch, and so physical evidence and a motive, and the suspect, what's his name, Ghorpade, places himself at the scene. What else could we need? What are you looking for?"

"Nothing, sir. I mean I don't know."

"These are delicate times, Sartaj," Parulkar said. "Pushing too hard, without sufficient reason, on that family could lead to, let us say, sensitivities." What he meant was that for an outsider, a Sikh, to push a little was to push a lot. It was true, even though the Patels were Gujaratis and so outsiders themselves. There were outsiders and outsiders. To say, I was born in Bombay, was very much besides the point. Sartaj nodded. "Meanwhile," Parulkar said, "there's something else I have to speak to you about . . ."

He stopped as Shaila came in with a tray. Sartaj watched him as he bent forward to pick up his steaming mug of tea, because he had never known Parulkar to be delicate about business around his daughters. In this house filled with women they were clinically straightforward about death and mayhem.

"There is something else," Parulkar said after Shaila had swung her plaits out of the room.

"Sir?"

"I got a call from Shantilal Nayak last night."

"Sir." Nayak was an MLA who lived in Goregaon. He was the sitting home minister, and he had come to Sartaj's wedding mainly as a guest of Megha's family.

"He mentioned some papers."

"Papers?"

"That you were to sign?"

Sartaj felt, suddenly, a rush of hatred for the rich. He hated them for their confidence, their calm, how they thought everything could be *managed*. But he said, "Yes, sir."

"Sartaj," Parulkar said, leaning forward a little. "Sartaj. If I could, I would have given anything to change it all."

"Yes, I know," Sartaj said finally. It was true.

At the door Parulkar put a hand on his shoulder, and Shaila came running out to take his wrist again in both of her hands.

"Don't get wet," Parulkar said. "It's cold."

Sartaj nodded and splashed down to the gate. Then he turned around and came back. "What is *alacktaka?*"

"What is what?" Parulkar said.

"*Alacktaka.*"

"Never heard of it."

"It's something you colour your lips with," Sartaj said.

"My lips?"

"Not yours, sir. I meant generally. Men use it to colour their lips."

"This is general somewhere?"

"That's what I want to know," Sartaj said. He felt absurd standing there with his raincoat flapping around his knees and the water dripping from his eyebrows, and he turned abruptly and left them there, feeling their looks of enquiry on the back of his neck all the way down the lane. On the way home, under the bleak surges of anger, there was a nibbling doubt, an obsessive circling around something that was unknown and elusive. He now had facts about the deceased and his family, and these were quite ordinary and commonplace, repeated in any other family down the street or somewhere across the country. He knew something about the killer, if that was what Ghorpade was. They were two ordinary men who came together on a Bombay street corner one night. But Sartaj remembered the Rolex watch, and he was certain he knew nothing about the man who wore it, nothing that would explain the silky artifice of the thing, that would show how the commonplace and ordinary became Chetanbhai Ghanshyam Patel. He didn't know this and somehow it felt like a debt.

Sartaj had put aside notions of debt the next time he went to the Bandra station. There was no option other than winding up the investigation and charging Ghorpade with murder, this was clear. He said this to Moitra, who nodded and said, "Yes, well, you'd better take a look at him."

In the lockup the three other occupants were leaving Ghorpade well alone. He was lying on his side, his face against the wall, curled up. The air in the cell was cool, still between the old smooth stone of the walls.

"He can't keep any food in his stomach," Moitra said. The whole holding area smelled of vomit.

"Ghorpade," Sartaj said. "Eh, Ghorpade." Ghorpade lay unmoving.

"We'll send him to Cooper Hospital this evening," Moitra said. "But we have his statement anyway." She meant that the hospital was no guarantee of his survival. "Come on, I want to finish up early tonight."

In her office, while they stamped and signed papers under a picture of Nehru, the phone rang. "Hel-lo," Moitra said softly. Sartaj looked up at her, and she changed to her usual clipped voice, "Hello."

"Is that Arun?" Sartaj said.

"Yes," she said, holding a palm over the mouthpiece and regarding Sartaj with a steady glare that dared him to be funny. "So?"

"I have a question for Arun." Arun was her husband, a professor of history at Bombay University.

Moitra was still wary. "You do?"

"Yes, ask him what *alacktaka* is."

She mouthed the word, feeling it out to see if there was a joke in it. Then she took her hand off the mouthpiece and asked. "He says he's never heard of it," she said after a pause. "He says what's the context?"

"I've forgotten," Sartaj said. "It's not important anyway."

So after all, on paper, it was going to be an open and quickly shut case, not even worth a headline in the afternoon papers, but still Sartaj studied Chetanbhai Ghanshyam Patel's chequebook as the jeep wound its way north through afternoon traffic. The entries were routine, three hundred and eighty-three rupees for electricity to BSES on January 28, nine hundred and ninety five rupees to the ShivSagar Co-op. Building Society on January 29, one hundred and twenty-five rupees to the Jankidas Publishing Company on February 1, two hundred and ninety-two rupees to the Milind Pharmacy the same day, and Sartaj bent the book and the pages flurried by, the same names and the same little amounts again, BSES, Hindustan Petroleum for cooking gas cylinders on April 15, one hundred and twenty-five again to the Jankidas Publishing Company on May 1, two hundred and forty-eight to Patekar College on May 14. There were no large amounts, no huge payments to cash, nothing that indicated danger, or even excitement. Finally Sartaj took a deep breath and closed the book and put it back in his pocket. It was time to give it up. There were other cases to follow, which meant, he knew, other puzzles that would distract him from himself, so there was no reason to cling to this one. It was time to give it up.

And yet when he faced Kshitij, Sartaj had to force himself to pull out the chequebook and hand it over. "We will formally file charges tomorrow morning," Sartaj said. "I came to tell you. It is a man named Ghorpade."

When Kshitij had opened the grandiose door to the apartment, he was holding a dumbbell, and was dressed in a white banian and shorts which hung off his thin waist onto his angular hips. His chest heaved up and down as Sartaj told him about Ghorpade. His face was suffused and contorted, and when Sartaj was finished he nodded. He tried to speak and the breath came and went.

"I will get in touch shortly," Sartaj said. They looked at each other and then Sartaj turned away. He paused, feeling as if he should say a word of comfort to this boy in his loneliness, and finally uttered with a smile that felt false, "Building the body, *haan?*"

Kshitij nodded. "Good," Sartaj said. "Good."

As Sartaj shut the lift door he heard the boy's voice. "*Vande mataram.*"

Sartaj paused with his finger on the button marked "G." Kshitij was standing with his hands by his sides, his back straight. Feeling slightly ridiculous, Sartaj came to attention, and Kshitij and he looked at each other through the metalwork of the door. It was an old-fashioned slogan Sartaj had heard all his life, mostly in movies, but he could never say it without a surge of belief. "*Vande mataram,*" he said. Hail to the mother. And despite himself, unwillingly, he felt again, in his chest, a havoc of faith in the devious old mother he was saluting, and in the same moment, despair.

The sound of the rain was endless. It was still early afternoon but it was dark in the station house. Sartaj sat at his desk, loose limbed, and watched water stream down the panes of his window. Under the torrent, there was a strange quiet in the station house. It was as if everyone and everything were waiting.

Parulkar came in and walked over to the window. The collar of his shirt was bunched up around his neck, and he looked damp and uncomfortable.

"I had another call from Nayak this morning," he said. "At home, this time."

"I'm sorry, sir," Sartaj said.

Parulkar walked around the room, nodding gently to himself. Finally, from behind Sartaj, he said, "I don't understand. Why don't you just sign the papers and let it finish? What are you afraid of?"

And Sartaj, who was watching how the water on the window made the world outside a vague blur of brown and green, said without wanting or meaning to, "I'm afraid of dying."

Parulkar put a hand on his shoulder, for a moment, with an awkward sort of fumbling movement. Sartaj twisted in the chair but already Parulkar was walking towards the door. His shoulders were hunched up as he pulled violently at his belt, and all the way out of the door his face was turned away.

There was a weariness in Sartaj's arms and legs now, and his eyes, even after he closed them, felt hot and scratchy. Every breath was labour now, because he was afraid of the silence. He was too afraid even to feel contempt for himself.

Sartaj Singh lay flat on his back on the floor of his apartment, in a white *banian* and red pyjamas, arms wide to the sides, and contemplated death. He had these words in his head, "to contemplate," and "death." Between them there was a kind of light, a huge clear fearful sky in which he was suspended. When the shrill of the doorbell called, it took him a full minute to descend from this thin and deadly atmosphere, to lift his weightless body off the floor. Then there was a stagger to the door as he rubbed his eyes. In his blankness he found the rubbing pleasurable, and he felt keenly his knuckle on the eyelid, so that when the door swung open against his shoulder and he saw her, he had trouble recognizing the scene he had imagined a thousand times. "Hello, Megha," he said finally, his hand still up to his face. She waited, until he understood the formalities now between them. "Come in, please," he said, and hated the words.

She walked stiffly, her shoulders high, and with a large black purse held hard against her hip. She stood next to the furniture they had chosen together, in a black skirt and high heels, stylish as always and with the closed face of model on a runway. "Sit, Megha," Sartaj said. He pointed at the green sofa, and she arranged herself with her hands held in front of her, the purse standing straight up on the coffee table in front of her like a bulwark. Sartaj sat on a chair across from her and held his hands tightly across his stomach. He opened his mouth, and then shut it again.

"Rahul told me he told you," Megha said.

"Told me what?" Sartaj said, even though he knew. His voice was loud. He wanted her to say it, the word. So that his pain would hurt her, as it always had. But she said it easily, as if she had been practising.

"I'm getting married."

"Is that why you came? For that?" With the jerk of his head he meant the papers on the dining table behind him, but in the sudden snap of the motion he had also the policeman's brusqueness, the coiled promise of angry force. She shut her eyes.

"No, I didn't come for that," she said. When she looked at him now her eyes were wet, and he felt inside the unhitching of pieces of himself, things drawing apart and falling away. "I came because I thought I should tell you myself." A tiny shrugging motion with her shoulder, and a hand drawing up and touching her mouth. "I didn't want you to hear about it like that, from someone else."

The sunlight in the room dappled the familiar sofa and made it unreal. Sartaj was aware now of the great distances to the surfaces of his body, the strangeness of the hand that lay like a knurled brown slab in his lap. He slumped in his chair, trembling.

"What are you smiling at?" Megha said hesitantly.

Sartaj thought about it. "How did we get so old?"

He laughed then, and after a moment she with him, and the sound sped around the room, over the photographs, the few knick-knacks on the shelf, the stained dining table. They both stopped suddenly, at exactly the same moment.

"I'm sorry," she said.

He struggled himself upright. "Do you want some tea?" he said.

In the kitchen he had to wash the pot, and then the teacups as the water burbled. Then he stood ready with the sugar, alert and concentrated, and the smell of the heating milk and the leaves, and the wisps of steam, sent him reeling into the first morning of their marriage, the first time they had woken together, the profound heat of her skin against him, and her confession that she did not know how to make tea. I told you I can't cook, she giggled into his neck. But *tea*, Sartaj said, pretending to be angry, but after that he had always made tea in the morning. Now the heat from the stove spread across his knuckles, and he remembered the newspaper splayed across the table between them, and buttery kisses, and he felt his heart wrench, kick to the side like a living thing hurt, and he fell to his knees on the dirty floor, held his head between his hands, and wept. His sobs squeezed out against all the force of his arms, and the wooden doors on the cupboard under the washbasin rattled faintly as he bent and curled against them.

He felt Megha's hands on his shoulders, and her breath on his forehead as she whispered, "Sartaj, Sartaj," and he turned away from her, from his own embarrassment, but his strength was gone, and she pulled his head back, into the solid curve of her shoulder. He shook again and she held him tight, hard, and he felt with piercing awareness the pain of her forearm against the back of his neck. He was gone, then, vanished into the familiar fragrance of her perfume, unknown for so long, with its flowers and underlying tinge of salt. He was perfectly still. Her lips moved against his cheek, murmuring, something that he couldn't quite hear, and then he felt the brush on his mouth, a gift of softness and then the shifting suppleness, what he always experienced as a question. He kissed her desperately, afraid to stop or pause because then she would stop. But she wasn't stopping, she held his face in her hands, her long palms strongly on cheeks and chin, and sipped at him with little murmurs. Despite himself, Sartaj curved against her, an arm up and around, and he felt the weight of her breasts against his side, and she laughed into his mouth, not here, not here.

They almost made it to the sofa in the drawing room. He walked behind her, and he watched the sheer cloth of her skirt flap faintly against her legs, and her neck under the pinned hair, and the straight back under the expensive white cloth, and he reached with both hands to hold her by the upper arms. Again the vivid shock of the flesh. She fell back easily against him, offering him her neck. Under his nuzzling she squirmed and said, "The curtains." He stumbled back, dizzy, found the curtains and pulled. When he turned around into the sudden dimness she was sitting on the sofa, her hands together on her knees. "I'm going to marry him," she said, and her voice was small. Sartaj navigated towards her, one step and then another, and they peered over the sudden distance. He knew it was true and there was nothing he could say to it. He tamped down his entirely unreasonable anger and searched for words. Then she giggled. He followed her eyes and there was the unreasonable bulge in his pyjamas, his red *shamiana* she had called it once.

This time they found each other somewhere over the coffee table. He dragged her over it, one hand on her back and the other in her hair. Once they would have delighted in the lingering discarding of clothes, the slow fall of silk, the shifting of cotton and slow revelations, but now there wasn't the time. He laboured with the complications of her skirt as she shrugged off her blouse. Her pull at his *nada* dug into his side but his pyjamas came down efficiently with a single movement of her wrist. "Sar-taj," she said, and took his hands away from her skirt, and with two clear snaps it came away, and then she was against him. Now he dared to look at her face, and in the dark flush of her cheeks there was that concentration, that singular look of intent purpose he had not seen for a long time, and he was no longer afraid. Under his thumbs her nipples bloomed and she shivered helplessly and smiled.

But he buckled under the scrape of her fingernails on his thighs. She was arrogant now, full of secrets and sure, very sure, as he slid to his knees and onto his back. She pressed with her hands on his shoulders, pushing him down, straddling and hovering over him, her breasts a maddening lightness on his chest. Again her fingers moved over his stomach, scuffing, and his face contorted, saying take pity on it, my thing my muscle my cock, take pity on its loneliness, and she grasped him in her hand. She leaned low over him, breathing in the agonized relief in his exhalations. When she looked down along the length of their bodies, he looked with her, and saw her hand grasping hard, and springing from her fist, him, each pulse distinct. They had argued and talked and laughed about what to call their parts, she hated *lund* and *chut,* how vernac and crude and vulgar she said, cock and pussy and fuck felt foreign in his mouth, he said that to her and she laughed fondly and said all I want in your mouth is me and thrust her breast against his lips, me by any other name. But now she groaned, a curious groan mingling hunger and joy and defeat and yearning and she snaked down fast moving like heat over his skin and she took him in her mouth. She reached with her neck, mouth wide open, and took him in. *Me by any other name.* His mind drunken reeled and she made greedy little noises, slobbering, and he heard his own voice calling, and her head bobbed and weaved, and in the confusion of pleasures he remembered *a long walk along a sandy beach the feeling of the sunrise ahead,* and raised his head and saw with wonder her lips on him. The stretch of the flesh and beautiful and grotesque. His gasps in his mouth. A burning warmth against the side of his chest through the thin silky cloth on her hips. With his right hand he reached down and pulled pins from her hair. It uncoiled reluctantly and dropped slowly to his stomach.

When she looked up her face was blurred, her eyes hazy from wine. "Condom?" she said. "Condom?" He was still running back, retreating from the edge she had brought him to and relieved she had stopped, and as always the way she pronounced the word with the flat "um" baffled him. "Condom?"

"In the bedroom," he said finally. He followed her, followed that movement of her haunches, that slight jiggle which still and now made his heart surge in tender ferocity. He found the unopened condom packet easily, in the table next to the bed. She lay back on the bed, twirled off her panties in a single arcing moment that bent her like a bow and back. Orange light spilled through the curtain on the west-facing window, across her belly and into the shadow below. His fingers fumbled at the plastic.

"Give," she said. She took it from him as he tumbled onto the bed. She kissed his tip with a swirl of tongue, then rolled the rubber down. Then she was over him, squatting. She held him and he thought of the other man viciously. Look where she is now. Look. But who is the cuckold, which is the husband, and he felt despair in his throat, like black and bitter iron. But then he cried out in love, from the scalding oily embrace of her. She took him in, a fraction, just so much, so little. His hips bucked and she put a hand on his stomach. Don't move. He knew her pleasures. Her engulfing would last an eternity, little by little. She was absolutely still, not moving at all but yes slipping down eighth by infinitesimal inch. On her face an expression of indescribable luxury. Even during the first time together, which had been her first time ever, she had been confident. Afterwards *she says ah that wasn't too good but I think it's going to get better and rolls herself in a yellow silk sari.* Sartaj saw now that this was the last time, and again flickering shadows of hopelessness chased the pleasure up his spine. He opened his eyes wide, to see her breasts light and golden in the slanting light, against the black brassiere, and he wanted to touch them but he knew not yet. Her mouth was open and he knew she was on the same razor edge between excruciating delight and impatience, holding by the will on to time. For in time there was joy. Children's shouts tumbling into the room but here the harsh breathing. In Benares *he is overwhelmed by time as an owl-faced shopkeeper displays for Megha his saris, he throws them in the air with a flourish and the silk billows, red and gold and deep blue and green, and Sartaj laughs as the colours float and fall but he is full of loss and afterwards on the street she asks. It's nothing, he says. Nothing.* Now she exhaled, a wail, "Sartaj it's so good." He considered the nuances of "it," distilled the traces of regret and exultation in her voice, but now with another grateful sigh she gave up, gave in, reached with a right hand to their joining, under her, above him, and with a finger strummed at herself, at the centre. Through her flesh he felt the vibration. Which he remembered. When *she finds out about him and someone else she cries and leaves for two weeks and three days. Later when he finds out about her, much later, he cannot believe it cannot see it in his head and then wants either to die or kill someone.* She flick flickered with her finger and he could hear it in her breathing and nothing else was moving and he raised his head to watch and she leaned down suddenly and kissed him and her tongue moved in and out of his mouth furiously. He felt fucked and was grateful. She spoke into his mouth now, a cry, something, and then shook and came down on him the rest of the way, and trembled defencelessly on him, and he held her. Until she was still.

But with his hands spread wide on her buttocks and his face in her neck, her shoulder, he found his rhythm. She stirred and moved with him. There was the fleeting awkwardness, a move this way and that and an unsatisfactory impact and a farting sound from between their bodies, but then she pushed herself up on his chest, palms spread, hair falling over his face, and together they had the movement, and he was

moving in and out slicked from the sweet pocket of contentment, his thumbs on nipples pulled from the brassiere and
rolled, and she made now small sounds on every stroke,
halfway between protest and welcome, between all worlds, and
Sartaj somewhere aware of the bed below, the roof, the building, and what they were doing high in the air above the earth,
the eager grinding of the bodies, he in the body and out of it,
mind moving and not moving, sweat on her forearms, *me by
any other name,* the moving sun, and then she looked down at
him with eyes shining with wonder, and he held her by the hip
and strained up to her, rising off the bed and reaching in her,
saying Megha, and she rolled down to meet him, and at the
closest point of their meeting he felt the spill, ecstatic and
alive, and in a last moment of thought he asked, is this me? Is
this you?

The condom made a sad plop on the floor next to the bed.
As he turned over Sartaj had the sensation of time starting to
stir again. He lay on his side, put a hand on Megha's stomach
and watched his fingers move with her breathing. She had an
arm over her eyes, and he blinked hard, trying to read the set
of her chin. He could feel the throbbing of his own heart. She
turned to him suddenly. "We must be mad," she said, but there
was no sadness in her. She smiled and touched his cheek with
the tips of her fingers. "I have to go." He watched her walk
across the bedroom, past the white wall with its filigree of
shadow, and he knew he would remember this image forever,
this person, this shimmering body moving away from his life.
From the bathroom he heard the sound of rushing water.

Sartaj was no longer angry, or despairing, but as he lay on
the sheets he was possessed of a certain clarity, and he could
hear the world ending. In the huge distances of the red sky, in
the far echoes of the evening he could feel the melancholy of
its inevitable death. He ran a hand over his chest, and the slow
prickling of the hair was distinct and delicious. He got up,

walked into the bathroom. Megha was standing under the shower, his blue shower cap on her head, and was lathering her stomach absently. He took the soap from her, led her by the hand into the bedroom, to the bed. He had her lie down on her back, and smoothed away the soap from her body with his fingers. He bent his head to her breasts, and found cool beads of water and underneath an evasive smoothness. He tongued the nubbly brown nipples and she stirred under him restlessly. As he trailed down her body she tugged at his *patka*. It came off finally and with her fingers in his hair he put a hand under one knee and lifted the leg up, away. He heard her breath, sharp, and as always the close curl of her labia against each other, under the soft slope of black hair, was once more strangely unknown to him, familiar and yet astonishing. He kissed her thigh, in the crease, and there was the lush smell of her, round and full and loamy in his nostrils. The flesh to the centre flushed and trembled and thickened under his tongue. In and into the sudden salty heat he lapped, hungrily, following the twisting trail of her shakes, losing sight of the secret and finding it again. She held his head and moved him and herself to the place she wanted and then away from it. His fingers dabbed and stroked through the folds and in the plump fluttering confusion there was time and its thousand and one tales, *first flirtation, vanilla ice-cream eaten dripping from her fingers,* and *a Congress election poster outside the restaurant window while they quarrelled* and he clung to none of them, they drifted and vanished and he sometimes himself and then vanished, his tongue moved and his lips and his fingers under her bottom, and then he heard her rising cry, and he knew she had her right index finger in her mouth, biting. Finally she drew him up and kissed him, licking his mouth and fingers. This time he put the condom on himself. They moved together and the bed creaked under them. His body bent over her and he looked back over his shoulder at their tangled shadows, rising and falling, and then down at her and at their hair mingling. He bent down to kiss her, and when he came away she was crying. With a groan he touched her cheek but she put a hand on his wrist. "Don't stop," she said. "Don't stop. Don't stop." And so he went on. In the twilight she raised a hand to his mouth and he could see her tears. And so then a moment when everything was lost, but her.

Afterwards it was dark and they said barely a word to each other. At the door she raised her cheek to his, and for a moment they stood like that. When she was gone he shut the door, and came back to the sofa, and sat on it, very still. He felt very empty, his mind like a hole, a black yawning in space, and he searched desperately for something to think about. He thought then of Kshitij, and his mother, and his father, and the boy's anger, the resentful line of his shoulders, and Sartaj began as if from a great distance to see a shape, a form. He sat on the sofa and thought about it. Outside the night came.

"*Alacktaka.*"

The word hurt Sartaj's ear. His heart was racing and he had no memory of picking up the phone.

"*Alacktaka.*"

"What?"

"We found out for you what it is." It was Shaila, and she was whispering with great excitement.

"Who is we?"

"Me and my friend Gisela Middlecourt. We went to the library yesterday afternoon." Then there was the sound of a struggle. "Gisela, stop it."

Sartaj waited for the giggling to subside, and then said, "Why are you whispering?"

"Listen," Shaila said. "We're sort of interested in things to paint lips with."

"You are?"

"Of course we are," Shaila said. "Be quiet and listen. So we wondered what *alacktaka* was. Gisela said we should look in the *Britannica*. It wasn't there. Then we looked in the *Oxford*. No. Then we thought, all right, the Urdu-English dictionary, which is down the reference shelf, you know."

"No, I don't know," Sartaj said, resting his head on his knees.

"Obviously you don't. It wasn't there. So then the Persian-English dictionary. Still no. Then we found the Sanskrit-English Dictionary, Ety, Ety-mologically and Phil-lolo-gically Arranged, by Sir Algernon Algernon-Williams, M.A., K.C.I.E., and Principal A. S. Bharve, published 1889."

"Shaila, what's the point?"

"You're not grateful in the very least."

"For what?"

"*Alacktaka*. Page 232 of the Sanskrit-English dictionary. *Alakta*, rarely *Alacktaka*. Red juice or lac, obtained from the red resin of certain trees and from the cochineal's red sap. Used by men and women to dye certain parts of their bodies, especially the soles of the feet and lips." Now there was another bout of stifled laughter. "R. 7.7. Mk. 4.15. Km. 5.34."

"What's that?"

"*Rig Veda* 7.7. That's a reference. Sister Carmina told us. Do you know what *Km.* is? No, I'll tell you. Sister Carmina didn't want to tell us. It's the *Kama Sutra,* which she says isn't in the library. But Gisela's parents have a copy which they think is hidden away on top of their shelf. We looked it up. It's there, Chapter 5. Advice to the young gentleman, man-about-town. After your morning bath you put on balms and *alakta*, before you go out. I'll read it to you."

"Shaila?"

"What?"

"Don't." Sartaj was staring at the top of his own head,

which he could see in the mirror on the wall. He was wondering what Chetanbhai Ghanshyam Patel put on in the morning. What was his aftershave? Sartaj rubbed the skin on his wrist, under his *kara*, remembering again the heavy silkiness of the Rolex. Where was Chetanbhai's copy of the *Kama Sutra*?

"Why are you quiet? Are you thinking? What are you thinking about?" Shaila chirped into Sartaj's ear, very interested.

"Never mind what I'm thinking about," Sartaj said. "You put that book back where you found it. And don't read any more." He could hear them laughing as he hung up.

Taking a deep breath, Sartaj plunged into the swamp. Above, the morning sky was low and dark, heavy with black clouds. The water came up fast to his thighs and then to his waist, and he clutched dizzily at the reeds to keep his balance. Things moved under his feet and the water lapped against his shirt, but finally he was able to take a step, and then another. The surface of the water was covered with a foamlike scum, and there were rags and drabbles of paper stuck to the reeds. After another step the thick green plants closed behind him and he could no longer see the buildings across the road. He was trying to make a circle but he could no longer tell where he was.

He pushed ahead, moving aside the matted stalks with his hands. His face was covered with moisture and the breath burned in his chest. Something buzzed against his cheek and then he saw a flash of white to his left. He tried to turn and something gave way under him and he fell full length into the water. As he came closer he saw that the white was a smooth form, like stone, that came out of the liquid, and as he struggled he tried to place it in his memory, he was sure that he had seen it before, and then it turned over in his vision and took on a new form, like a cloud, and he saw that it was the Apsara's shoulder, and that she lay face down in the water, almost covered but held up by the criss-crossing reeds and the thrust of the swamp itself. He reached her and panted as he strained to turn her over. Her smile was eternal and untouched by what she had come to. He looked around for the buildings and the pathway, but could see nothing, and then he tried to imagine Chetanbhai's wife bringing out the Apsara and throwing her into the muck. It was impossible and improbable, but he could see without any effort Kshitij dragging out the white form, like a corpse, in the darkness of the early morning, not looking at the Apsara's eyes, her swollen lips, and tipping her into the water. What he couldn't form within himself was a logic for it, a first cause, a reason why. Not yet, he said, yet, and then he began to look for a way out.

"You smell," Kshitij said when he opened the door to Sartaj's urgent knocking.

"Of shit, yes," Sartaj said, walking into the apartment, which was clean now, neatened and stripped of its gaudiness. The paintings were gone, and the books on the shelf were a different lot, thicker with gold writing on the spines.

"Did you fall into a gutter or something?" Kshitij said, looking at the puddles of water on his floor. "Hope you didn't swallow anything. You need medical attention if you did."

"Not quite. Not quite." The swamp was used as a gutter by the labourers who built the apartment buildings, and some of the servants who worked in them, and Sartaj understood Kshitij's pained look of distaste, but he was reading the titles on the shelf. "*A History of the Indian People*," Sartaj said. "Was your father a great reader?"

"Not really, no," Kshitij said.

"Your mother?"

"No, she's not."

"I see. And you?"

"Yes, I read. But is something wrong?"

"I'd like to see that chequebook I gave to you. If I may."

"What is this? I thought you had the man."

"I have the man. Where is it?"

There was a moment then in which Sartaj saw the possibilities clicking in Kshitij's eyes, and fear, and then Kshitij shrugged and laughed. "All right. No problem."

When he had it, a minute later, Sartaj held the chequebook by his fingertips, away from his body, and flicked through the pages. "I'll keep this," he said.

"Sure. But why?"

Sartaj looked at him, considering. Then he leaned forward and said deliberately, "I'm very interested in your father's reading habits."

The Jankidas Publishing Company turned out to be a man, a woman, and two computers in a garage. The garage was at the rear of an old four-storied building in a lane near Bandra station. Lines of fresh clothes hung from every balcony above the garage, and as Sartaj, now dry and no longer fetid, unlaced his shoes he was aware that at least three women were watching him from different homes above, their laundry forgotten. He had called Katekar from home, while he was changing, and had him waiting outside Chetanbhai's building in plain clothes, ready to shadow Kshitij. There was an excitement in his blood now, a hunter's prickling on his forearms. As he tugged at the lace on his left shoe there was again that darkened stirring in his mind, something falling into shape, barely recognizable yet. But moving. The "Remove Shoes Please" sign had been done in a fancy curled typeface on red paper, and inside Mr. Jankidas was eating his lunch near his computer, under a purple sign that announced, "We Believe in God and Cash. No Credit Please." Mrs. Jankidas, who wore steel-rimmed spectacles like her husband and looked very much like him except for her full head of hair, held a tiffin from which she occasionally served out *puris* and *bhaji*. Mr. Jankidas sat cross-legged in his chair, quite content, and it was as perfect a scene of domestic tranquillity as Sartaj had ever seen. He broke it with some satisfaction.

"I am aware of some transactions between you and a certain Mr. Chetanbhai Ghanshyam Patel," he said. "Who is unfortunately in the position of being the deceased in a very serious case of murder."

"It's more serious than the average murder case?" Mr. Jankidas said. Sartaj liked him.

"It appears to be," Sartaj said. "It may turn out to be very complicated. Which is why I must appeal to you. This Mr. Patel was in the habit of writing cheques to you. Monthly, that is, as far as I can tell."

"He was our client," Mr. Jankidas said.

"Satisfied, no doubt. What did he purchase from you?"

Mrs. Jankidas tilted her head slightly and Sartaj saw the look of command that passed between them.

"We promise our clients confidentiality," Mr. Jankidas said. "It is, you understand, part of the terms."

Sartaj leaned back in his chair. He was quite comfortable in the air conditioning. "Is this allowed, to operate a business in a garage in this building? According to the building society rules? What about municipal rules? I wonder." He was addressing himself to Mrs. Jankidas. "I must remember to find out." He turned his head to look at the other signs in the room. Mr. Jankidas was a believer in signs. Dust Is the Enemy of Efficiency. Customer Is our Joy. When Sartaj looked back Mr. Jankidas was ready to talk.

"We provide multiple services. Brochures. Business cards. Company papers. Legal typing. Invitations. Wedding cards. If you need, please."

"And?"

"Also we publish a magazine."

"Yes?"

"We function as a stage, you see. For the exchange of information. Mutual communications."

"What kind of information?"

Mr. Jankidas bent over in his chair and fished beneath the computer desk. He brought out a magazine with slick covers, all red and yellow, resplendent with many typefaces. On the front a young woman looked straight into the camera, under the title in green, *The Metropolitan*. Sartaj had seen it before, at railway book stalls, the pages stapled together securely. He took it from Mr. Jankidas and opened it and read, in the middle of a column, "R-346. (M) *Bombay*: I am 32 year old, Engineer man working as a Class-I Gazetted Officer in a Central Govt. Establishment. 168 cms, 72 kgs, heartily welcome bc, cpn from frank, good-looking, bm ladies-couples l-nw, no bars. Cfndt assured-expected, pht appreciated. H: Games, nature, outing. LK: English, Hindi, Marathi."

"What's a 'bm'?" Sartaj said.

"Broad-minded," Mrs. Jankidas said suddenly. "H for Hobbies, LK for Languages Known."

"Languages. Of course," Sartaj said. "I see, I see." Of course he didn't see at all, but he pushed on. "I take it Chetanbhai was a customer for this."

"Yes," Mr. Jankidas said. "They ran one ordinary ad every month."

"They?"

Mr. Jankidas picked up a ledger, ran a finger down a ruled page, and pronounced, "M-434."

Sartaj found M-434, towards the back of the magazine. "*Bombay*: In absence of true and loving friendship, life is nothing but one long process of getting tired. Let's join up! Come together to explore the fascinating future. An educated, charming, very friendly couple is inviting like-minded singles/couples to make the life a colourful span of sweet surprises, tender thrills. Melodious moments, fabulous felicities and warm welcome are all waiting for you. What are you waiting for?"

"It was the same ad every month," Mr. Jankidas said.

"It must have had results," Sartaj said.

Mr. Jankidas held up his hands. "We don't know. We just forward the letters, for a small fee of course."

"You see," Mrs. Jankidas said. "Mutual communications."

Sartaj drove his motorcycle to Colaba in a daze of wonder. He looked at the people passing by, at their faces, marvelling at their calm, their public banality. A woman in a red sari waited at a crossroad for a bus to pass, holding a netted bag full of potatoes. A taxi driver leaned on his cab, spilling tobacco into his palm. Noticing Sartaj's stare, a girl in a green and white school uniform looked away. But Sartaj was asking merely if she, they, how many of them had colourful spans of sweet surprises. He knew he had finally heard Chetanbhai Ghanshyam Patel's voice, and he felt revived and childlike, as if he knew nothing. "Melodious moments," he said to himself. "Melodious moments." After he parked he pulled the photograph of Chetanbhai and his family from the file, and sat looking at it, at Chetanbhai's round face, the sweetness of the smile on his face, the pride in his wife's eyes as she looked into the camera, secure in the thickness of her gold bangles and her family, confident of the future. And behind them Kshitij, unsmiling but earnest, and on the right of the picture, a flash of white just inside the frame, the curve of a soft hip.

Finding the parking lot that Chetanbhai had used was simple. Getting the two brothers who sat shifts in the wooden booth, handing out tickets and change, to remember the Patels was simple: they were excited by the thought of being part of an investigation, and the elder, who worked Saturday days, remembered, instantly, the red Contessa.

"That's them," he said, when Sartaj showed them the photograph. "Them two."

"Which way did they go?" Sartaj said.

"Always there," the man said, pointing with a rigid finger. "There."

Sartaj had a general direction, and so he started. The shopkeepers were busy with tourists, and there was commerce everywhere, from the stacked statues of Krishna and the men leaning in doorways muttering prices for illegal substances barely out of Sartaj's hearing. "Who has time to look nowadays, baba?" one stallkeeper said, wrapping a pair of *chappals* for a Japanese couple. "People come and go." But then he looked at the photograph and remembered them. They had never bought anything but they had been walking by for years. They had become familiar to him because of their regularity.

Around the corner from the *chappal*-seller, from his rows of footwear, there was an alley's length of beer bars. Sartaj went into the first, into the air-conditioned darkness, and found a patient line of women in shiny green and red *churidars*. They shook their heads at the photograph deliberately, back and forth and back again, and their lack of expression was complete and carefully maintained. Sartaj nodded, thanked them, and went on to the next bar. Finally, at the end of the road, near the seafront, there was a hotel used mainly by visiting Arabs. In the lobby, the men standing by the ceiling-high picture of an emir knew nothing, had seen nothing, weren't interested. "We are guides, you see," the oldest one said, as if that were a scientific explanation for not seeing anything. "Guides for the Arabs." He straightened his red tie and looked very serious. Sartaj smiled at the gentle mockery, nodded, and went on to the desk clerk, who knew nothing, but the *durban* outside remembered the Patels. He had always thought they lived somewhere nearby.

By late afternoon Sartaj knew he was getting close to the destination. He overshot the trail only once, when they took a left, and it took him an hour to come back and find the direction again. Now he was striding briskly, along a back street lined with faded four-storied apartment buildings. Though the road was crowded with parked cars, it was quiet, shaded with trees, so that Sartaj could feel the lost elegance in the names of the buildings and in the circular balconies that must have been all the rage. To the left, in the shadow of a *neem* tree, behind a gate with a plaque — "Seaside Villa" — a man with white hair knelt among flowers. Sartaj walked by him, then turned and came back.

"You," he said, crooking his finger.

The man pushed himself up and came to the gate, dusting his hands on old khaki shorts.

"Your good name, please," Sartaj said.

"A. M. Khare, IFS retired." Despite his torn *banian* there was the assurance of having travelled the world.

"Mr. Khare, have you seen these persons?"

"Not once but many times. He talked to me about my flowers."

"What kind of flowers are those?"

"Orchids. They are very hard to grow."

"Did he know anything about flowers?"

"No, but he complimented me particularly."

"Did you observe where they went after they talked to you?"

Khare shrugged. He seemed embarrassed. "Yes."

"Yes?"

"To the building there" — pointing with his chin — "called *Daman*."

On the second floor of *Daman*, Sartaj found a boarding house, which was really a large flat, with thin partitions making tiny rooms let out mostly to trainees at the Taj. But, Mrs. Khanna said, there was a deluxe suite, on the floor above, next to her own rooms, which she hired out very rarely and only to people known to her. Mrs. Khanna wore a green caftan and smoked

rapidly, and spoke in a no-nonsense style designed to intimi-
date tenants. She nodded at the photograph.

"Known them for years," she said. "Regulars. Nice people.
Paid in cash, advance."

"For what?" Sartaj said. "Who came to see them?"

"I don't ask questions. Not my business."

"But you notice things."

She shook her head, deliberately. "Not my business."

"Let's see the room."

There was a long passageway from Mrs. Khanna's flat to the
suite, with a locked door on either end. The inner door opened
into a small room filled up by a coffee table and four old
chairs. On the wall there was a painting, ruins on a cliff, over a
river.

"See," Mrs. Khanna said. "With attached bathroom. Very
nice."

Sartaj followed her into the bedroom. The green curtains
were drawn and it was very dark, and Sartaj felt his head swim
in the sudden quiet. Over the bed, a village belle flashed dark
eyes at him over the edge of her stylized yellow *dupatta*. He
reached down to the cassette player perched on the headboard
and popped out the tape. There was no label. Sartaj put it back
in the player and pressed a button. Mehdi Hassan sang: *Ranjish
hi sahi. . .*

"Is this his tape?" Sartaj said.

"Yes. Mr. Patel's tape."

"And the paintings?"

"Also his. He said the room was very sparse." She looked
around the room, gesturing with a cigarette. "He was, he was a
very *shaukeen* type of person, you see."

"Yes, a lover of the fabulous felicities."

"What?"

But Sartaj was drawing back the curtains. Mrs. Khanna
watched keenly as he went through the bedroom and into the

small bathroom, which was sparkling clean. She was clearly amused as he bent over to look behind the commode.

"It's cleaned every day. Or when it's used," she said. "Nothing left over. Nothing to find."

"Very commendable," Sartaj said. "Are you sure you never saw any visitors?"

"No. Separate door there, opens out in front of the lift. They come and they go."

"And this boy in the picture? Mr. Patel's son? Have you ever seen him? Did he ever come here?"

"No."

"He's dead, you know. Mr. Patel is murdered. You know?"

"I read the paper."

"What is your idea about it?"

Mrs. Khanna was holding her cigarette carefully in two extended fingers. Nothing moved except the smoke. "I'm not curious," she said. "Not my business. Don't want to know."

Sartaj searched the room. The mattress was clean, the floor underneath swept, every surface was clean and polished, and the rubbish bin empty. Mrs. Khanna was a good housekeeper. In a drawer in the bureau next to the bed there was an opened packet of Trojan condoms, "Ultra-Fine."

"These? Mr. Patel's?"

"Perhaps," Mrs. Khanna said.

"American. Very expensive."

"He was *shaukeen*."

Sartaj looked at the bureau, under it. He peered behind the headboard of the bed, then to the left, behind the bureau. It was close up to the wall. He put the tips of three fingers behind the wood and tugged. Then with a flicker of pain his fingers came away and the bureau sat, battered and unmoving. He squatted, gripped low by its legs and pulled. A grunt, another one, and it shifted. Now he was able to get behind it, to look. There was something between the green wood and the baseboard. He reached down into the crack, searched with his fingertips. He brought it up and saw that it was a photograph, a Polaroid. He wiped away the dust, and the colours in it formed an image, and he turned it this way and that, and saw then that it was a woman's body, naked but blurred, the brown of the skin hidden in parts by a moving smear of white, as if a sheet had been pulled off and she had turned away, all the frame filled with fast motion. Her face was hidden by a hand, an upflung arm, the chin barely visible as a suggestion, but there was her hair, long and thick and luxuriant. And the curve of a naked hip.

"Do you know who this is?" Sartaj said.

Mrs. Khanna considered the matter. "No," she said. She was bored. There was much in the world she didn't want to know about, and the naked body was no news to her.

"Did you ever see Mr. Patel with a camera?"

"No."

Sartaj was looking at the picture, trying to read what he could see of the forehead, the chin. Was it protest? Or laughter? Mrs. Khanna watched him, and he saw that she was faintly amused by his attention to the picture. He held up the family photo of the Patels. "Are you sure you never saw this boy?"

"Told you, I didn't."

"This is a dangerous position you're in, you realize? Running a house of prostitution without license?"

"Nobody prostitutes anything here."

"Still it would bear investigation."

"Investigate if you want. I'm not involved."

"You mean you don't want to be involved."

She shrugged. Sartaj shook his head, and turned away. When he was at the door, she said, "All right."

He turned back to her. "What?"

"I'll tell you," she said. "Because I didn't like the little bastard in that photograph. He threatened me. But if you try and get me involved I'll deny everything. I won't sign anything, and I won't appear anywhere."

"Yes, fine," Sartaj said. "Tell me. What about the little bastard?"

"He came here," Mrs. Khanna said.

"When?"

"I don't know, nine, ten days ago."

"Alone? What did he want?"

"Yes, alone. First he wouldn't tell me who he was, but said that he wanted to see the room that Mr. and Mrs. Patel hired. I said I didn't know any Mr. and Mrs. Patel, and why should I let him into any room. Then he began to argue, and I told him to take himself out of my house before I had him thrown out. Then he asked if they had left anything in there, anything at all, and I said I was tired of talking to him, and called Jaggan from downstairs to throw him out. Then he started shouting, abused me. *Randi,* he said. So Jaggan gave him a shake."

"Then?"

"Then he said he would come back. With friends. Come back with your whole *paltan,* I said. We'll see you, he said. The *Rakshaks* will take care of your kind. They know you and your type. They know how to handle whores like you." Mrs. Khanna studied the end of her cigarette thoughtfully.

"He said the *Rakshaks*?" Sartaj said.

She tipped her head to the side. It was a strange gesture, full of resignation. "Yes, that's what he said. They're absolutely mad, those bastards. Capable of anything. So I let him see the room. Why take trouble on unnecessarily?"

"True," Sartaj said. "What did he do in the room?"

"He went through it," she said. "Just like you, searched it, opened drawers, looked under the bed, in the bathroom. Looked in the rubbish bin. Like he was checking it for something. Evidence. Clues. Things left behind."

"I see."

"But he was shaking and his eyes were red. Speaking under his breath to himself. Mad."

"Yes, mad. Did he find anything?"

"No, nothing. He was their son?"

"Yes."

Mrs. Khanna stubbed out her cigarette in an ashtray. "Chetanbhai was a good man," she said. "Poor Chetanbhai."

On his motorcycle, with metal trembling against his thighs, Sartaj thought of bodies. He tried to picture his own, and found it curiously blurred, his knowledge of it dulled and patchy. He had known it forever, but what were his shoulders like in pain? The back of his thighs in sleep? Megha he knew, the pulse on her wrist and the one that beat hard on her throat, but each time they settled against each other, had settled, he had felt compelled to take stock anew. Like a man afraid of memory dying. The loud blatting of the engine beat on his ears. He tried to imagine Chetanbhai Ghanshyam Patel naked, as he had been under the sheet at the morgue, a round face and a sloping chest, a paunch, thighs splayed apart. In his life had somebody watched him in the morning, awoken him with an invading caress? Sartaj tried to imagine his own parents, and his mind turned. It turned and stopped, as firmly as the bike stopped in grinding rush-hour traffic, in front of the temple at Mahalakshmi. His mother he saw in her gentle plumpness, her slow walk, her pleasure in afternoon talk and tea. He remembered his father's vigour, the energy the old man took such pride in at fifty, bounding up the stairs, roaring with unexpected laughter at his son's infrequent jokes. But had they lain against each other late at night, satiated but unable to sleep? Touching with a holding hand? These were only words, and Sartaj was unable to see it. It was impossible to imagine. There was no photograph that he could construct, rising the colours out of his childhood, marking here and there with lines until the shapes became bodies.

Katekar was waiting at the end of the lane when he reached the Narayan Housing Colony, smoking a *bidi* near a *paan*-seller's kiosk. Sartaj was wearing his dingiest civvies, but Katekar looked sceptical as Sartaj strolled up, relaxed and studiedly casual. Katekar was carefully nondescript in shiny rayon pants, and there was nothing in Sartaj's wardrobe that could equal the bland horror of his shirt. Sartaj accepted the criticism, because since training he had known he was not very good at shadowing, and his turban was only part of the problem. It was his walk and the cast of his shoulders — he had found it difficult always not to swagger, to fade away into the crowd.

"The mother's gone," Katekar said, looking away and pulling on the *bidi*. They were two friends passing the time on a weekday evening. "He drove her to Bombay Central this evening. She caught the Saurashtra Express to Okha. That's in Gujarat."

"I know. They've started running," Sartaj said. "That's very good. Then?"

"He didn't wait for the train to leave," Katekar said, his face stiff with disapproval. "Just put her in the compartment and came back here and went up. Just got back. He's up there."

"Right," Sartaj said. "Go back to the station house. Rest. Well done."

Katekar nodded. "With care, *sahib*. Something strange is going on here."

"I know," Sartaj said. He watched as Katekar pedalled away on an old Hero bicycle. In many ways, care had come hard to Sartaj, because in his pride he had believed that he would win the things he wanted by just asking. But now, older, he had found patience. He found a table behind a window at a restaurant called East Haven near the intersection and ordered dinner. He regretted the *ragda-patis* after the first bite. It had that searing hotness of all the cheap restaurant food that he and

Megha had once lived on. It was incredible to him that they had actually enjoyed it, in Formica-paneled dives like this one. Now the place filled up quickly with T-shirted teenagers, and Sartaj listened intently to them, and pushed a piece of bread around his plate. The road outside was crowded with cars and scooters and through it all he could see the gate through which Kshitij must come, but an hour passed, and then two, and there was no sign of him. The groups of friends changed at the tables around Sartaj, and outside on the tiny patio, and it was a slightly older crowd now, less raucous, with none of the rapturous pubescent laughter of the early evening, but still there was no sight of Kshitij, or any mention of him in the lengthy gossip that wound and unwound in the smoky air. They all knew each other, as everyone had in Sartaj's colony, and he remembered sitting like this, shoulder to shoulder in an endless round of silly *phattas* and cups of tea. And the girls who came in and sat at their own tables but not too far away. Sartaj wondered if Kshitij would stay up there all night, behind the brassbound door, without even the Apsara for company, and then gave up the thought instantly: no one could stand that hideous loneliness of that apartment's four bare walls. He would come, sooner or later.

At eleven East Haven was nearly empty, and the waiters had stopped asking Sartaj if he wanted anything. The traffic was no longer the mad snarl of the evening, and yet Sartaj missed the car completely. It had passed and was already long out of sight behind a bus when Sartaj saw in his memory the red Contessa with the shadowed figure behind the wheel. He ran out to his motorcycle, leaving a hundred on the table, and cursed the machine as it coughed and hung. By the time he came out at the mouth of the bazaar the Contessa was far ahead, a pair of red dots far ahead in the dark, and now his anger at himself for expecting a walking man made himself come up on it fast, too fast. Before the next intersection he found the right distance, two cars behind and to the left, and whenever there was a lit-up stretch of road he switched off his headlight, so that there would be no regular illumination in the Contessa's rearview mirrors to attract attention and suspicion.

But there was no sign that the driver ahead knew of the shadow: the car went steadily, not too fast or too slow, through the Andheri subway and north on the highway on the other side, past the Sahar turnoff, past the right turn for Film City, and still further north, and Sartaj exulted in a growing certainty: this was too far away and too late to be innocent. And in the next moment he remembered the joy of pointless and endless rides, not so long ago, and he rebuked himself for having become, completely and deep in the bone, what he had thought he would never become, a policeman like his father, and his father before him.

The car stopped in front of a new apartment building, in a development so new that there was still the rolling shape of a wooded hillside behind it. Sartaj switched off his engine and coasted gently to a halt, crunching across gravel as a figure got out of the Contessa and walked in through the double gates. There was a cool breath of air from the hill as Sartaj pushed down the kickstand and edged closer to the car, keeping his back against the low wall that ran around the building. There was that sound of night that was always lost in the city, insects and calling birds, and the size of the sky. Two men came out now, through the doors, each carrying something heavy, dark bundles that they loaded into the dickie and then the back seat. They went back and forth, carrying the square boxes to the car, and now Sartaj could see the glint of Kshitij's glasses. When the car was full, they got in, and now the sound of the engine was very loud, and the glaring circle of the headlights moved towards Sartaj. He took a deep breath and stepped out into the road, holding up his hand.

He leaned them against the hood of the car and patted

under their arms and over their backs. He let them see the pistol under his bush shirt, and Kshitij frowned.

"What do you want?" he said. "Why are you doing this?"

"Shut up," Sartaj said. He walked around the car, and the back seat was full of the bulky packages. Sartaj's heart was thudding. The dickie opened smoothly, and Sartaj felt around in the box on top. There was only paper, pamphlets of some kind. He held the box by the edge and pulled it out, tipped it over onto the road, and the small stapled notebooks spread across the asphalt. There was nothing else in the box.

"Why are you doing it?" the other boy said. He was larger than Kshitij, more confident in his body. "That is only our literature."

"Whose literature?"

"Us," the boy said, gesturing at himself and Kshitij, and then at the building. "Us, the *Rakshaks*."

"You're a *Rakshak*?" Sartaj said to Kshitij.

"Yes," Kshitij said, standing up straight. "I am."

All of Kshitij's resentment made sense now, his dense anger just under the innocuous surface, all of it barely concealed. Except, of course, to a man vain enough not to believe that he could be despised for what he was, for his beard, for his turban. But Kshitij no longer was hiding his contempt, his keen scalpel-edged hostility. His face was eager with it.

"You have no right to do this," his friend said. "We are a cultural organization."

"This?" Sartaj said, bending down to pick up one of the pamphlets. "This is your culture?" There was a line drawing of a goddess on the cover, superimposed over a map of India, and the words "The Defender" underneath. He had seen the magazine before: it was a call to arms, a hearkening back to a perfect past of virtue and strength, and an explanation for every downfall. "You defend nothing. You are attackers."

"We attack only those who attack us. And those who attack our culture."

"What is your name?"

"Pramod Wagle," the boy said, puffing out his chest.

"Pramod Wagle. I want to see what's inside," Sartaj said. He pushed them towards the building, and as they came up to it two men came out of a door and watched silently. On the ground floor, next to the unfinished lobby, there was a double door with the same goddess painted in full colour over the door, and she wore a sari of radiant white. Now there were three other men in the corridor, watching. Inside, the apartment was divided into an office, which contained a large cyclostyle machine, and a dank gymnasium, with mirrors on the wall, and a rack of *lathis*.

"Everything is legal," Pramod Wagle said. "We are a registered organization."

Sartaj was fingering the long length of a *lathi*, following the dark sheen of the wood. "Yes," Sartaj said. He had seen, four months before, a man killed with a *lathi* in a fight, his head had been split open, but Wagle was correct, it was legal. So was everything else. "Come on," Sartaj said to Kshitij, and turned to the door, but in the corridor outside it was they who watched him, a solid phalanx of dark faces, completely silent. They stepped aside to let him pass, but exactly that one moment too late that let him know that they could do anything they wanted, despite his pistol and any other thing.

"Drive to the police station," Sartaj said. "I will follow you on the motorcycle."

"Why?" Kshitij said.

"There are certain questions we must ask you."

"Am I under arrest?"

"No," Sartaj said. Just behind Kshitij his friends made a crowd, pushing against each other's shoulders.

"Did your father own a Polaroid camera?" Sartaj said. In the boy's silence, his absolute stillness, there was absolute fear. Sartaj leaned over to him and spoke in his ear. He could smell, faintly, hair oil. "I have the photographs, Kshitij. I could pull them out now in front of everyone and show them to you."

"All right," Kshitij said finally. His voice was loud. He turned to Pramod Wagle. "It's all right. Just some questions."

But at the station he refused to answer questions. Somehow, during the drive to the station, with Sartaj's single light blinking and bobbing in his rearview mirror, he had decided that there were no questions he could answer. He sat with his arms folded across his chest, clenching his jaw. "Why are you asking me anything? You have the man in jail already. I want to see a lawyer."

"Come on, Kshitij," Sartaj said, leaning back in his chair. "Come on." He had Kshitij sitting in his office, across the desk from him. Behind Kshitij, Katekar sat in a chair against the wall, slumped but alert. "We know everything. We don't need you to say anything really. We know every last thing. We know what your mother and father did. Here, look at this advertisement. Strange, isn't it? Good, ordinary people. Doing this kind of thing. Unbelievable, if we didn't have it in black and white. Then, we have the woman who runs the house where they rented a room. A cheap whorehouse, really, it is. This woman, the manager, tells us all kinds of things. And also we have, finally, the photographs. Colour Polaroid photographs. Like life itself. Can you imagine? Disgusting photographs. Disgusting things they are doing with god-knows-who-all. To do things like that and then take photographs. . . . I wouldn't have believed it myself if someone had told me. Only when one sees with one's own eyes can one believe. Is that what you were burning in the rubbish heap?"

Kshitij was staring at the brass plate on Sartaj's desk, which announced his name in blocky ornamental letters. He seemed to be reading it back and forth. Behind him, a slow and very faint smile spread across Katekar's face.

"So what happened, Kshitij?" Sartaj said. "Did you find the photographs? Did you see them?"

"I don't know what you're talking about," Kshitij said.

"Did you see your mother in these photographs?"

"I don't know what you're talking about."

"With other men, Kshitij?"

"I don't know what you're talking about."

"Doing things, Kshitij?"

"I don't know what you're talking about."

"A mother is pure, Kshitij. After all she is a mother. But your mother, Kshitij. What is she? In a whorehouse? And your father? To take pictures? What did you see, Kshitij? We'll find out, you know, Kshitij. We're investigating, we have our people asking questions in Okha. We know she's gone to her brother's house near Dwarka. Samnagar, the place is called, isn't it? We'll bring her back. In handcuffs to jail. The world will know then. All your friends. Everyone will know everything about her. So you might as well tell us now. Maybe we can keep it all quiet. What happened? Did you see these photographs and get angry?"

"I don't know what you're talking about."

"Did you see something horrible in the photographs, Kshitij? Of course it was horrible. Your parents. Your mother." Sartaj stopped, swallowed. Then he leaned in close. "Did you see your mother with some stranger? Sucking on him?" The light in the room was yellow, and outside the stillness of night, and small sounds from far away. Sartaj could see the outline of his own head, his turban, in Kshitij's eyes, and he knew he had on his interrogation face with the opaque eyes, and in his body, in his arms and legs, there was the uncurling of a virulent hunger, an angry need to know. There was also somewhere sympathy and disgust and horror, but all that was faint and far away and battened down, safely subterranean.

"I don't know," Kshitij said. And then he stopped. There was no motion in his body, but a kind of rippling, like the surface of water in which no current can be seen. Through the night he grew more inert, like a stone sinking into the worn cloth of the chair, and yet somewhere in the sunken eyes, in the base of the throat, there was that agitation. At two in the morning it had begun to rain, and Sartaj left him to Katekar and walked outside, along the corridor that ran beside the offices. There was that usual late-night talk and movement at the front of the station, the drunks on their way into the lock-up. Sartaj stretched, and reached with an open palm into the rain. His *kara* moved slowly on his wrist. There was the steady drip of water onto his skin. He and Katekar would keep the suspect up all night, taking turns, wearing at him with the repeated questions, beating at him with half-knowledge and insinuations, until in the early day he broke in exhaustion. It was likely. Many did.

He heard a shuffle behind him, the sound of feet. It was the head constable, bringing the night's phone messages. The first was a ten-thirty message from Rahul, asking for a call back. The second the usual late-evening call from Sartaj's mother, and the third was an intimation from Cooper Hospital. Ghorpade was dead. He had died at midnight after a day of discomfort and difficulty with breathing. Sartaj put the slips of paper in his pocket, scratched at his eyebrows, and then he walked back into his office. Katekar was leaning over the suspect, looming over him and letting him smell sweat and tobacco. But Kshitij had found from somewhere a small reserve of fortitude.

"If you are going to charge me with something, charge me," he said. "File an F.I.R., get a warrant. Otherwise what is all this? You're doing this because I'm a member of the *Rakshaks*."

Sartaj sat behind his desk. He twisted his watch around his wrist, once, twice. His cheeks felt congested with rage.

"Katekar, this *chutiya* thinks we're idiots," he said. "And he thinks he's very smart. Take him down to the detection room and take some of his smartness out of him. Give him a good taste of what we do to smart *chutiyas* around here."

Katekar had Kshitij by the scruff of his neck and out of his chair before the boy had time to react, even to open his mouth. As he turned Kshitij away, Sartaj forced himself to raise a hand: easy, no marks. Katekar slammed Kshitij through the swinging doors, and pushed him down the corridor. "*Chala*," he shouted, and there was a terrible anger in his voice.

Sartaj squared the papers on his desk and tried to work. It was raining heavily now, and the water softened all sounds. After a minute or two he gave up, sat back, and put his hands over his face. When the phone rang, he let it ring six times before he picked it up.

"Sartaj Singh."

"Did you take money?" It was Rahul, and his voice was feathery and high.

"What's wrong, Rahul? Are you crying?"

"Ravinder Mama came for dinner today. They were talking about you. They asked if you had signed the papers yet."

"Yes?"

"Megha said not yet. Then Ravinder Mama said you probably were waiting for money. He said you were all for sale. So I called him a name. Daddy told me to shut up. I threw a plate on the ground and left."

Sartaj shut his eyes. "No, I don't take money." But Sartaj then remembered all the things he had been offered because of his uniform, that he had taken, suits at half-price from a tailor near Kala Ghoda, meals with Megha at a five-star restaurant, miraculous train reservations in the middle of summer. A smiling road contractor had once brought over a cannister of *ghee* to Sartaj's grandfather's house as a Diwali gift, and the old man had tipped the cannister over the contractor's head. But life moved in jerky half-moments, in the empty spaces between big decisions, and Sartaj had been unable to resist the specially discounted shoes at Lucky's. Italian style, the proprietor of the shop had said again and again, Italian style. That evening long ago Megha and Sartaj had taken Rahul out for a birthday dinner, the thirteenth, and Rahul had noticed the shoes, and Sartaj had promised him a pair, and then told him stories of detection. Sartaj sat in his chair, and his lips moved: And I arrested a man for a crime he didn't commit, and that man is dead, and life is very long, and investigation is one way to get through it, but to call it justice is only half the truth. "No, I don't take money," he said into the mouthpiece.

"Did you talk to Megha?"

"Yes, I talked to her. Rahul, it's, it's not going to work."

"Why?"

"We're not suited to each other."

"Like you couldn't communicate?"

"Yes. That's it," Sartaj said, grateful for the phrase.

"You should've learned how to communicate."

"Yes."

"What was that?" Rahul said. There had been a sudden surprised yowl that echoed faintly down the corridor.

"A cat outside, I think."

"A cat?"

"A cat."

"Okay." As always, Rahul believed him. Rahul had a whole and unadulterated faith that was beautiful in its clarity: he believed. Now Rahul was trying to help. "These things happen in life, you know. Between men and women. I'll always be here, you know, to help or anything you need."

"Thanks, Rahul," Sartaj said, his voice thick. "I know that."

Megha hadn't believed. One morning at breakfast she had put

down a newspaper crowded with angry headlines, and had asked, for the third time in a month, do you really hit people? Torture them? Her brow was heavy with doubt, and he knew that the easy answer would no longer service. Yes, he said, sometimes it's necessary. It's a tool, an instrument. That night and the next night she had slept on the very far edge of the bed. When he had touched the back of her neck at breakfast she said, without looking up, I hate the world you live in. He had wanted to say, it's your world also, but I am thirty-one years old and I live in the parts you don't want to see. I live there for you. But he had quietly picked up his briefcase from the table in the hall and had shut the door behind him without another word. That had been one of their many silences.

Now Sartaj walked down the corridor, towards a certain room in his world. As he walked he could see the curving pools of light from the bulbs, fading into darkness in the yard, and from beyond the shuffling sound of leaves under the fall of rain. He stepped through a door, and then another one. Katekar had Kshitij strapped face down on a bench. The bare feet hung over one end. The room was bare but for that bench and a chair, and had curving ceilings and a single ventilator high on the wall and, high up, higher than a man's uplifted hands would stretch, a thick white metal pole that went from one wall to the other. In his hand Katekar had a *lathi*, with the wood shining a heavy brown in the yellow light.

Sartaj pulled the chair and sat in front of Kshitij, one leg crossed over another. Kshitij's face was red.

"I'm sorry that you're making me do this, Kshitij," Sartaj said. "I hate to do this. Why don't you just be sensible and tell me what you saw, what you did? Did you scrub down the car, Kshitij? Why? What was in it?"

Kshitij's eyes were amazed, as if he were seeing something that he had never imagined. He seemed to be thinking, contemplating some new but essential truth he had just discovered. Sartaj tapped him gently on the cheek.

"You know, Kshitij," Sartaj said. "I spoke to a lot of people about your father. Everybody loved him." Now Kshitij looked up, straining his neck, his mouth working. "Everyone liked him, you know. His business colleagues said he was dependable, hard-working, dedicated. They thought he had come far and was to go far. In your building, they said he took his neighbour's troubles on his shoulders like his own. Always he was willing to help, not only with advice but practically. At the weddings of other people's sons and daughters how much work he did, they said. In times of grief a good friend. Generous and happy. Fun to be around, always singing, always playing his *ghazals*, always ready for a movie or an outing. A good husband in a happy family they said."

Kshitij's eyes were watery and a trickle seeped from his left nostril. "He was *not* a good man." His voice came out thick and anguished. In all his years Sartaj had never seen a face so full of pain as this one.

"What did he do, Kshitij?" Sartaj said, leaning over close. In his stomach there was a bubbling, nausea, but he had to go on. "What did he do? Tell me. I know he wasn't good, he fooled them. What did he do?" It was the beginning of a confession and he felt it coming. But Kshitij teetered at the edge for a moment, found himself then, and with an appalling effort pulled himself back. Sartaj saw the struggle as the face settled, went from disarray to control.

"I have nothing to say," Kshitij said.

Sartaj sat back, shrugged. "Then I can't help you," he said. "I'm very sorry for that." He waited until Kshitij looked up, then nodded at Katekar. "Go ahead," he said, and got up.

He was halfway across the room when he heard Kshitij's voice, loud now. "What's the matter, bastard? Can't hit me yourself?"

Sartaj turned, then looked around the room. Next to the door there was a row of black metal hooks, and from one of the hooks hung a worn strap, a piece of a heavy industrial belt meant for machinery, four inches wide, attached to a wooden handle. Sartaj felt in his arms a painful pulsing of blood. He took the *patta,* turned around, and with all the swing in his shoulder brought the strap up and around and onto Kshitij's buttocks. And then again. The sound it made was like two flat pieces of wood dashing together. He had his arm back again when he heard, through the rushing in his ears, Kshitij's voice. "What?" he said. He stopped, took a deep breath, and stepped up to the bench. Finally he could make out the words.

"You can't hurt me," Kshitij was saying.

"Oy, did you hear the noises you were making?" Katekar said.

"That was only the body," Kshitij said, and Sartaj could see the drops of spittle darkening the dirty floor.

"I'll hurt you, *bhenchod,*" Katekar said.

"You can't hurt me," Kshitij said. "Or kill me. Only my body."

Sartaj could see the eyes, shining and focused, looking straight ahead, straight through the grimy wall, at something a thousand miles and a thousand years away. He dropped the *patta,* stumbled to the door, which rattled under his shaking hand, and as he fled to the cooler outside air, he could hear Kshitij chanting, "*Jai Hind, Jai Hind.*" But outside, in the corridor, the sound of the rain was loud, and the voice was lost in the water, and Sartaj leaned against a pillar, leaned lower and out above the bending hedges, and retched into the darkness.

When he was able to stand straight, he saw that Katekar was watching from the other side of the pillar.

"I'm all right," Sartaj said.

Katekar nodded, then turned back to the doorway.

"Katekar," Sartaj said. "No more. Just talk to him."

"No? You don't think he'll talk if we give him a little more?"

"Not this one."

Katekar nodded. "What could we do to him?" he said. "He's already in hell."

Sartaj sat on a bench in the corridor, one leg over the other, looking out at the greying sky. He watched Katekar walking up, stretching his right shoulder and then his left.

"This one's not talking, sir," Katekar said.

"Yes, I know," Sartaj said.

"He's one of those, sir," Katekar said. "Gets stronger."

"It's all right," Sartaj said. "Sit."

"Sir?"

"Sit down, Katekar."

A moment, and then Katekar sat, his legs apart, his hands on his knees.

"Did you always want to be a policeman, Katekar?"

"My father was, sir."

"Mine also."

"I know, sir."

The rain had stopped. There was a silence like Sartaj had never heard before.

"My back is going to hurt," Katekar said.

"Is going to hurt?"

"It doesn't hurt now," Katekar said. "But it will. Not this month perhaps, or the next. But then someday soon it will. It'll start and get worse."

"Is it the muscles? Or a disc?"

"The doctors say it's nothing. They give me pills and tablets and it still hurts. Then my wife sends me on pilgrimage to Pandharpur. I walk with the *palkhi* of Dnyaneshwar. There are hundreds of pilgrims. I tell nobody I am a policeman. Nobody can tell one from another. We walk during the day and it is very hot. For the first day and the next and after that my legs hurt and squeeze and become tight. My feet swell and blister and it is difficult to get up the next morning to walk. The sun is very hot and it is all a plain, no trees and just a straight road. The walking is hard. We walk all together. The days pass and it seems like it will never end. Everything is forgotten but the walking. At night the pilgrims sing songs. There are discourses. But usually I fall asleep early on the hard ground and dream of walking. Then I wake up in the morning and walk. Of course I don't believe in any of it. My wife sends me. But when it is over after fifteen days, I cannot remember when my back became better but always, it no longer hurts. I come back to the city, tired. But my back is all right. For a while. Then it starts to hurt again."

Sartaj thought he should say something, but then the moment for speaking passed and they sat quietly next to each other. There were the distinct shapes of trees now, the walls, the top of a building across the way. Soon the colours would appear, the huge sweep of green, covering everything.

Samnagar was full of television aerials and *pucca* houses, and its share of modern amenities, Sartaj knew, was testimony towards the entrepreneurial and adventuresome spirit of its sons and daughters. Rupees and dollars and pounds sterling had updated everything except the old .303 Lee-Enfields his escort carried, which meant a certain reassuring traditionalism in the local crime. He couldn't quite decide whether the enigma he carried in the case file inside his briefcase was old or new. Go yourself, Parulkar had said. We don't have time to get her down here, we can hold the boy for only two days, three maybe, there is much political pressure. Already there are calls for your transfer.

So Sartaj had gone. "Bad road," the driver said. "Water." The house they were looking for was six miles away from the village, from the town it was becoming. The metalled road vanished after the first mile and a half, and between the fields of cotton a rutted path rose and dipped. Now, ahead, it vanished beneath a sheet of water.

"We walk," Sartaj said. He stopped caring about his pants in the first three steps, and then splashed forward furiously. The clouds piled up ahead of him, black and dense. He had a sensation of feeling quite small, under this arching sky and long silence. They walked past a grove of trees and a ruin, a single wall with a door and a window in it. As he walked, Sartaj realized a bird had been calling, again and again.

The house, when they reached it in late afternoon, was set between hedges at the intersection of three fields. There was one young constable, dozing on a *charpai* in front of the house. He woke up scrambling for his cap, panicked by Sartaj's high official presence, but managed finally to say, "She's inside."

She sat alone in a room inside, on the ground in a corner, in a widow's white and also an attitude of despair so sharp that Sartaj stopped at the door, all his eager volition to get at the heart of it gone, vanquished completely. "She hasn't said a word since she got here," her brother whispered into Sartaj's ear. "Not one." It was obvious. Her hair hung around her face and to the floor. She was staring at a point on the ground a foot ahead of her, and she didn't look up as Sartaj took off his shoes, or as he came and squatted next to her. He leaned close to her and spoke into her ear. He told her he knew everything. He told her what he knew and then conjecture as truth, the old policeman's trick: yes, this is how it happened, Kshitij found out, he saw photographs, he quarrelled with his father, something happened, something was said, correct, do you remember, but now he saw the images as he told her and he was afraid she would say, yes, that story is how it happened, he was suddenly afraid. But she looked straight ahead at the floor and he wasn't sure she heard him at all. Then he had nothing else to tell her. He stopped, and he could hear the bird calling outside. He came close to her, so that her hair tickled his nose, and he said, "I want to know how it happened. How you came to this. Kshitij said his father was not a good man." She looked at him then, and her face was homely and common to any street. Sartaj put the Polaroid down on the ground in front of her. "This is you. Did he force you to do this? Did your husband force you to go to that room in Colaba?"

She shook her head.

"Don't be afraid now," Sartaj said. "It's all over. He forced you?"

Her gaze was level, and through her grief Sartaj could feel her pride. "No," she said. "No. He didn't force me. Nobody forced me." She held him by the wrist and spoke to him, her breath hot against his cheek. She spoke fast in a Kutchi he didn't completely understand, but he understood that there was no compulsion, no solution so simple as a bad man, only a series of fragments, dinner at the Khyber with her husband and her son, their honeymoon long ago in Khandala, a train ride and an upper berth together in a crowded compartment, at breakfast he must have a glass of cold milk, a movie in Bangalore and a quarrel during interval, and Sartaj knew that what Chetanbhai and Ashaben had done together was as complete and as inexplicable as what had happened between him and Megha, real and true and impossible to tell afterwards. Somehow it had happened. Not somehow but anyhow. Things happened, Sartaj thought, one after the other, and what we want from it is a kind of shape, a case report. Now Ashaben looked up at him, holding him still, with that confessional need, and he had seen it before and he knew what it required. "I understand," Sartaj said, and understood nothing.

Before he left, he said, from the door, out of a sense of duty, "Will you testify? Would you sign a statement?" She began to weep.

As they began the trek back to the jeep it began to drizzle.

They splashed on, and then the gusts began to spray the water from the puddles up into their faces. Finally they ran for the grove of trees, past the ruined wall, and at the centre of the grove it was possible even to sit on the ground. It was damp but it was comfortable. Sartaj could see, still, through half-open eyes, the wall, the angle of the doorway. The bricks were small and oddly shaped. Sartaj had taken history in college, but he had no idea if the wall was fifty years old and English, or from a Moghul serai. Or from the other Dwarka, Krishna's ancient city, sunk now, the story said, below the waves somewhere to the south. As he sat on the ground, Sartaj could feel the earth against the back of his thighs, grainy against his calves.

"What kind of tree is this?" Sartaj said, leaning back against the trunk.

"Mango, *janaab*," the seniormost of the constables said. "Rest, *sahib*. There is plenty of time."

Sartaj was thinking of the plaster Apsara, bobbing in the water near the Narayan Housing Colony, west and north of Andheri West, Bombay. He thought of her sinking and then rising a thousand years later to confound some historian's calculations, and he laughed. He thought of the curve of her shoulder and the drops fell through the leaves above him. His eyes closed. He thought of Megha, and he tried to answer the question, Rahul's question, his own, and he said what happened to us was that we loved each other, and we were unkind to each other, and impatient, and unfaithful, and disappointed, and yet we wanted it for forever, but these are only words, and then came a flowing stream of images, dense with colour and the perfume of her hair, and it carried him. He felt himself floating and it felt easy, but then a moment of wild fear, he was sinking, he clutched and held on to himself, tightly, tightly, but then he felt his pride quicken, the word reverberated suddenly, *alacktaka*, and he made himself, he let himself go, and he was plummeting, down, into darkness.

The Rolex slid easily between Sartaj's fingers. There was pleasure, distinct and unmistakable and undiluted, in the silky fall of it against his skin, in its weight, substantial and unexpected. Under his hands there was Chetanbhai's case file, closed. It was over, according to the file, and there was a murderer who had died in the hospital. Kshitij had left that morning, walking slowly to his friends at the front of the station, and they had watched Sartaj with careful regard as he watched them.

Sartaj picked up the phone and dialled. He swung around in the chair as he listened to the steady ringing, half a dozen rings, then ten. In the glass of the map case he could see the shape of his turban.

"Hello, Ma," he said. "*Peri pauna.*" She had walked painfully across the drawing room, holding her hip, he knew this.

"*Jite raho, beta.* Where have you been?"

"Casework," he said. As she spoke he reached back far in memory, trying to find the earliest fleeting fragment of her. He remembered her in Dalhousie, a cold mountain day, her white sari in a white chair on a patio in the sunlight, the rising mountains behind, the cold white peaks far ahead. He running up to her. How old had she been then? Young, younger than Megha.

"Ma," he said.

"Yes?"

He wanted to say something to her about his father. Something about the two of them together, what they had said to each other as they walked behind him down a twisting mountain road, under the unfamiliar hill trees, leaning towards each other.

"What, Sartaj?"

He swallowed. "Nothing, Ma."

"Is something wrong?"

"No, not at all, Ma."

After he put the receiver down, Sartaj turned back to his desk, gathered up the file. As he stood up, the watch warming in his fist, he remembered suddenly his mother getting up from the kitchen table, walking behind his father, who bent over a newspaper and a cup of tea, and her hand as it brushed over the heavy shoulder, touching for a moment her husband's cheek. The small swing of the woman's hair as she walked away. And the small smile that flickered on the man's face.

There was a doorway in Sophia College Lane, across from Megha's building, where he used to wait when they had first met each other. He was hiding in it again, now, in a new uniform, and that other long-ago self felt foreign somehow, another Sartaj, faintly puzzling. There was music drifting down from a window above, a *ghazal, ye dhuan sa kahaan se uthta hai,* and the swirling rush of cars below on Warden Road. He listened to the music, and when Megha first came out of the building he didn't recognize her. Her hair was cut short, above the shoulders, and she was wearing dark glasses and she looked very stylish and young. She paused with her hand on the door of the Mercedes, raised her head up, looked about as if she had heard something. Sartaj stepped back into the shadows. Then she got in, the door shut, and the car moved off quickly, past Sartaj. He had a glimpse of her profile, and then it was gone.

He straightened up. He walked across the road, to the gate where the same gatemen waited. The first time he had visited her in her home, in what he thought were his best and dazzling jeans, they had stopped him and made him wait while they checked upstairs.

"*Sahib,*" one said. "You haven't come for a long time."

"Yes," Sartaj said. "Will you give this upstairs? In *Memsahib's* house?" This was the divorce papers, each page initialled, the last signed and dated and witnessed.

"Of course." As Sartaj walked away the gateman called, "Will you wait for a reply?"

"No need," Sartaj said. He had Katekar and the jeep waiting below, at Breach Candy, but he wanted to walk for a while. A van passed with that ugly throbbing American music that Sartaj could feel in his chest. A school bus passed, and three girls in blue uniforms smiled toothily at him from the rear window. Sartaj laughed. He twirled his moustache. In the blaring evening rush he could feel the size of the city, its millions upon millions, its huge life and all its unsolved dead. A double-decker bus ground to a halt at the stop across the street, and people jostled in and out. On the side of the bus a poster for a new movie proclaimed: "Love, Love, Love." Somewhere, also in the city, there was Kshitij and his partymen, with their building full of weapons and their dreams of the past, and Sartaj knew that nothing was finished, that they remembered him as much as he thought of them. A light changed just as Sartaj was about to cross the road, and the stream of cars jerked ahead madly, causing him to jump back, and the sidewalk vendors and their customers smiled at him. He smiled also, waiting his moment. Then he plunged in.

Artha

"NOW WHERE EXACTLY is it that you go?" said
Ayesha one evening in April. Ayesha I've known since
college, and she knows me well, and when I told her, she said,
"A dingy bar that far away, a bunch of old guys, and one oldie
telling stories? Stop *phenko*-ing, *yaar*." She thought I had a
woman hidden away somewhere, otherwise why would I leave
her and the Crimson Cheetah and the overpriced beer for
some *ghati* bar. She had been working for one of the new cable
TV companies for almost a year, so her new friends were all
models and account executives and what she called "personali-
ties," and sometimes they were so hip I couldn't understand
what they were saying to each other.

"It's true, a few old guys," I said. "Really." So she came with
me. Ayesha, once she gets curious about something, telling her
no just makes her believe you have something she needs to
know about. And anyway it pissed her off, the idea that somewhere in the city there might be a club that didn't want her, so
I think she was actually a little disappointed when Subramaniam made a place for her at the table and lit her cigarette. By
the end of the evening she was calling him Uncle Sub and teas-
ing him about why he never brought Mrs. Subramaniam to the

bar. I hadn't even known that there was a Mrs. Subramaniam. Ayesha came back two days later, and she brought two of her friends with her, both television-types in very high heels. They said they were going to produce a men's talk show on Zee TV.

So we had a sudden new crowd at the old bar. The balcony filled up with journos full of horrific election-time tales from the interior, and the younger Maruti 1000 kind of stockbrokers, and also a certain hotel-trainee group who always said, "*Hamara* group has the most fun, man," and Subramaniam still sat in his corner, and the rest of us grumbled, and I muttered about how they were going to sell the place to some fucking dairy farmer's son who would give it some *maha*-groovy name like The Purple Ant Farm and drive us all out with beer prices only foreign-bank imperialist-*choosoing* scum could afford. But really we all enjoyed it quite a bit, the free *papad* suddenly got better, and one day we came in and the tables were covered with pink plasticky tablecloths that squeaked under our elbows. It was all quite dazzling.

Now, that evening, Subramaniam had been telling Ayesha that she must get married.

"But, Uncle," she said, "suppose I do get married to somebody." She said "somebody" as two separate, very long words and rolled her eyes up to the fan. "Suppose I do, where are we going to live? Outer Kandivli?" I knew for a fact she had never been to Kandivli. "As it is," she said tragically, "the only half-decent PG one could get was in bloody Bandra."

"People live," Subramaniam said. "Somehow."

"How?" Ayesha said. "How?"

I had been watching him for weeks, him in his corner, watching us and all the others, and so I filled his glass again. "Yes," I said. "How?"

He laughed at me, his shoulders shaking. He picked up the glass and drank.

"All right," he said. "Listen."

A year or two ago (Subramaniam said) I travelled from Delhi to Bombay on the Rajdhani. This was a troubled time, we huddled in the half-empty train as it sped through the cities, watching for fires and crowds, and afraid of the rumours that flitted from one coach to the other. There was only one other person in my compartment, a thin young man in a white shirt and black pants. We had the lights off, so I saw his face illuminated in flashes by the lights that whipped by in the tearing wail of the wind. The angular shadows raced across his body, and I saw fragments of his face, tired eyes under thinning hair, unexpectedly rich lips, like a dark statue's pout, and slim hands holding each other. All put together, there was a comforting everyday ordinariness in the person who sat across the aisle from me, knee to knee, as we yearned towards our homes through our country's nocturnal madness. We were speaking —I admit it — of Beauty and Art. When I said that phrase, those words, "Beauty and Art," he laughed shortly.

"I could tell you a thing or two about that," he said.

"Do," I said. "Please." We went across a bridge then, with that sudden hollow mournful note to the train's racheting, and he watched me.

"Because I'll never see you again," he said. "My name is changed, and also the others, slightly. But everything else is true."

"Yes, I understand," I said. "Please tell me."

And so he told me a story. On that train, that night. This is what he told me.

Twenty rupees and twenty paise is not so much (the young man said), but it's exactly worth a man's job, and his career, and so his life. We knew this that afternoon when Das called and told us we had thirteen days to find the problem and fix it.

"Then I have to tell my bosses," he said, and left it at that, which was very polite of him, considering that he had taken our bid for their inventory and accounting software against bigger companies, and that too in an organization where they thought calculators were flashy and unreliable compared to a good abacus.

"They'll throw him out, Iqbal," Sandhya said.

There was no use saying no for the sake of comfort, because it was obvious. "Not if we find the bug," I said. Das had pushed our bid through, against all the old men who owned the company, and now if they found out this program written by a woman was not only crashing but losing money here and there, just disappearing it into outer space, they would have him out on the street before the quarterly meeting was over. Not to forget our payment, which was only a third in our pockets yet.

"Shit, Iqbal," Sandhya said. "Thirteen days."

"Let's find it then. Twenty rupees and twenty paise."

"Right," she said, straightening up in that torn and tattered chair she loved, and smiling at me. "Let's find it."

She was trying to be a leader, like those people in the management books she kept buying from Crossword, but I could see she was tired to the bone. Putting in a new software application will do that to you, because something always goes wrong on the site, what works at home never works there, and the damn users always have one idea after another, and they tell you to change this and that, as if you can wave a wand and it's all done, and you can't even tell the bastards they okayed this exact design three months ago. Plus this was our first solo project, our first very own thing for Mega Computers, Ltd., and let me tell you, looking at Sandhya I could see that running your own company sounds fine until you actually run it. And besides I wasn't much help.

"What do you mean you aren't any help?" Rajesh said later

that night. He had been waiting for me as usual at the bus stop on the corner of Carter Road. "You're there all day and most of the night, working for her."

It was past eleven, and most of the shops were shut. I could feel a swelling from the sea against my face, a hint of coolness. I put an arm around his shoulder.

"But not all of the night," I said, touching his hair with the tips of my fingers. He shrugged my arm off. We walked on, and I said, "I help with the kid, and the accounting, I pay the bills, I even keep the mother quiet, I make tea for the painter, but I can't help her with what she does."

"You're a programmer," he said sullenly. "You said so."

Even our quarrels were familiar and shapely now. We fit each other snugly. I put my hand on the back of his hip, with a finger looped through a belt loop, and told him again that I coded high and she coded low, that when I cranked out my bread-and-butter xBase database rubbish I was shielded from the machine by layers and layers of metaphor, while she went down, down toward the hardware in hundreds of lines of C++ that made my head hurt just to look at them, and then there were the nuggets of assembly language strewn through the app, for speed when it was really important, she said, and in these critical sections it was all gone from me, away from any language I could even feel, into some cool place of razor-sharp instructions, "MOV BYTE PTR [BX],16." But she skated in easy, like she had been born speaking a tongue one step away from binary.

"Me-ta-phor?" Rajesh said. "You've been speaking to the painter."

We were on the rocks now, under the seawall, and I made a big show of finding my footfalls in the darkness, even though I knew each jagged outcrop a little better than the steps to my room in my house, my parents' house. The rocks bulked up above us, and in the darkness there were the huddled shapes of bodies, couples in the niches and the shadows.

"Of course I've been speaking to the painter," I said, facing out to the sea. "I can hardly help it if he's in the flat all the time. Sandhya is madly in love with him."

"He's in all the time, is he? Talking about me-ta-phors?" He pulled me back so that I settled against him, as always with the lovely surprise of the taut muscles of his chest and thighs, shaped and solid. His eyelashes moved like feathers against the rim of my ear. "You like the painter when he talks about me-ta-phors?"

I laughed quietly, and turned my face for a kiss, for his lips a little bitter with the day but welcome and hungry and supple. "Not only then," I said, still laughing, and then gasped from his hand scooping roughly under my belt. "Not only. But so do you like him." Rajesh wasn't talking then, but touching with careful tenderness the contour of my collarbone, and I was starting to move in a tight frenzy under the distant movement of the tide, with a sound caught in my throat, and as long as I could, a glance and another for the top of the seawall, where sometimes the policemen strolled.

Afterwards, Rajesh was depressed. He slouched down the road, and I walked behind, watching the shape of his back. Rajesh worked out at a *bhaiyya* gym near his house in Sion, in a pit of fine sand surrounded by gleaming wrestlers. I had gone there and watched him once, the dense chocolate length of his body under the buzzing tubelights, and the white *langot* pulled tightly between his buttocks. I watched the whirl of the weights and told the wrestlers he was my best friend.

"I'm sick of this," Rajesh said.

"What?" I said, but I knew.

"Screwing on the rocks," he said. "I'm thirty-two years old. I want to fuck in my flat."

His flat wasn't his flat, but a flat that he wanted, in a building off Yari Road. It was a rectangular yellow building, with a staircase that ran around the insides, and red doors every few yards along the long dim corridors. Rajesh's flat was a narrow entrance passageway, a bathroom to the left, a kitchen ahead, and a single twelve-by-twelve-foot room to the right.

"So how much is it today?" I said.

"Twenty-two lakhs," he said, and added hopelessly, "and sixty-five thousand."

He checked Bombay prices every week, with a kind of grim pride as they climbed and spiralled away.

"The most expensive real estate in the world," he said expansively. "Pricier than Tokyo and New York."

So there might be a room in Tokyo or New York for a programmer and a postal clerk, or at least a better fantasy—this is what I wanted to say, but I reached for his hand and held it until we got to the bus stop with its quiet row of exhausted shopworkers and drivers and cooks. We sat there, hand in hand, looking just like two best friends, until the bus came, with its despairing midnight grinding of gears, and then I couldn't stand anymore the look on his face and reached forward and crushed him as hard as I could into my arms, and found his stubbled kiss for a moment amidst the sudden jostle of the passengers on and off. He shook his head at me, but with a tiny bit of a smile. Then the bus pulled away and I was alone.

The painter was crouched on the floor of his room, clutching at the spread-out sheets of a newspaper, when I reached Sandhya's house the next morning. Rajesh and I always called him the painter, mainly because neither of us had ever met a painter before, but his name was Anubhav Rajadhakshya, and he was tearing at *The Times of India*.

"Bastard," he said, his face an inch away from the newsprint. "Bastard, bastard, bastard."

"What's wrong, Anu?" I said. I stepped over the scattered

sheets, to the back of the room where he had a canvas tilted up on an old desk, in front of the big window that went across the whole length of the wall.

"What? Iqbal . . . Nothing, it's nothing."

The long canvas had colour in it at the top, a wash of red and yellows and black. In the painting, in the background, there was a poster for *Deewar*, that one, you know, Amitabh Bachchan with the coolie's rope around his neck and legs wide apart. In front of it there was a man, a real young man with a cigarette, leaning against the wall, not coloured in yet.

"All balls, Anu," I said. "Don't try to be so cool and careless. You look like you want to kill somebody in the paper. What's the deal?"

"Fuck you also, Iqbal," he said, and settled back on his heels. "All right. Listen to this. 'Mr. Vidyarthi's installation is a succinct comment on the restricted imaginative life and the repressed, bubbling anger of the lumpen. He artfully uses elements of Bombay street kitsch to achieve a nearly absolute expression of spatial nullification and emotional withdrawal. A series of incisions on the rear wall leak sheets of water — a potent psycho-symbolic image of unconscious energy leaking into and through artistic expression, yet unnoticed by the installation's absent inhabitants. His project is the crystallization of emptiness.' Now look at this." This was a grainy, shadowy picture of a room filled with pieces of wood, brass utensils, a sagging *charpai*, a torn mattress, torn movie posters, and framed pictures of gods and goddesses, and some other stuff hanging from the roof that I couldn't quite make out. There was a wall with cracks running across it.

"And so?" Anubhav said. "Succinct comment, you think?"

"If it's in *The Times of India*," I said, "it must be true."

"*Maderchod*," Anubhav burst out. "Why do I even try with people like you? It's the most silly, the most facile, easy bullshit I've ever seen. It's, it's completely lacking in talent. That fucking Mahatre is so impressed by the simple fact that it's an *installation* that he thinks it must be really mod and good. Fuck. Fuck. Fuck." By now he was shredding *The Times* and tossing the pieces about as he walked back and forth, and I was trying to hide my smile as I edged carefully out of the room. Anu's habit of thinking he was smarter and better than everybody else always made it easy to fuck with his trip. Or maybe it was that he thought that the rest of us were a little more stupid than him. Either way he was sexy when he was all angry and running about giving speeches about art and life.

In the long corridor outside Sandhya's mother was shuffling her slippers along. I sang, "*Namaste*, Ma-ji," and she threw a glance over her shoulder and crept on, holding her sari carefully an inch above the gleaming stone. She didn't like me very much, and I knew that not very behind my back she called me *kalua* and *musalta* and *kattu*, which was true enough, my skin was blacker than theirs, not by a little but much, and I was Muslim, and I was very definitely circumcised, and they were very exalted Brahmins of the green-eyed Maharashtrian variety and so very pure. I suppose I should have hated Ma-ji for thinking of me quite straightforwardly as low-caste in Muslim disguise, but then there was my father every evening going on about "kafirs" and "dirty Hindu buggers," which last made Rajesh laugh always, because dear father knew not what he said.

Ma-ji turned the corner slowly, into the kitchen where she liked to harass Amba *bai* about her cooking. She went, whispering prayers under her breath, mixed, I could swear, with occasional curses directed at Anubhav. She looked at me usually with a kind of vague distaste, but she detested him truly, and I could see why, because I had said much the same things to Sandhya — he was a shifty painter with uncertain income and slippery intentions — but Sandhya thought he was Bohemian, and so now he used one of the rooms in her house as his studio. When she first used that word, "Bohemian," she explained it to me, but pretty much as I could work it out it meant somebody who lived with his parents and didn't have a place to hang his brushes and didn't want to get married, which made me a Bohemian also, but she didn't find that very funny. She told me I was ignorant and uncultured. She — under Anubhav's supervision — had been buying art books at Crossword also, big glossy affairs, each of which cost more than a dozen management texts put together. This is the trouble with people who get their first good sex when they're thirty. You tell them the truth and they talk about culture.

Now, though, she wasn't thinking of culture. She was leaning into the bluish-white glow from a seventeen-inch monitor, motionless as a stalking crane and as acutely alive, fingers lightly on the keys. I shut the door to her office behind me, said her name once, then again, and it wasn't the jet-like roar of the old air conditioner that kept her from hearing me.

"Sandhya," I said again, a little louder. I had learnt not to tap her on the shoulder — it was like waking a sleepwalker, and scarier for me than for her, that sudden strangled sound she made, and the absence in her eyes. "Sandhya."

She turned to me finally, slowly and reluctantly. When she hadn't slept much, her skin became translucent somehow, so that you saw how small she really was, and how her will and velocity pushed always against the delicacy of her body, and also the cost.

"Trains ran late this morning," I said. It was necessary to talk of exactly nothing for the first minute or two, until she had left the shimmering world where wisps of code slid noiselessly against each other, until she inhabited firmly the person in the chair in front of me. "Also there was an accident near the Pedder Road flyover."

Her regard was square-on but dispassionate, cool and uninterested. "Budget will be presented tomorrow in Parliament," I said, and finally her eyes narrowed and she saw me, saw me really, I mean.

"Iqbal," she said. "*Kaisa hai*?"

"I'm alive," I said. "But you're looking a little hard-labour this morning, dear. When did you sleep?"

"Four," she said, passing a hand over her face. "Don't be mean." This meant she had perhaps slept at four and woken up at six to get Lalit ready and off to school, or had maybe not slept at all, but tossed about on the double bed for a while, twisting some function or procedure inside out as the sky lightened outside.

"Go take a bath," I said, and dragged her chair towards the door.

"Iq-bal," she said.

"Tihar Jail is not a good look during the day, Sandhya. And think of what the worshipper-of-beauty would say."

"He's here?"

"Yes."

"He's not a beauty-worshipper, Iqbal," she said wearily. "He's a serious artist." She slumped out of the door. I spun her chair back against her desk and began to clean, starting with her keyboard, which as always was muddy with tea stains. The room was jammed with hardware — we ran a Novell server with four terminals, all the way from an old XT to a Pentium 166, and we had two printers, one ancient wide-carriage Epson dot matrix, and a Laserjet that had recently started to vibrate violently every thirty pages or so. We had a reed *chick* over the window to keep out the heat, but in the afternoons the air conditioner roared alarmingly, and my toes near the grey computer chassis under my desk would start to get warm. Then there were the manuals stacked above the desks to the roof, and boxes of disks and tapes, and accordion-like thicknesses of printouts, and the chairs back to back. Even if we could have afforded two more coders for our free terminals we had nowhere to put them, because we understood completely that two in that room was already one too much, and four would lead to murder. I did my best with the manuals and the printouts, stacking them evenly against the wall, and put pens in cups and threw away crumpled pieces of paper. Then I straightened out our steno pads and cleaned the phones with an old towel. Finally I wiped off our screens. When I finished with the room I had something that wasn't quite order, and far from beauty, but a place where you could live one more day. Then I got to work.

Sandhya came in with her hair in a towel, wearing a white *kurta* and jeans. She sat at her desk and the keys started clicking, and meanwhile I opened envelopes and wrote up invoices and typed out cheques. The minutes passed, and when I turned my head, I could see, over Sandhya's shoulder, the lines of black letters moving up and down the white screen, too fast for me to read. She had a bad habit, when she was debugging, of also polishing up, snipping here and there to make everything tighter, and now she sat wrapped in the glorious mantle of her concentration, her cheekbones purified by her devotion. Elegance, elegance, she said to me always. My code was patchy and twisty and knotted together, like MTNL phone wiring, and if it worked I didn't really care if it was creaky, but that was the difference between us, and one reason why I loved her so.

"All right, genius," I said, rubbing her shoulders. "Time for a break."

I kept rubbing, and finally she leaned back, away from the keyboard.

"Shit," she said. "How long has it been?"

"Hour and fifteen minutes."

"Went like a flash."

It always did. We had an arrangement that I would stop her every hour for a ten-minute rest period, which she had agreed to only when she had started getting cramps in her arms and shoulders so bad that it would stop her working for half a day at a time. She was still peering at the monitor, though.

"Why's this thing crashing, Iqbal?"

"I don't know," I said, and spun her chair around. She tilted her head back and drew her knees up to her chest and made a tight little smile.

"He came yesterday evening," she said. "After you had left."

I recognized the grimace and I knew who he was. He was her ex-husband, Vasant, who behaved as if he were even now not only her husband but still her all-holy *Parameshwar*, with the resulting godly duties of visiting suffering and pain upon her. "What the hell did he want?"

"He was angry about Anubhav again."

I looked at her keenly, checking, and she turned her face away. Vasant had hit her only once after the divorce, but the Anubhav thing made him rage, and he was capable of anything. "And?"

"He said he would go to court to show that I was an immoral woman. Of loose character. Not fit to raise Lalit."

"Please. He should be the last one to talk. If we went to court what-all we could show."

"Yes. That's what he said anyway. He was very abusive."

"Bastard."

"Yes. Anyway. Back to work."

She spun her chair around and a moment passed and then slowly the keyboard began to click. I listened to it, waiting for the usual headlong swiftness. *Parameshwar* is a word I heard in real life for the first time from Ma-ji, when I first started to work for Sandhya. Until then I had heard it only in movies, but Ma-ji wanted Sandhya to stay with Vasant, in spite of everything, she really said it, because he was *Parameshwar*. You must learn to endure, Ma-ji had said to her own daughter, and although I was the new employee and everything, I had wanted to scream at her, endure how much, for what? I never did, though, all the way through the complications of the divorce, through Vasant's threats, his attempts to snatch the flat from her, to drive her away from her own father's property, her loneliness, her fear for her son being taken away from her. I had never asked my mother either, my mother who taught me eternal patience and *sabr* in the name of another saviour. Endure. How much, for what?

The next evening we all went to an arty party. The party was actually called an opening, for someone who was a friend of Anubhav's whose name I didn't recognize. This was on day two of our countdown, eleven days left and the bug still hiding somewhere, flitting elusively just beyond Sandhya's grasp. Sandhya was wearing a black power suit and a new silk scarf, bright red, and her hair swept over her cheek and to her shoulder in a long elegant line. Rajesh and I clapped when she model-walked out into the drawing room and twirled for us. But she slept in the cab, despite the heat and the blaring traffic jam, her head swaying on the back of the seat. When her mouth lolled open, Rajesh reached over and gently nudged it shut. "Mad girl," he said, grinning, and for the rest of the ride he held her by the shoulder and kept her steady. Despite all his grumbling about my hours and my late-coming, during her trouble he had offered to put out *supari* on Vasant. Five thousand rupees only, he had said, making a pistol barrel with his fingers, *tap-tap*, two in the back of the head and you won't even hear of the *maderchod*'s memory again. I'd laughed at him, and had told him he was cute when he was dangerous.

At the Pushkara Gallery we woke Sandhya, which was no easy task, because in the three kilometres and forty minutes of the ride she had fallen deep into sleep. She woke up with a start, paid the cabbie, checked herself in the rearview mirror, stepped out onto the pavement with her little black purse held in front of her, and then we followed as she marched in, past the gleaming glass door held open by a *durban,* her shoulders moving smartly in time with the clipping of her heels. Rajesh and I looked at each other as we trotted behind, because normally we would have been a little scared of going into a place like that, but with Sandhya leading we were afraid of nothing, not even the very little look a woman gave us as we came in, a woman dressed in a Rajasthani *ghagra* and *choli* with mirrors all over, and a black rural-type *bindi* on her forehead. It's the little looks that rule the world. But we, despite our sweat-stained fifty-percent-rayon shirts, were in past the *durban* and his door, and so Rajesh and I, we found our usual place at these things, with our backs to a wall and not very far from the bar. Sandhya was off looking for Anubhav in the crowd, which was floating from here to there and laughing and trilling, and, I have to say, smelling really good. Soon we had glasses of champagne, which was our very new vice, with its thin little taste of foreign wickedness. We drank it fast.

"What's that one looking like a calendar for?" Rajesh said, turning his eyes towards the mirrored one, who was still giving us those deadly looks now and then. I think maybe she owned the place.

"It's Rajasthani, idiot," I said.

"So?"

"Means ethnic, you know."

"I don't. Ethnic *manjhe?*"

"Ethnic means real. Like from a village."

He looked baffled, but then Sandhya came leaning through the crowd, dragging Anubhav behind her. Anubhav was wearing a white silk *kurta,* very traditional, with a black shawl draped over one shoulder, and if someone tells you beauty doesn't matter, they've never been to an arty party. Anubhav wasn't good-looking exactly, but he had curly black hair cut in a thick halo around his head, a fine long nose, lovely brown eyes, good height, and as I looked around, squinting through a silvery champagne haze, I saw how everyone looked longingly at him, at the comeliness of his expensive English-medium arrogance, at the impervious grandeur of his self-regard. Standing next to him, we were peasants.

He nodded at us. I raised my glass, and he ever so slightly gave us his shoulder and began to talk to some people on the other side of Sandhya. A feeling passed like a shadow over Rajesh's face, not disappointment or resentment but a single flicker of hope. I wasn't jealous—it wasn't desire, not that at all—no, I felt it also, the eternal dazzlement of the outsider. I touched Rajesh's hand and raised my glass at him and we drank. Then a man passed us. He was a small man, dressed all in white, but when he walked through the crowd it drew apart for him. His gaze passed impersonally over me as he went.

"You know him?" It was Anubhav, raising an eyebrow at Rajesh. "I saw him look at you."

"Who was he?" I said.

"That was Ratnani," Rajesh said. I shook my head. "Ratnani, Ratnani Construction. Really, Iqbal, sometimes you're so stupid. Ratnani's built half the big buildings in the city."

"Ah," I said. "Of course."

"So how do you know him?" Anubhav said. "Tell me, *yaar*." He was standing next to Rajesh now, a hand on his shoulder. Rajesh shrugged and made a show of emptying his glass. But I could see he was pleased.

"I work for him," Rajesh said.

"I thought you worked for the Post Office," Anubhav said.

"No," Rajesh said. "I work for Mr. Ratnani."

I laughed, and snorted a gulp of champagne into my nose. Anubhav watched me splutter and dab at myself. "You're a liar," he said to Rajesh. And he turned away.

"No, I'm not," Rajesh said. He said it quietly, but he was angry, and I believed him. I put a hand on his arm. What he was saying, what I suddenly believed, made no sense. But he was looking past me, at Anubhav.

"Hundreds of people in Bombay work for Ratnani," Anubhav said. "So maybe you did something for somebody who works for him."

"Not like that," Rajesh said. "I work for him directly. Even to his house I've been. I could introduce you."

"Sure," Anubhav said in English, smiling. "Sure."

"Come on," Rajesh said, and he shrugged me away. He took Anubhav by the arm and led him through the crowd. I followed, frantic now, I don't know why, pushing through and leaving a trail of outraged glances and whispers. Rajesh and Anubhav moved in a half-circle through the room, but Ratnani was nowhere to be seen. They stood in a corner now, craning their heads. I was staring at Rajesh, trying to catch his eye, and past him I saw Ratnani shoving open a black door. Rajesh followed my glance and saw the white shoulder and white pants, and then the door closed.

Inside the bathroom Ratnani's whites were overpowering. The walls were black marble, the floors were black, the urinals were black, even the mirrors somehow had a black tinge to them. I could see Anubhav's reflection repeated again and again in the glass. The room was so large and cool and luxurious I would have been afraid to piss in there. But Ratnani was standing in front of one of the urinals, his legs spread wide, his head thrown back. He looked as if he were thinking of something very important. The sound of his urination was loud.

"*Salaam, sahib,*" Rajesh said.

Ratnani turned his head, looked at Rajesh for a moment, then turned back to his reflection in the wall. "*Salaam,*" he said.

"I'm Rajesh Pawar, sir."

The tinkling slowed and stopped. Ratnani hunched his shoulders, and I heard the sound of his zipper. He turned to the row of washbasins. "Good," he said. His face was wide and dark and heavy, and his hair receded on both sides of his forehead, leaving a narrow peak.

Rajesh stepped forward, turned a tap on. Ratnani leaned forward, soaped and washed his hands. When he finished, Rajesh handed him a small white towel. "I work for you, sir."

"Really?" Ratnani said, drying his hands. "That's good."

"You remember I came to your house, sir?"

"Many people come to my house."

"But I came with . . . "

Ratnani handed the towel to Rajesh, and looked at him directly. His eyes were calm. "I've never seen you before," he said. Then he turned, stepped past Anubhav, and pushed the door open. Before the door could shut behind him, Anubhav had gone through it. Then Rajesh and I were alone, he with the towel still in his right hand.

"Rajesh," I said.

He turned away from me, towards the basins. I put a hand on his shoulder and he jerked it off, took another step, further, his face turned away, and it was absurd but I had the sense that he was crying. I had never seen him cry. So I pushed through the black door, back into the noise, and Sandhya and Anubhav were standing nearby, their heads close together. I walked over to them, and we were then surrounded by a sudden knot of people, they laughed and shook hands with Anubhav and Sandhya and me, I saw white teeth shining, and diamonds, and a face receded away from me, floating like a flower on the swell of clinking chatter.

I blinked, and I heard Anubhav's voice, raised high: "Nice work, Vidyarthi. Interesting. Really interesting." A waiter came through the crowd, holding up a tray. I turned away, a new glass in my hand, and the roiling crowd carried me along as I drank. I went as hopelessly as, as a man without a friend in the world. The cold liquid came past the constriction in my throat and stumbled me and I laughed, and laughed again. I stood in the centre of the long room and held the glass in front of my face and drank slowly and carefully. When the glass was empty I went back to the bathroom and found it empty. I pushed at the door to each of the stalls and found them unoccupied. Outside, I saw Sandhya, just her red scarf and the angle of her cheekbone through a commotion of shoulders. I pushed my way through, and she was talking to the mirrored woman and a man with his hair held back in a ponytail. They were standing on two sides of her, with her face close between theirs.

"Sandhya," I said, putting a hand on her shoulder. "Where's Rajesh?"

"Not now, Iqbal," she said.

"But Rajesh."

"I haven't seen him." She and the other two looked at me for a long moment. "I'm buying, Iqbal."

What, I wanted to ask, and with what exactly, but the man took Sandhya by the elbow and the ethnic woman pointed to something on the opposite side of the gallery, and they went, all holding on to each other. I took another glass off a tray and trudged along. I was suddenly heavy with exhaustion, and the light came in spirals, circling around my head. As I leaned close to a canvas the colours breathed across its surface, filling my eyes with a roseate brightness.

"If you stand further away you can see what it is," somebody said loudly into my ear.

"I want to see what it's made of," I said, and I heard footsteps tapping away. I could feel myself swaying back and forth, towards and away from the intricate pattern of ridges and valleys snaking across the orange and the green. Then there was a hand on my shoulder. I shuffled myself around, and it was the mirrored woman. I leaned towards her chest, wanting to see myself, and she backed away, her nose wrinkling.

"Don't be afraid of me," I said. "Not like that. Just want to see."

Sandhya appeared behind her, rolling her eyes. "All right, Iqbal," Sandhya said. "Home. Come on." She took my hand and towed me through the crush, and now they all stepped back to let us pass. I snarled, and laughed when they stepped on each other's feet.

Outside, on the sidewalk, the ethnic woman caught up with us. "Talk to you tomorrow, Sandhya," she said.

"Absolutely," Sandhya said.

"Lovely meeting you, darling." She fluttered her fingers and shut the door firmly behind her.

"Where's Rajesh?" I said.

"I didn't see him in there," Sandhya said. "I think he's gone."

"I can't go without him," I said, but she cut me away from the glass door, nudged me to a Maruti parked under a poster for *Droh Kaal*.

"Don't *do* anything," she said. "Stay here. I'll be back."

It was dark now. The hood of the car was hot, and the air moved snugly against me, and I felt sweat running down my back. I shut my eyes and breathed deeply, once and again, against the constriction, against the sopping weight of myself. But still I could feel my skin burning, heavy and inescapable, and I opened my eyes and I could see the bluish square of the door, like a crystal, and the faint golden and silver shapes floating within. And then the music, ethereal and distant, which must have been always there but only now in my ears. I listened to it carefully. As if it were trying to tell me something. I turned my head and saw another man leaning on a car, a driver, I thought. He lit his cigarette and in the sudden flare I saw his tired face, a thin moustache. We waited together.

Then the door opened and Sandhya came up quickly to me, shaking her head. "He's not here. He's gone."

"He just left?"

"I'm going to put you in a taxi," she said.

"I can take the train."

"Don't be silly. I'm going to put you in a taxi." And she did, literally, holding on to my arm, and lowering my head into the seat. She folded a hundred-rupee note into my shirt pocket, and shut the door without a word.

"Where do you think Rajesh went?" I asked, but we were already halfway down the block, and the driver turned his head to look at me, but he had no answer, and neither did the city, my city which went by swiftly and gleaming in the dark. We swept over the long arc of Marine Drive, through Kemp's Corner, down Pedder Road, Mahalaxmi, Worli, Mahim, and the concrete loomed above, white in the moonlight, higher than I ever remembered, and I lay helpless under its weight, crushed by its certain beauty.

"Parameshwar, Parameshwar." Ma-ji exhaled softly as she lowered herself onto the far end of the couch, next to me but far away. I was sitting in the long passageway, puffing viciously at a cigarette, against my pulsing headache and anger and desolation. I had given them up four years ago, but now I had decided that Rajesh had left me at the Pushkara Gallery, left me — and I knew this somehow even before I woke up — for some fancy prancing rich boy. In his anger and sulks, he had gone, gone, despite his workingman's muscular solidarity and his accusations about me, me, telling me always to go back to my Malabar-Hill-Fair-and-Lovely-brand queens that I liked so much. So now I pulled on the foul taste, a tonic for the bitterness in my heart, and even the miracle of Ma-ji choosing to sit beside me, even if at arm's and a leg's length, it amused me worth nothing, less than nothing, and I sat blowing smoke.

"Twenty-two thousand for *that*," she said, and it was all clear. That was the painting the mirrored woman (whose name turned out to be Miss Viveka Gupta) had brought to the house that morning, wrapped in double and triple sheets of newspaper and carried by two men in shorts and bare feet, and twenty-two thousand was the price, in white only and all by cheque, and since I was the one who cut the drafts and quarrelled always with Sandhya about how she scattered and flung about her own money like pigeon-feed, I was now Ma-ji's friend against waste and frippery. She had spent the morning watching from the door of the drawing room, as Miss Viveka supervised and her *mistris* took down the framed poster of the Eiffel Tower from the long wall, used a level to pencil-mark heights and angles, and as they hung up the twenty-two-thousand-rupee masterpiece. All the time Ma-ji had cursed under her breath.

"It's art, Ma-ji," I said.

She looked at me as if I were mad. "Art? And what, we are *nawabs*?"

"I think you are, Ma-ji," I said. "Definitely, at least *rajas*."

She looked at me out of her watery grey eyes, the white *pallu* wrapped tightly about her head, not quite sure whether to be flattered or infuriated, and she glanced at the drawing room door, and I could see that the invisible and mighty presence of the twenty-two-thousand-act-of-genius was tilting her rapidly towards breaking our tiny truce, but then Lalit came running out of the kitchen and saved me.

"Iq-bal Uncle," he said, flinging himself forward on his grandmother's knee. "I want an aquarium."

"A what?"

"An aqua-ri-um, Iq-bal *ghonchu* Uncle," he said, as Ma-ji smoothened his hair down with both her hands. She worried always about the parting in his hair. "For fish, don't you know?"

"I know, I know," I said. "But where you got this crackpot idea from?"

"From the sea," Lalit said. "In there." He shrugged away his grandmother's arms without looking at her, but easy and gentle, and pulled on my sleeve until I stood up and let myself be dragged to the drawing room door. He stood next to me, leaning on my leg, and pointed at the painting on the wall.

"The sea," he announced, with the pride of someone who had created it.

It was a square canvas, about five feet each way, and with a wash of green and blue that seemed to seep off the painting, into the air, so the whole room seemed suddenly marine. There were dark shadows in it, that came and went as you looked. I suppose it was the sea if it was anything.

"The sea," I said. "And so you want an aquarium?"

"Of course," Lalit said, laughing at my backwardness. "For fishes."

"Of course," I said.

"It's going to cost a lot, this aqua-ri-um," Ma-ji said under my shoulder. She always took an age to go from here to there, but just when you stopped watching her she would turn up with startling suddenness, blowing curses over your skin. Now, again, as my pulse jangled, she boxed her hands over Lalit's ears and whispered, "And this painting, so much money. Such bad habits she's teaching him."

Lalit was hanging on to my shirt, leaning forward towards all this, through the drawing room door, which he wasn't allowed to enter. The drawing room contained Sandhya's new Swedish-looking sofa and couches with white cushions, her glass-topped coffee table, her crystal imported from America, her new blue carpet with the Persian pattern on it, her flowers which looked so real you couldn't tell. It was a perfect room, and none of us were allowed to enter it. Even Sandhya hardly went in there.

"Careful, Lalitya," I said. "Don't cross the line."

Now the phone rang and my heart lifted. It rang again, and I wanted to go to it, but Lalit was still a weight against my leg, and Ma-ji was muttering behind me somewhere, and I was flooded with relief and trying to remember to be angry. The ringing cut off abruptly, and I started slowly down the corridor, carrying Lalit with me. Then I heard Sandhya down the hall.

"Iqbal!" she said. "Another crash. It's Das. Another crash, and this time the whole system's frozen."

She appeared in the door to the office, her face stricken. I gathered up my tools, and waited by the front door, by the orange statue of Ganesha, while she dressed for the outside world. From where I was leaning against the wall, I could see Anubhav working in his room. He was wearing shorts and a T-shirt, and he was squatting on his heels, holding a thick brush with a long grip, and it moved over the canvas with a whirring sound. The brush moved back and forth, and I could see the splatters of paint on his knees. He was working hard, had been all day, harder than I had ever seen.

"Eh, Anu," I said. "Listen." I said his name two more times, and then walked into the room and tapped him on the shoulder.

"What?" he said, still looking at the canvas.

"Last night. Did you send Rajesh out of the gallery? To get cigarettes or something?"

"What, me? No." He turned his head and looked up at me. There were tiny dots of paint on his face.

"Did you see him leaving?"

"No. After that bullshit in the bathroom with Ratnani I don't know where he went. Why?"

"It's nothing. I just don't know when he left."

"He was high, man. Telling stupid stories like that. Must've fallen asleep somewhere on the way home."

Anubhav turned back to his painting. Rajesh's lies weren't very interesting to him. I had believed Rajesh, and I was afraid.

"Come on," Sandhya said, coming down the hall in a green

suit. Outside, the sudden blaze of the sun hurt my eyes. The traffic ground past us in a solid stream, and all the taxis were full. We waited. I turned and looked up at the building, at the four stories of long curving balconies. It had been built in fifty-four, when they had built balconies everywhere, and those rounded corners, but now there were only chips of yellow paint left here and there, and most of Sea Vista was now black. The cars were dragging past us in starts and stops, inch by inch. Then it all stopped with a blare of horns, and we waited.

You can lose yourself in hardware. It takes only a twist or two, some pressure maybe, to break a coax cable, but tracing a cable break is long and careful hours with a crimping tool and terminal pings and NIC tests. When Sandhya and I got to the factory everything, each last terminal, was frozen solid, a cursor blinking hysterically from each screen. So she brought down the server and I got to work, walking each black cable length, looking for sharp bends, cuts in the casing, anything. The factory, which was called Sridhar and Sons, Ltd., was built on a big L-shaped plot in the Okhla Industrial Estates behind Nataraj Studios. I followed the cable through the executive cabins in the building at the front of the plot, under desks and over partitions ("a terminal on every manager's desk and so instant information," we had told them), around the production sheds where with great whines and clatters they made what they called custom high-heat high-performance parts for oil technology applications, which meant nothing to me except as data from which we missed twenty rupees and twenty paise and more, again and again and now and then, and probably now again, and I went then back out again into the sunlight, following the cable, which went outdoors in its protective plastic shell which snaked over the wall covered with red splatters of *paan,* across the small yard littered with *bidis,* and into the raw materials shed at the back of the plot, where sheets of metal and coils and tubes were stacked to the ceiling, with the cable slung above, over the tubelights and back down to the little room, a cupboard, really, carved out of the wall between the storage area and the accountant's office, and in this closet we had one terminal, and the server. Sandhya sat coiled in front of it.

"Seek errors," she said, and I could hardly hear her above the rattling air conditioner which hung precariously above the door. "Seek errors, seek errors. And our tables are corrupted."

"And twenty rupees and twenty paise?"

"Gone, this time thirty rupees and fourteen paise, gone again."

"The cable looks all right. I'll run terminal checks."

I did, one by one by one all the way out to the executive cabins, and then I went back to raw materials and checked the power and the UPS, and then I opened up the server and pulled the hard disk controller. The machine was a big tower, which we had pushed up all the way against one side of the room, next to the terminal, both against a locked door which opened into the accounting offices, and even then I had to send Sandhya out into the passageway when I opened the case. I leaned my back against the wall and worked the board out, cleaned the gold contacts, settled it back in, checked for a firm seat, all gone home and snug in the slot, hooked in the cables, stared helplessly at the lovely design, at the exact fit of the components against each other, how can it not work, and then closed it up and went outside. We had already replaced the controller twice, and the hard disk once.

Sandhya was leaning against the door.

"It's all working," I said.

"I know," she said. "It must be software. Has to be. Let's go home."

And then, suddenly, I was overcome by sadness. It came out of the endless azure sky and settled in my bones. I looked out at the yard, at its scattered pieces of paper, the two workers squatting against the wall with their bare knees shining, at the scattered bits of smoke around their heads, and I was hopeless.

"All right," I said, but when I went in to pack up my screwdrivers, Manishi-ji came out of the accounting office and pulled us in for a cup of tea.

"A cup of tea only," he said, waving us towards the two chairs in front of the foot-high platform that took up most of the room. He and the other accountant, Raunak-ji, had little inclined desks that they sat behind, on either side of the platform.

"O Raju," Raunak-ji called, and when Raju came in, a boy of about fourteen in oversized khaki shorts, Raunak-ji said, "Two *chai,* 'pecial, and biscuit."

"No, really, nothing to eat," Sandhya said.

"Nonsense, *beta,*" Manishi-ji said. "You've been working hard. Must keep up the energy."

And Raunak-ji nodded. When I had first seen them, seated on their thrones behind the desks, I had thought they were twins, or at least brothers, with identical balding heads and pained expressions and thick round specs. They were both in their mid-fifties and wore white shirts and the same Bata sandals. They lived in their dank room lined with blue ledgers from floor to ceiling, balancing and balancing away, and I wondered if they knew about the twenty rupees and twenty paise. So I smiled, in spite of the sludgy bitterness in my veins, and Sandhya did, through her taut sheen of fatigue, and she talked to them about the stock market. They argued and laughed together, and I watched them. The only colour in the room came from the big safe against the wall behind them, an old Godrej painted a rusty red and covered with those little metal locket-type pictures of Ganesha and Lakshmi and Shiva with magnets on the back. There were so many gods and goddesses on the safe that you saw the red only in patches, and there was even an Air India Jumbo flying up the front of the safe, winging right through the holiness.

Then Raju brought the tea in, and we ate the biscuits as he poured. I found myself very hungry and took large bites. Raunak-ji dipped his biscuits in his tea and chomped with sturdy teeth. I ate and tried not to think of Rajesh.

Afterwards, we walked down the street to the corner, stepping through the pools of light under the streetlamps, turned left to the highway, and waved down a rickshaw amidst the headlong rush of trucks. As we got in, a black Ambassador pulled to a halt behind us. It was Das, on his way back to the factory after a day of meetings in the city. Sandhya told him what had happened. "Sir," she said. "We are working on it day and night. We will solve it, never fear."

"Yes," he said, and sat back in the seat. The car crunched off in a swirl of dust, and I was sadder still. He had the look of a man going to his execution, a man who has accepted that this unbelievable thing is going to happen, and is now settling accounts in his mind. I think he was quite past fear.

On the second day I gave in to panic. I mean on the second day that Rajesh was gone I gave up all hope of indignation and frankly drowned in dread. At exactly ten-thirty I was unable to work anymore, and I turned in my chair and looked at the back of Sandhya's head. She was writing code in quick little flurries of keytaps. I picked up the phone and dialled a number that Rajesh had told me never to call, and listened to thirty-four rings. Personal calls are not allowed, Rajesh had said, and anyway they're a nosy lot, those fellows who work at the Post Office, they would ask too many questions. I listened to the shrill ringing and counted. Finally, a voice said, "Chembur Post Office."

"Parcel Office," I said, and waited. There was a longer ring now, insistent. I lost count but I held the receiver hard against my head and waited.

"Yes?" a woman said.

"Parcels?"

"Yes."

"Is Rajesh Pawar there?"

"No."

I knew I had another question, but I was silenced by stories that appeared abruptly in my head, complete tales of disaster and horror. She hung up.

I concentrated on my finger, the finger that tapped the bar on top of the phone, brown against black, the finger that pressed the keys. I made each movement deliberate and then again waited. This time I asked for the supervisor. "You are who?" the woman said.

"Supervisor, please," I said.

I had to tell her my name, and also that it was about a missing registered letter, and the line was cut off once and I had to call back, but finally he came on and I asked about Rajesh.

"Your good name?" he said.

"Iqbal Akbar," I said.

"And you are who?"

"I'm a friend."

"A friend?"

"Of Rajesh."

"A friend of Rajesh."

He said that with some satisfaction, as if he understood everything. Whatever he did understand, it persuaded him. "But this is very strange, if you are a friend," he said. "Rajesh Pawar hasn't worked here in eight months. He just walked out one afternoon. He was sorting parcels and then he just got up and left. No resignation letter, nothing. Very improper. But how is it you do not know?"

I put the phone down. I pressed my temples with my

knuckles as hard as I could and tried to squeeze it all away.

"Listen, Sandhya," I said.

But she was away, deep into the machine. I put my hand on her shoulder and waited, my heart tightening like a fist.

"*Haan?*" she said, jerking out of her trance. "What? What?"

But suddenly I didn't want to talk about Rajesh. A question about him, now, would give shape to my fear, put it in the world and make it real. "How did you meet Anubhav?" I said.

A moment passed, and another, I asked again, and then she said in a drugged voice, wrapped around silences like a call from the other side of the moon, "He helped me buy a book at Crossword."

"What book?" I knew the answer, but I wanted something, a word, a story, a plank or two to prop against my collapse.

"Picasso book," she said. "It was a book about Picasso."

"But what did you like about him?" I think there was something in my voice, a sob, and she swivelled in her chair, bumping against my knees, and looked at me, blinking.

"What is it?" she said.

So I told her. She took charge then. She shut down her compiler, and sent me outside to put on my shoes and wait by the front door. I watched Anubhav paint. When Sandhya stuck her head in his door to say that we were going out for a while, he didn't turn his head to say his "*Haan,* okay, see you later." He was painting rural scenes. In a canvas leaning against the wall, there was a mud hut and a pile of hay and a hard yellow sky. And a bony, elongated cow peered at me from an easel to the side. I thought, he's been working hard. Sandhya waved at his back and I blinked at the cow and we left.

We caught the local from VT to Sion. In the train, which was mostly empty because of the hour, I turned my head and leaned my head against the bars on the window and cried. The incredible length of Bombay sped by, those endless sprawls of buildings, huts and shacks, children squatting and shitting by the tracks, refuse, the crowded grey roads twisting and winding between, all of it blurred but fearsome in its strength, in its very life that grew it unstoppably. I had a plea in my throat, a half-formed call for mercy. A supplication, my mother would have called it. Then, filling my head, a roar as the train went through a station without stopping, faces only a few feet away dimmed by the ferocious speed.

At Sion station we got into an autorickshaw. I had Rajesh's address written out in my diary, but I had never been to his house before, so we went slowly, stopping now and then to ask directions. "All the way around to the back of the Rupam Cinema Hall," a man driving a DHL van told us. "Then you go straight, Dharavi side." So we went around Rupam, which was crowded for a matinee of *Zanjeer*. A revival, I thought, Rajesh will be angry he missed it. We drove on, and the road became narrow, and finally we stopped. Sandhya paid off the autorickshaw and then we walked. The lane was actually a road, but the stalls had pushed out from the shops on either side, so that you could only walk in the very centre, brushing shoulders. They were selling suit pieces, baby clothes, kitchen utensils, plastic hair bands. After a while we left the bazaar behind and turned right, into a road lined with *chawls*, great greyish buildings continuing forever. Sandhya was wearing a black suit, and she began to walk faster as people turned to look at her. I stopped one of them, a thin grandfatherly man with white handlebar moustaches, and asked for the Saraswati Shinde Chawl. He looked at Sandhya, shading his eyes, and said to me, "Come, I'll show you." He turned and led us up the road, around a curve, and to it. "Here," he said, gesturing with a tilt of his head. "Here."

It was a four-storied building, enormous, built around a central courtyard, balconies running all the way around on the inside. There was a small tree in the centre of the courtyard, a patch of unexpected green. The sun came down hard into the land, and I was trembling.

Rajesh's father was short, heavyset. He came eagerly to the open door of No. 312 when we knocked, tugging his *banian* down over his belly. He slumped into stillness while Sandhya told him that we were friends of Rajesh, and watching his stubbled, disappointed face, I thought he looked much smaller than I had imagined him from Rajesh's stories. His wife came out through a narrow door behind him then, wrapping a blue *pallu* around her shoulders. She sent him away to put on a shirt, and seated us on a *takath* that almost filled the shallow breadth of the room.

"Dilip has gone to the police station," she said in Marathi-accented Hindi. "We have reported this yesterday."

I was looking at the calendar on the wall behind her, at a picture of the pristine arc of Marine Drive, hidden by her shoulder. She was looking at me, and I tried to speak but found that I could say nothing. There was a battered black table fan perched in a niche in the wall next to the *takath*, and I could feel the streaming air moving slowly across my back.

"I'm sure there will be some news soon," Sandhya said.

"You, you know Rajesh for very long?" Rajesh's father said to Sandhya. His shoulders filled the doorway as he buttoned a striped shirt. He looked uncomfortable asking the question, and I coughed and forced myself into speech.

"No, actually, I'm Rajesh's friend. For the last two years. A little more, maybe. Mrs. Gore is my boss and has met him also. We saw him on Tuesday night." I realized I didn't know the Hindi for art opening. "He came to a painting show with us."

"For what?" Rajesh's father said.

"A show of paintings."

"Iqbal is Rajesh's *best* friend," Sandhya said suddenly, her eyes moist. "They are, they are *old* friends." She stopped abruptly.

They were puzzled by me, by their son's unexpected Muslim friend who talked about paintings. But I knew about them. I knew that his name was Shivraj and hers Sharda, that they had an elder son named Dilip who worked as a clerk in a cooperative bank, and I knew that the young woman who emerged now with a rattle of cups and glasses was Dilip's wife Mamta, that she was tiny in size and meek in appearance but had a tongue as sharp as a fish-knife, that Dilip and Mamta went every Saturday afternoon to Juhu beach, that she had a yearning for blazing spices.

"Please take," Rajesh's mother said hoarsely. She leaned forward, and still standing, handed the teacups to us. They were in fear, but they were certain about their hospitality, and so we drank the water out of little steel cups, and then the tea. There was a blue plate piled high with *chiwda,* and Rajesh's mother held it out to us. "Please take," she said. A group of children had followed us up the stairs, and I could hear their feet on the floor outside, their whispering. I put a palmful of *chiwda* into my mouth, and looked at the strip of wall between Rajesh's mother and father. We sat in silence. I knew that Rajesh slept on the *takath* that we were sitting on, and that his father slept on a mattress on the floor next to him. Since their marriage, Dilip and Mamta had the one room inside, and Rajesh's mother the passageway next to the kitchen. I had imagined the room and it was exactly as I had imagined it, but I hadn't known about the calendar, or the steel cups.

Dilip came back from the police station an hour later, and to his mother's eager questions he said, only, "Nothing." And then he walked with us to the train station. I said goodbye to Rajesh's parents, to the narrow length of the room and its muted light, to Mamta, and then we walked down the staircases, around and back on the balconies, past the dozens and scores of identical rooms, with the children following behind us. I stumbled after Dilip, staring at the blue check on his shirt collar, wondering how with his thick glasses and his retreating air of meekness he could be Rajesh's brother. On the street Sandhya walked between us, and finally she looked up at him and asked, "Did you know Rajesh hasn't been to the Post Office for work in many months?"

Dilip looked away, then back. "Yes. Only now we found out. I have not told my mother yet. Also . . ."

"Also?" Sandhya said.

"Today one sub-inspector said they had received information that he was involved with some bad people. *Bhai log* he worked with."

"What?" I said.

"Yes, *bhai log*." He grimaced as he repeated the phrase. In my mouth I tasted the small cleverness of the words, the mean wit with which the city's gangsters described themselves: the fraternity, the band of brothers.

"How much I didn't know about my own brother," Dilip said. "How much more don't I know?"

Sandhya said nothing, and I stared straight ahead, and we walked on, through that road dense with other people and a thick haze of unreality. I stared at the gouts of red *paan* stain at the foot of a wall, and forgot how I had come to be there. Time passed, and I was paralysed by an ecstasy of wonder. I was filled with a glory of questions like a blinding blue light. I could not tell you how much of the day stumbled past us. Finally, outside the train station, Dilip and Sandhya and I stood near a long yellow wall, leaning towards each other against the ceaseless flow of faces. He held me by the elbow, and shouted over the afternoon rush. "How did you meet Rajesh?"

"I met him while we were exercising," I said. The lie came easily. I had a certain fluency at lies.

"Of course. He was always building his body," Dilip said with pride. "He was second in a competition last year, you know."

I knew. We said goodbye to Dilip and bought tickets. On the platform, we waited, and I tried to remember the truth of meeting Rajesh. I had met him, as I remembered, on a New Year's Eve when I had eight hundred and twenty rupees in my pocket from a birthday envelope from my grandmother. It was in a bar called the Ramanand behind the Taj, which during the day was crowded with office workers eating *bheja* curry and *faluda*, but by evening was taken over by men, only men. I had had one Hayward's Ale, and when I noticed him standing in the crush, I gathered all my beery courage and motioned to the empty chair across the table. I had one more beer, and bought him one. When we told each other our full names we looked at each other for a moment and noted and dismissed the difference in our religions in one smile, that was all. Afterwards we walked outside on the waterfront, drifting happily with the holiday thousands. The charge at Vertigo was fifty rupees each, and the wait was half an hour, but inside there was the happiness of a beat that I could feel in my chest, *choli ke peechay kya hai,* and bodies and bodies, a mirrored ceiling in which danced the happy faces of men. We danced, and I bought another beer and leaned against the wall, and Rajesh stood in front of me and was pressed against me by the delirious jostle. He was very sure of himself. He held his beer with one hand and rested the other on my belt buckle. My stomach trembled, and he grinned, his eyes blue in the disco light, and he said, "*Dandi mein* current *hai?*" That was wrong, I stuttered, because you can't have current in wood, it was a wrong manner of speech, it couldn't be true, but he grinned even more widely and let his hand move, and I was wrong, and maybe there was current in the *dandi* after all. We passed the next year in meetings and quarrels and separations and phone calls. We argued about cricket and movies and broken promises and faithlessness and disease and death, but on the next New Year's we were together again, against the same wall in Vertigo. I leaned my forehead against his shoulder, against the curving-in from the chest and the tight bulk of the biceps, and he whispered into my ear, "Bastard, you like me just for my Maharashtrian muscle." I thought of what he had done a year ago, at his blunt roughness, and laughed at him. But what he said was true, and a little more than true, and much less than true. I pinched the tendon under his shoulder. "And you?" I said. "Why do you like me?" "For your beauty," he said, and cupped my cheek in his hand. I wanted to believe it and couldn't. "It's true," he said, and kissed me.

Things settle and sink. I spent the next two days buying and setting up an aquarium. I learnt about air, and the lack of it, and what there is to know about food for fish. I learnt about which fish eat each other. Lalit and I cleared a place in his room, near his bed, moved aside his toys. After I carried in the aquarium, we laid in the gravel, siphoned the water in while Ma-ji stood in the doorway and talked about doom. Then the fishes, and then Lalit and I sat on the ground and watched them, their sudden turns, their cool black eyes. There was a sunken boat at the bottom of the sea, a shattered green hulk through which they flitted, in and out. This especially delighted Lalit. He made up stories about how it sank, terrible tales of storms and sea-monsters. Me, I allowed myself one phone call every evening to Dilip, just before I left to go home. I waited every day as they sent someone up from the tea-shop, feeling a constant motion at the bottom of my heart, deep where it had gone while the world went on. Dilip came on always and said, "*Haan*, Iqbal?" After he told me that there was no word of Rajesh, he talked often of other things. I think that, oddly, he was trying to comfort me. We spoke one day of cricket, and on another about a hit movie neither of us had seen. The next day

Sandhya said we were to have a party on Saturday, two days away. I said nothing, but I must have looked so poisonous that she began her defence immediately.

"Don't say anything," she said. "It's very important to Anubhav. It's Mahatre-ji's birthday."

"Mahatre-ji?"

"He's the *Times of India* critic, you know. Anubhav's already told him and invited some people."

"How many people?"

"Forty-fifty, he said. For dinner."

Forty, or maybe fifty, for dinner, in two days meant that I could have said a lot about Anubhav, a full day or two of dissection, but I wasn't in the mood. My pleasures were gone from me. "I'll get it done," I said.

"Thanks, Iqbal," Sandhya said. She turned and walked down the corridor towards the office, stretching her shoulders.

"Sandhya," I said, and she stopped. "I never saw any Picasso book around here," I said.

"Anubhav has it at his parents' house, I think," she said.

We looked at each other, down the dark hall, and we were both too tired for my customary shake of the head and her embarrassed little smile. I took the Amarson's shopping bag from the kitchen and got to work on Anubhav's party. The main dishes I would get catered from Bhaktawar's down the street, but between Ma-ji and myself and Amba *bai* we would manage the snacks, and also the rice and *chappatis* and the sweet-dish, I went through the usual scrimping and saving out of habit. I started on the customary trek out to Abdullah's in Mahim for the Scotch, mainly because I wanted the comfort of their reassurance that it was all actually real foreign whisky, not rebottled local stuff. I wanted to hear them say it again, as before, before the world changed. I must tell you that the city was for me full of Rajesh. This is I suppose commonplace, but for me it was astonishing that I saw him behind the pillar near the autorickshaw-queue at Mahim station, that he was in the car stuck in the traffic next to me at Mori Road. I thought I heard his voice in front of a stationery store and I whirled, violently, and two schoolboys in grey shorts watched me, their mouths open and red from the ice-*golas* they were eating. It was noon, and I shut my eyes and turned slowly through the heat. When I opened my eyes I felt as if I were looking at the road from a cavern deep inside my body, from a small place of shade far away. I thought, then, I cannot tell you why, that I would take an hour and go to Rajesh's *bhaiyya* gym. I knew Dilip had been there, and everywhere else already, with all the proper questions, and I had no hope of finding out anything, but I remembered Rajesh whirling the huge *joris* behind his back, his grip on the wooden handles, his whistling breath and the sweat, the shiny colour of his skin under the tubelight.

What I thought of as a gym was actually an *akhara*, the *Akhara Pratap Singh* as I now saw, in the sunlight, from the board on the wall that ran around it. It was a small plot of land between two buildings, an open shed with a tin roof on bamboo poles, a pit of fine soil under a broad spreading *neem* tree. There were the *joris* to one side, and some other equipment I didn't know, and a small shrine at the top of the plot. The man who met me at the gate said Guru-ji was eating, which I could see, Guru-ji was sitting crosslegged on the ground and eating from a *thali*. His student, who was a boy really, went and whispered into his ear as he drank from a tall brass tumbler, and I could see the teacher's eyes watching me gravely. He waved me over. I started, and then had to stop when the student pointed at my feet. I bent, took my shoes off, and walked across the yard. I could feel the earth under my toes, clean and grainy.

"Rajesh you're looking for also?" he said. Guru-ji's Hindi was difficult for me, accented and turned in a strange Northern way. "Sit."

There was nowhere but the ground to sit on, so I bent

awkwardly and sat next to him, my knees high.

"I remember you," he said. "You came once with him." He had bright little eyes in a round face, a smooth bald head, and grey in his stubble. His stomach, which he rested a hand on as he spoke, looked round and hard under his *kurta*. "Yes." He sat at ease on the ground, as if he had been planted in it.

"I did," I said. "Once. It was a long time ago. My name is Iqbal."

"Yes, what was your name? Iq-bal? I was surprised to see Rajesh then. Since then I haven't seen him. I told his brother that."

"What do you mean? I thought he came here every other day."

He laughed. "Oh, not here. When he was a boy he did. Then he came every day. But now he only goes to that body-building club." He said the word in English, as "badi-beelding."

"What bodybuilding club?"

"At the corner of Atreya Lane. Many of them go there now, and to other ones. To become big with the machines. Here, I ask too much of them. I ask them to be pure. I am an old man. I've heard them say it, Kaniya Pahalwan is an old man and he asks too much. I do. But to have a body of one colour, you must drink a bitter cup."

He said, *sharir ek rang ka*. A body of one colour. "I don't understand," I said.

"*Sharir ek rang ka.* Not huge slabs of meat hung together on a wire. Like parts on a car. Pieces and pieces. No. All this, this, this, this," he said, touching his stomach, his heart, his head, "all one. To be all one you must sacrifice. You must be pure. You must eat pure. You must think pure. But they pay money over there to become big. I charge no money. I ask them to pay of themselves."

"Do you know if Rajesh was, was involved in anything bad? Bad people?"

"Rajesh was a good boy. But I hear anything can happen at these clubs. All kinds of people go to become big." He looked down at his *thali*, which was empty, wiped clean. "Rajesh was a good boy," he said. "And I am an old man. Do you know, when I first opened this *akhara* here, forty years ago, this was all an open *maidan*?" The sweep of his arm took in the *akhara*, the lane, the buildings, and what lay beyond. "My buffaloes grazed right there. Now everything is built up. Even this land they want."

"Who?"

"They who own that building, and that. They have asked me many times. Perhaps the next time there is trouble in the city, and there will be trouble in the city, I'll find all this gone, burnt down. If I'm here when it happens, maybe my wrestlers will find me here, two holes in my head." He pointed at his head with two stiff fingers. "One more poor victim of unfortunate Hindu-Muslim riots. Maybe I should go back to my village. Retire." He used the English word, "retire," and he laughed. "It is a village called Rudragaon, near Benares. Have you been to Benares?"

"No."

"Sometimes I cannot remember if I've been to Benares." He laughed again, with his cheeks full and round, and the shadows from the *neem* moved like a web over his head and shoulders. He didn't look very frightened.

"I must go," I said. "Back to work."

"I hope you find Rajesh."

"He was a good friend."

He nodded his head from side to side. I got up with a click in my knees, and he reached out and rested a palm on my shin. "Come back and do some *bethaks* with us, Iq-bal. This *akhara* is open to all. No money."

I smiled at him and walked past the wrestling pit, and I left him there under his *neem* tree. All that afternoon, as I bought soda and Scotch and extra glasses, I thought of Rajesh doing *bethaks*, squatting and rising in a ceaseless rhythm, his arms swinging forward and back, going to the balls of his feet and then back to his heels as he rose. I counted the first three hundred and then just watched him, the shining dark skin, his eyes radiant and calm, the brown earth rich with sweat, his face as if in prayer. *Sharir ek rang ka.* When all my buying was done, on the way back, I stopped the taxi on Atreya Lane, and looked in the door of the bodybuilding club, which was one dark room at the back of the ground floor of a commercial building. It was full of long rusty bars, dumbbells, and mirrors, and there was a tower with pulleys on it. There was a two-in-one on a windowsill, and some very loud music, and the room was empty. Then the taxi had to move because a truck was trying to get around the compound, and I ran back, and we went on. I held the carton full of bottles steady with one hand and wondered why Rajesh had taken me to the *akhara* and not this other place. When we had left the *akhara*, that night, after he had touched Guru-ji's feet, he said as we walked down the lane, "That's a *neem* tree." I nodded, silenced by desire. "It's a good place," he said. I nodded again, fast. "A really good place," he said. "I feel at peace here." I had agreed, too blinded by love, and longing, to know what he really meant. Later that night, with the sea pounding in my ears, I had run my tongue over his stomach hungrily. I felt the small soft prickling of the hair against my lips, my nose. And the tenderness of the skin. He held my head delicately in his arms. I had felt a desperation to know him, to hold something essential. *Sharir ek rang ka.* I sat in the taxi and wondered what it was that I had kissed. I thought of my own body, and asked, had he found peace in me? And the bottles rattled against each other with tiny bell-like sounds, and I felt an ache in my wrist.

Late that night I came back to the gym on Atreya Lane. Now there was a man in a khaki uniform sitting on a stool by the door. It was past ten, but I could see through the door that the room was crowded with heavy-shouldered men in *banians* and T-shirts. The music was heavy and loud.

"Members only," the doorman said.

"I want to talk to your manager. Owner?"

"Nobody is here. Members only."

"Will your manager be coming later tonight? Anybody? Who is in charge?"

He shrugged. He was chewing a *paan,* and now he turned his head and spat into the darkness.

"I'll wait here," I said, pointing to the gate. "When whoever is in charge comes, you tell him that I want to talk to him." I groped about in my pocket and held out a twenty-rupee note. He chewed, and looked disinterestedly at the first button on my shirt. I walked to the gate, and leaned against the cracked concrete. Above my head a streetlight made buzzing noises. I waited, and now and then men came out of the gym, carrying bags. For all of them I had the same question, "Do you know Rajesh Pawar?" I believed the first one when he shook his head and hurried away, looking at the ground, but when none of the first four knew him I grew angry. I snapped out my question at the next one, and he looked at me carefully. I was afraid then, because he was very big, with a neck so thick that he had to turn his whole body to look at me. But he said, quietly, "No," and walked away. I asked each one who went in or out, until midnight, and the doorman watched me from his stool. A little after twelve he got up, stretched, and began to shut the door. I hurried up to him.

"Manager?" I said.

"Didn't come," he said, and spat past my knee. He shut the door in my face. I looked at the chipped paint on the wood for a minute, then went home. I walked most of the way, even though twice I could have caught the bus if I had run a little, to the stop. I was punishing myself, I think. I felt that I could have done more, should have. I entered the house very late, fell exhausted into my bed without taking off any clothes, and dreamt of childhood.

The next morning I made my usual call to Dilip. He began our usual small talk, but I cut him off, and asked, "Who are those people that Rajesh is supposed to have worked with?"

"Who?"

"The *bhai log*. Who are they? Do you know any names?"

"Iqbal," he said. I could feel, over the line, his fear. It was there, present, as thick as the exhaust fumes on the street outside. "Why do you want to know such things?"

"Tell me," I said.

"I don't know anything specific, you understand," he said. "But I have heard the name of Govardhan *bhai*."

"What else?"

"Nothing," he said. "Be careful." And then he hung up.

I went back that evening to Atreya Lane. Again the doorman at the gym regarded me with infinite boredom. But when I said, "I want to see Govardhan *bhai*," he straightened up.

"Wait," he said, and disappeared. A few minutes later he came back and led me inside, past the loud room with the muscles straining against weight, and into an office at the back. There was a man sitting behind a desk, a man with a thin moustache, about forty, in a plain white shirt. And another one, younger, heavyset, standing next to the desk.

"You're asking about Govardhan *bhai*?" the man with the moustache said.

"Are you Govardhan *bhai*?" I said.

"No, no, I'm not him," he said. "I am merely a friend of Mr. Rajan here, who is the owner of this establishment." He waved a hand in the air. But Mr. Rajan was leaning over to light his cigarette, and when the match flared I knew where I had seen the man with the thin moustache before: outside the Pushkara Gallery, when I had been waiting for Sandhya, and I had thought he was a driver. Until this moment I had had a brittle kind of courage, a thin belief that nothing had happened to Rajesh, and that nothing would happen to me, but now I was very afraid. He pulled at his cigarette and watched me.

"Your good name, please?" I said.

He smiled and shook his head, nodded at Mr. Rajan, who left the room, shutting the door behind him. "Doesn't matter," he said. "Yesterday you were asking about Rajesh Pawar. Already the police has been here, with his brother I think it was. You are?"

"His friend."

"His friend. Very good. Name?"

"Iqbal. Iqbal Akbar."

"Iqbal," he said. "That's a good name for a friend to have. I had a friend named Iqbal once, long ago."

"Do you know where Rajesh is?"

He raised his hands, palms upward. "No. Why would I?"

I was breathing fast, and the room seemed dark to me. I said, very fast, "Because I saw you outside the gallery the other night. I think you work for Ratnani. I think Rajesh also worked for Ratnani. Rajesh met you here, in this place. He started working for you and Ratnani."

"Interesting story. What does he do for me?"

"I don't know." I shook my head. "He's strong. Maybe he kills people?"

He laughed, throwing his head back. "You're mad," he said. "*Arre*, Rajan," he called, not very loudly, but the door behind me opened instantly and Rajan appeared behind me. "Throw this madman out. And don't let him in again."

I tried to struggle, but Rajan had one of my arms twisted behind my back, and I discovered again what I already knew: I am not very strong.

Even at that time of night it took me only an hour and a half to find out where Ratnani lived. You can search in this city forever for a poor man, but the mansions of the rich are landmarks. I made phone calls, and told the friends that I got on the line to make more phone calls, and before long I knew that Ratnani lived off Pali Hill Road, near KetNav, in a bungalow at the very end of a dead-end lane. Behind a high wall covered with creepers. As I paid off the autorickshaw driver and walked up the lane I could see a huge metal gate let into the wall, and high over the wall, the exotic turrets and lovely red tiled roofs of the castle that Ratnani had built for himself. I pounded on the gate with my fist and it rang loud, like a huge bell. The man was right: I was a madman. Sweat poured down my face and I lashed with both fists on the iron. A little window opened in the middle of the gate, and eyes peered out at me. "What?"

"I want to see Ratnani," I bellowed.

"Don't shout, you bastard," I heard behind me, and then I was on my knees, holding my head. Under my left hand the top of my ear and the side of my head throbbed with pain.

"Who the hell is he?" I heard.

When I managed to focus my eyes I saw three uniformed guards with *lathis* in their hands standing over me. To the left there was a man in plain clothes, with hair cut very short and a very straight back. In his hands he held a Sten gun, the muzzle pointed directly at me. And stepping through the gate there was the man with the clipped moustache from the Atreya Lane gym.

"You again?" he said, mildly. "Never mind," he said to the armed man, who was jerking glances over his left shoulder and right, and looked ready to shoot. "It's all right. I'll take care of him."

He put a hand under my elbow and pulled me to my feet. I was still looking at the gun, which looked heavier than anything I had ever seen in the movies, and my legs gave out from under me. "Steady," my moustached friend said. "That's Mr.

Ratnani's police protection. You made him nervous." He was walking me towards a black Matador van parked at the head of the lane. "You'll get yourself in real trouble if you keep pulling this kind of crazy stunt."

He put me in the back of the van, tapped on the black plastic partition, and the Matador jerked forward.

"Are you a policeman also?" I said.

"No, I'm not a policeman," he said. He had one arm along the back of the seat, and was sitting back, quite relaxed. "You were a good friend to this Rajesh Pawar. Very loyal. I like that. But take my advice. Go home and forget about it. Otherwise you'll end up in a ditch. *Tap-tap*. Dead."

Outside the van, separated from us by thin lightly tinted glass, a family drove past, three children laughing in the rear seat. And on the other side of the road, there were shops, brightly lit. Inside, I looked at this man, at his angular profile.

"*Tap-tap*," I said. "He did work for you, didn't he? Did he kill?"

"What, Rajesh?" he said, smiling. "He was too big."

"You know him then."

"You boys, you watch too many movies. Size is what you think it's all about. Silly. Now you, you would make a good shooter. You look like nobody. So you look like everybody. That's what a shooter needs. Walk up in a crowd, behind your target, and *tap-tap*, that's all. *Bas*. Disappear into the crowd. The big fellows, all they're good for is scaring people. Destroying houses and huts and slums. Clearing land. If anyone dies, they die — it's incidental."

"Is that what he did for you? For Ratnani?"

He was quiet then, and he looked straight ahead, and in the occasional flashes of light I could see his thoughtful face.

"Is Rajesh all right?" I said.

We were speeding along a stretch of empty road now. On every bump we swayed first in one direction and then the other, as if in time. He didn't say a word, and then it occurred to me that I was going to die. I had heard that things like this happened, that people like this existed, that shattered bodies were found in the city parks, but it had been always far away, something for Rajesh to fantasize about. Now I was in a van in the middle of the night, alone with this man and the driver I hadn't seen, and it was really happening. Here was my knee rattling against the side of the van. My hand on the rough cloth of the seat. And currents of pain along the side of my head. I tried to say something, I'm not sure what, and I whimpered. A small sound, but high and quite distinct and audible. He looked at me, then, and I was paralysed and the air rushed against the window behind him. His eyes were black and cool.

Finally he nodded and slapped his hand on the partition, once. The van skidded quickly to a halt. He pushed open the door, got out, and crooked a finger at me. I had to make a conscious effort to move myself the breadth of the seat, every inch of it. We were on a seafront, not a beach but just a wall, dropping sheer to rocks below. He bent forward, grabbed my arm, and pulled me out of the van. I took a step, and then sank to the ground. My legs were bent under me. I sat.

"Are you afraid?" he said.

I nodded. I was looking out at the dark sea, and I didn't want to turn my head to look at him.

"Good," he said. And then I felt his hand on the top of my head, his palm cupping the crown, his fingers holding gently. "I know who you are, Iqbal Akbar. By tomorrow I will know where you live. Who lives with you. Understand?"

I tried to nod but he held me.

"Don't ask questions about Rajesh. Don't make noise. You'll get eaten and nobody will even notice you're gone."

Then I felt his hand leave me. I waited. There was a crunch of gravel, and with a great effort I turned my head. My neck hurt.

"Your friend named Iqbal," I said. "What happened to him?"

He had his hand on the door, and he swung himself into the van. I couldn't see him anymore. "He died," he said. "It happens."

The door clanked shut, and the van swung away. From where I sat there was only the sea in front of me, but still the glow from the city fell across the water, and I could see the rocks far below, and the waves.

On the afternoon of the party the house was full of the smell of food. Lalit made himself sick eating the *bhajiyas* the *bai* was cooking up, and then I had to keep him from feeding *bhajiyas* to the fishes. He didn't believe that the *bhajiyas* would make the fish sick, but he did believe, with certainty, that they would make the fishes crazy and they would start eating each other. He helped me lay out paper napkins on the table in the drawing room, arranging them in a circular pattern exactly and with great care. At seven Sandhya came in, drying her hair with a towel.

"Crash," she said.

"Bad one?" I said. I stood up, and the side of my head throbbed.

"Terminal freeze, but the server didn't lock. I told them we would come over to the factory tomorrow morning to pick up the backup tapes." She had them backing up every two hours, so that we could look at the data files immediately before and after a crash.

"I'll go now," I said.

"It'll take you an hour and a half to get there, same to get back. It's late, Iqbal." She looked up at me, her head tilted to one side. I had told her my ear was swollen because I had stumbled in the crowd on a railway platform and had fallen against a pillar.

"No, really, I want to," I said. "One day left only." That Monday was when Das would pull our plug. To this there was no answer, and so I went. Really I wanted to get out of the house, to travel. I had felt sick all day, the smell of the frying had drifted into my clothes, I could feel it on my tongue. It was actually an hour that it took, and when I arrived the factory was dark. The gateman shone a torch into my face, and let me in with what I thought was a look of sympathy. I had a feeling that plugs had already been pulled.

I went around to the back, and the door to the raw material shed was ajar. I pushed it in, stepped into darkness lit only by the glow from the door of the accounting office. As I stepped up to the door Raunak-ji rose from his desk, his face alarmed.

"It's me," I said. "Just came to pick up the tapes."

"Ah, my boy," Raunak-ji said, a hand on his heart.

"He's very nervous always," Manishi-ji said, shrugging. "Go ahead, Iqbal." He waved a hand at me.

"What's wrong?" Raunak-ji said, pointing at my head as I turned.

"I fell," I said.

"You young fellows. So careless."

I smiled, and felt my way to the server closet. There was a light switch on the inside of the door that flared up a single bare bulb above my head. As the circles floated in front of my eyes I squinted at the machine and fumbled at the front of it for the tape, and in that dazzle of colour there was still the image of Raunak-ji and Manishi-ji, and their room, the rows and rows of ledgers and the safe. Then I froze, my fingers aching on the cold metal. Then I could make myself move and I went through the door and back to theirs. I leaned against the side of the door.

"Manishi-ji," I said. "I have to run a backup, it'll take a few minutes, but I was wondering . . . Some of that *chai*, perhaps? And something to eat?"

"Of course, of course," he said.

"Yes, yes," Raunak-ji said, getting up.

"Raju's not here?"

"Never mind that," Raunak-ji said. "You do your work, young fellow."

"Thanks," I said. I nodded, and then backed away from the door. I had looked at Raunak-ji and Manishi-ji, and I had tried not to look at the safe, but as I went back to the server room I carried an image of it, a slightly blurry painting in my head. There were the two of them, then the ledgers, the desks, an uncapped fountain pen, a long grey pad, the safe with its covering of gods and goddesses, and in the middle of it all, an empty space, a shape outlined by everything else, by all the others, something gone, an absence, a hole with a form, wings. I closed the door behind me, stood jammed up against the machines, which stood against the other locked door to the accounting office. I leaned over and looked at the front of the server, tried to look behind the computer, but it stood less than an inch away from the wall and I could see nothing. There was no question of moving it, because it stood, steady and firmly set, in the special exactly fitting table with half-inch flanges that we had ordered the factory *mistri* to build. I reached over to the top of the tower, tiptoeing, and ran my hand over the edge I couldn't see, over the other side of the computer, between metal and wood. My fingers passed over something, roundly pointed and smooth. I traced back and felt the shape, hooked it between my middle finger and forefinger and pulled. It came slowly, sticking to the metal, pulling towards it, clinging to it. But finally it came away and I held it in my hand: silvery, its wings outstretched in hungry flight, nosing through my fingers, the big Jumbo from the safe, with the Air India maharaja bowing at me. I turned it over, and the dark strips of magnet on the belly of the plane, and on the wings, gathered up the light, dense as empty space against the white.

I—after a while, a few moments, I don't know how long—I put the plane back, slid it down behind the tower where I had found it. The magnets kissed the metal with a small sucking sound, and as I leaned close to the machine I could feel their pull, and I thought I felt it in my fingertips, the random destruction, the corruption of our files on the hard disk, particles moving on metal and twenty rupees and twenty paise gone. I stood up straight, swallowed. Then I started my backup, and went outside to the accounting office, and I sat in a chair. Then Raunak-ji came in with a glass of tea and a plate of *bhajiyas*, and I drank and ate. I made myself sick with eating.

"How long have you worked here?" I said.

"Twenty-nine years," Manishi-ji said. "I have one year seniority."

"Eight months," Raunak-ji said. "Seven-and-a-half, actually."

Manishi-ji laughed, shaking his head, and I laughed with him. "Are you married, Manishi-ji?" I said.

"Of course I'm married," he said. "You young people are absurd. You're not married, Iqbal?"

"No, I'm not," I said, at which they both looked perturbed. "Children, Manishi-ji?"

I had never seen them before, not really. That evening, I learnt about Manishi-ji's son, who had a shop at the airport in Dubai, and his daughter, who was married to an engineer in the PWD, and the death of Raunak-ji's wife the year before of cardiovascular congestion. I ate with greasy fingers, and in that room stacked with ledgers I listened to their lives, and laughed with them, and found that I loved them. When I said, I must go, they said they would leave with me. I waited as they locked up the accounting office, and then waited again outside as they struggled with the lock on the raw material shed.

"Ooof," Manishi-ji said. "Here, let me try."

"Go ahead and try," Raunak-ji said. "You after all are the lock expert."

"Move, no, a little."

They were standing shoulder to shoulder, peering at the

huge lock, turning the key back and forth. I was standing behind them. Over us, on the wall, a tubelight flickered on and off. In that blue light I looked at their bent backs, their shoulders, and I saw how even their necks were the same, stubbled and slight, with greying hair above, and shiny pates. I saw how the human head is made, the little hollow at the top of the neck, where the skull rests on the body. Is that the place? Is that where the flesh is vulnerable? Is it so easy? Do you just raise the pistol, point it up into that hollow? *Tap-tap. Tap-tap.*

"There," Manishi-ji said. "What's so difficult about that?"

"If you're so good at it," Raunak-ji said, "you do it from tomorrow."

They walked with me to the gate, each with a hand on one of my shoulders.

"Take some rest," Raunak-ji said.

"Relax," Manishi-ji said. "Everything will be okay."

As I walked down the lane towards the highway they both waved. When I turned the corner their hands were still raised.

I could hear the party as the lift came up the shaft, the clink of glasses and that enticing hum of voices behind closed doors. I let myself in and squeezed my way through the crush in the corridor. There was a familiar face here and there, Anubhav's arty friends, but many I hadn't seen before. In the kitchen Ma-ji and Amba *bai* were standing in front of sizzling *karhais*, tossing *bhajiyas* onto plates.

"Did you see how they eat?" Ma-ji said. "Hungry as dogs."

"Who are all these people?"

She shook her head and threw handfuls of vegetables slathered in *besan* into the burning oil. I turned, went to the office, where I left the tapes on a shelf, checked on Lalit, who was sleeping the uneasy stomach-clutching sleep of the greedy, and finally found Sandhya in the drawing room. She turned sideways to get through two painters, raising a tray high above her head, and whispered fiercely into my ear, "We're going to run out of Scotch." It was true: on the table where I had put out the drinks three bottles were empty. Even as I watched a documentary filmmaker emptied a fourth. I tried to get back to the door, but found myself working my way around the back wall, near Sandhya's blue painting, where Anubhav was sitting on the sofa and talking to a man dressed in a white bush shirt.

"True, true, too true," Anubhav was saying. "Mahatre-ji, that is just so much commodity fetishism."

Mahatre took a mighty gulp of his drink and said, nodding, "Mere decoration."

On Mahatre's left there was a woman in a white sari talking to Miss Viveka. The ponytailed fellow was leaning on the back of Miss Viveka's chair, talking to two men in long *kurtas*. The blue of the painting was reflected in all of Miss Viveka's mirrors, and the colour seemed to stain the dim lamplight. I gave up trying to get back to the door, and went instead to the table, where I found a bottle and poured myself a double peg. My stomach was heaving from all the grease I had eaten, and I drank the Scotch with hope, feeling it burn down like an elixir. I took another sip, and saw Sandhya again, bringing more food to the table.

"Do you think I would make a good killer, Sandhya?" I said to her.

"What?"

"Nothing. What's wrong?" I said. Normally she enjoyed this rattle and roll, all this laughter and welcoming people into her house. Das's deadline was on us and as far as she knew on Monday we were dead, unless a miracle happened on the Sunday, but there was no joy in her at all, nothing. She was putting plates from the tray on the table, slamming each one down. "Tell me," I said.

She pulled me close to her, and whispered with astonished hatred, "He's *screwing* her. He's screwing *her*." She jabbed with her head over her right shoulder towards the far corner of the room, through the crowd, and I knew exactly who she meant. I went back, holding my glass high up, and now Anubhav was standing near the wall, leaning back with his legs apart. To his left Miss Viveka was talking to Mahatre, smiling up at him. Anubhav and Miss Viveka weren't facing each other, actually they were facing away from each other, not back to back but angled a little, outwards and away, but there it was, it was true. I knew it was because of the precise three inches between them, not touching but not exactly far, because of the laughter in their conversations and their occasional glances back at each other, their happiness and that feeling of safety in their now-and-then glancing shoulders. I knew it because they weren't looking at each other. It was exactly how Rajesh and I used to stand.

So I stood in the blue light and emptied my glass. Then I had another. Afterwards I went out into the building compound below and vomited all over somebody's Maruti Zen.

I woke up with a Jumbo jet roaring through my head. I sat on the edge of my bed, with my hands over my eyes, and decided I had to tell Sandhya about Raunak-ji and Manishi-ji, tell her now. But the phone was dead, so I pulled on some clothes and staggered out into the sun. As I went down the street each step went through my heels to the top of my head, and I was heavy with regret. I thought of their lives, and their children, their years and years of work, and I stopped in the middle of the road and turned back once, but then I went on. At the Grand Video Store I asked to use their phone, but Ahmed Raza, whom I had known all my life, said, "Iqbal, all the phones are dead. Go home." I didn't move. My legs ached. "There's some trouble in the city. We're going to close the shop."

I watched as he slammed down the shutters. "Go home, Iqbal," he said. But I thought of Sandhya spending another

day, a Sunday, teary-eyed at her computer, and so I went on.
Even that was an evasion. I went on mainly because I wanted
to give what I knew to somebody else, get rid of it. Around
me the city's Sunday emptied. Have you ever been at the beginning of a riot? You feel it coming, gathering in silence. There
was the bazaar hustle of a holiday morning, and then suddenly
all the shops were closed. The street was blank and yawning,
and a woman's slipper lay at a crossroad. I looked up and all
the windows were vacant. I walked on. The road dipped
between plots covered with bricks and coils of steel cable
which towered above my head. I could feel the fear, the terror
in the empty lanes and the sky overhead. I was not afraid, but I
was not brave. I felt that I had a question. I thought I would
turn a corner, and I would see Rajesh swaggering down the
road towards me, an iron rod in his hand. I wanted to ask: will
you kill me, Rajesh? Will you kill my Muslim mother and my
Muslim father? Will you take our land then, our needle-point
of land in this wilderness? Will you live happily in it then?
Could you? Tell me, tell me, I said. Tell me. Across a creek
filled with black, sludgy water, a line of buildings extended a
serrated edge across the horizon. Now there was a quick flurry
of barks, a howling that echoed back and forth among the
walls and the buildings and then vanished, sunk in the silence.
I walked on. A sudden cluster of shacks spilled down from the
road to an unseen precipice, twisted together like some memory of a village, obscenely tiny and squeezed against each other.
The road was fearsome because I had never been able to look
to its end as it stretched far away, endless and quiet. I had
never seen how long it led. I walked. Over the rooftops a column of smoke stretched into the sky. In my heart I saw flames,
and Guru-ji face down in the middle of his *akhara*, stretched
across the fine sand. My mouth worked, open and shut, open
and shut. I turned a corner and saw a dog. He turned in the
middle of the road and looked at me over his shoulder. He was

yellow in colour, ugly and lean, filthy, and I could hear his breathing. I went past him and then he began to walk next to me. I stopped, bent down as if to pick up a stone, raised my hand, and he cringed and lowered his head to the ground, but didn't run. I turned, and stumbled away, and he came with me. The sun was overhead now, and I didn't know where I was. I remembered my mother's Allah and Ma-ji's *Parameshwar* and thought, tell me, lord, tell me, master. The dog stopped short and looked over his shoulder again at me. I laughed. The city curved away from us, stretching like hills as I put a hand to my eyes, valley after valley, always higher.

It must have been afternoon when I saw the blood. My body felt as light as air, and I floated now from shadow to shadow. All the time there was the harsh huffing of the dog, and his trotting pace next to me. I thought first that it, the blood, was a smear of oil on the ground. Then as I came closer the sun tilted and I saw the colour, going from red to black. It was quite large, a shape like something had exploded on the ground, and droplets leading away. There were rivulets where it still ran shiny. I hung above it, feeling a sensation of dropping. The dog mewled uneasily behind me. I looked around and it was another nondescript street, the same buildings and the same shuttered shops. The huge shadows came towards me and I felt my heart turn in bitterness. I stepped away but now I could no longer see where I was going. I felt my way to a wall and keeping a hand on it I pushed myself forward. Finally I could walk no more and I crouched with my back against concrete. The dog stopped, then came forward and circled me, moving his head back and forth. Finally he dropped to his haunches and sat in front of me, close, facing away. I could hear the breath sliding in and out of his throat, and also my own, insistent and unstoppable. The fur on his back was dirty and matted, and underneath I could see the pinkish flesh. The sight of it filled me with disgust but I was finally able to raise a hand, to let it down slowly on his shoulder, and his ears pricked but he kept still, and we stayed like that, next to each other. Under my fingers I could feel his heart beating.

It was night when I awoke, and the dog was gone. I pushed myself up, and as I tried to calculate where I was, going a little way down this street and then that, I was picked up by a police van. I pointed at my head and told them I was staggering because I had been assaulted and injured by a stranger. They cursed me much, cuffed me about a little, but on the whole they were quite generous—they dropped me right at the head of my lane and told me to stay home and not get into trouble. The next day the newspapers said that the situation was normal, that absolutely nobody had been killed, only a few scattered injuries, and so I went to work.

"I asked him," Sandhya said as soon as I came into the office. She looked at me, her eyes enormous in her face. "I asked him and he said yes, they had made love. He said it happened. Then he just went back to work." When I had passed by the studio Anubhav had been leaning into a canvas, his brush busy, intent and focussed. Sandhya here, on the other hand, looked as if she were about to curl over and collapse.

"Listen," I said. "I have something to tell you also."

So I told her. I told her about Manishi-ji and Raunak-ji and the safe and the magnets and the Jumbo jet. She jumped up, sat down twice, walked around the room, and then she picked up the phone and called Das. He was already in his meeting, and she insisted and shouted on the phone, and then we waited.

"What assholes," she said. Her face was flushed. "What did they think? We weren't trying to get rid of them. It wasn't as if they were to be *cancelled*."

"They've been there for thirty years, Sandhya," I said.

"That's no damn excuse. Things change. Everything changes."

I shrugged. The receiver burbled into her ear, and she began to speak. She told Das. For some reason I couldn't stand to hear it, so I went out into the corridor, into Lalit's room, and I sat on his bed and watched the fishes circle in the water and dash through the wreck at the bottom. Half an hour later I heard the office door open, and Sandhya came in.

"He says he'll look into it," she said. "He was pretty angry."

"Yes," I said.

"I think he's going to throw them out."

"He'll have to."

"At least we got a better program out of it."

"Better?"

"Come look."

We went into the office, and she booted it up, and I sat at her desk and ran it through its paces. It was better, it was leaner, faster, more elegant looking. Where screens had scrolled, they now snapped, lookups happened in a flash, every process was twice or three times as fast. It was beautiful. She had gone close to the metal and come out with a kind of perfection.

"Beauty," I said. "Really, beauty, man."

"Shit, Iqbal," she said, and I turned around. She was sitting in my chair, chewing on her collar, twisted with remorse. "I mean, they weren't bad guys. They were probably just scared."

"Yes," I said. "Quite scared."

"Maybe I can tell Das we'll retrain them," she said.

"Yes."

"Maybe he doesn't have to fire them." She picked up the phone and dialled. "Maybe they just did us a service, you know, made us work harder. We don't have to be like that . . ." As she was talking I watched her face. She spoke and she listened to herself speak. The words got slower and slower. "We don't have to be like that . . ." Then she was absolutely still. I saw something happen in her, like a change in the light when the sun moves. She put down the receiver, carefully, deliberately. She looked at me straight. "Fuck them, *yaar*," she said. "Let them burn."

Then she got up, marched down the corridor, went into Anubhav's studio, picked up the Rural Cow and threw it out of the window. Then she threw him out. I mean she told him to get the hell out of her house and not come back. He started to argue, but meanwhile the Rural Cow had landed on the bonnet of somebody's car, and so people were shouting from underneath, and Anubhav went running down to save his cow. While he and the car owners were shouting at each other, Sandhya was pacing up and down the room, leaning out of the window now and then to tell him a thing or two, with Ma-ji egging her on. After a while she grabbed the Rural Mud Hut and threw it out of the window too, and then Anubhav began shouting at her from below. By now all the neighbours were out, leaning on their balconies, and from the ground floor the Khan twins came out in their identical red tracksuits, to tell Anubhav that they had known Sandhya *didi* since they were this high and they weren't going to stand for any damn bastard shouting at her. So now that began to develop into a full-fledged shouting match of its own, and all in all it was soon a full-scale old-style Bombay *tamasha*, with people watching from every balcony and window in every building, up and down the road, laughing and giving advice and yelling at each other. Then, and I tell you I'm not making this up, Vasant suddenly came rumbling down the street on his motorcycle, and of course began taking the part of the injured ex-husband and scattering abuse this way and that, and soon enough he threw a punch at Anubhav, and then Sandhya ran down too and the confusion was general. I was watching the circles swirl below, and then Ma-ji appeared under my elbow. She was trembling all over, every part and limb of her, and her face was a furious blotchy pink, and she was smiling.

"Here," she said. "Help me pick this up."

It was an earlier painting, not one of the rural series. I helped her get it onto the windowsill. With a huge peal of laughter she heaved it over. So then I helped her throw out his Sennelier paper and Schmincke crayons and tubes of oil paint, and drawings and paintings and glossy art magazines, all of which I remembered well because I had written the cheques for every last thing, and the crowd below was clapping now each time some art came falling out of the sky. I saw a portly *havaldar* heaving his way down the street, his mouth wide open. I leaned out of the window and saw Anubhav looking up.

"Ma-ji," I said, "ask Anubhav where the Picasso book is."

"Who?"

"Picasso."

So I pulled up a chair, helped her onto it, and she leaned over the balcony railing and boomed in an unbelievably loud voice, "*Pee-kasso kahan hai, maderchod?*" The *havaldar*, who was arresting everyone below, looked up at this question, momentarily paralysed by the sheer power of the voice. "*Pee-kasso kahan hai, maderchod?*" Vasant took this opportunity to try and run, and the *havaldar* plunged after him, and meanwhile, above, "*Pee-kasso kahan hai, maderchod?*" I tried for a minute to explain to Ma-ji that the question she was supposed to be asking was not exactly "Where's Picasso, motherfucker?," but she was standing on the chair with such fierce exultation in her arms, having so much fun, and now the kids below were chanting with her, that it seemed beside the point, and maybe that was the question after all. "*Pee-kasso kahan hai, maderchod?*"

Afterwards, as we tried to calm ourselves down, and Ma-ji moaned from a backache, Sandhya put down her cup of tea and said to me, a little teary still, "Why is everything so *low*, Iqbal? Why is everything made of money?"

"I don't know," I said. "Maybe money is made of every-thing." She looked at me, puzzled. I didn't quite know what I meant, myself, so finally I had to admit, "I don't know what that means."

"Maybe you're just trying to make a me-ta-phor," she said, and we both burst out laughing.

Look, there are the lights of Surat station. Who can tell what will happen? But perhaps tomorrow you and I will pull into Bombay Central. Then, on the platform I will raise my hand in farewell, and we will not see each other again. I will go straight to Sandhya's house to drop off these contracts, which are for a big project in Delhi. It turned out, once we got the system sta- bilized, and money no longer disappeared from the ledgers of Sridhar and Sons, that Das was quite a complicated fellow, with contacts here and there, so now we've expanded a little, and we have a new office, not very big really, two more people working for us, perhaps one more soon. I travel to Delhi often. We are not quite mega yet, but we are bigger.

What happened to Manishi-ji and Raunak-ji, you want to know, of course. When Das confronted them they first denied and denied and denied everything. When Das got angry and threatening, Raunak-ji broke down and confessed, and then they both begged forgiveness, and said they only wanted to serve the company. He had them both out of there that after- noon, and a week later they both filed suit against the compa- ny, saying they had been framed, hoodwinked out of wages and pensions, discriminated against because they were trying to expose fraud and deception and embezzlement. It drags on.

Also Anubhav drags on. Yes, I wish I could tell you that Sandhya never saw him again, that he was exiled forever. But you know life never does the things it should. He had a big show at the Pushkara Gallery, and a grand opening. We hear Miss Viveka got a new haircut for the event. Mahatre gave Anubhav's paintings a review that I can only call a rave. He said Anubhav had created a searing vision of the realities of rural India. On that first night alone, Ratnani bought five paintings. Since then, in the last month, Sandhya has had lunch with Anubhav twice. She says to talk things over. Both you and I know what's really happening. The trouble with beauty is you can't give it up, not ever. So I know tomorrow she'll tell me about another lunch, trying not to look guilty. I'll try to be nice, and we'll take Lalit for a walk, and he'll stroll between us, skipping, holding both our hands.

When I'll get home it'll be late. I won't switch on the light, because my brother and his wife will be asleep on the drawing room floor. I'll edge around them, holding my suitcase to the side. I'll hear my father's snores from the bedroom, perhaps my mother's sleepless shiftings. I'll find the two steps up to my room without effort, and once I've shut the door I'll switch on the light. This used to be a balcony once, so it's oddly shaped, long and narrow. I'll take my clothes off and lie on the less-than-single bed, with the light on. I'll think of Anubhav. A man named Vidyarthi told me that Anubhav got that good review from Mahatre because Anubhav even serviced Mrs. Mahatre. Vidyarthi used that word, "service." I tell you this not because I believe it, but in the interests of showing you the world of art as I know it, a certain aesthetic completeness, you see, and to tell you what I do not believe. Anubhav Rajadhakshya is surely a whore, a leech, and a liar, but there is something I owe him. I owe him for his talent. I believe this. As I lie on my bed, I will look to the foot of the bed, and on the small table at the end I will see a painting in a frame. The frame is mine, the painting is Anubhav's. After I had helped Ma-ji throw out his paintings and his materials, the next day, I helped her clean out the room. Behind a cupboard, rolled up and forgotten, I found a painting of a young man leaning on a wall, in front of a poster for *Deewar*. The painting had a swirl of yellow and red at the top, a pavement in pencil, but Anubhav had worked on the man a little since I had last seen the painting, on the swirl of smoke from his cigarette, on his face. I saw that it was Rajesh. So I took it. I took it, not paying the high prices that Ratnani gave, but I told myself I had given enough to Anubhav. Maybe not enough but something, a service here and there.

I will lie in my bed and look at the painting. I'll wonder what it is on the canvas that is Rajesh. Yes, I wish I could tell you we found him, that we knew what had happened. But life never does what it should. After eight-and-a-half months we know that he worked with some *bhai log*. I now know the name of the moustached man at the gym, and that he is known to Ratnani. This we know. But only this. In this life, the sub-inspector said, some people just vanish. I said: I know. These facts, and the theories that I made up to explain it all to myself, those plots that gave me comfort and a comfortable kind of terror, they've been bleached white by the ferocity of my attention. They rattle around in my head with a dry click-ing noise. But the painting is life itself. So I'll lie in my bed and look at the painting. I'll look at the curve of the hip, the shirt sleeves rolled up on the swell of the biceps. At the shadowed eyes in black, and the curl of hair on the brown forehead. I will lie in my long narrow room and look at the strong fingers holding the white cigarette and wonder what it is in the shapes that is Rajesh.

When I wake it'll be dark in the room, the lights will be off, and I'll know that my mother has come into the room, drawn a sheet to my chest, sat next to me with a hand on my forehead for a while. Alone, I'll look for the painting in the dim shifting light. Now I'll see only a glimmering in the dark, a white that comes out of the shadow. I'll know that Rajesh is not in the lines, that the body is not in the colour. But there is that colour that moves through the body, *rang ek sharir ka*. There is that glow. I know what it is. It is the absence in my heart.

Shanti

I HATE SUNDAY EVENINGS. It's that slow descent into the dusk that oppresses me, that endless end with its undertaste of death. Not so long ago, one Sunday evening, I flipped the television off and on a dozen times, walked around my room three times, sat on the floor and tried to read a thriller, switched on the television again, and the relentless chatty joyousness finally drove me out of the house. I walked aimlessly through the streets, listening to the long echoes of children's games, tormented by a nostalgia that settled lightly over me. I had not the slightest idea of what I was looking for, but only that I was suddenly aware of my age, and it seemed cruel that time should pass so gently and leave behind long swathes of unremembered years. I walked, then, along the long curve of the seawall at Haji Ali, and came along towards the white shape of the mosque floating on the waters.

Then, at the intersection, I didn't know what to do. I stood, too tired for another long journey and too restless still to go home, and I was swaying a little from side to side. Then I felt a gentle tap on my shoulder. It was Subramaniam.

"Come along," he said. "I'll give you a drink."

He was carrying a tattered *thela*, and we stopped along the way to fill it with bread, marmalade, and bottles of soda. He lived in an old, shabby building near Tardeo, and we went up four flights of stone stairs worn thin in the centre. Inside the door marked "Subramaniam" in brass letters, I bent to take off my shoes, and I could see the space was cool and large. There were those old high ceilings, and walls hung with prints. I sat in the drawing room on a heavy teak couch, on worn cushions, and wriggled my toes on the cold marble. Subramaniam came in carrying a bowl of chips.

"New brand," he said, smiling, and he put the bowl down on the table at my elbow. Then he poured me a drink. He sat in an armchair that creaked slightly, and raised his glass at me.

"Haven't seen you in a while," I said.

"Yes," he said. "Unfortunately my wife has been unwell."

"Sorry," I said. "I hope it's nothing serious."

He raised his shoulders in that awkward little shrug of his. "At a certain age everything is serious, and nothing is serious." He drank, and then put down his glass on the table with a crisp click. He looked keenly at me. "How is that Ayesha?"

"Yesterday, she was very bitter about a patriotic movie she saw," I said. "She is in despair about the state of the country. What are we, she said. For a cynic she despairs a lot. She's my friend, but I don't understand her, not really."

He nodded. "Listen," he said. "I want to tell you a story."

A train drifting across a field of yellow grass. This is what he saw first. A plume of black smoke turning slowly in the white glare. He had gone up the long slope in front of the station, across the three tracks, and then up the rise, to the ridge which had turned out to be much, much further than he had thought. When he had reached it, and gone across, he had found himself on an endless plateau, a plain dotted with scrubby bushes, an endless flatness that vanished into the sky. So he had turned around and come back. He had already forgotten what he had hoped to find on the other side of the ridge, but for two months he had looked at it curling in the distance, and finally he had taken a walk to see the other side of it. Now the sun burnt on his shoulders. Now he came back over the ridge and saw the train drifting across a field of yellow grass.

It was 1945 and he was twenty years old. His name was Shiv, and he had a twin who was dead, killed in Delhi the year before when a Hindu procession had gone the wrong way. The newspapers had regretted the continued communal violence in the city, but had reported with relief that on this day there were only six dead. One of the six was his, one body identical down to the strangely short fifth toe on the left foot. He had never known the bitterness of small statistics, but now he carried it everywhere in his mouth. He had it now, as he stumbled with aching calves, back from his walk of no purpose. The day yawned before him. He lived with his sister and her husband in a large bungalow a minute and a half's walk from the station. In the house there were a dozen novels he had read already, his B.Sc. degree framed on a wall, and two small children he could not bear to play with. He had come to live with his sister and her station-master husband after his silences had frightened his parents. His sister had loved him most, had loved him and his brother best after their birth at her eight years, and even now, grief-stricken, she found happiness and generosity enough in the safety of her home to comfort him. But the day, and life itself, stretched on forever like a bleak plain of yellow grass, and he felt himself walking, and the train drifted with its fantastic uncurling of smoke.

The train slowed imperceptibly as he walked. It must have, because he became aware that it was paused, halted at the station. But even then it moved, shimmering in the heat haze, a long red blur. Then, again, it was stirring, drifting across the yellow. He had no sense of his own movement, only of the shuffling of his feet and the sweat trickling down his back, and somehow the train was drawing away from him. Then he was at the station. He crossed the tracks and climbed onto the main platform. He went past the sign that proclaimed "Leharia" and its elevation of seven hundred and eighteen feet, past the station master's office and the second class waiting room, past the door to the ticketing office and the passengers sprawled on the green benches, and to the arched white entrance to the station. There he stopped, unsure. He looked out across the tracks and there was the slow slope and the far-away rim. He had gone to the edge of his world and come back and he didn't know what was next. The train was now a single oblong to the west. He looked down along the tracks to the west and then back to the east and the thought occurred to him suddenly that he could wait for the next train, and it was a short step off the platform onto the black rails, a drop of three feet. The train would be moving very slowly but it had a great momentum. It could not be stopped. He recognized the melo-drama of the thought, and was also surprised that he had not had it before. There was a certain relief in it. It seemed now inevitable, at least as an idea, and he determined that he would wait for the next train to see what happened. That would be the three-thirty from Lucknow.

Now that there was a plan he was released from lethargy. He was suddenly full of energy and very thirsty. There was a *matka* of water in the first class waiting room. He walked now with a snap, and he waved smartly at Frankie Furtado the assistant station master, who was looking, from a barred win-dow, after the receding smudge on the western sky with an expression that was usually taken for commendable railway concentration and proper seriousness. He was actually — Shiv knew — dreaming of Bombay, and now Frankie returned the wave with but a slow raising of the fingers of one elegant hand that rested on an iron bar. There was an entire matinee's worth of tragedy in the single motion, and Shiv smiled a little as he drank the lovely clayey water. It was crisp and cold and the ladle made a deep belling sound as it dipped under the dark surface.

He poured the water into his mouth. It splashed over his neck and chest, and he let it fall on his face, and when he heard the laugh he choked. When he stopped coughing he turned and saw the figure by the window. At first all he could see was hands held together, the furled drapery of a grey sari from knee to ground. Then in a moment or two he could see her. She was thin, very young. She wore no ornaments, not a bangle, no earrings. The eyes were large, there was a thick plait falling over a shoulder, and now she looked down and put a hand over her mouth. Shiv put the ladle back in the *matka*, and it dropped with a rattle into the water. He backed to the door, edged through it, blushing, and then stood on the platform wiping his face.

"Who is that in there?" he asked Frankie Furtado, whose face lit up at the question. Frankie was really a movie star trapped by his railway father and railway grandfathers and various railway uncles in Leharia, which he always called Zinderneuf. He had explained with shining eyes the sentimental possibilities of desert forts, marauding Bedouin, stolen jewels, and violent death. Now he was bright eyed about chance meetings while whistles echoed.

"Second class passenger," Frankie said. "But I put her in first class because she is very beautiful."

"Yes," Shiv said. Actually she was rather plain, but Frankie was dedicated to romance.

Frankie ran his finger down a list on a board. "Mrs. Shanti Chauhan," he said.

"Fine," Shiv said, unaccountably irritated. He walked down the length of the platform, trying to find again his imperturbable velocity of a moment ago. At the end of the platform he waited, sitting on a green bench. He fanned himself with a folded *Times of India* and tried not to think. But as always the images skipped and skittered at the back of his head. He spread the newspaper across his knee but then was drowned by the vast turbulence of the world, its fires and refugees and ruined cities. A letter-writer called "Old Soldier" wrote, "Whether these men of the so-called Indian National Army were prompted by a version of patriotism, or gave in to fear of unspeakable persecutions by the Japanese, is scarcely to the point; that they took up arms against their former comrades is certain. They betrayed their vows to their units and their army and their king, and a soldier who is false to his *namak* can expect only two things: court-martial and the ultimate penalty." Shiv saw them falling, their bodies riddled and holed. He shuddered. So he shut his eyes and with a slow twist of fear in his stomach gave himself up to the uncertain currents of memory. Then Shiv's nostrils were full of Hari's smell, the slightly pungent aroma of life itself, cotton and perspiration and flesh, springing muscle, the same hair oil he used himself but sweeter on Hari. Now Shiv opened his eyes and his face was covered with sweat. There was a whistle, softened by distance.

He stood up and waited. He felt very small now, and under the huge sky he waited for the two events to come together, the busily grinding three-thirty from Lucknow and himself. He could see them moving closer to each other, the loco on its tracks, and his life, brought to each other in a series of spirals. He took a step forward and now it was a matter of another one to the edge. He could see the train, a black circle, huffing smoke and getting bigger. He began to think of calculations, of the time it would take to put one foot in front of another, of velocity and braking distance. He noted the red fragments from a broken *khullar* next to the tracks and determined that he would jump when the shadow of the train fell on them. That was close enough. The train came faster than he had thought it would, and now the sound enveloped him. He felt his legs twitch. He watched the red clay and then at the last moment turned his head to look down the platform. He saw in the swirl of colours a grey figure, motionless. He jerked his head back, felt the huge weight of the engine, its heat, and began his step forward, seeing the black curve of the metal above him, slashed in half by the slanting sun, the rivets through the iron, and then he staggered back, pulled himself back, an arm over his head.

Shiv found himself sitting on the ground, knees splayed outward. The bone at the base of his spine throbbed. He picked himself up and hurried past the first class compartments as the train screeched mournfully. She was stooping to pick up a small brown attaché, and he was sure she saw him coming. But she turned her face away, an expression of anger on her face, and walked resolutely towards the door of a carriage, where Frankie Furtado stood with his clipboard. She went past his smile with her eyes downcast, into the carriage, and afterwards sat in a compartment with half-lowered shades. Shiv stood outside, wondering at himself. He could see her arm. Twelve minutes passed, and then Frankie waved a green flag, leaning suavely to one side, and quite suddenly the train was gone. Leaving only a black wisp fading, and Shiv with his questions.

Frankie had an alphabetical list of names: "Madhosh Kumar, Magan Kumar, Nand Kumar, Narendra Kumar . . ." He read from these every evening when Shiv visited him in his room behind the National Provision Store, in his desert lair, his lonely eyrie festooned with pictures of Ronald Colman. Frankie was the handsomest man Shiv had ever seen, with his gently wavy hair and his thin moustache and fair skin, and they were trying to find a screen name that would encompass and radiate all the mysterious glamour of his profile. Usually Shiv enjoyed the distraction of holding the name up to imaginary bright lights, of writing it into the magazines which Frankie collected and hoarded with incandescent seriousness. "Nitin Kumar Signs with MovieTone," or "Om Kumar Dazzles in Megabuster" were all tried, tested and classified and estimated and measured, and found wanting in the analysis. This discussion took place always on the little *chabutra* in front of Frankie's room, with the spokes of Frankie's bicycle glinting in the moonlight. There were a few bedraggled bushes at the bottom of a brick wall, and a *chameli* tree overhanging the wall from Lala Manohar Lal's garden. The Lala's two daughters were of course in love with Frankie, but tonight even the sight of them hovering on the rooftop across the way like two bottom-heavy nightingales took nothing from Shiv's enormous yearning.

He was filled with a longing so bitter that he wanted all over again to die. He felt as if he was gone from himself. This was not the numb descent towards an inevitable stillness, no, not that at all. Now, in the darkness, Shiv felt a quickening in the night, a throb like a pulse that moved far away, and he was acutely aware of the smallness of the *chabutra* and how tiny Frankie's room was, with its one sagging *charpai* and the chipped white plaster on the walls and the crudely shaped green windows that could never completely close. Even the moonlight didn't hide the dirt, the dishevelled ugliness and cowpatties of a small *mofussil* town one step away from a village.

"Have you seen her before?" Shiv said. His voice was loud. He was angry, and he didn't know quite why.

"Yes," Frankie said. He stood up straight, alive with pleasure. "Twice before. She comes through every two or three months, I think. Looking so beautiful and so alone."

"Going where?"

"I don't know. She catches a *tonga* outside the station. I think to the cantonment. Her attaché has stencilling on it."

Four miles from the station there was a brigade headquarters and, further away, an aerodrome.

"She's married," Shiv said. "Probably going to visit her army husband."

"Air force," Frankie said. "And why would she be visiting instead of staying in a lovely air force bungalow? And when she showed me her ticket I saw that she had others. Connections to all over the country, man. Why?"

"I don't know," Shiv snapped back. "I don't *know*. And why would it matter to you and me anyway? She's a married woman."

Frankie raised an eyebrow. He put a hand on his hip and his shoulder rose and fell in a long exaggerated shrug. Shiv saw that it was a gesture too large for life, impossible in its elegance, but in the silver light it was entirely conceivable and exactly right, as if the world had suddenly changed, moved and become just a little larger, just enough to contain Frankie Furtado. Frankie, who swept his hair back now and turned majestically away, ridiculous and beautiful. Shiv shut his eyes, pressed on them until he felt pain.

Frankie sang: "*Kahan gaya ranchor? Duniya ke rahane valon bolo, chcheen ke dil mera, kahan gaya ranchor?*" His voice was good, light and yet full of intensity, and ample and rounded with its delight in its own skill. Shiv fled from it.

A cut on the palm of a right hand. Small, not too large, but ferocious in the straightness of its edges, in the geometry of its depth. Another on the left forearm, from the same straight edge. This is what Shiv remembered. As he walked home along a dusty lane he remembered the dark pearls of blood frozen on the pale skin. In the morgue he had found the cuts unbearable to look at, this damage, these rents in the surface and the lewd exposure of what lay underneath. Now he clung to the still shape as the only reality. It was the world stripped of all its fictions, this dead body on a grey stone slab, the smell. In only a minute or two, in a lane off Chandni Chowk, a whole life came

to merely this, all of Hari's idealisms, his Congress membership
and his Nehru-worship, his belief in change and the careful
asceticism of his three khadi *kurtas* and his blushing appetite
for mangoes, all of it gone to an odour of rot. All of it ready for
the fire. Shiv held out an arm in the darkness and took careful
steps with his fingertips on a wall. In the memory of the dead
body of his brother there was a certain safety. There was a certain logic there, a brilliant lesson about the nature of the world.
This Shiv knew. In Frankie's falsities, in his fantasies about the
past and the future, there was certain disaster. To believe
Frankie, to believe in him, that he could exist in Leharia, Shiv
knew, was to risk an unfolding in his own chest, an expansion
of emotion that would let in, once again, a certain hell of hope
and remorse. He had left this behind.

"Did you have a good evening?" Shiv's brother-in-law,
Rajan, liked to sit in an armchair in the courtyard of their
house after dinner. Shiv could see the curve of his bald head,
and the rounded shapes of his shoulders.

"Yes," Shiv said, and shut the door to his room behind him.
He knew Anuradha *akka* would hurry out of her bedroom in a
moment, and want to give him food. He was unspeakably
rude, and they were used to this. They had patience. But Shiv
lay on his bed and wrapped death around himself. He could
hear a bird calling outside, solitary and plaintive. Shiv knew
that finally the bird would stop crying out, his sister and her
husband would stop whispering to each other and sleep, the
house would settle into a late silence, a quietness that would
echo the slow creaking of trees into his head. He would feel his
self, his soul turn and turn inwards, again and again, until it
was as thin-drawn as a wire, shiny and brittle. It was not a
good feeling but he knew it well, and it was better than everything else. He waited.

He found that he was waiting for her. As he cycled around

town, from one tuition to another, he anticipated each turn in the rutted lanes, even though on the other side of each corner there was always the same pool of stagnant water, the same goat leaving a trail of perfect black pellets, the same two familiar *dehati* citizens of Leharia with their flapping *pajamias* and "Ram-Ram, Shiv Bhaiyya." At the station, Shiv sat on platform number one and watched the trains. Frankie smiled fondly and hummed *Mere piya gaye Rangoon* under his breath every time he strolled by. Rajan believed that Shiv had at last and only naturally succumbed to the charm of steam, that he had become a lover of the black beauties that raced across the horizon, an aficionado of their hulking grace and their sonorous power. He came and sat beside Shiv often, in the quiet moments of the day. "Beyer Garrat loco, latest model, 1939. Used only on the express. Look at that! The total heating area, including the superheater, is more than four thousand square feet."

Shiv listened to the tales of the trains, and imagined the tracks arrowing across the enormous plains to the north, and to the south across the rocky plateau, and hairpin turns over vertiginous ridges, and through black deserts. He thought of her sitting by a half-closed window, her hands in her lap, and wondered what she was doing. Who was she? Where was she going? Why did she return? As the questions came he understood that everything had changed. Now, at night, instead of long wakefulness and empty, tiring slumber for an hour before dawn, he found a twisting, sweaty, dream-ridden sleep. He saw long visions of childhood, fantastic and drenched with blood, and also adventures in forests, and unspeakable seraglios in which *apsaras* with long black hair twisted against each other. He was hungry all the time, and ate his sister's *uttapam* with a relish that made her beam and write gladdened letters to his parents. And one evening in August he actually asked Frankie Furtado to sing *Kahan gaya ranchor*. Frankie tilted himself against the wall next to a window, a slim streak of white against the black, black clouds, turned his face to the light, and sang as the rain billowed over the green fields.

Shiv believed that he would know, somehow, when she came back, that he would sense her presence in the twisting lanes. Even as he laughed at the Frankie influence on his thoughts he believed this. But when she came he missed her entirely. He was unfastening the cycle-clips from his calves outside the station when Frankie came running out and found him.

"Where were you? She's here," Frankie said, clutching hard at Shiv's shoulder. "She's here."

"Where?" There was a solid sheet of water falling from the crenellated roof of the station, spattering loudly against the flowerpots below.

"On the 24 up. She had to wait quite a while for a *tonga*, all this rain, I suppose. Then finally she left ten, fifteen minutes ago."

Shiv threw his leg over his cycle and skidded out into the rain. His plastic cap tumbled away and splashed into the mud but Shiv rode on, spraying an arc over the road. He rode hard, leaning against the pedals, feeling the water pull at the wheels in the deep parts. The rain hit him violently in the face, coming straight and parallel to the road, and he laughed. His chest was drenched and cool, but under his raincoat he was sweating. He cycled through the main bazaar, where the little shops looked cozy under the darkness of the rain. Then he struggled against the long slope where the road opened out into the orderly rows of the Civil Lines and the cantonment, and the wind pushed against him, but then he saw the shape of the *tonga* ahead, sailing on the water. He pedalled madly, and then he came up on it and slowed. He could hear the muffled clip-clop, the swish of the wheels. There were small curtain-like pieces of cloth drawn around the back of the *tonga*, but he could see her feet on the backboard. Shiv went along now, not near but not too far. He listened to the rain, and the sound of his own breathing, in and out. He had no idea what to do next.

Shiv stopped at a big double gate. There was a wide curving drive leading up to the square white building Shiv knew was the military hospital. He could see, as he blinked his eyes against the sting of the drops, the *tonga* stopped next to a balustraded entranceway, the dripping horse, her attaché case, and her, as she hurried, head bent, through the doors. Shiv waited, cold now, shivering. Finally, when it was dark and he could only see the rows of lighted windows, glowing and unreadable, he turned and wheeled his cycle home, coughing.

He woke up the next morning with a fever. His sister saw it in his reddened eyes and careful walk, but he burst past her protestations and rode to the station. It was very quiet now, no rain, and the silence was wet and fresh and everywhere green, and he felt himself lost under the enormity of the smooth grey sky. Frankie was waiting for him at the entrance to the station.

"She's in the waiting room," Frankie said.

Shiv nodded impatiently. He walked down the length of the platform, past the fire buckets filled with sand and the two coolies wrapped in checked red sheets and a cloud of *bidi* smoke. Outside the waiting room, he stood for a moment, running hooked fingers through his tangled hair. His eyes burnt drily. He pushed the doors ajar and went in, keeping his gaze on the floor. He found the *matka*, and as he dipped into the water with the ladle he found that he was really thirsty. He poured into a glass, drank, and turned.

"Hello," he said.

She said nothing, and looked solemnly at him. He realized suddenly what it must take from her, how much courage and strength to travel the length and breadth of the country alone, in these times.

"My name is Shiv Subramaniam," he said. She looked down, and he was then ashamed of persecuting her as many others must have done on her travels, and he edged away toward the door. But Frankie was backing in, carrying a tray with a teapot and cups.

"Mrs. Chauhan," Frankie said, swooping down on the small table in front of her. "Tea for you." He laid out the cups with smart little movements. "There. Mr. Subramaniam, who is our esteemed Station Master *saab*'s brother-in-law, will serve." He looked at Shiv. "Please." Then he bowed to Mrs. Chauhan, and was gone.

For a moment Shiv stood absolutely still. He felt dizzy. Then he stepped up to the table, bent over, and picked up the teapot. He was angling awkwardly at the waist and the teapot felt very heavy, but he poured one cup, and then the other. He put the pot down.

"Sugar?" he said.

"No," she said. Her voice was oddly husky. She took the cup and the saucer and held it in her lap. Shiv stood stupidly still, and then realized she was waiting for him. Quickly he picked up his cup and saucer, and tried to keep it steady in his trembling hand. He took a sip, and it was very hot and he usually took sugar, lots of it, but he drank rapidly and watched her. Finally she raised her cup and drank.

"You've come here before," he said.

"I go to the hospital at the base," she said.

"Ah," he said. His legs were shaky, and very carefully he sat on the chair to her left. Looking at her directly, he saw that she was very thin, that the way she held her head alertly above her bony shoulders gave her a kind of intrepid dignity.

"I'm looking for my husband."

"Your husband?"

"He's missing in Burma," she said. "He is a pilot."

There was nothing to say to this.

"He is a fighter pilot," she said. "He was in the first batch of Indian fighter pilots in the RIAF. He was flying a Hurricane over Burma in 1942. They were protecting transports. They were attacked by Japanese fighters. The last his wingman saw of him was the plane losing height over the jungle. The plane was smoking. That was all they saw."

She was speaking in an even voice, and the sentences came steadily after one another, without any emotion. It was a story she had told before.

"So, at the hospital . . . ?"

"I talk to the men who come back. Before it was only a few. Now they're all coming back. From the prison camps. And the others, from the INA." She looked at Shiv. "Somebody must have seen him, met him. Only today I met a soldier from the Fourth Gurkhas who said he had heard about a fighter pilot in a camp on the Irrawaddy."

She had complete confidence. The names of the units and of the faraway places came to her easily.

"So I'll go to the army headquarters in Delhi, find out who was in that camp. Talk to them."

She nodded. She finished her tea, and put the cup back on the tray. Then she folded her hands in her lap, and it seemed she was now content to wait, either for the train, or the man from the Fourth Gurkhas, or a flier in a plane above the trees. There was again that strange quietness, as if the world had paused. Again Shiv felt that he was vanishing into the huge wash of grey above, the sudden and endless green to the horizon. He shut his eyes.

"The man in the hospital told me he had seen the most evil man in the world."

Shiv opened his eyes. "Who? The Gurkha told you this?"

"No, no," she said impatiently. "The man in the next bed. He was from the Twenty-third Cavalry."

And then she told him the story of the most evil man in the world. Shiv listened, and the words came to him through the burning of his blood and the din of his pulse. The shadows drifted in the room and then she was finished. Then Frankie came in and said the train was near, and they walked down the platform, and Shiv held her attaché case in his right hand, and walked slowly behind her. They stood on the platform until the train came, and when the train pulled away neither she nor Shiv waved or raised a hand.

Frankie walked up to him. "You don't look very well," Frankie said.

Shiv fainted.

His sister was pressing a glass against his lips. Shiv choked on the hot milk and turned his head away from the bitter metal of the glass.

"You have to drink, Shiv," Anuradha said. "There is this weakness you have to defeat."

He raised himself up against the pillows, and his body felt light, ready to float. He drank the milk, and saw that Frankie was sitting at the far end of the darkened room. Shiv finished, and handed the empty glass to Anuradha, still feeling the hot liquid burble in his throat. After Anuradha left, Frankie opened the window a little, so that Shiv could see the swirling sky. And there were still the steady drops splattering on the stone outside.

"Crazy man," Frankie said. "But you'll be all right. Just a little flu you've got."

Shiv tilted his head, yes, and the room moved around him.

"She was talking to you for a long time," Frankie said, smiling. "I saw. Very seriously. What was she telling you?"

"She," Shiv said. He stopped for the friction in his throat. He tried again. "She told me about the most evil man in the world."

Frankie turned, came and sat next to the bed. "What do you mean?"

Shiv didn't quite know. What she had told him, how she

had told him, that day yesterday was now left to him only in fragments. He remembered it now only across the dark sea of sleep, lost behind the distant horizon of sunset and illness. He reached back and held only slivers. But there was something else in his throat, complete and whole. "I think this is what she told me." He cleared his throat. It hurt.

I touched my mother's feet and she sent me to war with an *aarti*. "Ja, beta," she said. And so I left her, and the smell of incense, and went. My grandfather and my father had served in the Twenty-third Cavalry, and there I went. Our colonel McNaughten said our job was to kill Germans, and we killed them. We are fighting evil, he said. In the mess there was a cartoon of Hitler crushing Africa under his jackboots. So we killed them on Ruweisat Ridge, on the Rahman track, on the Aqaqir ridge. I saw huge stony fields and burning tanks and trucks and upended guns till the eye could see no more. Long black columns of smoke and oily burning at the root. We killed them. And they killed us. Mahipal Singh, Jagat Singh, Narain Singh. Kirpal Singh in the night when we ran into the First Life Guards and they shot us and we shot them.

On the Tel the Germans tried a counterattack. They came at night down a narrowing slope, after a barrage with what they had left. Across a narrow wadi, facing the slope, the 1/9th Suffolk had dug in. They had machine gun positions and anti-tank and mortars sighted in on the slope. All night the Germans came and the Suffolk cut them down. They could hear the Germans calling to each other. Then the light of flares and the Suffolk firing. The Germans came and tried and tried again and then again. All night it went. Then in the morning the Suffolk counterattacked, and then they opened up and let us through, followed by Bren gun carriers. I was driving the lead armoured car, not only in the troop but in the regiment. We came down the Suffolk side of the wadi with the wheels and tracks crunching on the rocks and we could see the bodies of the Germans covering the slope opposite. They had fallen so close, so many, that it was as if all the rock were covered with faded olive cloth, a green carpet. German bodies. Of course not all of them were dead. But we had killed them. We bounced into the bottom of the wadi and the engine growled and we struggled against a lip of rock and the heavy wheels bit into the ground and rocks crumbled and sprayed and then we were almost over and then I stopped.

I stopped the car, I brought it to a halt. Through the driver's slit, through the armour plate, not six feet away and ahead, a German was looking at me. He was very young, propped up on an elbow, that strange golden-white hair, and he had the bluest eyes I had ever seen. He was looking at me. He had the bluest eyes I had ever seen, against the dust-covered face, eyes the colour of a sky you or I had never seen. I could not tell if he was dead or alive, and he was looking at me. "Damn it, Huknam," Captain Duff crackled into my ears. "Push on." But I could not tell if the man with the blue eyes was dead or alive, and he was looking at me. "Huknam, you're holding up the whole advance," Captain Duff shouted, and I thought of the troop behind me, and then the regiment, and the army and armies and all the countries beyond, all held up behind me. So I let in the clutch and the man with the blue eyes was looking at me for a few seconds more and then we went over him and up the slope and the regiment followed. The engine was thundering in my ears as we crunched up and up but as we went up I could not have heard it but I heard them, them outside on the ground calling out. "*Mutti*," they said. "*Mutti*." We came up over the ridge and they had nothing left, but thirty-four miles on and the next day we came into a line of anti-tank guns. They were very close to the ground and well-camouflaged and they caught us well, two other cars in our troop burning in the first minute. We saw the muzzle-flashes and tumbled one, but then there was a whang behind and above me and I was deaf, and I raised my hatch and jumped out. The sand was on fire and there was a burning behind my ears and on my shoulders. I fell down and got up and ran as I could and then I knew my shoulders were on fire. I rolled and rolled and finally it was out. The car exploded and I never saw any of them again, not Captain Duff or the others. It must have been an eighty-eight.

They put me in a field hospital and finally in Cairo they cut my left arm off. When I had jumped off the car I hadn't known but it had been shattered all to pieces. They cut my arm off and it was strange but I felt no pain, not then and not afterwards. But there was something else. When finally I could walk I went into the courtyard of the hospital, I liked to sit on the bench there. There were birds in the roof and in the rafters and they came down to be fed, and there was a fountain. One day I sat on the edge of the fountain, which was dry. But there was a Rajput who brought out a bowl of water for the birds and put it, the bowl, into the fountain. In this bowl of water I saw that my eyes had turned blue. I went inside and found a bathroom with a chipped mirror and still my eyes were blue. My eyes were blue and as I looked at the man, the man who was before me, I saw that his face was cruel and the eyes were blue and still, neither alive nor dead, strange in the brown face. He had the bluest eyes in the world. And this was how I met the most evil man in the world.

When Shiv finished he was exhausted. He lay back on the pillows and let his eyes shut. Yet he was afraid to sleep. He felt Frankie pull the sheet up and lay it over his chest.

"Did she see him?" Frankie whispered. "Did she see his eyes."

"Yes," Shiv said. "She saw him and she said he had the bluest eyes she had ever seen, not only for an Indian but for

English or German or anything else."

After a moment, Frankie said, "Sleep."

Shiv stretched under the sheet, turned his neck against the pillow. He felt tired but better, achy but relaxed. He knew he would get better. He slept.

Shiv got so much better that his parents started talking about marriage. He splashed around town on his cycle, singing. He laughed at the yellow furrows that his wheels carved deep in the water. His sister and her husband were relieved and then a little concerned, made uneasy by the sudden change, but in Delhi his parents were convinced that all was now well and it was time for him to settle, everything should be settled. Meanwhile Frankie Furtado watched the trains eagerly, even the ones that were not going towards Bombay. He told Shiv that he would use a network of assistant station masters throughout the country to find her, to trace her movements and predict her return. But Shiv was confident that she would come back, and soon. He said to Frankie, "Not to worry, my friend. She'll come back." Frankie looked disappointed as his dream of a clandestine spy network vanished, but still, a month and three days later, it gave him tremendous satisfaction to discover her name on a list of advance reservations. He found Shiv on platform three, where he was sitting with his arms flung over the back of a bench, looking out at the slow wind swaying the tall grass.

"My friend," Frankie said. "Eleven hundred hours tomorrow."

"What?" Shiv said.

"Eleven hundred hours," Frankie said out of the side of his mouth, his hands in his pockets and looking away significantly.

Shiv looked up and down the empty length of the platform. "Yes, that, but what?" he said.

Frankie raised an eyebrow, and Shiv burst out laughing. "What, her?"

"Yes, yes, her," Frankie said, a tremendous smile on his face and not a spy anymore.

Shiv got up, put his arm through Frankie's, and led him down the platform. "Frankie Furtado," Shiv said. "You're a madman."

Frankie flung his hair back, and raised a declamatory hand to the sky. "I have drunk of the chalice of wine," he said. "And I am mad." And Shiv thought that Frankie was indeed mad, and he was mad too, and if there was wine the world must have drunk it too.

The next day, though, Shiv was very rational, very cool when she stepped from the train. "Mrs. Chauhan," he said, and carried her attaché case to the *tonga*.

"What did she say?" Frankie said, pulling at Shiv's elbow as the *tonga* pulled away. "What did you say?"

"Nothing," Shiv said. Frankie was stricken. "Don't worry, Frankie. She'll come back and I'll tell her something."

"What?"

"I don't know. Wait and see."

The next day Shiv found her again in the waiting room. Again Frankie brought in a tray with cups and a teapot, and again Shiv poured. She drank the tea without speaking, as before, but afterwards she cleared her throat.

"Did you find anybody from the camp on the Irrawaddy?" Shiv said.

"Yes," she said. "But he wasn't in that camp. But there was some other news, of an escape at another place. So many of them are back."

Shiv nodded. They had come back in thousands, from the army, from the prison camps, and from the other army which had fought against its former comrades. And they had hope for her, each of them, and despair.

"But," she said. "But I met somebody, a woman."

"Yes?"

"At the bus station at Bareilly. She was a Congress-*walli*."

Shiv nodded. He started to say, my brother was also, but it caught in his throat. "Yes," he said.

"She told me something."

"Yes?"

"She told me about a woman who ran backwards into the future," she said.

Afterwards, when she, Mrs. Chauhan, had gone, gone away on the train without a wave or a backward glance, Frankie put an arm around Shiv's shoulder and walked him to the end of the platform. "So?" Frankie said. "So how did you get along?"

"Swimmingly," Shiv said.

"Tell me all. What did she tell you? Learn anything new?"

"Nothing about her, really."

"But you were in there so long. What, then?"

"Take a walk, Frankie?"

"Where? There? No, you must be crazy."

But Shiv could see that Frankie was dying to know, to be told, and so of course Frankie came along with Shiv, in spite of the green grass stains on his white pant legs, and they walked up the slope a far way. And Shiv told him what she had said.

Zingu heard a speech by a politician. Zingu had been coming home to his hut at the end of the day, and it was dark, and so Zingu stood in the dark behind a broken wall and listened to the politician. The politician stood under a petromax lamp and said that all men were equal. The townspeople applauded. Zingu went home in the dark, and he slept quietly, but in the morning he told his wife not to go to work. He told her that there was no need to carry shit anymore. This is what they did, Zingu and his wife. They cleaned the latrines of the twice-born by hand and carried it away on their heads in baskets. But Zingu said his son would be a judge. He told his wife that all men were equal. His wife told him that he was crazy, and took her stinking basket and went to the village. But they killed Zingu anyway, and his son. He wandered around with his son saying all men were equal, and so they caught him in the open fields behind Dhiresa's mansion and cut Zingu and his son to pieces. One of them held up Zingu's foot at the end of a *talwar* and said, look at the size of this thing. All men aren't equal. And that was the end of Zingu, and his son.

But that's not the end of it. Because in Dhiresa's mansion, on the roof, his daughter-in-law Janamohini was drying her hair. In the winter sunlight Janamohini was lying on a *charpai* on the roof, her long, long black hair spread like a cloud, wet and curling and shining and dark. She was young and beautiful and loved, and the mother of two sons and one daughter, and through the delicious sunny sleep of the contented she heard far away the snick and whick of the swords as they cut Zingu. She stretched reluctantly out of her drowsy dreaming, feeling the welcome soreness in the muscles from the night before, sat up, and looked out over the parapet and saw Zingu's foot at the end of a sword. She covered her face and screamed, and many people came running up, uncles and aunts and cousins, and comforted her, and told her it was nothing. And then she was content, and smiling again, and she ate well that night.

But in the darkness, from the roof, she saw a glow. There were fires in the fields. She saw campfires in the fields, and figures dancing about them. She watched them, for a long time, and she could hear singing. She could hear music. Finally her husband called out to her from the courtyard below, and she went down the stairs. She was happy, she laughed and played with her children, yet later she slipped out of the house, by the small door inset into the spiked gate at the back of the house, and she went into the fields. Janamohini walked for a long time, guided by the glow shining off the sky, and finally she found her campfires. There was indeed music, and singing. There were people dancing near the fires. Janamohini saw they were of despised caste, that they were celebrating a wedding, that they were drinking liquor and eating meat, and the music was happy and they welcomed her, and so she danced with them. She drank their liquor and ate their meat. And she whirled around the campfires.

But then her husband and his brothers, who had found the open door, came and took her back to Dhiresa's mansion. Janamohini screamed and fought, but the husband said there had been no campfires, no dancers, no liquor, no meat. He said there had been nothing at all. Now Janamohini shrieked, my feet, my feet, look. She said her feet were pointing the wrong way. Upside down they are, she said. Look. And she began to walk backwards. They tried to stop her, but she walked backwards, faster and faster. She began to run backwards. Her husband wept, and she said, can't you see? If I go fast enough, back and back, I will leap into tomorrow. And her husband wept.

They tried many exorcists then, many a priest, two Tantrics, and a doctor from the town. But Janamohini always walked backwards after that, looking for tomorrow.

But that's not the end of it. Because on that night, no, the next morning, when the people in Dhiresa's mansion woke up, the aunts and uncles and cousins, they saw that Janamohini's hair was white. During that night, and that night only, all of her glorious hair, all of it long and luxurious and oiled and to her knees, all of it, turned white. From the scented clinging black of love it went to the white of madness. All in one night. All this happened in one night.

"And," Shiv said, "she, Mrs. Chauhan, that is, she said she asked the woman who told her this, is this true?"

"Yes," Frankie said. "And the woman said?"

"The woman said—yes, it's true, I tell you it's true, because Janamohini was my mother. I saw her hair turn white, she said, I saw it white in the first light of the morning. All of it white. And I am twenty-two and my hair is white. And perhaps my daughter's hair, if I have a daughter, will be white also."

"And it was white, her hair? The woman who told Mrs. Chauhan this?"

"White, yes. She was young but her hair was white as salt on a beach, as metal in the moonlight, as the sun on a flag."

"That's white," Frankie said. "Poor Zingu."

"Poor Zingu."

They walked back towards the long length of the station, with the huge mottled sky above, and the wind pulled at their shoulders.

"What about her, Shiv?" Frankie said. "Did you find out anything about her? The husband?"

Shiv thought, his head tilted back to the grey glory of the clouds. "I don't think so," he said.

"You didn't ask?"

"No."

"Don't you want to know, Shiv?"

Shiv shrugged. He knew he was smiling awkwardly. "I know it's strange," he said. "And I suppose I do want to know. And I suppose I'll find out. But right now, today, I just like her name."

"Shanti?"

"Yes."

Frankie put his hands in his pockets, hunched his shoulders, and laughed. "Some people fall in love with dark eyes. Others with pale hands glimpsed beside the Shalimar. Why not a name then?"

"It's a good name."

"I know," Frankie said, and put an arm around Shiv's shoulder. "But, brother, a fact now and then is a good thing."

"You're talking about facts, Frankie the lover?"

"Lovers are practical, my young friend."

"Really? That's interesting. It means, I think, that I'm not a lover."

Frankie nodded gravely. But as he looked away Shiv saw that he was smiling. The grass made a sighing sound as they walked.

Now Shanti—and this was how Shiv thought of her—came to Leharia often. As the trial of Dhillon and Sahgal and Shah Nawaz was argued in Delhi, and lawyers and advocates and judges jousted with each other to establish once and for all who was traitor, who was hero, she followed anecdotes and hints and the visions of delirious men up and down the country. Now she pursued the merest whisper, a shadow seen on a jungled hillside years before, a fevered groan floating across fetid bunks laden with dying men. But each time she came she told Shiv of something that she had heard on the way, the things that came to her on all the ways that she went, some incident, some episode, told to her by an old man, a young bride, a favourite son, an angry daughter-in-law, a mother, an orphan, and all of it true, true, and true. She told him about The Ten Year Old Boy Who Joined the Theatre Company of Death, The Woman Who Traded in Oil and Bought a Flying Racehorse, The Farmer Who Went to America and Fell Through a Hole to the Other Side of the World, The Moneylender Who Saw the True Face of the Creator, Ghurabat and Her Lover the Assassin Who Wept, The Birth of the Holiest Nun in the World and The Downfall of the Mughal Empire. And each time Shiv said, it's true. Of course it's true.

But one day in January she had nothing to tell. Or perhaps she hadn't the strength to speak. She sat in her usual chair, an empty teacup in her lap, and her eyes fluttered shut as Shiv watched. He saw the way her mouth trembled and the slump of her shoulders from the taut line he had come to know. He took the cup from her and put it on the table, and with the tiny rattle she opened her eyes.

"They let them go," she said. "They went home."

"Who?"

"Dhillon, Shah Nawaz, and Sahgal."

The papers had exulted in huge black letters: "GUILTY, BUT FREE!" They had gone home, the three, heroes or traitors, finished with it one way or the other. They had been convicted, cashiered, but finally they were told, you're free, you can go. They would go home, and even if nothing was finished, not ever, they would batten away the memories and find new beginnings. All of them were going, going home. Shiv thought of them, the thousands and thousands of them, jostling and jolting across the country in trains, in busses and bullock carts. He pulled a chair toward Shanti, set it squarely in front of her. He sat down in front of her, his hands in his lap. At the back of his neck there was a trembling, as the words pulsed in his chest, exerting a steady pressure against his heart: you're free, you can go.

"I heard something," Shiv said.

"What?"

He cleared his throat, and for a moment he felt fear, blank and overpowering, and he was afraid of speaking, he felt profusion pressing up against the clean prison he had built for himself, but then he looked into Shanti's eyes and he spoke. He told her what he had heard. Afterwards they sat in silence, and Shiv was grateful, because his shoulders ached and he was very tired.

When she was in her compartment, settled in the window, Frankie came strolling down the platform to announce that the train was delayed for twelve minutes. Shanti nodded, but Shiv was too lost in a sudden panic of emotion to say anything. He felt terror and joy mixing in his stomach, and a slow creep of pleasure at the sunlight across his shoulders, and grief. Frankie looked at him, and then took him by the arm and led him away.

"This time you were talking," Frankie said. "And talking and talking. About what?"

"I was telling her something."

"*You* told her a story?"

"Yes."

"Tell me."

Shiv tried. He opened his mouth, and tried to form the words, but they were gone from him. "I can't," he said, trembling. He gestured at his throat, meaning to explain the tumult under the skin.

"All right, sure," Frankie said, baffled but quick to the chase. "I'll ask *her*."

And he did. Frankie stood by the window, his head cocked to one side. Under the long flutter and hiss of steam, Shiv could hear her words.

Amma woke in the morning and cleaned the house. She cleaned the storerooms, the rooms around the courtyard, she swept the dark mud floors and wiped the mantlepieces and the tops of the doorways. She put new wicks in the lanterns and filled them with oil. She washed the red brick of the courtyard and emptied out the ashes from the *choola*. And the children going in and out of the house, through the big door with iron hoops, told their mothers, Amma's cleaning. And the women of the village said, one of her children is coming.

It was a small house, with a granary at the rear and a good well. Amma's grandfather had built it in some time so far away that she thought of it as beyond numbers. He had built it solid and strong, and she came back to it after her school-teacher husband died of typhoid. She came back with four children, two sons and two daughters, the oldest just eleven, to this village called Chandapur, and here she lived and grew old. Her name was Amita but the village called her Amma. She could not read or write, but she educated her children. There was money, just so much, from the farming of her land, and she lived quietly and with a simplicity that was exactly the same as poverty, but she sent her children to school in the city. In her house books were sacred. She wrapped them in red cloth and stacked them on a bed in the biggest of the rooms in her house. Amma lived in a village and ate only twice a day but her children went to boarding school. Her eldest son went to Roorkee and became an engineer. Amma went sometimes to the cities, north, south, east, and west, to visit her children, but came back always to her house in the village, fiercely alone and happy.

It was this engineer son who came home that day. He sat on a *charpai* in the courtyard and spoke to the men from the *panchayat*, who came and sat around him in a circle and smoked. There were women in the kitchen, helping Amma and laughing with her. She had a wicked tongue, and liked to talk. They could hear her laughing in the courtyard, as they listened to the engineer. There were children running in and out of the house. The engineer was telling them, everyone, about the end of the war. He was wearing a white shirt, dark blue pants, and his hair came up on his forehead in a wonderful swell which the villagers, knowing too little, couldn't recognize as stylish. He had a high querulous voice, and he was telling them about the American bombs.

"The bomb killed a city," he said. "There were two bombs. Each finished a city." He snapped his fingers, high in the air. They looked at him, not saying a word, and he felt the stubborn peasant scepticism gathering around his ankles, that unmovable slow stupidity. He was irritated, rankled now as he used to be when his mother laughed at his modernisms. *Aji-haan,* she would say, unanswerable. It baffled him that his most sophisticated explanations of cause and effect were defeated easily by snorting homespun scepticism, sure-yes, *aji-haan.* He could see her now, standing in the sooty doorway to the kitchen, her arm up on the wall, listening. "Fire," he said. "Whoosh. One moment of fire and a whole city gone."

"How?" It was Amma. Her hair was white, and she was wearing white, and she had a strong nose and direct eyes. The engineer looked up at her, a glass of milk in his left hand. "If you break a speck," he said. He didn't know how to translate "atom." "You release energy. Fire." Amma said, "How?" Now the children were quiet. Amma took two steps forward. "How?" The engineer gestured into the air. "It's like that thing in the *Mahabharata*," he said finally. "That weapon that Ashwatthaman hurled at Arjun." "The Brahmasira?" Amma said. "That was stopped." "Not this one," the engineer said, turning his hand palm down. "They used it." Then the food was ready and he ate.

Nobody noticed until the next morning that Amma had stopped talking. "What happened?" the engineer asked. "Why aren't you talking?" A little later he asked, "Are you angry with me? Did I do something?" Amma shook her head but said nothing. She refused to talk to her friends, and to their children. Now some people thought she had taken a vow of silence, like Gandhi-ji, and others thought that she had been witchcrafted by some secret hater. The engineer was annoyed, and then concerned. He wanted to take her to the city, to a doctor. She put a hand on the ground and shook her head. But she wouldn't talk, couldn't. Finally he left, her son. In the weeks after her other children came, one by one, and still she spoke to nobody. She smiled, she went about her daily business, but her silence was complete and eternal.

First it was just one child, Nainavati's daughter, eight years old. Her skin cracked on her hands. Her mother rubbed her skin with *neem*-leaf oil, and held her close. The next morning the cracks were open, a little wider, and spreading to the elbows. And that afternoon Narain Singh's son had it too. There was no bleeding, no pain, only the lurch of Nainavati's heart when she looked at her daughter's hand and saw the white of bone at the wrist. A week later all the children in the village were splintered from head to toe. Looking at each other they wept with fear, and their parents were afraid to hold them. Pattadevi said it first. One morning her baby, ten months old, gurgled against her thigh, and Pattadevi raised her head, forgetful and so smiling, and she saw the pulsating beat of a tiny heart. Pattadevi shut her eyes tight, and in her anguish she said, "Amma's son brought it home, with his Japanese bomb." That was then the understanding of the village, true and agreed upon.

Finally the horror was that they grew used to it. The months passed and they were shunned by the neighbouring settlements, and certainly they did not want to go anywhere. Life had to go on, and so they tended the crops, saw to the animals, built and repaired, and lived in a sort of bleak satisfaction, an expectation of precisely nothing. On the three hundred and sixtieth day Amma came to the *panchayat*.

They were sitting at their usual places under the *pipal* tree, the old men, and the powerful, and then the others. They fell silent when Amma walked among them, surprised by her appearance in an assembly of men, and a little afraid of her, her witchy quiet and her confident walk. She sat under the pipal tree. In her hand she had a letter.

"What is that, Amma?" the *sarpanch* said. "A letter from your son? What does he write?" He took the letter from her, as he usually did, tore it open, and began to read. "Respected mother . . ."

"I want to praise," Amma said.

"What?" the *sarpanch* said, dropping the letter.

"The kindness of postmen, their long walks in the summer sun, their aching feet. The mysterious and generous knowledge of all those who cook, their intimate and vast power over us. The unsung courage of young brides, their sacrifices beyond all others, their patience. The age of trees, the years of their lives and their companionship. The sleeping ferocity of dogs—I saw two kill another last week—and their stretching muscles, their complete and deep and good happiness with a full stomach and a long sleep."

The *sarpanch* opened and closed his mouth. Before long all the women gathered too, with their children, and the whole village listened to Amma.

"The long song of those who drive trucks on the perpetual roads. The black faces of the diggers of coal, and their wives who try ever not to hear the sound of rushing water under their feet. The staggering smell of the birds that clean bones, their drunken walk with its anxious greed. The roofs of the village houses in the morning, seen from the *ghats* above the river, and the white glimmer of the temple above the trees. The roaring familiarity of the dusty brickmakers with fire. The painful faith of unrequited lovers."

The villagers listened to her. One of the children noticed it first. He tugged at his mother's hand, but she was rapt. He held her index finger and pulled it to and fro, and the gold bangles on her wrist jingled, and she looked down. He held up his arm to her, and she saw the cracks were gone. Then others saw it too. No one could see it happening, not one fissure or the other closing, but if they looked and looked away and looked back, they could see the skin becoming whole. And Amma was talking. She praised the sky, the earth, and every woman in the village, and each of the men, even the ones known for sloth, or cruelty. Then they brought her food, and water, and she talked.

When she finished talking the next day the children were well. Much later, the *sarpanch*, who was sitting on a *charpai* in her courtyard, said to her, "Well, Amma, your son brought the sickness, and you fixed it."

"What did you say?" Amma said, and for a moment the

sarpanch was afraid that for all his dignity she would throw the teacup she was holding at his head. "My son brought it?"

"You have to admit that he came, and then they were sick."

But Amma rolled her eyes. "*Aji-haan*," she said, and that was that.

By the time Shanti had finished telling the story, the train was an extra two minutes late, and Rajan came out of his office and looked angrily down the platform. Frankie waved his flag and the bogie began to move. Shiv walked beside the window, and he watched the shadows from the bars move across Shanti's face. With every step he had to walk a little faster.

"Will you marry me?" he said.

"What?"

"Will you marry me?"

A shudder passed over Shanti's cheeks, a twist of emotion like a wave, and she turned her face to the side in pain, as if he had hit her. But then she looked up at him, and he could see that her eyes were full. He was running now.

"Yes," she said.

He raised a hand to the window as she leaned forward, but the train was away, and the platform came suddenly to an end. Shiv stood poised at the drop, one hand raised.

"Is it true?" It was Frankie, eager and open-faced. "Is it true?"

"What?"

"Your story, you stupid man, is it true?"

"Of course it is," Shiv said, waving his arm in front of Frankie's face. "It is. Look."

Frankie was looking past the arm with a deductive frown. "What happened to you? Why are you grinning like that?"

"She's going to marry me."

"She is? She? You mean you asked?"

"And she said yes."

"But where is she going now?"

"I don't know."

Frankie raised his arms in the air, clutched at his hair, threw down his red flag and green flag and stomped on them. "God help this country, with lovers like you," he said finally. Then he took Shiv by the arm, and took him home, to Frankie's lair, and began to plan.

Two months and three days later, in a train to Bombay, Shanti slept with her head on Shiv's knee. They were in an unreserved third class compartment, and Shiv was thinking about the four hundred and twenty-two rupees in his wallet. Next to the notes he had a folded yellow slip of paper with the address of one Benedicto Fernandes, who was Frankie's first cousin and an old Bombay hand. In the sleeping dimness of the compartment Shiv could see the nodding heads and swaying shoulders of his fellow travellers, two salesmen on their way back from their territories, a farmer with his feet propped up on a huge cloth bundle, his wife, a muscular mechanic, and others. They had made space on the one berth for the newlyweds.

They had been married in a civil ceremony in Delhi. This after Shiv had written to his father, "My Dear Papa," and "I must ask your blessing in a momentous decision," and had received a curt reply telling him to come home, and containing no blessing, or word of affection. He had written again, and this time received two pages of fury, "disobedience" and "disgrace to the family" and "that woman, whoever or whatever she may be." Meanwhile Anuradha was tremulous, and Rajan had muttered about what one owed to one's parents, and what a bad influence that Furtado fellow was. But finally Frankie had saved them. He had found Shanti, her letters and Shiv's had gone to his address, and he had made the arrangements, set up their rendezvous, lent money, and had gone with Shiv to wait for the night bus at the crossroads.

"What if they do something, Frankie? What if you lose your job?"

"All to the good, my friend. I shall be free." In the moon-light Frankie threw his head back. They stood arm in arm, with fields and bunds stretching away on all sides. Frankie was humming something, a song that faded gently under the chit-tering of the crickets. When the headlights appeared to the east, appeared and disappeared, Shiv said, "Thanks, *yaar*."

"*Yaars* don't say thanks," Frankie said. Then the bus roared up to them, heavily full of passengers, and luggage, and a half dozen goats. Frankie found a place for Shiv's suitcase on the roof, and a space for him to squat in the doorwell. Shiv hugged him, hard, and Frankie held him close.

"Go," Frankie said.

"Frankie, come to Bombay," Shiv said as the bus pulled away. Frankie raised a hand, and that was the last Shiv saw of him, in a silvery swirl of dust and a fading light.

Now Shiv looked down at the head on his knee, at the rich thickness of the dark hair. It occurred to him that they hadn't kissed yet. After they had signed the register they had both paused, and then Shiv had thanked the registrar. Then they had gone to the station, awkward in the tonga, each keeping to one side of the cracked leather seat. Shiv had seen kisses in the movies, but he hadn't ever kissed anyone. He looked around the compartment, and then, with the very tips of his fingers, he touched Shanti's cheek. It was very soft, and he was over-come by a knowledge of complete unfamiliarity, of wonder-ment, and complete tenderness. "Shanti," he whispered under his breath. "Shanti." How strange it was, how unknown. How unknowable.

Shiv's fingers moved over her cheekbone, and now she stirred. He watched her come awake, the small stirrings. Then she tried to stretch, and found the hardness of his hip, and the end of the berth, and woke up. He could see memory coming back, shiverings of happiness and loss. She sat up, rubbed her face. He smiled.

"Do you have a photo of yourself?" she said.

"What?"

"A photo. Of yourself."

"You woke up thinking about this?"

"I went to sleep thinking I don't have one."

Shiv leaned back, raised his hip with a curl of pain through his back, and found his wallet. Under the four hundred and twenty-two rupees and behind Frankie's cousin's address he found a creased snapshot.

"Here," he said. "Actually it's Hari. But it doesn't matter. We're identical."

She was looking down at the photo, smoothing away the ridges. "No, you're not."

"Yes, we are."

"No, really, you look different. Very different. See?"

He looked, and there was the well-known twist of the torso, the smile. He knew exactly and well the leaves behind the hair, the tree, and the garden.

"Maybe," he said. "Maybe."

"It is," she said, certain. "You are." She took the photo from him and opened her purse, found a small black diary and put the picture away.

"How about one of yourself?" he said.

She hesitated, then opened the diary to the back. In the picture she gave him she was laughing, leaning towards the lense. But in front of her, there was a smiling man, very handsome, dark hair and keen pilot's eyes, and her hand rested on the epaulettes of his jacket.

"You're different, too," Shiv said.

"I was younger, yes," Shanti said.

"More beautiful now, I meant," Shiv said, and she smiled at

him, and he wanted very much to kiss her but the compartment was stirring now. They sat back and away from each other as the travellers awakened themselves with thunderous yawns. Shiv put the photo in his shirt pocket, and raised the shutter on the window. He leaned into the fresh wash of air, the glad early grey of the land. You are changed, Shiv thought, and I am, and we are all something new now. And then he looked up, and saw the red sun on a ridge, and he was filled with excitement and foreboding. The mountains here were unfamiliar to him, different in their age, their ridges, and the shape of their rivers.

"We must be near Bombay," he said.

One of the salesmen leaned over to the window, scratched at an armpit, looked about with the certainty of a professional traveller, and shook his head. "No, not quite," he said. "Not yet, *beta*."

Shiv laughed. He looked at Shanti. She was laughing with him. "We'll get there," he said.

Now there was night outside. In the dark I wiped at my face, and listened to the clear clink of ice in Subramaniam's glass. There was something I wanted to say, but it seemed impossible to speak. Then I heard a key turning in the door.

"That must be my wife," he said, and got up. "She and her friends have a Ladies' Tea on Sundays. Where they drink anything but tea." A light came on in the corridor.

"Are you sitting in the dark?" she called, and another light flickered, a lamp just inside the room. She had the same white hair as him, and round gold-rimmed glasses, and she was wearing a dark red sari.

"This is young Ranjit Sharma," Subramaniam said. "From the bar, you remember."

"*Namaste, namaste,* Ranjit," she said in answer to me. "Sit, sit. And you, you've been giving him those horrible chips? Has he been eating them, Ranjit? And drinking? He's not supposed to, you know. And did you go to Dr. Mehdi's for the medicine?"

He hadn't, and so she shooed him out, and I made her a drink. She drank Scotch and water and talked about horses. Also about a long vacation that they were to take, and their reservations.

"You're feeling better, then?" I said.

"Me? Me? Oh, I see. You mustn't believe a word he says, you know." She took off her glasses. Her eyes were a lovely flecked brown in the lamplight. He had said nothing about her eyes. "The medicine is for him, not for me."

"Is it serious?"

"Yes."

"I'm sorry."

She shrugged, just like him, and I thought they looked exactly like each other, transformed by the years together, and I tried to smile.

"Don't be sad," she said. "We've had our life, our Bombay life. Come on, you'll stay for dinner. But you'll cut onions before."

It is night, and I am walking in my city. After dinner, Subramaniam came down to the road with me, and walked a little way. What happened to Frankie, I asked. Did he come to Bombay and become a movie star? For a long moment Subramaniam said nothing, and we walked together. No, he said, no, to tell you the truth, Frankie died. He was killed. Those were bad times. But there was somebody else who came to Mumbai and became a movie star. When I come back from vacation, he said, I'll tell you that one. You had better, I said. At the *naka* he shook my hand. Goodbye, chief, I said.

I am walking in my city. The island sleeps, and I can feel the jostling of its dreams. I know they are out there, Mahalaxmi, Mazagaon, Umerkhadi, Pydhuni, and the grand melodrama of Marine Drive. I have music in my head, the jingle of those old names, Wadala, Matunga, Koliwada, Sakinaka, and as I cross the causeway I can hear the steady, eternal beat of the sea, and I am filled with a terrible longing. I know I am walking to Bandra, and I know I am looking for Ayesha. I will stand before her building, and when it is morning I will call up to her. I might ask her to go for a walk, I might ask her to marry me. If we search together, I think, we may find in Andheri, in Colaba, in Bhuleshwar, perhaps not heaven, or its opposite, but only life itself.